MUSIC THEORY TRANSLATION SERIES

CLAUDE V. PALISCA, EDITOR

ON THE MODES

Part Four of
Le Istitutioni Harmoniche, 1558

GIOSEFFO ZARLINO

TRANSLATED BY
VERED COHEN

EDITED WITH AN INTRODUCTION BY
CLAUDE V. PALISCA

YALE UNIVERSITY PRESS, NEW HAVEN AND LONDON

The preparation of this volume
was made possible by a grant from the
Translations Program of the National Endowment for the Humanities, an independent federal agency.

Designed by James J. Johnson
and set in Garamond Roman by
The Composing Room of Michigan, Inc.
Printed in the United States of America by
Murray Printing Company, Westford, Massachusetts.

Library of Congress Cataloging in Publication Data

Zarlino, Gioseffo, 1517–1590.
  [Istitutioni harmoniche. 4a pt. English]
  On the modes.

  (Music theory translation series)
  Bibliography: p.
  Includes index.
    1. Music—Theory—16th century.   2. Musical intervals
and scales—Early works to 1800.   I. Cohen, Vered.
II. Palisca, Claude V.   III. Title.   IV. Title:
Institutioni harmoniche.   V. Series.
MT5.5.Z3813   1983   781'.22| 83–2477
ISBN 0–300–02937–3

10 9 8 7 6 5 4 3 2 1

Contents

Introduction

Of the four books of Gioseffo Zarlino's *Le Istitutioni harmoniche,* Part III, on counter-point, and Part IV, on the modes, are oriented toward the practicing composer and musician, while Parts I and II establish the theoretical foundation on which the later books are built. Part III was published in translation in this series in 1968. We are now able to complete Zarlino's *Practica* with this translation of Part IV, which in the original lacks a title and we are calling simply *On The Modes.* We aim with this translation, as with Part III, *The Art of Counterpoint,* to enrich the resources both of the historian of theory and of the musical analyst who seeks to apply contemporary criteria to the music of the mid-sixteenth century.

The book on the modes marks a new stage in Zarlino's thought. Whereas the book on counterpoint was wholly rooted in the practice taught by Adrian Willaert, the chapters on the modes emerge largely from Zarlino's own researches into sources often external and somewhat alien to the rest of the *Istitutioni.* Willaert's works remain the most quoted examples for modal practice—thirty-two citations in these chapters—but the most important source is a theoretical work that Zarlino never acknowledges: Heinrich Glarean's *Dodekachordon* (Basle, 1547). Glarean, long dissat-isfied with the received doctrine on the eight modes of plainchant as a tonal system for polyphony, completed in 1539 his exposition of the system of twelve modes.[1] Adding to the modes of plainchant that had been recognized as early as the ninth century—the eight on the finals D, E, F, and G—he canonized four more that in practice had existed in the guise of modes with cofinals or irregular finals. These four are the authentic and plagal modes whose finals are A and C.

Several concepts derived from the classical music theory transmitted by Boethius and Gaffurio helped Glarean to legitimize these four modes. One concept was the species of consonance, which takes into account the arrangement of tones and semitones within the span of a consonance.[2] For example, the consonant interval of

---

1. For a history of Glarean's work, see Clement A. Miller, "The *Dodecachordon:* Its Origins and Influence on Renaissance Musical Thought," *Musica Disciplina* 15 (1961): 155–66. See also Miller's translation of Glareanus: *Dodecachordon,* translated, transcribed and edited by Clement A. Miller, Musical Studies and Documents 6 (American Institute of Musicology, 1965), p. 9.

2. Boethius, *De institutione musica,* ed. Gottfried Friedlein (Leipzig, 1867), 4. 14, p. 337. Boethius figured the species descending, i.e., fourths, a-e, g-d, f-c; and fifths: b-e, a-d, g-C, f-B; the octaves: a'-a, g'-g, etc., to b-B.

the fourth is a compound of two tones and a semitone, which may be arranged ascending in three ways: tone-semitone-tone, semitone-tone-tone, and tone-tone-semitone. Consequently the fourth is said to have three species. Similarly the fifth has four species, and the octave, seven species. Glarean followed Gaffurio in numbering the octave species from A, the species of fifth from D, and the species of fourth from A.[3] Thus Glarean built each authentic modal octave on its final with a fifth as the base and a fourth above it. Since there are four species of fifth and three of the fourth, twelve combinations are possible, but only six are diatonic, those in which semitones are separated by at least two but not more than three whole tones. The potential combinations are shown in Table 1. The plagal modes were conceived as joining at the final a fourth below and a fifth above. Again out of twelve such combinations, only six are usable. Thus twelve modes are possible, six authentic, and six plagal.[4]

Another concept that Glarean derived from classical theory is the division of the octave by arithmetic and harmonic means.[5] If the octave is expressed as the ratio between two string lengths, as 12 (for the lower note) and 6 (for the higher), then the arithmetic mean is 9 and the harmonic mean, 8.[6] Measured up from the lower limit

---

3. Franchino Gaffurio, *De harmonia musicorum instrumentorum opus* (Milan, 1518), Book I, chaps. 11–13. See the translation by Clement Miller in Musicological Studies and Documents 33 (1977), pp. 58–60. The tradition of numbering the fourths from A, fifths and octaves from D stems from Hermannus Contractus, *Musica*, ed. Leonard Ellinwood (Rochester, 1952), pp. 26–31. It persists in music theory through the middle ages and Renaissance, including Marchettus of Padua, *Lucidarium*, and Aron, *Trattato della natura et cognitione di tutti gli tuoni di canto figurato* (Venice, 1525), chap. 1. Glarean, evidently, did not know their work. Cf. *Dodekachordon*, Book I, chap. 8; II, 3.

4. Glarean, *Dodekachordon*, Book II, chaps. 3, 7.

5. Boethius, *De inst. mus.* 2. 12–17.

6. Zarlino describes the method for finding the harmonic mean between two terms of a ratio in Part I, chap. 39. First find the arithmetic mean, which is half the sum of the two terms. Then multiply both terms by the arithmetic mean to get the ratio in larger whole numbers. Finally multiply the two original terms to get the harmonic mean between the larger numbers. Thus, if the interval is a fifth in the ratio 6:4, then the arithmetic mean is 5; the converted larger term is $6 \times 5 = 30$, the smaller term, $4 \times 5 = 20$, and the harmonic mean is $6 \times 4 = 24$. More simply stated, the harmonic mean between two terms is the product of the term divided by the arithmetic mean.

Let the two terms be a and b. Then the arithmetic mean is

$$\frac{a + b}{2},$$

and the harmonic mean

$$\frac{ab}{\frac{a + b}{2}}$$

or

$$\frac{2ab}{a + b}$$

Zarlino avoided this simpler solution, because in the case of small numbers, such as 6 and 4, it results in a fraction, in this case 24/5.

Table 1. The Modal System of Glarean

Species of 8ve	Species of 5th	Species of 4th	Harmonic division	Arithmetic division	Names	Mode No.
1. A-a	1. A-e	2. e-a	A-e-a		Aeolian*	9
	1. d-a	1. a-d		A-d-a	Hypodorian (Hyperaeolian)	2
2. B-b						
	2. e-b	2. b-e		B-e-b	Hypophrygian	4
3. c-c′	4. c-g	3. g-c′	c-g-c′		Ionian*	11
	3. f-c′	3. c-f		c-f-c′	Hypolydian	6
4. d-d′	1. d-a	1. a-d′	d-a-d′		Dorian	1
	4. g-d′	2. d-g		d-g-d′	Hypomixolydian	8
5. e-e′	2. e-b	2. b-e′	e-b-e′		Phrygian	3
	1. a-e′	2. e-a		e-a-e′	Hypoaeolian*	10
6. f-f′	3. f-c′	3. c′-f′	f-c′-f′		Lydian (Hyperphrygian)*	5
7. g-g′	4. g-d′	1. d′-a′	g-d′-g′		Mixolydian	7
	4. c′-g′	3. g-c′		g-c′-g′	Hypoionian*	12

*Indicates Glarean's additions.

of the octave, the arithmetic mean is its fourth, the harmonic mean, its fifth. Glarean followed the precedent of Franchino Gaffurio[7] also in applying the theory of means to the modal octaves. Glarean defined the authentic modal octave as mediated by the harmonic mean, the plagal octave as mediated by the arithmetic mean. Of the seven species of octave, one, B-b, lacks a harmonic mean, and one, F-f, lacks an arithmetic mean. This eliminates the possibility of a final on B, as there is no perfect fifth above it for an authentic mode, and no perfect fourth below for the corresponding plagal.[8] (See Table 1.)

Thus, whether by the method of joining species of fifths and fourths or by harmonic and arithmetic mediation, Glarean could defend the acquisition of four new modes, two authentics and their plagals, with finals on A and C.

Since the ninth century, certain musical theorists had associated the plainchant modes with the Greek tribal names, Dorian, Phrygian, etc. Most medieval and renaissance theorists, particularly Italians, however, avoided these names, referring to the modes simply by numbers from 1 to 8. But Gaffurio, an aspiring humanist, revived the Greek names in his *Practica*[9] and spoke of the eight modes as if they were identical to those of antiquity. Glarean adopted these names, and consequently faced the task of baptizing four new modes. With the help of the early fifth-century Roman

7. Gaffurio, *Practica musice* (Milan, 1496), Book I, chap. 7. See the translation by Clement A. Miller, Musicological Studies and Documents 20 (1968), p. 45; or the translation by Irwin Young (Madison, 1969), pp. 40ff.

8. Glarean, *Dodekachordon*, II, 3, 15.

9. *Practica musice* (Milan, 1496), I, 9ff.

encyclopedist Martianus Capella,[10] the second-century Aristoxenian Greek music theorist Cleonides,[11] the third-century Greek grammarian and anecdotist Athenaeus,[12] and again Gaffurio,[13] Glarean was able to associate the Aeolian with the A-octave and the Ionian with the C-octave. Having, after much research, assigned these names to the new modes, Glarean was confident that he had reconstructed the modal system of the ancient Greeks.

Zarlino adopted Glarean's theoretical underpinning for the dodecamodal system, but not all his classicizing analogies. Zarlino stressed certain features that fitted the new modes into the natural harmonic order: the harmonic and arithmetic divisions; the primacy of the authentic form because of its more sonorous arrangement of the fifth below the fourth; and the symmetry and completeness of the twelve-mode array.

If Zarlino did not credit Glarean, it may be because he wanted silently to snub his predecessor's fanciful recreation of the ancient system. How many modes the ancients had and their names and natures made no difference to Zarlino, since "we now use the modes in a manner very different from the ancients" (chapter 10). The lengthy historical section (chapters 1 to 8) was his response to the elaborate network of links that Glarean had spun between the ancient and modern modes. The Greek modes, Zarlino showed, were named after different peoples according to their preferences for stylistic complexes that embraced meter, rhythm, verse form, particular instrumental accompaniment, melodic form, harmony, and affective content. The modern modes, on the contrary, sidestepped considerations of rhythm and meter, clinging only to the melodic and harmonic factors.

Zarlino brought a wide range of reading to this discussion and a more perspicacious study of the Greek musical treatises than Glarean. Zarlino's Greek was not as good as Glarean's, but he used it more resourcefully, and he sought out whatever translations into Latin or Italian were available. Although he was not accustomed to cite translators by name, they may be assumed to be those whose texts were published. Giorgio Valla issued a Latin translation of the *Introduction* of Cleonides and the *Section of the Canon* by Euclid in Venice in 1497.[14] The *Harmonics* of Claudius Ptolemy was translated into Latin by Antonio Gogava,[15] and, although not published until 1562, Zarlino may have seen it before finishing his book. Together with Ptolemy's, Gogava published the *Harmonics* of Aristoxenus, but Zarlino made no use of this until years later. Plutarch's *On Music* was issued in a Latin translation by Carlo Valgulio in 1507.[16] No translation of *On Music* by Aristides Quintilianus was available; so

10. Martianus Capella, *De nuptiis philologiae et mercurii*, ed. Adolf Dick (Leipzig, 1925). See the translation by William H. Stahl and Richard Johnson, *Martianus Capella and the Seven Liberal Arts* (New York, 1971), II.

11. Giorgio Valla, *Cleonidae harmonicum introductorium* (Venice, 1497).

12. Athenaeus, *Deipnosophisti*, Latin translation by Noël dei Conti (Venice, 1556).

13. Gaffurio, *De harmonia*, IV, 11.

14. See above, n. 11

15. Antonio Gogava, *Aristoxeni musici antiquiss. Harmonicorum elementorum libri iii. Cl. Ptolemaei Harmonicorum, seu de Musica lib. iii . . .* (Venice, 1562).

16. *Charoli Valgulii prooemium in musicam Plutarchi ad Titum Pyrrhinum* (Brescia, 1507); *Plutarchi*

presumably Zarlino studied the original. A lengthy quotation from this in Greek is creditably transcribed and translated in Chapter 6, though the Greek text has a few obvious scribal or printer's errors. Of Gaudentius' *Introduction* there was also no published translation.

Among the more general sources on Greek musical practice specifically cited, Aristotle's *Politics* and *Metaphysics* were available in Latin translations, the first by Leonardo Bruni, the second by Bessarion.[17] The Dialogues of Plato were available through Marsilio Ficino's Latin versions.[18] Athenaeus, *Deipnosophists,* was translated into Latin by Noël dei Conti (Venice, 1556) on the basis of a text edited by Marcus Musurus and published by Aldo Manutio in 1514. The *Onomasticon* by the grammarian and lexicographer Julius Pollux was issued in Latin by R. Gualtherus.[19] The fantastical, yet informative, writings of Lucian, a second-century sophist and rhetorician, were published in the Latin of Jacobus Micyllus from as early as 1519. The geographical treatise of Strabo known by its Latin title as *De situ orbis* was translated by Guarino Veronese.[20] The *Bibliotheca historica, or Universal History from the Mythical Beginnings to the First of the Gallic Wars* by Diodorus Siculus, was partly translated by Poggio Bracciolini before 1455[21] and published in 1472.[22] Among other Greek works, Zarlino must have known the famous encyclopedia *Suidas* from the Latin of Aemilius Portius (Geneva, 1530), and the writings of the church fathers, particularly the *Stromata* of Clement of Alexandria, from which he quotes liberally.

Zarlino did not neglect the Latin authors,[23] whether those who wrote extensively on music, such as Censorinus, Cassiodorus, Martianus Capella, and Boethius, or those who touched on it only briefly, such as Apuleius, Fabius Quintilianus, Cicero, Pliny, Valerius Maximus, Statius, Josephus Flavius, the poets Ovid, Horace, and Vergil, and the tragedian Seneca. Zarlino identified many of his ancient sources in the marginal postils of the 1573 edition, which the translator and editor have utilized (and when necessary corrected) in the footnotes. The standard English translations of many of these Greek and Latin works are cited in the bibliography, but, unless quoted in the text of the translation, not usually in the footnotes.

Zarlino communicated a view of musical practice and theory in antiquity that was more authentic and credible than Glarean's ingenious reconstruction or Gaffurio's

---

Chaeronei philosophi historicique Opuscula (quae quidem extant) omnia . . . Musica clarissimi Carlo Valgulio Brixiano interprete (Basel, 1530).

17. Bruni's translation of the *Politics,* dating from 1438 (see R. R. Bolgar, *The Classical Heritage and Its Beneficiaries* [Cambridge, 1954], p. 434), was published by Eucharius Silber (Rome, 1492), and Bessarion's of the *Metaphysics,* from 1455, by Henricus Stephanus in Paris, 1515. Both were republished in numerous editions of the collected works.

18. Plato, *Opera omnia, interpr. Marsilio Ficino* (Florence, n.d.)

19. *J. Pollucis Onomasticon, hoc est instructiosimum rerum et synonymorum dictionarium, nunc primum Latinitate donatum. R. Gualthero . . . interprete* (Basel, 1541).

20. Rome, 1469 or 1470.

21. See Bolgar, p. 435.

22. *Diodori siculi historiarum priscarum a Poggio in latinum traducti* (lib. i–v; Bologna: Balthazarus Azzoguidis, Ugo seu Rugerius et Dominius Bertochus, 1472).

23. See the citations in the footnotes to the translation.

eclectic quilt of quotations. He judiciously claimed no sure knowledge of the ancient modes, declining to say how many there were, in what order they should be named, how many steps each had, how large or small these steps were, or what intervals separated them, for about all these things the ancient authors differed. The Greeks and Romans did not cause many parts to sound together; this he gathered from their notation, which did not indicate more than one tune. From Boethius it was evident that the modes did not differ in interval content, the same constitution of notes being moved up or down, with the result that one mode was like another except in pitch. So far as calling the first modern mode Dorian, the second, a tone higher, Phrygian, and the third, a semitone higher, Lydian, this was contrary to Ptolemy's order, in which these were all a whole tone apart. His succession of modes would only be possible placing the Dorian on C, where Zarlino later, in the *Dimostrationi,* proposed to start the series.

Although Zarlino shows occasional sparks of understanding of Ptolemy's system, he disappoints the modern reader by not correcting the impression given by Boethius that Ptolemy added an eighth mode, the Hypermixolydian.[24] Ptolemy emphatically denied the necessity of an eighth mode, because he linked the number of modes to the seven octave species, to produce which in the central octave only seven tonoi were required.[25] Although aware that Ptolemy's modes transposed the same scale up and down, Zarlino did not recognize the function of the octave species in the system, blaming Cleonides for reversing the order of the modes, when in fact he was dealing not with modes but octave species. Zarlino attributed much of the difficulty to the fault of the scribes who so corrupted the manuscripts of the treatises of Ptolemy and Aristides Quintilianus "that little can be gained from them" (chapter 6). In the end Zarlino was forced to confess that "the ancient modes have little or nothing to do with our purpose, especially since we now use modes in a manner very different from that of the ancients" (chapter 10).

If in his historical chapters Zarlino proved himself a keener humanist than Glarean, in the central chapters on the modern modes Zarlino revealed, besides, a more sensitive musicality than his Helvetian predecessor. Modality to Zarlino, a composer instructing composers, was the backbone of polyphonic structure. As against Glarean's vague concept of *phrasis,* which revolved around each psalm-tone's characteristic rise toward its reciting tone, Zarlino provided the young composer with a variety of constraints for hitching his part writing to a chosen mode: the characteristic ranges of the authentic and plagal modes; the shaping of melody through their proper species of fifths and fourths; the initial notes and the regular cadence steps, which are the same, namely, the final, third, and fifth of the authentic mode for both it and its plagal form; and the final itself as the locus of the closing cadence of a piece.

The keystones of Zarlino's chapters on the individual modes are the two-part examples, each a specimen of modal clarity and contrapuntal decorum. The imitative

24. Boethius, *De instit. mus.* 4. 17 (Friedlein ed. 348. 3).
25. Ptolemy, *Harmonics* 2. 9. See the translation by Ingemar Düring, *Ptolemaios und Porphyrios über die Musik, Göteborgs Högskolas Årsskrift* 50 (Göteborg, 1934), p. 75.

subjects carefully outline the species of fifths and fourths, the leap of the fifth frequently answered by the leap of the fourth, a "modal" answer of which no notice is taken in the text. Initial notes and cadences are limited to the three regular steps: the final, and the third and fifth degrees up from the final. The range usually fills out the modal octave, qualifying the mode as "perfect," but often the range is "superfluous," that is, the authentic modes exceed their octave upwards and the plagal downwards. The "common" mode, which combines the authentic and plagal ranges in a single voice, is also illustrated, as in Example 13, upper part, or Example 14, lower part. There are no examples of "mixture"—the blending of the characteristics of a mode with another that is not its collateral, called "commixture" by most other theorists.[26]

These are textbook examples, to be sure, but they betray Zarlino's infatuation with his own theories. The internal cadences are too "regular"; not a single example of the "irregular" cadences that he countenances on any step of the mode occurs. Even the evaded cadences incline toward the regular endings. The third mode, Zarlino admits, is special; it is "somewhat hard" if not mixed with the ninth, which requires cadences on A. Yet Example 15 shows internal cadences only on B (m. 8), E (m. 17), and G (m. 23). Zarlino was probably moved to insist on the regular cadences by his theoretical bias for the harmonic and arithmetic means that divide the species of fifth into two thirds.

Zarlino's theory of modal cadences represents a notable departure from previous norms. Although he was probably not aware of the work of Johannes Tinctoris[27] on the subject, he must certainly have known the treatise of Aron on the nature and characteristics of the modes.[28] However he never cites it, or for that matter the writings on music of almost any modern author. In a series of chapters dedicated to cadences in the various modes, Aron specified the "orderly" (*ordinate*), or "natural" (*naturali*) or "true" (*vere*) cadences in each mode, and those that were "discordant" (*discordanti*) or "contrary" (*contrarie*). He based these choices on plainchant practice, that is, the endings in "Introits, Graduals, Alleluias, Offertories, Postcommunions, Antiphons, and Responsories" (chapter 18). In these endings Aron included the *differentiae,* options for closes of psalm verses and their doxology to suit the beginning tones of the accompanying antiphons. He posited the general principle that a composition may close on regular finals, irregular finals, that is cofinals, and according to the "differences of the *saeculorum.*"[29] Aron's recommendations for modal polyphonic cadences do not always conform to the traditional allowed *differentiae* but were obviously guided by them. It is instructive to compare the cadences recognized by Aron

26. See, for example, Johannes Tinctoris, *Liber de natura et proprietate tonorum,* ed. Albert Seay, Corpus scriptorum de musica 22 (1975), chap. 13, "De commixtione tonorum," p. 78. The term, "mixed," was reserved for the modes Zarlino calls "common," in which an authentic is combined with its complementary plagal. See in Tinctoris: 22, "De mixtione tonorum," p. 84.

27. See above n. 26.

28. Pietro Aron, *Trattato della natura et cognitione di tutti gli tuoni di canto figurato* (Venice, 1525).

29. Aron, *Trattato della natura,* chap. 1. For a convenient chart of the differences recognized in sources dating from around 1100 to the sixteenth century, see Leeman Perkins, "Mode and Structure in the Masses of Josquin," *Journal of the American Musicological Society,* 26 (1973): 200–01, Table 1.

Table 2. Cadence Preferences in Aron and Zarlino

Mode	Aron		Zarlino	
	Orderly	Discordant	Regular*	Irregular
Mode 1	d f g a	c' e'	d f a d'	any other
Mode 2	A c d f g a	e b c'	a f d A	any other
Mode 3	e f a b c'	C d	e g b e'	any other
Mode 4	c d e f g a	b c' d'	b g e B	any other
Mode 5	f a c'	c d e g b d'	f a c' f'	any other
Mode 6	c d f a c'	e g b d'	c' a f c	any other
Mode 7	g a b c' d'	d e f	g b d' g'	any other
Mode 8	d f g c'	c e a b d'	d' b g d	any other
Mode 9			A c' e' a'	any other
Mode 10			e' c' a e	any other
Mode 11			c' e' g' c''	any other
Mode 12			g' e' c' g	any other

*Zarlino names and cadences of the plagal modes in descending order.

and Zarlino. (See Table 2.) The absence in Zarlino's cadence preferences of A, c', and a in Mode 3 and a in Mode 4 is conspicuous, because c' is the reciting tone or *repercussio* of Mode 3 while a has the same function in Mode 4. Equally anomalous is b in Zarlino's list for Mode 4, a close Aron considered discordant. Also oddly missing is the reciting tone c as a cadence in Mode 8, while b, deemed discordant by Aron, is included.

It is significant that Zarlino ignored the choices that plainchant practice handed down, as if for him harmonic considerations outweighed melodic factors. The harmonic bias may account for the appeal that Zarlino's preferences had for Tigrini,[30] Artusi,[31] Burmeister,[32] and Calvisius,[33] among later authors. On the other hand, Pontio,[34] a conservative, yet highly original, theorist, resolved the question of modal cadences more traditionally, recognizing for each mode primary, secondary, transitory, and inimical cadences, thus retreating in the direction of Aron's prescriptions.[35]

30. Oratio Tigrini, *Compendio della musica* (Venice, 1588), Book III, chaps. 6–19.
31. Giovanni Maria Artusi, *L'Arte del contraponto ridotta in tavole* (Venice, 1586), p. 43.
32. Joachim Burmeister, *Musica poetica* (Rostock, 1606), chap. 6.
33. Sethus Calvisius, *Melopoiia* (Erfurt, 1592), chap. 14.
34. Pietro Pontio, *Ragionamento di musica* (Parma, 1588), pp. 94–121.
35. For a detailed account of how later authors, particularly Burmeister and Calvisius modified Zarlino's theory, see Bernard Meier, *Die Tonarten der klassischen Vokalpolyphonie, nach den Quellen dargestellt* (Utrecht, 1974), pp. 86–102. This book, of which an English translation of a revised edition is being prepared by Ellen Beebe for publication by Broude Brothers, is also recommended for the study of other aspects of later modal theory. See also Harry Powers, "Mode," in *The New Grove Dictionary of Music and*

One reason why Zarlino may have deemphasized the plainchant tradition is suggested by his comments on Mode 9. He defends this new mode against those who deny its existence because it is not represented among the "intonations of the psalms," that is, the psalm tones (chapter 26). The psalm tones, he insists, are one thing, the melodies composed in the different modes, another. Then in almost the same breath he justifies the finals of the new modes, A and C, by the fact that these are among the pitches on which *differentiae* may occur. The urge to rationalize the four new modes may have directed Zarlino away from criteria developed in plainchant practice and led him to suppress the reciting tone as a characteristic modal step for regular cadences.

Despite his insistence on the independence from antiquity of the church modes, Zarlino enumerated some of the traditional epithets for their ethos, which he was careful to report as opinions of others. The description of Mode 1 as intermediate between sad and cheerful, suited to words "full of gravity" and dealing with "lofty" and "edifying" subjects, recalls Glarean's identification of this mode as grave, prudent, dignified, and modest, which he based on the much touted attributes of the classical Dorian.[36] Yet the two Dorians had nothing to do with each other, as Zarlino knew. On the other hand, in qualifying the Third Mode as one that moved the listener to tears, Zarlino avoided any reference to the ancient Phrygian's capacity to incite men to battle. Concerning the Fifth Mode, Zarlino hedged: some claimed it aroused modesty, happiness, and relief from cares; yet the ancients (*antichi*) applied it to words of victory, for which reason it was called joyous, modest, and pleasing. Are these "ancients" the Greeks or the plainchant composers? In Chapter 5 Zarlino cited sources that called the Greek Lydian a lamenting mode and others who found it horrible, sad, and mournful; so he could not have meant the ancient Greeks. If the "ancients" are the composers of plainchant, the remark is not applicable to Zarlino's Mode 5, because they introduced B-flat into this mode, turning it into new Mode 11. A similar difficulty surrounds the qualification of Mode 6 as devout and tearful. The attribution of lasciviousness combined with cheerfulness and modesty to Mode 7 seems to stem from Aron.[37] Mode 8, reports Zarlino, is characterized by musical practitioners as having "a certain natural softness and an abundant sweetness."[38]

For Modes 9 to 12 Zarlino did not have previous Italian authors to lean upon; there were only the examples of the sacred and secular repertories, reports from antiquity, and Glareanus. The attributes Zarlino assigned to Mode 9—good cheer, sweetness, pleasant seriousness, softness, and suitability to lyric poetry—agree with Glarean[39] and Zarlino's own earlier report of what "some [Glarean] claimed" to be

---

Musicians (London, 1980), 12:406, Table 7; and the review of Meier's book by Leeman Perkins in *Journal of the American Musicological Society* 31 (1978): 136–48.

36. Glarean, *Dodekachordon*, II, 21.

37. Pietro Aron, *Trattato della natura*, chap. 25.

38. Glarean, on the other hand, speaks of "a tranquil dignity which both moves and dominates people," *Dodekachordon*, II, 22, Miller trans., p. 262.

39. Ibid., II, 17.

the qualities of the ancient Aeolian (chapter 5). With respect to Mode 10 Zarlino refers the reader to the attributes of Modes 2 and 4. Zarlino again agrees with Glarean on Mode 11, that it is apt for dancing;[40] indeed, he notes, most *balli* heard in Italy are in this mode. Mode 12, Zarlino, like Glarean, finds suitable for love songs but adds that it is thought to have something sad about it.[41]

The detachment with which he dealt with modal ethos, his carelessness in borrowing classical attributes, and the obvious dependence on Glarean, in whom he otherwise placed little faith, should persuade us not to take Zarlino's pronouncements on modal ethos seriously. More significant is a statement made in the book on counterpoint (chapter 10), where he divided the modes into two classes, according to whether the harmony built on the final yields a major or minor third. In Modes 5, 6, 7, 8, 11, and 12 the third is major, and these modes are cheerful and lively, "because in them the consonances are frequently arranged according to the nature of the sonorous number, that is, the fifth is harmonically divided into a major and minor third, which is very pleasing to the ear."[42] In the other modes, 1, 2, 3, 4, 9, and 10, the fifth is divided arithmetically "in such a way that often one hears the consonances arranged contrary to the nature of the sonorous number . . . with the result that I can only describe as sad or languid, and which renders the entire composition soft."[43] The importance of these remarks lies not in their adumbration of the major-minor system, in support of which they have usually been cited, but in that Zarlino, contrary to attributions of emotional qualities he made in Part IV on purely melodic grounds, here ascribes affective qualities to modes on the grounds of simultaneous combinations or chords. If the species of fifth that is central to both authentic and plagal forms dominates, as it should, the melodic structure of the parts, it is inevitable that the quality of its lowest third will permeate the harmony and mood.

The reasoning that led Zarlino to credit greater naturalness and numerical priority to the major-third modes led him eventually to revise the order and numbering of the modes and to incorporate this in the 1573 and later editions of the *Istitutioni*.[44] The reordering was an outcome of renumbering the octave species, which in the 1558 edition are figured starting with A-a. In his *Dimostrationi harmoniche*,[45] Zarlino proposed that the first octave species be that bounded by c and c'. The reasons are noteworthy. If a string and its segments are divided insofar as possible through the harmonic means, this is the species that results. For an explanation of the nature of this division, it is necessary to go to *Istitutioni* Part I, chapter 39 (see Figure 1). There Zarlino makes several harmonic divisions, first of the octave into a fifth below

40. Ibid., II, 20.

41. Ibid., II, 27.

42. Zarlino, *The Art of Counterpoint, Part Three of Le Istitutioni harmoniche, 1558*, trans. Guy A. Marco and Claude V. Palisca (New Haven, 1968; New York, 1976), p. 22.

43. Ibid.

44. Concerning the editions of the *Istitutioni*, see Palisca, Introduction to *The Art of Counterpoint*, p. xx.

45. (Venice, 1571), Ragionamento 5, Definitione 8, p. 270.

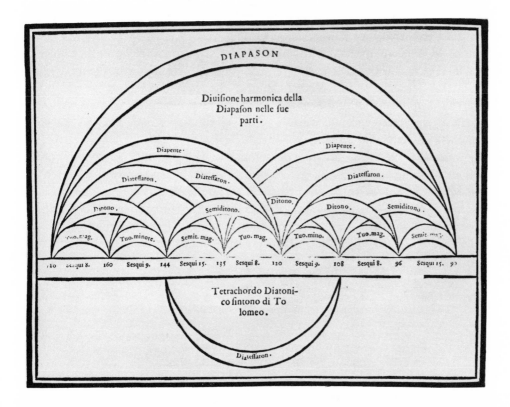

Figure 1: *Le Istitutioni harmoniche,* II, 39, Harmonic Division of the Octave in All Its Parts

and a fourth above. He then divides harmonically the fifth (the fourth not being susceptible of harmonic division), obtaining a major third below and a minor third above. Not only are the intervals so far all products of harmonic division, but they are, besides, superparticular ratios (3:2, 4:3, 5:4, and 6:5) and, as expressed in these root terms, they are contained within the *senario* or numbers 1 to 6.[46] If, then, fourths are measured off from each end of the fifth, this will divide the major third into two unequal whole tones, 9:8 to the left, 10:9 to the right, and the minor third into a major semitone, 16:15, to the left, and a major tone, 9:8, to the right. This division is "according to the harmonic and sonorous numbers," in which the larger interval is always the lower one, and tallies with the syntonic diatonic tetrachord of Ptolemy. Zarlino now divides the octave once again (this time arithmetically, though he does not say so), resulting in a fifth at the top. This fifth also is divided harmonically into a major and minor third. Meanwhile the upper boundary of the first fifth divides the major third into two parts, a 10:9 tone below and 9:8 tone above. Finally, the upper fourth from the first division is divided by measuring a major third from

46. Concerning the harmonic and arithmetic means, see above, n. 6; concerning the centrality of the *senario* to Zarlino's theory, see Palisca, Introduction, *The Art of Counterpoint,* p. xv.

the lower boundary and a minor third from the upper boundary. Not all these divisions are harmonic, Zarlino acknowledges, but they are all somehow a consequence of divisions that are harmonic. The results, shown in Figure 1, cannot be obtained except in the C-octave. (The main divisions are shown in Figure 2.)

The C-octave, Zarlino further claims in the *Dimostrationi,* was the first octave considered in music. Only after it was established were the notes Gamma, A, and B added at the lower end and d, e, f, g, aa at the upper end. For this historical argument, he offers no proof.

Adriano [Willaert], as interlocutor in the dialogue, now advances a further reason. Nothing appeared stranger to him in music than the fact that, given the syllables *ut, re, mi, fa, sol, la,* the first species of all the primary consonances began on the second syllable (that is, the species of octave on A, of fifths on d, and of fourths on a—all sung *re* in either the hard or natural hexachords). In the traditional species the syllable *ut* is reached only with the fourth species, but all the traditional species could

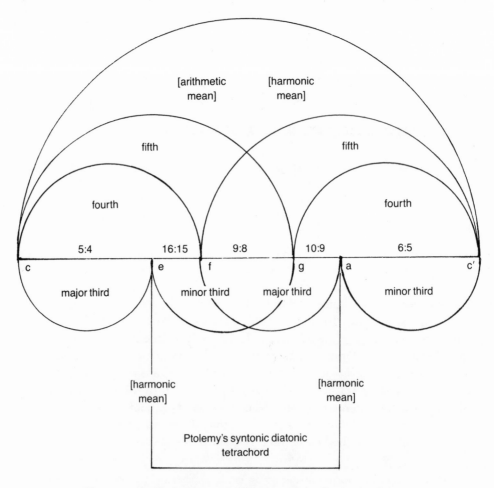

Figure 2: Zarlino's Harmonic Division of the Optimum Octave

not begin on the same note, such as A, for then the second species of fifth would be a diminished fifth, nor on D, for then the third species of fourth would be a tritone. All the species of consonance, however, can be started on c and completed without interruption.

Similarly, starting on c, the series of finals of the twelve modes can be fitted without interruption on the first six notes, c, d, e, f, g, a, and these finals would be sung on the syllables *ut, re, mi, fa, sol, la.* The sixteen notes of the gamut, from Gamma to aa (our G to a'), would then contain the plagal and authentic forms of all the twelve modes.

Finally, it occurred to Zarlino that, arranged in this way, the first, second, and third species were separated by a whole tone, as were the ancient Dorian, Phrygian, and Lydian. In Definition 14 he actually proposes that the first mode on C be called Dorian, that on D, Phrygian, and so on for Lydian, Mixolydian, Ionian, and Aeolian.

In the second (1573) and subsequent editions of the *Istitutioni* Zarlino adopted the numbering of the modes proposed in the *Dimostrationi*. However he never returned to the suggestion that the Greek names be applied to this new order. When using the more widely circulated 1573 edition the following equivalences of the modes should be kept in mind:

1558	1	2	3	4	5	6	7	8	9	10	11	12
1573	3	4	5	6	7	8	9	10	11	12	1	2

The chapter headings and numbering remain the same in the 1573 edition, but the material on a given mode appears under the heading of the new mode number. The following table shows the concordance of the contents of the chapters in the two editions.

1558	18	19	20	21	22	23	24	25	26	27	28	29
1573	20	21	22	23	24	25	26	27	28	29	18	19

Zarlino included several chapters at the end of Part IV that are not strictly about the modes but represent, rather, some concluding thoughts about musical composition, performance, and criticism in general. Two of these, Chapters 32 and 33, are among the few portions of this book that have been previously translated into English or any other language.[47] They have also occasioned more commentary than any other chapters of the fourth book, and this with good reason, for composers rarely expressed themselves on such secrets of the trade as setting a text to music or joining syllables properly to the notes when singing.

Chapters 32, on text expression, and 33, on text underlay, along with most of Part III of the *Istitutioni,* are believed to sum up teachings of Willaert. It is a compelling idea. Five works of Willaert, the only composer mentioned in chapter 32, are cited to illustrate various points. Another disciple of Willaert also wrote chapters on each of these subjects: Nicola Vicentino in *L'Antica musica ridotta alla moderna*

---

47. See Oliver Strunk, *Source Readings in Music History* (New York, 1950), pp. 256–61.

prattica.[48] Zarlino's instructions are at once more thorough and subtle. Whereas Vicentino associates minor consonances and slow motion with sad subjects and major consonances and fast motion with cheerful ones, Zarlino goes beyond this to point out that melodic motion with whole tones and major thirds as well as harmony containing the major sixth produces a harsh and bitter effect, while melodic motion through semitones and minor thirds and the harmony of the minor sixth induces a sweet, sorrowful, and soft affection. He also notes the greater virility of natural steps as against accidental steps, which are somewhat languid. The resource of the suspended seventh and fourth for expressions of bitterness is also noted. Both authors insist upon faithful rendering of long and short syllables, Vicentino paying greater attention to the nature of the language, whether French, Spanish, German, Latin, or Tuscan, each of which has its characteristic accents, syllable lengths, and steps and leaps.

Zarlino's chapter 33 on text underlay has been shown to be based on similar instructions in Giovanni Maria Lanfranco's *Scintille di musica* (Brescia, 1533).[49] The rules of Zarlino are essentially those of Lanfranco, expanded and brought up to date. Lanfranco numbered Willaert, along with Berchem and Costanzo Festa, among the *moderni,* on whose practices his treatise presumably was based. In a letter to Willaert he expressed admiration for his music: "I sing it and have it sung whenever I can get hold of it."[50] A later writer on the subject of text underlay, Gaspar Stocker, in *De musica verbali libri duo,* written between 1570 and 1580 and never published, credited Willaert with a new approach to text underlay:[51]

> Recently, Adrian Willaert seems to have begun, and happily so, a new music, in which he does away altogether with the liberties taken by the older composers [in matters of text underlay]. He so strictly observes well-defined rules that his compositions offer the singer greatest pleasure and no difficulties at all as far as the words are concerned. All modern composers follow him now.

Stocker makes a veiled reference here to the *Musica nova,* the collection published by Antonio Gardane of Venice in 1559. Zarlino cited several compositions from this collection, which contains music composed in the late thirties and early forties.[52] A

48. (Rome, 1555), Book IV, chaps. 29 and 39. See also Don Harran, "Vicentino and His Rules of Text Underlay," *Musical Quarterly,* 59 (1973): 620–32.

49. Don Harran, "New Light on the Question of Text Underlay Prior to Zarlino," *Acta Musicologica* 14 (1973): 24–56, where the relevant excerpts are given in Italian and English. For a complete translation of Lanfranco's treatise, see Barbara Lee, "Giovanni Maria Lanfranco's *Scintille di musica* and its Relation to 16th-Century Music Theory," Ph.D. diss., Cornell University, 1961, pp. 50–261.

50. Letter of 1531 quoted by Harran, "New Light," p. 53, from Rome, Bibl. Apost. Vaticana, MS Vat. lat 5318, fols. 192r–195v.

51. Edward E. Lowinsky, "A Treatise on Text Underlay by a German Disciple of Francisco de Salinas," *Festschrift Heinrich Besseler* (Leipzig, 1962), pp. 231–51.

52. Concerning the dating of this collection, see: Lowinsky, ibid.; Armen Carapetyan, "The Musica Nova of Adriano Willaert," *Journal of Renaissance and Baroque Music* [now *Musica Disciplina*], 1

recent study shows that Gardane, possibly under the influence of Willaert's circle, reached a new standard of accuracy and perspicacity in printing texts under notes as they should be sung.[53] Despite the dependence on Lanfranco's formulations, then, Zarlino's chapter 33 may be regarded as a faithful account of Willaert's principles of text underlay.

The translator of this book has sought to render Zarlino's text in an English style and vocabulary consistent with modern usage. But there are some special cases that deserve comment. *Harmonia,* when Zarlino meant by it agreement of sounds in the Platonic sense, is translated, as is normally done, "harmony." But it is left "*harmonia*" when it stands for the Greek *harmonia* in the sense of a modal scale, to distinguish it from Zarlino's *Modo. Melodia,* when it stands for the Greek general concept of *melos* as a composite of melody, rhythm, and text, is rendered "melos," otherwise "melody" or "music." *Modulatione* becomes "melody" or "melodic line." *Cantilena,* when it refers to plainsong, is translated "chant," otherwise "vocal composition," or simply "composition." For *Parlare* the translator has chosen "speech," for *Numero,* "rhythm," because in the present context the terms have these specific denotations.

As with Part III, *The Art of Counterpoint,* the 1558 edition was chosen as the basis of this translation. But for Part IV the compelling reason for selecting this version is that in it the modes and species of consonances are numbered in the conventional order. Despite the good case Zarlino made for renumbering them, it failed to gain acceptance, and today we still number the modes as in the 1558 edition. The paging in brackets in this translation follows the 1558 edition. When Zarlino added in the 1573 edition prose that the translator considered significant, she has given it in a footnote. The numbering of the musical examples is the translator's. Otherwise material introduced by her is in brackets, except for emendations, which are accounted for in the footnotes. The original note values have been preserved in the musical examples, but barlines were added between the staves. *Musica ficta* was applied by the editor. Chants named by Zarlino are located through footnotes in the most common modern chant books (which are listed below under "Abbreviations"), not because we assume that a modern published version is identical to that which Zarlino knew but to provide a handy reference to a melody that usually conforms to his description.

The English versions of classical quotations supplied in the footnotes are by the translator in consultation with Siegmund Levarie, of the City University of New York. The standard translations rarely served our purpose, being too free, particularly in musical terminology.

(1946): 200–21; Helga Meier, Introduction to *Fünf Madrigale venezianischer Komponisten um Adrian Willaert,* Das Chorwerk 105; and Anthony Newcomb, "Editions of Willaert's *Musica Nova:* New Evidence, New Speculations," *Journal of the American Musicological Society* 26 (1972): 132–45.

53. Mary S. Lewis, "Antonio Gardane and His Publications of Sacred Music, 1538–55," Ph.D. diss., Brandeis University, 1979.

The translator wishes to express her gratitude to Siegmund Levarie for his expert help, offered generously throughout her work on the translation; to Barry S. Brook, executive officer of the Ph.D. program in music at the City University of New York, for his continued interest and readiness to listen and give valuable advice whenever needed; to H. Wiley Hitchcock, William B. Kimmel, and Sherman Van Solkema of the City University of New York for their useful suggestions in matters great and small.

The editor acknowledges the assistance of M. Jennifer Bloxam in checking sources and classical references and other editorial tasks. Musical examples were scripted by A-R Editions through a computer program devised by Thomas Hall.

The preparation of this volume was made possible by a grant to Yale University by the National Endowment for the Humanities, Translations Program, Susan Mango, director.

Claude V. Palisca

List of Abbreviations

AR   *Antiphonale sacrosanctae Romanae ecclesiae pro diurnis horis* (no. 820). Tournai, 1942; reprint, 1949.

GR   *Graduale sacrosanctae Romanae ecclesiae de tempore et de sanctis* (no. 696). Tournai, 1938; reprint, 1956.

LU   *The Liber Usualis, with Introduction and Rubrics in English* (no. 801). Tournai, 1934; reprint, 1958.

PrM   *Processionale monasticum ad usum congregatione Gallicae ordinis Sancti Benedicti.* Solesmes, 1893; reprint, 1949.

WA   *Antiphonaire monastique . . . de Worcester. Paléographie musicale,* XII. Tournai, 1922.

LE ISTITVTIONI
HARMONICHE

DI M. GIOSEFFO ZARLINO DA CHIOGGIA;

Nelle quali; oltra le materie appartenenti

ALLA MVSICA;

Si trouano dichiarati molti luoghi

di Poeti, d'Hiſtorici, & di Filoſofi;

Si come nel leggerle ſi potrà chiaramente vedere.

¶ Θεῦ διδόντος, οὐδὲν ἰσχύει φθόνος.
Καὶ μὴ διδόντος, οὐδὲν ἰσχύει πόνος.

Con Priuilegio dell'Illuſtriſſ. Signoria di Venetia,
per anni X.

IN VENETIA M D LVIII.

LA QVARTA ET
VLTIMA PARTE
Delle Istitutioni harmoniche
DI M. GIOSEFFO ZARLINO
DA CHIOGGIA.

Quello che sia Modo.　　　　　Cap. 1.

EDVTO nella Parte precedente, et a sufficienza mostrato il modo, che si hà da tenere nel comporre le cantilene; & in qual maniera, & con quanto bello, & regolato ordine le Consonanze l'vna con l'altra, & etiandio con le Dissonanze, si concatennino; verrò hora à ragionar delli Modi. Et benche tale impresa sia non poco difficile (massimamente volendo io ragionare alcune cose di loro secodo l'vso de gli Antichi)si perche al presente (come altre volte hò detto) la Musica moderna dall'Antica è variatamète essercitata; come anco per non ritrouarsi alcuno essempio, o vestigio alcuno di loro, che ne possa códurre in vna vera, & perfetta cognitione; tuttauia non voglio restare di discorrere alcune cose; & con quel meglior modo, ch'io potrò, ragionando in vniuersale, & in particolare anco, di toccare alcune delle più notabili, secondo che mi soueniranno alla memoria, & anco mi torneranno in proposito; dalle quali li Studiosi potranno venire alla risolutione di qualunque dubbio, che sopra tal materia li potesse occorrere: Ilche fatto, verrò a mostrar dipoi, in qual maniera li Musici moderni li vsino; & dirò di quante sorti si trouino, l'ordine loro, & in che maniera le Harmonie, che nascono da loro si accommodino al Parlare, cioè alle Parole. Douendo adunque dar principio a tal ragionameto, vederemo prima quello, che sia Modo; acciò possiamo sapere, che cosa sia quello, di cui intendemo ragionare. Ne ciò sara fatto fuori di proposito; poi che'l Modo è il principal Soggetto di questo nostro vltimo ragionamento. Si debbe adunque auertire, che questa parola Modo, oltra di ogn'altra sua significatione, che sono molte; significa propiamente la Ragione, cioè quella misura, o forma, che adoperiamo nel fare alcuna cosa, laqual ne astrenge poi a non passar più oltra; facendone operare tutte le cose con vna certa mediocrità, o moderatione. Et bene veramente, imperoche (come dice Pindaro) ἔπεται δ' ἐν ἑκάϛω μέτρον. In ciascuna cosa è Modo, o misura; Ilche disse anco Horatio dopo lui;

Est modus in rebus, sunt certi deniq; fines;

Quos vltra citraq; nequit consistere rectum: Imperoche tal mediocrità, o moderatione non è altro, che vna certa maniera, ouero ordine terminato, & fermo nel procedere, per ilquale la cosa si conserua nel suo essere, per virtù della proportione, che in essa si ritroua; che non solo ne diletta, ma etiandio molto giouamento ne apporta. De qui viene, che se per caso, ouero a studio tal'ordine si allontana da tal proportione, non si può dire quanto offendi; & quanto il sentimento abhorisca questo tal'ordine. Hauendo adunque li Musici, & li Poeti antichi considerato tal cosa: perche gli vni, & gli altri erano vna cosa istessa (come hò detto altroue) chiamarono le loro compositioni Modi; nelle quali sotto varie materie, per via del Parlare esprimeuano, accompagnate l'vna all'altra con proportione, diuersi Numeri, o Metri, & diuerse Harmonie. Onde nacque dipoi, che posero tre Generi de Modi, non hauendo consideratione al Suono, ouero all'Harmonia, che nasceua: ma solamente alle altre parti aggiunte insieme; l'vno de i quali chiamarono Dithirambico, l'altro Tragico, & il terzo Nomico; di i quali le lor spetie furno molte; si come Epithalamij, Comici, Encomiastici, & altri simili. Considerando dipoi le Harmonie da per sè, che vsciuano da tali congiungimenti, perche riteneuano in in loro vna certa, propia, & terminata forma, le nominarono simigliantemete Modi; aggiungendoli Dorio, o Frigio, ouero altro nome, secondo il nome de i popoli, che furno inuetori di quella harmonia, ouero da quelli, che

più si

CHAPTER I

What Is a Mode

[293]

IN the preceding Part [of *Le Istitutioni harmoniche*][1] I sufficiently demonstrated the method that should be followed in composing vocal music, and showed in what manner and with what beautiful and regulated order the consonances are linked with one another and with the dissonances. Now I shall discuss the modes. This task is very difficult, especially since I want to discuss certain things according to the usage of the ancients. The difficulty arises because, as I have said at other times,[2] modern music is practiced differently from ancient music, and because there is no example or vestige of ancient music which can lead us to a true and perfect knowledge of it. Nevertheless, I do not want to refrain from discussing certain matters in the best way I can. I shall deal with these matters both in general and in particular, and shall touch upon some of the more notable points as they come to mind and as they become pertinent to the subject. From this discussion, scholars will be able to resolve any doubts which might occur to them in these matters. This having been done, I shall show how modern musicians use the modes and shall talk of how many sorts of modes there are, their order, and the manner in which the harmonies[3] generated by them are accommodated to speech,[4] that is, to the words.

To begin this discussion, we shall see what a mode is, so that we may know what it is that we intend to discuss. This is not beyond our purpose, for mode is the main subject of this, our last, discourse. It should be noted that the word "mode," in addition to all its many other meanings, properly means "reason," namely, that measure or form which prevents us from going too far in anything we do, making us act in all things with a certain temperateness or moderation. And this is truly good, because (as Pindar says), ἔπεται δ ἐν ἑκάστῳ μέτρον, "In everything there is mode, or measure."[5] The same thing was said after him by Horace:

> Est modus in rebus, sunt certi denique fines,
> Quos ultra, citraque nequit consistere rectum.[6]

1. *Le Istitutioni harmoniche*, Part III. In Gioseffo Zarlino, *The Art of Counterpoint*, trans. Guy A. Marco and Claude V. Palisca, (New Haven: Yale University Press, 1968; New York, W. W. Norton, 1976).

2. *Le Istit. harm.*, II, 4.

3. See Introduction, p. xxi for a discussion of this term.

4. See Introduction, p. xxi.

5. Pindar *Olympia* 13. 47–48.

6. Horace *Satirae* 1. 1. 106–07: "There are certain limits, beyond which on either side nothing right can exist."

This temperateness or moderation is nothing other than a certain delimited and closed order of operation through which the essence of a thing is preserved by virtue of the proportion found in it. This not only delights us but also brings us much profit. From this it arises that if order is separated from proportion, either by chance or by intention, the result is offensive and abhorrent to our feelings to a degree that goes beyond description.

Ancient musicians and poets, who were one and the same (as I have said elsewhere[7]), considered this matter, and called their compositions "modes." In these they expressed in words a variety of subjects, accompanied by different rhythms[8] or meters and different harmonies, proportionate among themselves. Hence they proposed three classes [generi] of modes, not in terms of the sound or harmony that came into being, but only according to the other parts [words and rhythm] joined together. One class they called "dithyrambic"; the second, "tragic"; and the third, "nomic." The species of these classes were many, such as epithalamian, comic, encomiastic, and others like them.

The ancients also considered the *harmoniae* themselves which emerged from these composites and likewise called them "modes," because they retained in themselves a certain intrinsic and limited form. They called them "Dorian," "Phrygian," or by other names, according to the name of the people who either invented a *harmonia* or who [294] used to enjoy one species of *harmonia* more than another. Thus the Dorian *harmonia* was named after the Dorians, who were its inventors, the Phrygian *harmonia* after the people who used to live in Phrygia, the Lydian after those of Lydia, and so forth. Since each mode had something intrinsic in its tune, and was accompanied by different rhythms, they called some modes grave and severe, some bacchanal and wild, some honest and religious, and others lascivious and bellicose. For this reason they took great care in joining the *harmonia* with rhythm, and these with the appropriate subject matter expressed in speech or spoken word, according to the nature of the subject matter.

Having considered all these things, the ancients categorized compositions according to the nature of the composite; for example, they used the name "tearful modes" for elegies, inasmuch as they contained sad and plaintive subjects. This can be seen concretely in the two volumes which Ovid wrote after he was sent into exile by Augustus,[9] as well as in almost innumerable works by other authors. It can also be seen in what Ovid wrote in the epistle of Sappho to Phaon, showing that amatory things are tearful and suited to elegies:

> Forsitan & quare mea sint alterna requiris
>   Carmina, cum lyricis sim magis apta modis.
> Flendus amor meus est. Elegeia flebile carmen.
>   Non facit ad lacrymas barbitos ulla meos.[10]

7. *Le Istit. harm.*, Proem; II, 6.
8. See Introduction, p. xxi.
9. Ovid *Tristia, Epistolae ex Ponto.*
10. Ovid *Heroides* 15. 5–8: "Perhaps, too, you may ask why my verses alternate, when I am better

Horace mentioned these modes, saying:

> Tu semper urges flebilibus modis
> Mysten ademptum.[11]

And Boethius, in Book 3 of *The Consolation of Philosophy,* said:

> Quondam funera coniugis
> Vates thraicius gemens,
> Postquàm flebilibus modis,
> Sylvas currere, mobiles
> Amnes stare coegerat.[12]

Cicero also commemorated these modes in the *Tusculan Disputations* when, mentioning at the same time the humble and depressed, he said: "Haec cum praessis et flebilibus modis, qui totis theatris moestitiam inferant, concinuntur."[13] In another place, mentioning the slow [modes], he said: "Solet idem Roscius dicere, se quo plus aetatis sibi accederet, eo tardiores tibicinis modos, et cantus remissiores esse facturum."[14]

Some modes were called "lamentful modes," as can be seen in Apuleius when he says: "Et sonus Tibiae Zigiae mutatur in quaerulum Lydij modum."[15] Others were called "sweet modes," as Horace shows in another place when he says:

> Me nunc Tressa Chloë regit,
> Dulces docta modos, &
> Citharae sciens.[16]

---

suited to the lyric mode. I must weep for my love, and elegy is the weeping strain, no barbiton is suited to my tears." The edition by Grant Showerman, Loeb Classical Library (London: William Heinemann, 1963), p. 180, has *requiras* for Zarlino's *requiris, elegiae* for Zarlino's *elegeia, lacrimas* for Zarlino's *lacrymas,* and *meas* for Zarlino's *meos.* The authorship of this letter has been disputed, but it is generally conceded to be Ovid's.

11. Horace *Odes* 2. 9. 9–10: "You always plead in tearful modes the dead Mystes."

12. Boethius *The Consolation of Philosophy* 3. 12. 5–9: "At the funeral of his wife, the Thracian poet sighed in weeping modes after he had compelled the woods to run and the mobile rivers to stand." The edition by E. K. Rand and S. J. Tester, Loeb Class. Lib. (London: W. Heinemann, 1973), p. 306, has *Threicius* for Zarlino's *thraicius.*

13. Cicero *Tusculan Disputations* 1. 44. 106: "They sang these words with dampened and tearful modes which carried sadness into the whole theatre." The edition by J. E. King, Loeb Class. Lib. (London: W. Heinemann, 1971), p. 126, has *maestitiam* for Zarlino's *moestitiam.*

14. Cicero *De oratore* 1. 59. 254: "The same Roscius likes to say that the older he grows, the slower he will make the modes of the tibia and the lower pitched the music."

15. Apuleius *Metamorphoses* 4. 33: "And the sound of Zygia's tibia was changed into the querulous Lydian mode."

16. Horace *Odes* 3. 9. 9–10: "The Thracian Chloe, learned in sweet modes and knowledgeable on the kithara, now rules me." The edition by C. E. Bennett, Loeb Class. Lib. (London: W. Heinemann, 1968), p. 212, has *Thressa* for Zarlino's *Tressa,* and Zarlino's third line is part of the second.

And Seneca also:

> Sacrifica dulces tibia effundat modos. [17]

Still others were called "sad modes," as can be seen by the authority of Boethius:

> Carmina qui quondam studio florente peregi
> Flebilis heu moestos cogor inire modos. [18]

Some modes were called "immodest," as Quintilian recalled, saying: "Apertius tamen profitendum puto, non hanc a me praecipi, quae nunc in scenis effoeminata, et impudicis modis fracta." [19] Other modes were called "rough" or "coarse," as is seen in Ovid:

> Dumque, rudem praebente modum tibicine Tusco,
> Lydius aequatam ter pede pulsat humum; [20]

Still others were called "discordant," and these are mentioned by Statius:

> Discordesque modos, & singultantia verba
> Molior. [21]

Lastly (leaving aside many other [types of modes] for the sake of brevity) some compositions were universally called "lyrical modes," as can be seen by the authority of Ovid, mentioned above. [22]

The modes were not expressed by voice only but were accompanied by harmony generated by some instrument, be it a kithara, lyre, pipe, or any other sort of instrument. There was a great difference among the modes, for the people of one province used one manner of verse and one instrument, and those of another province used another instrument and another manner of verse. The modes were different not only in instrument and manner of verse but also in harmony, because one people used

---

17. Seneca *Agamemnon* 584: "Let the sacrificial tibia give forth sweet modes."

18. Boethius *The Consolation of Philosophy* 1. 1. 1–2: "Once I completed songs with eagerness, now that I am weeping I am forced to initiate sad modes." The edition by E. K. Rand and S. J. Tester Loeb Class. Lib., p. 130, has *maestos* for Zarlino's *moestos*.

19. Quintilian *Institutio oratoria* 1. 10. 31: "I think that it must be more openly stated that it was not [the music] that I recommended. [The music] now on the stage has been made effeminate by immodest modes." The edition by H. E. Butler, Loeb Class. Lib. (London: W. Heinemann, 1969), p. 174, has *effeminata* for Zarlino's *effoeminata*.

20. Ovid *Ars amatoria* 1. 111–112: "While to the rude mode offered by the tibia-playing Tuscan Lidius struck the levelled floor three times with his foot." The edition by J. H. Mozley, Loeb Class. Lib. (London: W. Heinemann, 1962), p. 20, has *Ludius* for Zarlino's *Lydius*.

21. Statius *Silvae* 5. 5. 26–27: "Bring forth discordant modes and sobbing words."

22. Chapter 1, n. 10.

one sort of harmony and another used another sort. The modes also differed in the rhythms of the verse.

From this it followed that the modes were named after those people (as I have said above) who [295] took special pleasure in a particular manner or had been its inventors. Hence it is understandable that if a people, like that of Phrygia, heard some foreign manner, they declared it to be the mode of the province where it was used the most or where it had been discovered. For example, they named the Aeolian mode after the people of Aeolia, its inventors, for this mode was contained in a certain hymn composed in the lyrical mode with certain rhythms, and the Aeolians took pleasure in singing this hymn to the sound of the lyre or the kithara. According to the opinion of some (which I believe to be false), at that time the lyre and the kithara were the same thing. Such an instrument was also used by the Dorians, although they may have used another manner of verse and a very different harmony. Pindar attests to this fact when he calls a similar instrument Δωρίαν φόρμιγγα [Dorian phorminx], that is, Dorian kithara.[23]

We read in Horace:

> Sonantem mistum tibijs carmen lyra,
> Hac Dorium, illis Barbarum.[24]

The word *Barbarum*, which Horace intended for the Phrygian mode, shows that the Phrygians also used pipes. And they truly used to play this mode with such instruments, as I can show with many citations which I leave aside for the sake of brevity, except for one from Vergil:

> O vere phrygiae (neque enim phryges) ite per alta
> Dindyma, ubi assuetis biforem dat tibia cantum;[25]

And one from Ovid:

> Tibia dat phrygios, ut dedit ante modos;[26]

From these one can understand that what I have said is true.

The people who lived in Lydia also performed their harmonies on this instrument, and of this Horace is a witness, as we see here:

23. Pindar *Olympia* 1. 17.

24. Horace *Epodes* 9. 5–6: "Sounding mixed with tibias the song of the lyre, this one Doric, the other barbaric." The edition by C. E. Bennett, Loeb Class. Lib. p. 388, has *Sonante mixtum* for Zarlino's *Sonantem mistum*.

25. Vergil *Aeneid* 9. 617–18: "O you Phrygian women, indeed (for you are not Phrygian men), go over the heights of Dindymus, where to accustomed ears the double-reed tibia gives music." The edition by H. Rushton Fairclough, Loeb Class. Lib. (London: W. Heinemann, 1954), vol. 2, p. 154, has *adsuetis* for Zarlino's *assuetis*.

26. Ovid *Fasti* 4. 214: "The tibia, as it has before, presents Phrygian modes."

> Virtute functos more patrum duces,
> Lydis remisto carmine tibijs,
> Troianque, & Anchisen, & alma
> Progeniem Veneris canemus;[27]

Before Horace, Pindar, beseeching Jove for the sake of Psaumis of Camarina, winner of the Olympic games, says: "I come to you, O Jove, Λυδίοις αὐλοῖς," [with Lydian auloi], that is, with Lydian pipes.[28] Examples showing that the Lydians used the pipe are not lacking. We have the testimony of Apuleius, which is cited above,[29] and of many others, but those shown here will suffice.

From what has been said, then, we can understand that the ancient modes consisted of harmonies and rhythms performed by one sort of instrument, and that the differences between the modes lay in the variation of the harmonies, the diversity of the rhythms, and the manner of performance, namely, the type of instrument. And although some peoples conformed with others in regard to the harmonies or instruments, they differed in regard to the rhythms. If they were in agreement in regard to the rhythms, they differed in regard to the harmonies and instruments. Thus if they were in conformity in one or two things, they varied in the rest.

We see the same thing nowadays in different nations, inasmuch as the Italians use the same pattern of line, that is, [the same number of] verse feet or syllables, as the French and Spanish, namely, that of eleven syllables, but when one hears them sing, one perceives different harmonies and progressions. An Italian sings differently from a Frenchman, and a Spaniard sings in a manner different from that of a German, and of course different from that of the barbarian nations of infidels, which is obvious. The Italians and the French largely use the lute, the Spanish use the guitar [ceterone], which varies but a little from the lute, and other people use the pipe.

In regard to metrics, or versification, there are great differences among nations, their manners varying greatly from one to another. We may know this (to start at the beginning) from the fact that in some places outside Italy rhymed or blank verse of eleven syllables, similar to the Latin hendecasyllable, is not used, whereas in Italy, in France, and in Spain it is used very much. I believe that what is called rima [rhyme] in Italy comes from the Greek word ῥυϑμός, which means (as I have said elsewhere[30]) rhythm, or consonance, for it is from those correspondences and ties which are found at the end of the verses and which are called "cadences" [cadenze] that the consonance, or harmony, of the verse comes into being. The Italians do not use

---

27. Horace Odes 4. 15. 29–32: "Let us hymn with songs accompanied by Lydian flutes in the manner of the fathers the virtuous deeds of leaders of the Trojans, and Anchises, and the progeny of benign Venus." The edition by C. E. Bennett, Loeb Class. Lib. p. 346, has remixto for Zarlino's remisto, and almae for Zarlino's alma.

28. Pindar Olympia 5. 21.

29. Chapter 1, n. 15.

30. Le Istit. harm., II, 8.

these cadences very much in the manner of verse found in the *ottave rime,* or stanzas, or in the sonnets, *capitoli,* and other similar verses called "complete" [*interi*]. They utilize them more in canzonas and madrigals, in which many sorts of verses are used, such as those of seven syllables and similar others called "broken verses" [*versi rotti*].

Thus in Italy, mother of good and rare intellects, various manners of composing are used, as can be understood from the [diversity of forms, such as the] aforementioned *ottave rime,* or stanzas (whatever you want to call them), from the *terzetti, sestine,* sonnets, and *capitoli,* in all of which only one manner of verse is employed, namely, the complete verses. [The Italians then use cadences] in canzonas, [296] madrigals, and other similar verses, in which various sorts of meters are used in imitation of the odes of Horace. One must note, however, that the Horatian meters are without the cadences mentioned, whereas the Italians are bound to these cadences in the manner described, as can be seen in the learned and graceful canzonas of Petrarch and other most excellent men. I believe it is true that the learned Italian spirits have been the inventors of these cadences, inasmuch as I do not remember ever having found a similar way of composing with such cadences among the works of any other poet, either Greek or Latin, for all that the most learned Horace sang many odes in many different manners.

It is true that Latin poets (though not very frequently) have used similar cadences, or correspondences, in the middle and last syllables of some of their verses. These are called *canine* and are used by the Poet [Vergil] in the following verses:

> Ad terram misere, aut ignibus segra dedère.[31]

> Cornua vellatarum obvertimus antennarum.[32]

> Illum indignanti similem: similemque minanti.[33]

> Tum caput orantis nequicquam, & multa precantis.[34]

> Ora citatorum dextra contorsit equorum.[35]

Ovid also has observed this law in the following verse:

31. Vergil *Aeneid* 2. 566: "And flung themselves to the ground or dropped helpless into the fire." The edition by H. Rushton Fairclough, Loeb Class. Lib., vol. 1, p. 332, has *aegra* for Zarlino's *segra.*

32. Ibid., 3. 549: "We turn windward the horns of our stretched-out sails." The edition by H. Rushton Fairclough, Loeb Class. Lib., vol. 1, p. 384, has *velatarum* for Zarlino's *vellatarum,* and *antemnarum* for Zarlino's *antennarum.*

33. Ibid., 8. 649: "He looked indignant like one threatening."

34. Ibid., 10. 554: "Then as he pleaded in vain and begged much." Fairclough, vol. 2, p. 208, has *nequiquam* for Zarlino's *nequicquam.*

35. Ibid., 12. 373: "With his right hand he wrenched aside the jaws of the exerted horses." Fairclough, vol. 2, p. 325, has *detorsit* for Zarlino's *contorsit.*

Vim licet appelles, & culpam nomine veles.[36]

He has observed it in many other works as well which will not be cited here for the sake of brevity. Petrarch (as I believe) imitated this manner of composing, but arranged the cadences in a different way, rhyming the end of the verse with the middle of the following one:

Mai non vò piu cantar com'io soleva:
Ch'altri non m'intendeva: onde hebbi scorno.
E puossi in bel soggiorno esser molesto.[37]

The remainder of the poem proceeds in this way. Petrarch observed the same thing in the canzona *Vergine bella*[38] as well.[39]

Even if such a manner of composing with similar cadences is found among the Greek or Latin poets, it would be of little importance. For the first inventor of this manner of composing in Italian, even though he took the invention of some Greek or Latin poet, could pride himself as much as Horace prided himself on having been the first who discovered the way of composing lyrical verses in Latin in the manner of the Greeks. We can learn this about Horace from his own words:

Dicar, qua violens obstrepit Aufidus,
Et qua pauper aquae Daunus agrestium
Regnator populorum, ex humili potens
Princeps Aeolium carmen ad Italos
Deduxisse modos.[40]

36. Ovid *Heroides* 5. 131: "You may call it force, and veil the fault in the word."

37. Petrarch *Canzoniere* 105. 1–3: "Never more shall I sing as I used to, for she heard me not, hence I felt scorn; thus even in a beautiful spot one can feel ill at ease."

38. Ibid., 49.

39. Ed. of 1573: Sannazaro did the same in *Arcadia* in that part in the beginning where Ergasto, talking with the shepherd Selvaggio, says:

Menando un giorno gli agni appresso un fiume,
Vidi un bel lume in mezo di quell'onde,
Che con due bionde treccie allor mi strinse,
Et mi dipinse un volto in mezo'l cuore.

[Sannazaro *Arcadia* 1. 61–64: "One day leading my lambs beside a river I saw in the midst of those waves a beautiful light that bound me then with two blond tresses and painted in the middle of my heart a face." Most editions have *presso* for Zarlino's *appresso*, *trecce* for his *treccie*, *e* for his *et*, *mezzo al* for his *mezo'l*, and *core* for his *cuore*.

40. Horace *Odes* 3. 30. 10–14: "Where the violent Aufidus drowns me out and also where Daunus short of water rules over arrid people, I shall be called as the first who, from humble beginnings, knew how to lead an Aeolian song in the Italian modes." The edition by C. E. Bennett, Loeb Class. Lib., p. 278, has *regnavit* for Zarlino's *regnator*.

Tolomei also can pride himself on having been the first who expressed heroic verse, hexameter, and pentameter in Italian art.

Some claim that the most learned Florentine poet Dante Alighieri was the first inventor of *terzetti {terza rima}*, and Boccaccio of *ottava rima*. If therefore one wanted to give a particular name to these two manners of composing, desiring to name them after the country in which they were discovered, one would call both of them "Italian modes" (as Horace does in the passage above). If one wanted to name them after the region, one would call them "Tuscan modes." But if one wanted to name them after the inventors, one would call the first manner "Dantean mode" (so to speak), and the second manner "Boccaccian mode." In the same way, the kitharic and auletic nomes (as we have seen in Part II[41]) were named partly after the nation and partly after the inventors.

Even though in Italy there are many particular manners of verses, nevertheless the Greeks in our time, in addition to their other manners, have verses of fifteen syllables. An example of these verses is found in the works of Constantine Manasses, the great philosopher:

Ο τοῦ θεοῦ παντέλειος, καὶ παντοκτίστωρ λόγος,
Τὸν οὐρανὸν τὸν ἄναστρον παρήγαγεν ἀρχῆθεν.[42]

This means: "The word of God is perfect, and he who made all things in the world, in the beginning made the Heavens without stars." All the hexameters of Manasses are full of such verses, and [the Greeks] sing them according to their custom in a particular mode not used in Italy. Thus we can see from the Greeks and the Italians (not mentioning other nations) the differences in rhythms and harmonies that could occur in the modes of these nations at the time that music was in flower in Greece. For just as we see that each of these two nations in our time has a particular manner of verse and a particular manner of singing, so we should believe that the same was true among these nations in ancient times.

Although in our time some people of different nations converge on the same meter or verse feet and the same manner of composition in their songs, still they differ in the manner [297] of singing. These differences are found not only among different nations but also within the same nation and in the same region, as can be seen in Italy. For example, the songs called *villote* are sung in one manner in places near Venice and in another manner in Tuscany and in the kingdom of Naples. The same was once true among the ancients, for although the people of Doria and those of Aeolia used the same quality, or sort, of verse, and the same instrument, their harmonies were different in some aspects. From this we can understand the diversity of the names of the modes, for since the rhythm, instrument, and harmony differed from mode to mode, a diversity of names came into being. Hence I believe that the

41. *Le Istit. harm.*, II, 5.
42. Manasses *Compendium chronicum* 2A.

Dorian mode was different from the Aeolian, just as the Phrygian was different from the Lydian, and that they differed not only in regard to harmony but also in regard to rhythm, as can be understood from the varied effects generated by the different modes, which we shall see in due course.[43]

Thus we should not be surprised when we read[44] that Philoxenus, having tried to compose a dithyrambic poem in the Dorian mode, could never bring it to the desired end, because he was continually pulled to the Phrygian harmony suitable for this poem, the feet and rhythm of which are faster than those of any other kind of poem. The rhythms of the Dorian mode, on the other hand, are slower and more halting. Since there were different rhythms in the Dorian and Phrygian harmonies (as has been stated), it was impossible for Philoxenus to do anything that was good, just as it would be impossible, when dealing with the meters of Sapphic verse, to sing or lead in heroic verse. For Sapphic verse is composed of a trochee, a spondee, a dactyl, and, at the end, two trochees, or a trochee and a spondee, as in these two verses by Horace:

Mercuri facunde nepos Atlantis:[45]

and

Persicos odi puer apparatus;[46]

whereas heroic verse is composed of six feet alternating dactyls and spondees, as can be seen in each of the two following verses by Vergil:

Sed fugit interea, fugit irreparabile tempus.[47]

and

Parcere subiectis, & debellare superbos.[48]

I have pursued this discussion, perhaps longer than necessary, for no other reason than to enable the reader to understand more easily what was a mode in music. We can truly say that in ancient times a mode was a certain fixed form of melody,[49] composed with reason and artifice, and contained within a fixed and proportioned order of rhythm and harmony, adapted to the subject matter expressed in the text.

43. *Le Istit. harm.*, I, 5, 18, 19.
44. Aristotle *Politics* 1342b. 9–14.
45. Horace *Odes* I. 10. 1: "Mercury, thou eloquent grandson of Atlas."
46. Ibid., 1. 38. 1: "As a slave I hated the Persian apparatus."
47. Vergil *Georgics* 3. 284. "But meanwhile irreparable time flies away."
48. Vergil *Aeneid* 6. 853: "To have mercy on the humble, and to tame in war the proud."
49. See Introduction, p. xxii.

Modern musicians consider in their compositions only a certain order of singing and a certain species of harmony, and leave aside the consideration of the fixed rhythm or meter, for they say that this [aspect] belongs to the poets, especially now in our time when music is separated from poetry. However, as we shall see below,[50] modern musicians do consider this order [of singing and harmony] inasmuch as it is contained in one of the seven species of the diapason already shown,[51] divided harmonically or arithmetically.[52] Among these seven species there is a certain manner of singing which differs from one species to another, as we shall see, and this order of singing with differing manners or airs is called "mode" by the moderns. Some call it "trope," and some call it "tone."

We should not be surprised at those who want to call it "trope," because τϱόπος is the Greek word for "mode" or "direction." And if this term comes from the word τϱοπή, which means "turning" or "mutation," the name would make just as much sense, because one mode is turned and changed into another, as we shall see.[53]

"Tone" is not a bad term either, because the word "tone" (as Cleonides[54] shows in his *Introduction*) can mean four things. First, it may mean what the Greeks call φϑόγγος, which signifies any sound or inarticulate tone that does not move either up or down. Second, it may mean one of those two intervals shown in chapter 18 of Part III.[55] Third, it may mean a strong and sonorous voice, as when one says: "Francesco has a good, sonorous, and powerful tone," that is, a good, sonorous, and powerful voice. Last, it may mean that which has been discussed above, as when one says: "the Dorian tone, the Phrygian tone and the others," namely, the Dorian mode, the Phrygian mode and those that follow in order. Since the term "tone" is extended to several things, as we have seen, I have chosen to use the term "mode" and not "tone," in order to avoid ambiguity as much as possible.

In stating our definition of mode, we shall say with Boethius that a mode is a certain constitution in all the orders of notes, differing by pitch, and that this constitution is like a full corpus of melody[56] which arises from the conjunction of the consonances, such as the diapason, diapasondiapente, or disdiapason. Thus we find that one constitution comes into being from Proslambanomenos to Mese in which the intermediate notes or pitches are numbered. Similarly we find another constitution from Mese to Nete hyperboleon, always taking into account the intervening notes.

But [298] because these constitutions are really the various species of the

50. *Le Istit. harm.,* IV, 9, 11.

51. Ibid., III, 12.

52. See Introduction, p. viii.

53. *Le Istit. harm.,* IV, 17.

54. Euclid in Zarlino's text. Cleonides' *Introduction* was erroneously attributed to Euclid by many writers. The correct name is used throughout the translation. *Introduction* 12 (Meibom 19).

55. The large whole tone (9/8), and the small whole tone (10/9).

56. Boethius *De inst. mus.* 4. 15. Zarlino translates the phrase "plenum veluti modulationi corpus" as "un corpo pieno di modulatione." Concerning the term "modulatione," see Introduction, p. xxi.

diapason found from one letter to the other, as we have seen in chapter 12 of Part III, taking into account the intermediate notes, we shall say[57] that the mode is a certain form or quality of harmony found in each of the seven species of the diapason mentioned above. These seven species, when divided harmonically, give six[58] principal and authentic modes, from which, by arithmetic division, the collateral modes come into being. These collateral modes are called plagal or placal, as we shall see.[59]

57. Ed. of 1573: . . . as we also say in the Eleventh Definition of the Fifth [Discussion] of *Le Dimostrationi harmoniche,* and have also said above.

58. "Seven" in the 1558 edition. Corrected in the 1573 edition.

59. *Le Istit. harm.,* IV, 12.

CHAPTER 2   *The Different Terms That Have Been Used for Modes and the Reasons for Them*

ALTHOUGH I have called these manners of singing "modes," there have been some who have also called them *"harmoniae,"* some who have called them "tropes," some, "tones," and some, "systems" or "entire constitutions." There were many who called them *"harmoniae,"* and among them were Plato,[1] Pliny,[2] and Julius Pollux.[3] It is true (in my opinion) that Pollux differentiates between *"harmonia"* and "mode," for he takes "harmony" only for the concentus which is generated by sounds or by voices added to rhythm. Then he takes mode for the compound of harmony, rhythm, and word (a compound which Plato calls *melos*[4]), and shows how much mode differs from harmony. In our time the usage of music is very different from that of the ancients (as I have shown elsewhere[5]), for anything concerning rhythm is ignored, except for those harmonies heard in dances, which necessarily become joined with rhythm. Thus if we were to follow Pollux, we should use the term *"harmoniae"* rather than "modes." But we use the term "mode," for it is more common among musicians than is *"harmonia."* When Pollux, then, uses the term *"harmoniae,"* he does not disagree at all with Plato, for Pollux means the concentus which is generated by sounds or by voices joined with rhythm. When he uses for these the term "modes," he means *melos,* namely, the compound of harmony, rhythm, and words.

We should not be surprised that one and the same thing has been named in so

1. Plato *Republic* 398E–399C.

2. Pliny *Historia naturalis* 2. 20.

3. Pollux *Onomasticon* 3. 94.

4. Zarlino's "melodia" cannot be rendered "melody," as Plato's "melos" means "song" or "composition." See Introduction, p. xxi.

5. *Le Istit. harm.,* II, 4; III, 79.

many different ways, because it is not unsuitable for a single thing, when considered from different points of view, to be called by different names. Therefore when Plato and the others use the term "harmonies," it is possible that they do so because of the concordance of many sounds or voices dissimilar among themselves, and because of the conjunction of many consonances joined together, found [vertically] in several parts and [horizontally] in a single part. Thus ἁϱμονία, according to Quinitilian, is that concordance which is generated by the conjunction of many things dissimilar among themselves.[6]

If others used the name "tropes," it was also well put, for the modes are changed one into the other, higher or lower. Because of this quality, the modes are different from one another, since all the notes of one mode are lower or higher by the interval of a whole tone or semitone than the notes of the mode closest to it. The term "trope" was then used in consideration of the interchange of the modes when ascending or descending with the notes of one order into the notes of another. It is as if those who called them "tropes" wanted to say: "turned from low to high," or vice versa.

The name "tropes" is also appropriate if we consider the modes according to modern usage, namely, in regard to the inversion of the diatessarons, which are placed (as we shall see[7]) sometimes below and sometimes above the common diapente. Hence it seems to me not out of place that some called the two species mentioned above, namely, the diapente and the diatessaron, "sides" or "limbs" of the diapason, and that they called the diapason "body," because the change in the position of the diatessaron creates such a significant variance that it produces an admirable effect. From this it followed that some called the plagal modes "lateral," after one of the sides which changes position, namely, the diatessaron.

Those who used the term "tones" also acted with reason. One of them was Ptolemy, who said that perhaps the modes were so named because of the space of a whole tone by which the principal modes, the Dorian, Phrygian, and Lydian (as he shows in chapters 7 and 10 of the second book of the *Harmonics*), were distant one from another. Others claim that the modes were called "tones" because of a certain abundance of intervals, like the five whole tones in addition to the two large semitones in every diapason. Or else they say it is because of the last sound, or final tone, of each mode, by means of which tone and by the ascent and descent of the melodic line a rule is drawn for knowing and judging in what mode a composition, whatever it may be, is composed. But this last opinion does not please me, inasmuch as it does not have in itself any reason which the intellect can accept.

"Modes" are so named after the Latin word *modus,* which is derived from the verb *modulari,* [299] "to sing." Or perhaps the term is used because of the moderated order perceived in the modes, for it is not permissible, without offense to the ear, to go beyond their boundaries and to disregard the property and nature of each.

Those who used the term "systems," or "entire constitutions," one of whom

6. Quintilian *Institutio oratoria* I. 10. 12.
7. *Le Istit. harm.,* IV, 9.

was Ptolemy, began from the following premise: "system" means a congregation of notes, or sounds, that contains a certain ordered and complete melodic line or conjunction of consonances, such as the diapente, diatessaron, and others. In this manner, every mode is placed entirely in one of the seven species of diapason, which is more perfect than any other constitution.

CHAPTER 3   *The Name and Number of the Modes*

JUST as among all those who have mentioned the modes there exists (as we have seen[1]) a great variety of general names, so also a great variety exists of particular names. The same thing happens in regard to the number of the modes. For if we consider what Plato writes on such matters,[2] we shall find that he proposes only six modes and calls some of them mixed Lydian *harmoniae,* some high Lydian, some Ionian, and others simply Lydian. To these he adds the Dorian and Phrygian, praising only these two and approving of them above all the others as very useful to a well-instituted republic. In another place[3] he mentions only the Dorian, Ionian, Phrygian, and Lydian, and among these it seems that he praises only the Dorian, saying that it is more severe and better than any other mode.

Aristoxenus on his part (as Martianus Capella claims[4]) proposes fifteen modes: five principal modes, which are the Lydian, Iastian, Aeolian, Phrygian, and Dorian, and ten collateral modes, created by adding to each of the principal modes the two Greek prefixes ὑπέρ, which means "above," and ὑπό, which means "below." In this way, two other kinds of modes come into being, as, for example, the Hyperlydian and the Hypolydian, and so with the other modes in order.

Cassiodorus in his *Compendium of Music* proposes the same number of modes with similar names.[5] Writing to Boethius, he proposes five modes, namely, the Dorian, Phrygian, Aeolian, Iastian, and Lydian, and says that each mode has a high and a low [related mode], both named with respect to the middle one. Thus he implies that each of the modes mentioned above has two collateral modes and says that artful music is contained in fifteen modes.[6] In this he is in agreement with Martianus. But Cleonides, who also follows Aristoxenus, names only thirteen

1. *Le Istit. harm.,* IV, 2.
2. Plato *Republic* 398E–399A.
3. Plato *Laches* 188D.
4. Capella *De nuptiis philologiae et mercurii* 9. 935. Capella says that there are fifteen modes, but does not mention Aristoxenus in this connection.
5. Cassiodorus *De artibus ac disciplinis liberalium litterarum* 5.
6. Cassiodorus *Variarum libri* 2. 40. 4–5.

modes,[7] and Censorinus does the same.[8] Hence one sees two followers of the same author having very conflicting and varied opinions about the number of the modes.

Ptolemy, when discussing this matter,[9] proposes seven modes, namely, the Hypodorian, Hypophrygian, Hypolydian, Dorian, Phrygian, Lydian, and Mixolydian. To these he adds an eighth mode, calling it Hypermixolydian,[10] which is the mode called Hyperphrygian by Cleonides. Ptolemy did this so that the Greater Perfect System, namely, the fifteen notes from Proslambanomenos to Nete hyperboleon, would be comprised of the notes of these modes. Although he knew very well that there were many other modes besides these seven and the one he added (as is evident when he mentions the Iastian and the Aeolian, calling them "*harmoniae*"), nevertheless he did not want to go beyond this number. The reason may be that he had planned (in keeping with his purpose) to match each of the eight modes mentioned above to one circle of the celestial sphere, as can be seen in chapter 9 of the third book of *Harmonics,* and this in the manner in which the ancients also had assigned a name to each sphere, as Pliny shows in the *Natural History.*[11]

Julius Pollux agrees with Plato on the number of the modes, but disagrees on the names, for he proposes the [masculine] Dorian, Ionian, and Aeolian, and calls them "first *harmoniae.*" To these he adds the [feminine] Phrygian, Lydian, Ionian, and another one which he calls "Continuous" [*Continova*],[12] which is one of the *harmoniae* used in the music of pipes.

Aristides Quintilianus, in the first book of *De musica,*[13] proposes six modes, which he calls "tones." They are the Lydian, Dorian, Phrygian, Iastian, Mixolydian, and Syntonolydian, which we may call high Lydian. But the philosopher Gaudentius, having mentioned in his *Introduction* the Mixolydian, Lydian, Phrygian, Dorian, Hypolydian, Hypophrygian, and that which he calls "Common" [*Commune*], naming it also Locrian and Hypodorian, adds to these examples of the Aeolian and Hypoaeolian.[14]

Apuleius proposes five modes: Aeolian, Iastian, Lydian, Phrygian, and Dorian.[15] Lucian names four: Phrygian, Lydian, Dorian, and Ionian.[16] I shall not state

7. Cleonides *Introduction* 12. (Meibom 19, 20.) According to Cleonides the modes consist of one Hypermixolydian, two Mixolydians, two Lydians, two Phrygians, one Dorian, two Hypolydians, two Hypophrygians, and one Hypodorian.

8. Censorinus *Fragmentum* 12.

9. Ptolemy *Harmonics* 2. 10.

10. Although in *Harmonics* 2. 10, Ptolemy did describe a system of eight tonoi, including the so-called Hypermixolydian, he pointed out that this tonos was both misnamed and superfluous. See also below, chapter 7, nn. 1 and 4.

11. Pliny *Historia naturalis* 2. 5, 6.

12. Pollux *Onomasticon* 4. 65, 4. 78.

13. Aristides Quintilianus, *De musica* 1. 9, calls these *harmoniae.*

14. Gaudentius *Introduction to Harmonics* 19.

15. Apuleius *Florida* 4.

16. Lucian *Harmonides* 1.

what Boethius does, because we can see in chapters 14 and 15 of the fourth book [of *De institutione musica*] that he does not disagree in any way with the modes proposed by Ptolemy. Plutarch claims that there are only three modes, namely, the Dorian, Phrygian, and Lydian,[17] but he refers to them as principal modes, adding later that all other modes depend on these and are derived from them.[18] He said this because he saw that (as I have shown in chapter 14 of Part III) there were no more than three species of diatessaron, [300] and that from these three species of diatessaron the variety of modes arises.

There are many (and I leave out their names which are almost innumerable) who have mentioned only the Dorian, Aeolian, and Ionian as modes that are truly Greek. They have said this because, as Cicero shows, Greece was divided into three parts, namely, Doria, Aeolia, and Ionia.[19] This is also shown by Pliny in chapter 2 of the sixth book of his *Natural History*.

Others have incidentally mentioned some of the modes, as did Pindar, who named the Dorian after the Dorian kithara, and similarly the Aeolian.[20] And Horace, in various places, named the Ionian, Aeolian, Dorian, and Lydian.[21] Thus from the diversity of order, the variety of number, and the difference in names which exist in all these authors, one cannot draw anything but confusion of mind.

But however the modes are arranged and whatever their number and names, it matters little to us. It is enough for now to know that the ancients used their modes in the manner I have shown above, and that according to the usage of modern musicians, that is, according to the practice of placing the modes in one of the seven species of the diapason mediated harmonically or arithmetically, there are twelve modes, regardless of the number the ancients claimed. The reason for this is that the seven species of the diapason can be divided in twelve ways only and no more. Six of these divisions create the principal modes and six the collateral modes, as we shall see.[22]

It is difficult to determine how the disagreement arose among the [ancient] writers concerning the number of modes as well as their names and order, unless we wanted to say that this happened either because not all the modes were yet known in the time of a particular writer, or because the ancients mentioned only those modes which came into discussion at a convenient time and place.

We gather, then, from what has been said, that the principal modes among the ancients were six: Dorian, Phrygian, Lydian, Mixolydian, Aeolian, and Ionian. Al-

17. Plutarch *On Music* 8 in *Moralia* 1134A.

18. Ibid., 1136C–D, 1140F (Mixolydian), 1141B (Hypolydian), 1142F (Hypodorian, Mixolydian, and Hypophrygian). Plutarch mentions these without reference to the Dorian, Phrygian, and Lydian.

19. Cicero *The Speech in Defense of Lucius Valerius Flaccus* 27. 64. Cicero does not refer to Greece but to the Greek race.

20. Pindar *Olympia* 1. 17.

21. Horace *Odes* 3. 30. 13 (Aeolian), *Odes* 4. 15. 30 (Lydian). *Odes* 3. 6. 21 (Ionian), *Epodes* 9. 6 (Dorian).

22. *Le Istit. harm.*, IV, 12.

though Ptolemy[23] and Apuleius,[24] and others too, called the Ionian mode by the name Iastian, this signifies little or nothing, because each of these names is as valid as the other in the Greek language. Similarly, the Mixolydian mode was also called Locric or Locrian by Julius Pollux,[25] and Athenaeus took it for certain that the Hypodorian was the Aeolian.[26]

It is really very difficult to have a clear and perfect knowledge of the usage of the ancients, because it cannot be demonstrated in any way, this usage being so totally extinguished that we cannot find any vestige of it. We should not be surprised at this, for time consumes everything that is created. We should rather be surprised at those who believe that they can put into use the chromatic and enharmonic genera,[27] abandoned for so great a span of time, even though they do not know the style of these genera nor have any vestige of them. They do not realize that we do not yet have a full knowledge of the diatonic genus, and truly they do not know in what manner these modes were used according to the custom of the ancients. Hence I believe that even if they persist in examining the matter, they will find without any doubt, after having racked their brains with much effort and hardship, that they have thrown away time, a thing more precious than anything else. They will find that they have been deceived in the same way the alchemists have been in their desire to find what they will never be able to find, namely, that which they call "quintessence."

23. Ptolemy *Harmonics* 2. 1, 2. 16.

24. Apuleius *Florida* 4.

25. Pollux *Onomasticon* 4. 65, 4. 78.

26. Athenaeus *The Deipnosophists* 14. 624–25.

27. This is a veiled reference to Nicola Vicentino and his followers, whom Zarlino castigated in III, 72–80.

CHAPTER 4   *The Inventors of the Modes*

I T would not be out of place (if it could be done) to say who was the first inventor of the modern modes, because until now I have not found anyone who has done so. This, even though it is manifest to all who have read Platina[1] that it was Pope Gregory I, a most holy man, who ordered the singing of the introits, the Κύριε ἐλέησον (nine times), the Halleluya, and the other things that are sung in the sacrifice [of the Mass]. It is similarly clear that Vitalian, the first pope of this name, put the chants in order and added organa (as some claim) in consonance. But Leo II, a man expert in music, was the one who composed the chant of the psalms, that is, he found their intonations, and the way in which they are sung, and reduced the hymns to better consonance.

1. Bartolomeo Platina, *Historia de vitis pontificum* (Leyden, 1512), under Gregorius I, fol. 86r; under Vitalianus I, fol. 98v.

Damasus I had earlier ordered that certain psalms be sung in church, one verse by each chorus, and that at the end, the *Gloria patri* be added to the rest.[2]

All this has been said concerning the sacred chant, although its first inventor cannot be found. Concerning the invention of those modes that are in mensural music [*canto figurato*], and the invention of composing in the manner used at present, there is no doubt that we cannot be certain, although (as far as we know) it has not been long since the manner of composing in [301] mensural music was discovered.

The same difficulty arises concerning the inventors of the ancient modes; nevertheless we have some knowledge of the inventors of many of them. Pliny claims[3] that Amphion, son of Jove or of Mercury (as some say) and Antiope, was the inventor of the Lydian *harmonia,* in which (according to Aristoxenus in the first book of *Music*[4]) Olympus played the funeral music on the grave of the serpent Python, using the pipe. This *harmonia* was also used in the funeral rites of the virgin Psyche, as mentioned above.

Clement of Alexandria,[5] it is true, attributes the invention of the Lydian *harmoniae* to Olympus of Mysia, who was perhaps the same Olympus mentioned above, and others claim that the Lydian melody was discovered for no other purpose than for the function of funeral rites. It is also said that the peasants used this melody on forked roads and crossroads in honor of Diana, and in imitation of Ceres, who looked for the abducted Proserpine with great cries of anguish, as the Poet [Vergil] hints when he says:

> Non tu in triviis indocte solebas
> Stridenti miserum stipula disperdere carmen?[6]

From the above one can see that this function was not performed with many instruments, but with one pipe only, the inventor of which (as Apuleius claims[7]) was Hyagnis the Phrygian, father of the Marsyas who was severely punished by Apollo for

---

2. Ed. of 1573: And according to what John Gerson says, it was Ignatius, a most holy man and a martyr of Christ, who discovered the antiphons, as we may see in the following lines:

> Antiphonas dedit Psalmos Ignatius aptas.
> Monte prout quodam desuper audierat.

[Gerson *De canticis* 3: "Ignatius gave to the psalms apt antiphons, as he heard them from high up from a mountain."]

3. Pliny *Historia naturalis* 7. 56. 204.

4. Cited in Plutarch *On music* 17 in *Moralia* 1136E.

5. Clement *Stromata* 1 (Stählin ed., p. 225); in the Latin trans. by Gentianus Hervetus Aurelianus (Basel, 1566), p. 146A.

6. Vergil *Eclogues* 3. 26–27: "Uneducated one, were you not accustomed at the crossroads on a harsh-sounding straw reed to spoil the miserable song?"

7. Apuleius *Florida* 3.

his arrogance. The same function was also performed with the zuffolo [reed pipe or panpipes], the inventor of which (as claimed by some, and especially by Vergil) was Pan, god of shepherds. Vergil writes:

> Pan primus calamos caera coniungere plures
> Instituit.[8]

The Dorian melodies, on the other hand, according to the same Clement [of Alexandria][9] and Pliny as well,[10] were discovered by Thamyris, who was from Thrace. Clement also claims that the Phrygian, Mixolydian, and Mixophrygian melodies were discovered by the aforesaid Marsyas, who was from Phrygia.[11] Some claim, however, that Sappho of Lesbos, the ancient poetess, invented the Mixolydian melody, and some attribute this invention to Thersander, others to a trumpet player called Pythoclides.[12] Plutarch, relying on the testimony of one named Lysias, maintains that Lamprocles of Athens was the inventor of these melodies.[13] It is also claimed that Damon the Pythagorean was the inventor of the Hypophrygian,[14] and that Polymnestus was the inventor of the Hypolydian.[15]

I have not discovered the inventors of the other modes, but if the authority of Aristotle, as set forth in Book II of the *Metaphysics,* is valid on this matter, it may be said that Timotheus [of Miletus] was the inventor of the rest, even though Phrynis [of Mitylene], the perfect musician of those times, lived before him. For, as Aristotle says, if Timotheus had not existed we would not have many melodies.[16] But really it seems to me that the modes are more ancient than Timotheus, as one can see when reading many authors and examining them in regard to chronology.

It is not just very difficult to know which of the modes was discovered first; rather it is impossible, even though some claim that the Lydian was the first mode to be discovered. We could accept this opinion if the order of the modes posited by Plato, Pliny, Martianus, and many others was posited according to the order in which the modes were discovered. But really it is a weak argument, because we could say the same thing about any other mode which is placed first in any other listing, such as the

8. Vergil *Eclogues* 2. 32–33: "Pan was the first to arrange and connect several reed pipes with wax." The ed. by H. Rushton Fairclough, Loeb Class. Lib. (London: W. Heinemann, 1965), p. 12, has *primum* for Zarlino's *primus*, *cera* for his *caera*, and *pluris* for his *plures*.

9. Clement *Stromata* 1 (Strählin ed., p. 225); Latin trans.(see n. 5), p. 146A.

10. Pliny *Historia naturalis* 7. 56. 204.

11. Clement *Stromata* 1 (Strählin ed., p.225); Lat. trans. (see n. 5), p. 146A.

12. According to Plutarch (*On Music* 16 in *Moralia* 1136D), the invention of the Mixolydian is ascribed to Sappho of Lesbos by Aristoxenus, and to Pythoclides by "the writers on harmonics."

13. Plutarch *On Music* 16 in *Moralia* 1136D.

14. According to Plutarch (*On Music* 16 in *Moralia* 1136E), Damon of Athens is credited with the invention of the low Lydian.

15. Plutarch *On Music* 29 in *Moralia* 1141B.

16. Aristotle *Metaphysics* 2. 1.

Phrygian, which is put by Lucian first in order,[17] and the Aeolian, which is placed first by Apuleius.[18]

We shall now stop discussing these things and shall speak about the nature of the [ancient] modes. We shall talk about the properties of the modern modes at another time.

17. Lucian *Harmonides* 1.
18. Apuleius *Florida* 4.

CHAPTER 5   *The Nature or Properties of the Modes*

THE ancient modes, as we have seen elsewhere,[1] were composites of several things, and from the variety of these things a certain difference between the modes arose. From this one can understand that each mode retained in itself a certain indefinable variance, especially when all the things that went into the composite were put together proportionally. Thus each mode was capable of inducing different passions in the souls of the listeners, producing in them new and diverse habits and customs. Therefore, all who have written anything about the modes have attributed to each mode a particular property, in accordance with the effects which arose from it.

Thus they called the Dorian a stable mode and claimed that it was by its nature very fit for the ethos of civilized men, as shown by Aristotle in the *Politics*.[2] Lucian calls the Dorian mode severe because it has a certain severity,[3] and Apuleius calls it bellicose.[4] Athenaeus attributes to it severity, majesty, [302] and vehemence,[5] and Cassiodorus says that it induces modesty and preserves chastity.[6] It is also said that the Dorian is a mode which contains seriousness, and for this reason Laches, in [the dialogue of this name by] Plato, compared those who discussed or argued grave and severe things—such as virtue, wisdom, and other similar things—to the musicians who, to the sound of the kithara or lyre, sang not the Ionian, Phrygian, or Lydian melody, but rather the Dorian, which he considered to be the true Greek *harmonia*.[7] This was especially true when there were men worthy of such qualification, and when a certain consonance existed between the men and these qualities.

Since the Dorians used a somewhat grave and severe *harmonia,* with rhythms

1. *Le Istit. harm.,* IV, 1.
2. Aristotle *Politics* 1342b. 12–13.
3. Lucian *Harmonides* 1.
4. Apuleius *Florida* 4.
5. Athenaeus *The Deipnosophists* 14. 624.
6. Cassiodorus *Variae epistolae* 2. 40. 4.
7. Plato *Laches* 188D.

which were not very quick and words which contained severe and grave things, the ancients claimed that prudence was acquired by means of the Dorian mode, and that through it a chaste and virtuous spirit was induced in us. This was not said without reason, as can be understood from history. For (as Strabo relates[8]) King Agamemnon, before leaving his country to go to the Trojan war, put his wife Clytemnestra in the custody of a Dorian musician, because he knew that as long as the musician was near her she could not be corrupted by anyone. When the vicious Aegistus realized this, he removed the musician from sight, and acted on his own unrestrained desires. This may seem strange to some, but if they consider what I have said in [chapters 7 and 8 of] Part II, they will find that it is not implausible, for it is to be believed that the good musician impressed Clytemnestra continually with learned stories of virtuous deeds and contempt of vices, accompanied by appropriate harmonies. He placed before her many exemplary models of very chaste and well-mannered women, teaching her the path which she should follow in order to preserve chastity. He also entertained her with philosophical stories and very sweet songs, as was suited to a chaste and modest woman.

In such a manner, according to Vergil, the good musician Iopas entertained Dido with severe and grave songs.[9] This was customary among honest and chaste women, but not among those who were lascivious and less than honest, as we read in Vergil concerning the nymphs:

> Inter quas curam Clymene narrabat inanem
> Vulcani, Martisque dolos, & dulcia furta.[10]

Because of these effects, the ancients attributed the properties described above to the Dorian mode and applied to it subjects which were severe, grave, and full of wisdom. When they parted from these subjects and moved on to pleasant, merry, and light things, they used the Phrygian mode, its rhythms being quicker than those of any other mode, and its harmony higher than that of the Dorian. I believe that from this came the proverb: "From the Dorian to the Phrygian." This proverb is applicable when one passes from a discussion of very high and grave subjects to a discussion of light, low, and not very ingenious matters, as well as merry, festive, and also not very decent things.

Clement of Alexandria, following the opinion of Aristoxenus, claimed that the enharmonic genus, being an ornate and elegant genus, greatly suited the Dorian *harmonia,* and that the diatonic genus, being a more vehement and higher genus, suited the Phrygian *harmonia.*[11] The Dorian, then, was so venerated that no mode

---

8. Strabo *De situ orbis* 1. 2. 3., citing Homer (*Od.* 3. 267, 270.)

9. Vergil *Aeneid* 1. 740–46.

10. Vergil *Georgics* 4. 345–46: "Among them Clymene told of Vulcan's baffled care, of the woes and stolen joys of Mars." The edition by H. Rushton Fairclough, Loeb Class. Lib., p. 220, has *Volcani* for Zarlino's *Vulcani.*

11. Clement *Stromata* 6 (Stählin ed., p. 784), Lat. trans. (see Chap. 4, n. 5), p. 305A.

other than this one and the Phrygian was approved and admitted by the two wisest philosophers, Plato and Aristotle. This, because they estimated the other modes to be of little benefit and value, and because they knew the great benefit that the Dorian and Phrygian modes brought to a well-instituted republic. Hence they said that children should be instructed in music from a very early age.

The ancients also claimed that the Hypodorian had a nature different from that of the Dorian in every way. For they believed that just as the Dorian disposed people to a certain virile steadiness and to modesty, so the Hypodorian induced a certain laziness and indolence by the heaviness of its movements. Hence (as Ptolemy[12] and Quintilian[13] relate) the Pythagoreans had the custom, between morning and the time they went to sleep, of mitigating the exertions and cares of the mind from the past day by means of the Hypodorian; and at night, when they awoke from their sleep, they used to return to their abandoned studies with the help of the Dorian. Athenaeus (as I have also mentioned elsewhere[14]) thought that the Hypodorian was the Aeolian, and attributed to it the ability to induce a certain swelling and languor in the spirit, because of the somewhat soft nature of this mode.[15]

The ancients attributed to the Phrygian mode (as Plutarch shows[16]) the nature of sparking the soul and inflaming it with anger and wrath, and of provoking lasciviousness and lust; for they considered the Phrygian to be a somewhat vehement and furious mode, possessing a most severe and cruel nature, capable of rendering a man senseless. In my opinion, Lucian touched very well on the nature of this mode when he said the following: "Just as not all of those who hear the Phrygian pipe go crazy, but only those who are touched by Rhea and who, having heard the verse, remember the first affection, passion, {303} or perturbation [so not all of those who hear philosophy go away astonished and involved, but only those in whom there is a certain intrinsic incitement for philosophy]".[17] Ovid also hinted at this aspect of the Phrygian mode in the following two verses:

Attonitusque feces, ut quos Cybeleiä mater
Incitat, ad Phrygios vilia membra modos.[18]

Aristotle called this mode bacchic,[19] namely, furious and bacchanal, and Lucian called it furious or impetuous.[20] Apuleius, however, called it religious.[21]

12. Ptolemy *Harmonics* 3. 7.
13. Quintilian *Institutio oratoria* 9. 4. 12.
14. *Le Istit. harm.*, IV, 3.
15. Athenaeus *The Deipnosophists* 14. 625.
16. The marginal postil in the 1573 edition refers to Plutarch, *Politica*. Plutarch mentions the Lydian and Iastian in the essay on statesmanship (*Politica*) in *Moralia* 822C, but not the Phrygian.
17. Lucian *Dialogues of the Dead*. The bracketed part is an addition of the 1573 edition.
18. Ovid *Ibis* 453–54: "In frenzy sever your vile parts to the tune of Phrygian modes, like those whom the Cybelean mother excites."
19. Aristotle *Politics* 1342b. 2–7.
20. Lucian *Harmonides* 1.
21. Apuleius *Florida* 4.

The Phrygian mode (as we have seen[22]) was played in ancient times on the pipe [*piffero*: actually aulos], a very stimulating instrument, for which reason (according to some) the Spartans used it to call soldiers to combat. And (as Valerius relates[23]) compelled by the very severe laws of Lycurgus, the Spartans were careful never to go with the army to fight unless first well animated and aroused by the sound of this instrument played to the rhythm of the anapest, which is composed of three tempora, two breves and one long. From the two breves, which make for a more frequent and quicker beat, the Spartans understood that they had to assail the enemy with great drive; from the long they understood that they had to stop and resist boldly if they had not broken the enemy in the attack.

The same thing, as Tullius [Cicero] relates,[24] was also done by the Romans, who used to incite the soldiers to fight manfully not only by the sound of the trumpet but also by songs accompanied by this sound. Vergil shows this in the following verses:

> . . . quo non praestantior alter,
> Aere ciere viros, Martemque accendere cantu;[25]

in which he speaks about Misenus.[26]

The Italians used the trumpet, which was the invention of the Tyrrhenians,[27] as Diodorus [Siculus] claims.[28] Pliny claims that the inventor was one named Pysaeus, also a Tyrrhenian,[29] and Vergil touches on this invention in one word when he says:

> Tyrrhenusque tubae mugire per aethera clangor.[30]

But Josephus [Flavius], in the first book of the *Jewish Antiquities,* claims that the inventor of the trumpet was Moses.[31] Homer says that it was Dirce,[32] others, Tyrtaeus, and still others, Miletus.

22. *Le Istit. harm.,* IV, I.

23. Valerius *Factorum et dictorum memorabilium libri* 2. 6.

24. Cicero *Tusculan Disputations* I.

25. Vergil *Aeneid* 6. 164–65: "Surpassed by none in mobilizing men by wind instruments and in kindling by song the god of war."

26. Ed of 1573: Horace, speaking about Tyrtaeus, says:

> Tyrtheusque mares animos in martia bella
> Versibus exacuit.

[Horace *Ars poetica* 402–03: "And Tyrtaeus stirred up by verses the manly spirits for martial war."]

27. Etruscans.

28. Diodorus *Bibliotheca historica* 5. 40. 1. Diodorus says that the Tyrrhenians invented the salpinx (σάλπιγγα), which was therefore called "Tyrrhenian trumpet."

29. Pliny *Historia naturalis* 7. 56. 201.

30. Vergil *Aeneid* 8. 526: "And while the Tyrrhenian blast of the trumpet roared through the ether."

31. Josephus Flavius *Jewish Antiquities* 3. 291.

32. Not in *Odyssey, Iliad,* or hymns.

The Phrygian mode was expressed with the sound of the trumpet, which was harsh, quick, vigorous, and strong, as can be understood from the words of the ancient poet Ennius, who described the nature of this instrument in the following line:

At tuba terribili sonitu taratantara dixit.[33]

Having been induced to fight with great vehemence by the sound of the aforesaid instrument, the soldiers were induced to stop fighting by the slowness of the sound, that is, by the slowness of the movement and the seriousness of the mode. Alexander the Great was also called to arms by means of a pipe (as *Suidas*[34] indicates), as Timotheus recited the Orthian law in the Phrygian mode. Similarly, a young man from Taormina (as Ammonius[35] and Boethius[36] relate, and as I myself have mentioned[37]) was aroused by this mode.

For this reason, the ancients claimed that subjects which dealt with war and which were threatening and frightful would be suitable to the Phrygian mode, and that the Hypophrygian would moderate and mitigate the terrible and excited nature of the Phrygian. Hence some said that just as the Spartans and the Candiotes[38] used to arouse the soldiers to fight by means of the Phrygian mode, so they used to recall them from fighting by means of the Hypophrygian played on pipes. It was also claimed that Alexander [the Great] was recalled from battle by means of the Hypophrygian by Timotheus, reciting to the sound of the kithara, and that the young man from Taormina was appeased by means of this mode and by the singing of spondees.

Cassiodorus claimed that the Phrygian mode had the faculty of exciting men to fight and inflaming them with fury. He believed that the Lydian was a remedy for the toils of the mind, and, similarly, for those of the body.[39] But some claimed that the Lydian was suited to things full of lament and weeping, because it departed from the modesty of the Dorian, being higher in pitch, and from the severity of the Phrygian.

In the Lydian mode, as Plutarch relates,[40] to the sound of the pipe, Olympus sang the *Epicedia* on the grave of Python, these being verses which were sung in front of the grave of the dead. For in ancient times it was the custom to have someone sing to the sound of the pipe, or of another instrument, at the death of parents or of dearest friends, by means of which song the mourners present were induced to lament the death. This was done by a woman dressed in dark clothes, a custom which is also

33. Ennius *Annals* 2. 18: "And the trumpet with a terrible blast said taratantara."

34. A Greek lexicon (c. 970 A.D.).

35. Zarlino in the 1573 edition has a marginal reference to "Ammonius Predicabilibus.' The commentaries on Aristotle's *Categories* (sometimes known as *De praedicabilibus*) incorrectly attributed to Ammonius contain no reference to the Phrygian.

36. Boethius *De inst. mus.* 1. 1.

37. *Le Istit. harm.*, II, 7.

38. Cretans.

39. Cassiodorus *Variae epistolae* 2. 40. 4.

40. Plutarch *On Music* 15 in *Moralia* 1136C. The author cites Aristoxenus.

observed at present in some cities, especially in Dalmatia, at the death of honored men. Statius Papinius commemorated this custom, saying:

> Cum signum luctus cornu grave mugit adunco
> Tibia, cui teneros suetum producere manes,
> Lege Phrygum mesta.[41]

One sees that these [mournful] melodies were set in the Phrygian or Lydian modes, as can be learned from the authority of Apuleius cited above.[42] Because of the effects of the Lydian mode, some have called it horrible, sad, and mournful; Lucian called it furious or impetuous.[43] Plato proposed three sorts of Lydian *harmoniae:* mixed Lydian, high Lydian, and simply Lydian.[44]

[304] Some had the opinion that the nature of the Hypolydian was different from and contrary to that of the Lydian, and that it contained a certain natural softness and abundant sweetness. They said that it filled the spirits of listeners with happiness and merriness mixed with sweetness, and that it was completely removed from lasciviousness and every vice. Therefore they adapted it to subjects which were tame, civilized, and grave, and which contained profound, speculative, and divine things, such as those dealing with the glory of God and with eternal happiness, and those suited to entreating Divine Grace.

It was similarly claimed that the Mixolydian had the nature of inciting the spirit and restoring it. Apuleius called the Aeolian simple,[45] and Cassiodorus claimed that it had the power to render tranquil and serene a spirit oppressed by various passions, and that after these passions had been driven away it had the power to induce sleep[46]--nature and properties truly very similar to those of the Hypodorian. Thus one should not be surprised if Athenaeus, invoking the authority of Heraclides Ponticus, was of the opinion that the Aeolian was the Hypodorian, or vice versa.[47]

Some claimed that one could adapt to the Aeolian cheerful, sweet, mild, and severe subjects, because it had in itself a pleasant severity mixed with a certain cheerfulness and sweetness beyond the usual. They were of the opinion that, being an open and clear mode, the Aeolian was very suitable for the meoldic lines of lyrical verses. But if that which Heraclides [Ponticus] thought were true, the Aeolian would be very contrary to all these things, for it would have a different nature, as I have shown above.

41. Statius *Thebaid* 6. 120–22: "When the tibia roared on the curved horn the grave song for mourning which used to accompany the tender departed spirits according to the sad Phrygian custom." The edition by J. H. Mozley, Loeb Class. Lib. (London: W. Heinemann, 1928), p. 68, has *maesta* for Zarlino's *mesta*.

42. Chapter 1, n. 15.

43. Lucian *Harmonides* 1.

44. Plato *Republic* 398E.

45. Apuleius *Florida* 4.

46. Cassiodorus *Variae epistolae* 2. 40. 4.

47. Athenaeus *The Deipnosophists* 14. 625.

Apuleius called the Aeolian varied Iastian or varied Ionian[48] (the latter being just as valid). Lucian considered it cheerful,[49] because (according to the opinion of some) it was very suitable for dances and dancing. Hence the Aeolian mode began to be called "lascivious," and the inventors of this mode, who were the Athenians, a people of Ionia, lovers of cheerful and merry things, and students of eloquence came to be called "vain and trifling." Cassiodorus claimed that the Aeolian mode had the capacity to sharpen the intellect of those who were not very educated, and to induce a desire for heavenly things in those burdened by a certain earthly and human desire.[50]

These are the things which have been said concerning the modes. One perceives great variety among the writers, some claiming one thing and others another. I think that this variety may have originated from changes in the customs of a province; these customs changed in time, and thus gave rise to changes in the modes. I believe that some of the writers talked about those modes which preserved the essence of their first and pure simplicity, while others talked about those modes which had already lost their first nature. To give an example, we shall mention the Dorian mode, which, once honorable, grave, and severe, was changed by the change in customs, and came to be applied to matters of war. We should not be surprised at this, because if a change in customs comes into being from variations in harmonies, as is said elsewhere, it is not implausible that variations in harmonies and modes can come into being from changes in customs.

The differences among writers on modes could also stem from the lack of knowledge on the part of the writers of those times concerning this matter. It often happens in our times, too, that some propose to write things which they do not understand, and go back to the judgment and opinion of another, who sometimes knows less than they do about it. So they often take one thing for another and attribute to it some property which, while they consider it to be true, is as far from the true property as heaven is from earth. Many times we see that one thing is taken for another, as is evident in what Dio Chrysostomus writes concerning Alexander the Great in the *Commentaries of the Kingdom,* an example cited by many, in which he says that Alexander was compelled by Timotheus to take up arms by means of the Dorian mode.[51] Dio Chrysostomus, however, is the only one of this opinion, from what I have been able to understand, because Basil the Great[52] and many others before him claim that Alexander was forced to perform such an act by means of the Phrygian mode. But enough has been said about this, for it is necessary that we begin to discuss the order of the modes.

48. Apuleius *Florida* 4. Zarlino misinterpreted the text; this is surprising because in chapters 3 (n. 14) and 6 (n. 5) he interpreted the same text correctly.

49. Lucian *Harmonides* 1.

50. Cassiodorus *Variae epistolae* 2. 40. 4.

51. Dio Chrysostomus *Commentaries of the Kingdom* 1.

52. Basilius, "Sermo de legendis libris gentilium," in *Opera omnia,* ed. J.-P. Migne, in *Patrologia cursus completus . . . Series graeca,* vol. 31 (Paris, 1857): cols. 579–80A.

CHAPTER 6   *The Order of the Modes*

J UST as the ancients were of many opinions concerning the names and properties of the modes, so they had different opinions concerning the order and place of the modes, for some arranged the modes in one manner and others in another.

Plato, before anyone else, placed first in his order the mixed Lydian *harmoniae,* to which he added the high Lydian. In the second place he put the Ionian *harmoniae,* and those *harmoniae* which he called simply Lydian. In the third place he put the Dorian and Phrygian *harmoniae.*[1] It is true that one can say that Plato did not posit this order as natural, but rather as an order arranged by chance and accident, [305] according to what suited his purpose. For in another discussion he placed the Ionian first, then the Phrygian, added to them the Lydian, and put the Dorian melody in the last place.[2]

Some held to another order, for they placed the Hypodorian in the low part of the order, below every other mode, and the Mixolydian in the high part. Above the Mixolydian they put the Hypermixolydian, and above the Hypodorian they put the Hypophrygian. Above the Hypophrygian they placed the Hypolydian, then the Dorian, and then the Phrygian, and the Lydian was placed above these four middle ones, [that is, above the Hypophrygian, Hypolydian, Dorian, and Phrygian]. Among those who did this were Ptolemy[3] and Boethius.[4]

Others held to a different order, as did Apuleius, who placed the Aeolian before every other mode, and thereafter the Iastian and the others, as one sees in his order.[5] However, Martianus put the Lydian first, then added the Iastian and the other modes.[6] Others put the Mixolydian first, and among them were Cleonides[7] and Gaudentius[8] who are mentioned above.[9] Julius Pollux, in two places, put the Dorian first in order,[10] as did Plutarch[11] and Cassiodorus.[12] But Aristides Quintilianus placed the Lydian first,[13] as did Martianus, though Lucian put the Phrygian in the first place.[14]

1. Plato *Republic* 399A.
2. Plato *Laches* 188D.
3. Ptolemy *Harmonics* 2. 10.
4. Boethius *De inst. mus.* 4. 15–17.
5. Apuleius *Florida* 4.
6. Capella *De nuptiis philologiae et mercurii* 9. 935.
7. Cleonides *Introduction* 9 (Meibom 15).
8. Gaudentius *Introduction* 19.
9. *Le Istit. harm.,* IV, 3.
10. Pollux *Onomasticon* 4. 65, 4. 78.
11. Plutarch *On Music* 8 in *Moralia* 1134A.
12. Cassiodorus *De artibus ac disciplinis liberalium litterarum* 5. *Variae epistolae* 2. 40. 4.
13. Aristides Quintilianus *De musica* 1. 9.
14. Lucian *Harmonides* 1.

From this difference of opinion there follows nothing but great confusion of mind, and this occurs because some people writing on this matter held to the natural order when placing the modes one after the other, while others did not attend to such a thing and proposed an accidental order. The former were those who discussed these things according to the order of science and in a manner proven by reason, such as Cleonides, Ptolemy, Gaudentius, Aristides [Quintilianus], Boethius, Cassiodorus, and Martianus. The others discussed these things by chance, according to what suited their purpose; therefore they did not necessarily arrange the modes according to how they ought to be placed, one after the other, following the natural order, but rather they placed them in an order which was more convenient for them. Among those who did this were Plato, Plutarch, Lucian, Pollux, and Apuleius. It is no wonder that each of these should hold to a different order; we should rather wonder at those who treated the matter scientifically, and yet were so different in opinion.

But let us now stop wondering, because (as I have said elsewhere[15]) if there have been many sects in the other sciences, in music there were in those times two principal sects, one of which followed the doctrine of Pythagoras and was called Pythagorean, and the other of which followed the opinions of Aristoxenus and was called Aristoxenian. Since there were many different and diverse opinions among these people concerning the same thing, as some wanted it one way and others another, nothing arose from the variety of their principles but a variety of conclusions. Hence it happened that just as they differed in many things (as I have shown in some places when it suited my purpose), so they also disagreed on the number, place, and order of the modes.

If we consider what Ptolemy and Boethius wrote on this matter, we find that they placed the Mixolydian mode in the high part of their systems and claimed that the lowest note of each [mode] was called Proslambanomenos, the middle note, Mese, and the highest note, Nete. Boethius claims that the distances and intervals found in each mode are only of a whole tone or semitone.[16] But Cleonides in numbering the species of diapason begins the first species at the lowest step of the pyknon [gravi spessi], which he calls βαρύπυκνοι, from Hypate hypaton to Paramese, and says that the ancients called it Mixolydian. He begins the second species on the middle step of the pyknon, which he calls μεσόπυκνοι, from Parhypate hypaton to Trite diezeugmenon, and names it Lydian. He puts the third species in the ὀξύπυκνοι, namely, the top step of the pyknon, and calls it Phrygian. He calls the fourth species Dorian, the fifth Hypolydian, the sixth Hypophrygian, and the seventh he names not only Hypodorian but also Locrian and Common,[17] which Gaudentius also does, as is evident.[18] It is clear that Cleonides does one of two things: either he puts the Mixolydian mode in the low part of his monochord (as it really is) and the Hypodorian or Locrian higher up, or else he arranges the strings of the monochord in a way

15. *Le Istit. harm.*, II, 29.
16. Boethius *De inst. mus.* 4. 4, 14, 15.
17. Cleonides *Introduction* 9 (Meibom 15, 16).
18. Gaudentius *Introduction* 19.

different from that of other ancient musicians. Hence we now see justified the opinion on which I touched in chapter 29 of Part II, when discussing the opinion of the ancients regarding celestial harmony.[19]

But whoever wanted to talk about the way in which these modes were sung would have a difficult task: first, because no example of this can be found; and second, because, even though Boethius defines the interval from one note to the next in each mode,[20] Ptolemy[21] and Aristides [Quintilianus][22] posit different intervals, and neither of the latter two proposes the manner of proceeding, that is, when the modes were sung from low to high and when from high to low.

Although there are many handwritten copies of Ptolemy which show these intervals, nevertheless in them so many of the examples and other places are imperfect, either because of time or through the fault of the scribes, that little can be gained from them. It is true that in chapter 1 of the third book [of *Harmonics*] Ptolemy clearly applies to the Aeolian mode the diatessaron which is the ditonic diatonic tetrachord, but of the other modes I have not been able to find any such account.

[306] These intervals are detailed somewhat more clearly by Aristides [Quintilianus], so that they can be understood, though the copy which has come into my hands is so full of mistakes due to the ineptitude of the scribes that I could hardly make out the following few words. These I want to present as they are, so that one may appreciate the variety of the ancient modes and how much they differ from our modern modes. Aristides [Quintilianus] writes:[23]

Το μὲν οὖν λύδιον διάστημα[a] συνετίθεσαν, ἐκ διέσεως καὶ τόνου[b] καὶ τόνου, καὶ διέσεως καὶ διέσεως, καὶ τόνου[c] καὶ

19. In *Le Istit. harm.*, II, 29, Zarlino explains a controversy among the ancients concerning the movement of celestial bodies. The common premise was that the higher bodies moved faster than the lower ones, thus producing higher sounds. Others claimed that the lower bodies, being smaller than the higher ones, produced higher sounds. Zarlino explains that either opinion can be justified, depending on whether diurnal or annual movement is observed. Concerning the relationship between each of these opinions and the structure of musical instruments, he says:

Those who had the opinion that Saturn makes a high sound and the moon a low sound, placed the high notes in the high place, or right part, of their instruments, and the low notes in the low place, or left part. And those who were of the contrary opinion did it contrariwise, inasmuch as they placed the low notes in the high part, or right side, and the high notes in the low part, or left side.

Zarlino suggests the possibility that the high notes were in the left-hand side of Cleonides' instrument, and therefore his order of the modes was identical to that of Ptolemy and Boethius.

20. Boethius *De inst. mus.* 4. 4, 14–15.

21. Ptolemy *Harmonics* 3. 1.

22. Aristides Quintilianus *De musica* 1. 9.

23. The edition by A. P. Winnington-Ingram (Leipzig, 1963), p. 18, line 10 to p. 19, line 1, has the following variants from Zarlino's text: a. διάστημα] σύστημα   b. τόνου] διτόνου   c. τόνου] διτόνου   d. τόνου] διτόνου   e. καὶ διέσεως repeated   f. τριημιτόνου] τρι-

διέσεως. καὶ τοῦτο μὲν ἦν τέλειον σύστημα. Τὸ δὲ δώριον, ἐκ
τόνου καὶ διέσεως, καὶ διέσεως καὶ τόνουᵈ καὶ τόνου καὶ διέσεως καὶ διέσεως καὶ διτόνου. ἦν δὲ τοῦτο, τόνῳ τοῦ διὰ πασῶν
ὑπερέχον. Τὸ δὲ φρύγιον, ἐκ τόνου καὶ διέσεως καὶ διέσεως,
καὶ διτόνου καὶ τόνου, καὶ διέσεωςᵉ καὶ τόνου ἦν δε καὶ τοῦτο
τέλειον διὰ πασῶν. Τὸ δὲ ἰάστιον, συνετίθεσαν ἐκ διέσεως καὶ
διέσεως καὶ διτόνου, καὶ τριημιτόνουᶠ καὶ τόνου. ἦν δε τοῦτο
τοῦ διὰ πασῶν ἐλλεῖπον τόνῳ Τὸ δὲ μιχολύδιον, ἐκ δύωᵍ διέ-
σεων κατὰ τὸ ἑξῆς κειμένων, καὶ τόνου καὶ τόνου, καὶ διέσεοςʰ
καὶ τριῶν τόνων. ἦν δὲ καὶ τοῦτο τέλειον σύστημα. Τὸ δὲ
λεγόμενον σύντονον λύδϊον, ἢ διέσεοςⁱ καὶ διέσεωςʲ καὶ διτόνου
καὶ τριημιτονίου.ᵏ Δίεσιν δὲ νῦν ἐπι πάντων ἀκουστέον, τὴν
ἐναρμόνιον.

This means:

They have composed the Lydian span [*diastema*] of a diesis and a whole
tone and a whole tone, and of a diesis and a diesis, and of a whole tone and
a diesis; and this is a perfect system. But the Dorian they composed of a
whole tone and a diesis, and of a diesis and a whole tone, and of a whole
tone and a diesis, and of a diesis and a ditone; and this surpassed the
diapason by a whole tone. The Phrygian then they composed of a whole
tone and a diesis, and of a diesis and a ditone and a whole tone, and of a
diesis and a whole tone; and this was a perfect diapason. They composed
the Iastian of a diesis and a diesis, of a ditone and a trihemitone and of a
whole tone; and it was short of a diapason by one whole tone. The
Mixolydian then they composed of two dieses placed one after the other,
and of a whole tone and a whole tone, and of a diesis and three whole
tones; and this was a perfect system. That which was called Syntonic
Lydian[24] was composed of a diesis and a diesis, and of a ditone and a
trihemitone. Now the diesis in all of these should be understood as that of
the enharmonic [genus].

Thus from the words of Aristides [Quintilianus] we can understand that in his
opinion the modes differed not only in their intervals but also in the number of their
notes. Boethius, in chapter 4 of Book IV of his *Music,* proposed only eleven notes in
the Lydian, and in chapters 14 and 15 he proposed for each mode fifteen notes, to
which he added the Synemmenon tetrachord. But according to what we can under-

---

ημιτονίου   g. δύω] δύο   h. This edition supplies another καὶ διέσεως   i. διέσεος]
διέσις   j. διέσεως] διέσις   k. τριημιτονίου] τριημιτόνιον
24. High Lydian.

stand from the words of Cleonides and Gaudentius, cited above, each of the modes, when perfect, comprised one species of diapason, that is, eight notes.

Among the moderns, the following usage exists: they place the first and eighth modes within the fourth species of diapason, D to d; the third and tenth modes within the fifth species of diapason, E to e; similarly the fifth mode within the sixth species of diapason, F to f; and the seventh [and twelfth] modes within the seventh species of diapason, G to g. They place the ninth and second modes within the first species of diapason, A to a, or a to aa; and the fourth mode within the second species of diapason, ♭ [B] to ♭ [b]. Lastly they accommodate the eleventh and sixth modes within the third species of diapason, C to c, or c to cc, as we shall see further below. And the modes are twelve in number, not only among churchmen, but also among practicing composers, although the number is considered to be less than twelve by many people. I intend to discuss the modern modes in detail and to show in what manner each of them is used at present.[25]

25. *Le Istit. harm.*, IV, 18–29.

CHAPTER 7   *The Hypermixolydian of Ptolemy Is Not That Which We Call the Eighth Mode*

THERE have been some modern practitioners who have maintained as a certainty that the modern eighth mode that we use is the Hypermixolydian of Ptolemy, placed eighth in his order.[1] But really these people are grossly mistaken, because the eighth mode (as we shall see[2]) is contained within the fourth species of diapason, D to d, or between Lychanos hypaton and Paranete diezeugmenon, divided arithmetically, whereas the Hypermixolydian is contained within the first species of diapason, a to aa, namely, between Mese and Nete hyperboleon, as Boethius shows clearly in Chapter 17 of Book IV of his *Music*. Hence one can see the difference that exists between one and the other, and the error that these people commit.

1. As Ptolemy in *Harmonics* 2. 10 and 2. 8–9 clearly showed that he was vigorously opposed to adding an eighth mode to the seven he recognized, Zarlino must have based his statement about Ptolemy and the Hypermixolydian on Boethius, *De inst. mus.* 4. 17, where Boethus erroneously reported that Ptolemy added an eighth mode. In 2. 8 Ptolemy showed that an eighth tonos is unnecessary for intertonal modulation, and in 2. 9 he theorized that there should be no more tonoi than the number of species of octave, namely, seven. These points are conveyed clearly in the Latin translation of Antonio Gogava in *Aristoxeni musici antiquissimi Harmonicorum elementorum . . . Cl. Ptolemaei Harmonicorum* (Venice: Vincentius Valgrisius, 1562), pp. 96–101. This translation, commissioned by Zarlino while he was preparing the *Istitutioni*, may not have reached him in time to allow him to read it carefully, because the material on Ptolemy in Zarlino's present chapter is taken second-hand from Boethius.

2. *Le Istit. harm.*, IV, 25.

Some others have had the opinion that between the Hypodorian, which is lower than any other mode, and the Hypermixolydian, which is placed up high, there is no difference except that of pitch, for both are contained within the same species of diapason. But it seems to me that these people are in great error, for this would be like saying that Ptolemy reproduced above that which was placed below, without differentiating the harmony. This is not credible, because so great a philosopher as Ptolemy would not have been so lacking in judgment as to multiply a thing unnecessarily,[3] as would be the case here, much more so because this was a great discrepancy among philosophers. It should be said, then, that these modes differed [307] from each other not only in pitch but also in nature, in terms of melody, which was different, and that Ptolemy had intended this when he proposed the Hypermixolydian.

Others have wanted to call it Aeolian, and that, it really seems to me, without any reason, because in chapters 1 and 15 of Book II of *Harmonics* Ptolemy mentions the Aeolian, calling it Aeolian *harmonia*.[4] Some could perhaps ask for what reason Ptolemy did not add a collateral, or plagal, to the Hypermixolydian, and did not place the Aeolian in this order, nor the Ionian, which he called the Iastian *harmonia*. But because everyone reading chapter 3 of Book II of *Harmonics* will be able to find a sufficient reply to this doubt or proposed question, it does not seem to me to be necessary to repeat the answer here.

3. Glarean differs: Ptolemy's Hypermixolydian is "completely identical in nature" to the Hypodorian (*Dodekachordon*, II, 2). For Gaffurio too Ptolemy's Hypermixolydian does not differ from the first octave species in its internal relationships except in being higher by an octave (*Practica musice*, I, 7).

4. Ptolemy in 2. 1 (Düring ed., p. 43, line 19) speaks of "the so-called Iastian-Aeolian" (translated in Gogava, p. 83 as "appellatorum Iastiaeoliorum") but not in connection with the term "harmony." In 2. 15 Ptolemy gives tables of string lengths in the diatonic and chromatic genera only for the seven tonoi he admits into his system. The Aeolian is not mentioned in Ptolemy's text nor in Gogava's translation. The Iastian-Aeolian tuning of the kithara is mentioned in 2. 16, however.

CHAPTER 8

The Manner in Which the Ancients Indicated the Notes of Their Modes

WHEN it occurs to me that I have never found in the writings of any author, either Greek or Latin, even one example from which one could understand how the ancients made many parts sound together—unless they had a way of writing the notes of their modes or compositions separately and of indicating in what proportion they placed the voices apart from each other—it all the more confirms my belief that they never used to make many parts sound together, as I have shown in chapter 4 of Part II and in chapter 79 of Part III.

Furthermore, it is clear that the ancients did not use in their compositions those figures or characters, or those lines and spaces, shown in chapter 2 of Part III, which we use at present. They had (as Boethius says[1]) some signs which they placed above the syllables of their verses, and by means of these they understood how they had to sing, moving the voice up or down. These signs were placed in double lines, one above the other, and Boethius says that the signs placed on top were the notes or characters of diction, namely, of the words, and that those placed below were signs of duration [percussione]. He implies (in my opinion) that the former designated the pitch and the latter designated long or short duration, although one could have learned the duration from whether the syllable in the verse was long or short. The signs were different from each other, for a particular sign was allotted to each note, so that the sign of Proslambanomenos was different from that of Hypate hypaton and from that of any other note, and the sign of Proslambanomenos of the Dorian mode was different from the sign of Proslambanomenos of the Phrygian mode, and so forth.

But these signs were discarded because John Damascene, sainted Doctor [of the Church], discovered other new characters, which he adapted to ecclesiastical Greek compositions in such a manner that they did not signify notes, as did the characters or signs mentioned above, but rather demonstrated the interval to be sung.[2] Hence every musical interval had its own sign, so that just as the sign of the [ascending] whole tone differed from that of the [ascending] semitone, and the sign of the semiditone differed from that of the ditone, and so for the other ascending intervals, so also the signs of the [descending] whole tone, semitone, and other descending intervals differed [among themselves and][3] from the signs of the ascending intervals. To all these signs, duration was added in such a way that by means of these characters, or signs, every composition could be reduced and made much shorter than in our notation, as I can show in many of my compositions. And one could accommodate in this [notation] every one of those characteristics [accidenti] which can occur in a composition, whatever it might be, for I have used great diligence in accommodating all of these, when it suited my purpose.

But we should note, in order not to be led astray, that if we consider the words of Boethius which deal with the subject of the modes (found in chapters 14 and 16 of Book IV of his *Music*), we shall be able to understand two things from which, according to my judgment, two great difficulties arise. The first is that we shall not be able to find any difference in intervals from one mode to another, for Boethius claims that all the notes of the Hypodorian, as they stand, are moved higher by a whole tone to form the Hypophrygian mode, and that all the notes of this mode are in the same way moved higher by another whole tone in order to produce the notes of the melody of the Hypolydian. Boethius claims that if all these notes are then moved up by a semitone, the Dorian is formed, and so he goes on about the other modes. Under this procedure of obtaining the modes I cannot conceive of any difference between them, unless that, if all of them were arranged in order on the same

1. Boethius *De inst. mus.* 4. 3.
2. Ed. of 1573: . . . ascending or descending.
3. Bracketed phrase is from the ed. of 1573.

instrument, one would be higher than another by a whole tone or a semitone. However, all the modes would proceed by the same intervals. What difference, in Heaven's name, would exist between one mode [308] and another when in the low, middle, and high notes of one mode the same intervals were found as in the low, middle, and high notes of another? The only difference would be that the notes of one mode would be higher or lower than the notes of another by a certain distance. But what makes a difference between modes is not pitch, but rather the intervals which constitute them.

The second [point] is that from the words and examples of Boethius, badly understood, we can understand why modern musicians speaking on this matter have been very much deceived, for they believe that the modern fifth mode is the ancient Lydian, and they make it one whole tone lower than the seventh mode, which they call Mixolydian. They propose that the Lydian is contained within the sixth species of diapason, F to f, and the Mixolydian within the seventh species of diapason, G to g. These, however, are distant from each other by a whole tone, whereas Boethius clearly shows that the ancient Lydian is distant from the Mixolydian by a semitone. He similarly claims that the Dorian is a whole tone away from the Phrygian, something which Ptolemy also claims,[4] and that the Phrygian is another whole tone away from the Lydian. Yet the moderns claim that the first mode is the ancient Dorian, the third mode is the Phrygian, and the fifth mode is the Lydian. This turns out to be completely contrary to what the ancients maintained, because the first mode is distant from the third mode by a whole tone, and the third mode is distant from the fifth mode by a semitone.

Thus we can say that modern musicians are in great error when they call the first mode Dorian, the third mode Phrygian, and so on in the order in which they were arranged by Ptolemy and Boethius. If modern musicians want to call the modes by these [Greek] names (as if the modern modes were similar in some way to the ancient modes), they should call the eleventh mode Dorian, the first mode Phrygian, and the third made Lydian, rather than otherwise, because then the modes would be distant from each other by the intervals which Ptolemy and Boethius maintained.[5] One of the reasons (in case anyone is wondering) why I do not call the modes Dorian, Phrygian, Lydian, or other similar names, but rather first mode, second, third, and the others in order, is that I saw that the [Greek] names were used incorrectly. And although Franchino Gaffurio in his *Theorica*[6] maintains another manner of locating the modes, one higher or lower than the other, nevertheless he does not arrange the intervals of one mode differently from those of another but merely places the same

4. Ptolemy *Harmonics* 2. 10.

5. Zarlino deals with this problem also in *Le Dimostrationi harmoniche*, Fifth Discussion, Fourteenth Definition. In the Eighth Definition, he presents this matter as one of the considerations that prompted him to change the existing order of mode numbers, designating as first mode the one within the octave C-c, and thus keeping the accepted association of the Dorian with the first mode.

6. Gaffurio *Theorica musice* V, 8.

intervals higher, sometimes by a whole tone and sometimes by a semitone, and does not otherwise vary the melodic line.

This I wanted to say, not to speak against some of the ancient or modern writers, for whom I have and will always have the greatest respect, but rather to warn the readers and encourage them to consider this matter with all diligence, so that they may make [proper] judgments and always know good from bad and true from false in musical matters. I do not believe that it would be out of place to say that although Boethius was most learned in the speculative aspects of music, it might be that in practical matters he was not so knowledgeable. This can truly be confirmed by what has been said above and by what I have shown in chapter 13 of Part III about his discussion of the four species of diapente.[7] We should not be surprised at this, because everyone, inasmuch as he is human, may be mistaken in his opinion. And let us remember what Horace writes in the Epistle of *Ars poetica:*

Verum opere in longo obrepere somnum.[8]

This could be an excellent excuse for this most serious author, [Boethius], and also for everyone else who writes at great length.

7. In *Le Istit. harm.*, III, 13, Zarlino mentions another mistake by Boethius, saying: "Boethius, in chapter 13 of Book IV of *De musica*, puts the second species of this consonance [diapente] between the notes Hypate hypaton [B] and Parhypate meson [F]. This is a diminished fifth, for it contains two whole tones and two semitones."

8. Horace *Ars poetica* 360: "Truly in a long work it is natural for sleep to creep up." The edition by H. Rushton Fairclough, Loeb Class. Lib. (London: H. Heinemann, 1970), p. 480, has *operi* for Zarlino's *opere.*

CHAPTER 9

The Manner in Which the Diapason Should Be Harmonically or Arithmetically Divided

I stated above[1] that the twelve modes come into being from the harmonic and arithmetic divisions of the seven species of diapason. Before going further, I would like us to see how the diapason should be mediated, or divided, harmonically and arithmetically.

It should be noted that the diapason, which is the first consonance (as I have shown elsewhere[2]), is first divided by an intermediate note into its principal parts, the diapente and the diatessaron. These parts, which are often combined, yield two

1. *Le Istit. harm.*, I, 13; II, 39; III, 3.
2. Ibid., IV, 1.

Example 1.

[Harmonic division]   [Arithmetic division]

Diapente   Diatessaron   Diatessaron   Diapente

6 Sesquialtera 4 Sesquiterza 3   4 Sesquiterza 3 Sesquialtera 2

conjunctions, or unions, with either the diapente or the diatessaron below. One of the unions is not entirely good; the other is very sonorous and sweet. This sweetness arises when the diapente is placed below the diatessaron, for when these parts are joined and united in this manner, the extreme notes of the diapason are divided by an intermediate note which is the upper limit of the diapente and the lower limit of the diatessaron. Such a division, or rather conjunction, is called harmonic, [309] because the terms of the proportions which form the diapente and the diatessaron and which are 6, 4, and 3 stand in harmonic proportion to each other; that is, the intermediate note divides the two extremes in the required way, shown in chapter 39 of Part I.[3]

The other division is called arithmetic. It is not as good, because it is not as sonorous, the consonances in it not being located in the proper places. It is produced when the diapente and the diatessaron are united by an intermediate note in the opposite manner, namely, when the diatessaron occupies the low part and the diapente the high part. This division is deservedly called arithmetic, for the terms of the proportions which form the diatessaron and the diapente and which are 4, 3, and 2 are placed in arithmetic division, that is, the middle term, which is 3, divides the extremes, 4 and 2, in the way that the arithmetic division requires, as shown in chapter 36 of Part I.

The first union is much better than the second, because the order of the consonances in it is such that all the notes are in their proper and natural place, according to the nature of the forms of the consonances. In the second order, on the other hand, the consonances are situated in a manner that could be called accidental rather than natural. Therefore whenever a diapason is divided in the first way we say that it is mediated harmonically; when a diapason is divided in the second way we say (for the reasons mentioned above) that it is mediated arithmetically. We shall similarly speak of the division of the diapente into a ditone and a semiditone. The harmonic and arithmetic divisions of the diapason are illustrated in Example 1.

3. For a summary of Zarlino's instructions for finding a harmonic mean, see the Introduction, p. viii, n. 6.

CHAPTER 10   *There Are Necessarily Twelve Modern Modes; and How It May Be Proved*

IF, as practitioners claim, the modern modes come into being from the union or composition of the diapente and the diatessaron, we can show that these modes necessarily number twelve. They cannot be less, no matter how many ancient modes there were, because the ancient modes have little or nothing to do with our purpose, especially since we now use modes (as we have mentioned[1]) in a manner very different from that of the ancients. In order to show this, we shall take as a foundation that which we assumed above, namely, the union of the four species of diapente with the three species of diatessaron, shown in chapters 13 and 14 of Part III. As many as are the ways in which we can suitably unite the diapente and diatessaron, sometimes putting the diatessaron above and sometimes the diapente, that many is the number of the modes.

Beginning then in order: if we take the first species of diapente, located between D and a, and add above it the first species of diatessaron, contained within a and d, we shall undoubtedly obtain from this union or conjunction that which we now call the first mode, contained within the fourth species of diapason, between D and d. Similarly, if we take the same first species of diapente and add below it the first species of diatessaron, between D and A,[2] the result will undoubtedly be the first species of diapason, between a and A, which will contain what [310] we call the second mode. If we take the second species of diapente, contained within E and b-natural, and add above it the second species of diatessaron, placed between b-natural and e, we shall have what we call the third mode, contained within the fifth species of diapason, E to e. And if below the second species of diapente we add the second species of diatessaron, placed between E and B-natural, we shall have the second species of diapason, b-natural to B-natural, which yields a mode different from the first three modes, and which we call the fourth mode. Let us now take the third species of diapente, placed between F and c, and add above it the third species of diatessaron, placed between c and f, and we shall have within the sixth species of diapason, F to f, that which we call the fifth mode. If we take the same diapente and add below it the diatessaron F to C, we shall have the third species of diapason, [c to C], and with it that mode which we call the sixth.

In this manner we shall have six unions or conjunctions, namely, those of the first species of diapente with the first species of diatessaron, below as well as above, those of the second species of each, similarly below and above, and, in the same

1. *Le Istit. harm.*, IV, 1.

2. Zarlino names the plagal intervals in descending order, though not consistently. The reason may be that, as he says in *Le Istit. harm.*, IV, 15, upward motion is attributed to the principal mode and downward motion to its collateral. In *Dodekachordon*, I, 11, Glarean quotes a "little verse" concerning this matter: "An even mode tends to descend, but an uneven mode tends to ascend."

Example 2.

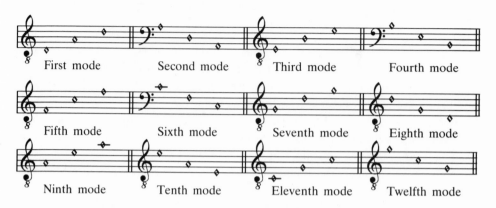

First mode   Second mode   Third mode   Fourth mode

Fifth mode   Sixth mode   Seventh mode   Eighth mode

Ninth mode   Tenth mode   Eleventh mode   Twelfth mode

manner, those of the third species, placed below and above, and by this means we reach six modes.

It remains now to match the fourth species of diapente with the first species of diatessaron, which can be done suitably. It should be noted that the species of diatessaron can be adapted and matched with those of the diapente in three ways: the first species of diatessaron can be matched with the fourth species of diapente, the second species of diatessaron with the first species of diapente, and the third species of diatessaron with the fourth species of diapente. These species cannot be joined together conveniently in any other way, as is clear to anyone moderately experienced in music.[3]

Taking, then, the fourth species of diapente, between G and d, we match it with the first species of diatessaron, d to g, and within the extreme notes of the seventh species of diapason, G to g, with its intermediate notes we shall have the mode called the seventh. If we again take the diatessaron located between G and D and set it below the [fourth species of] diapente, we shall have within the diapason d to D, the fourth species, the mode called the eighth. We shall now add the second species of diatessaron, located between e and aa, above the first species of diapente, between a and e, and within the first species of diapason, a to aa, we shall have another mode which, since it is different from the eight modes already mentioned, we shall call the ninth. Below this diapente we shall add the same diatessaron, between a and E, and we shall have within the fifth species of diapason that which we rightfully call the tenth mode. Finally, if we match the third species of diatessaron, contained within g and cc and placed above, with the fourth species of diapente, located between c and g, we shall have within the third species of the diapason, c to cc, the

3. Glarean gives specific rules for rejecting some of the combinations of the four species of the diapente with the three species of the diatessaron. He says (*Dodekachordon*, II, 3) that there are twenty-four possible combinations, but twelve of them are rejected for one of four reasons: (1) It has four successive whole tones. (2) It has five successive whole tones. (3) It has one whole tone between two small semitones. (4) It has two successive small semitones.

mode called the eleventh. But if we match these last two species in the other direction, placing the diatessaron in the low part between the notes c and G, we shall have the last mode, called the twelfth, contained within the seventh species of diapason, g to G, as seen in Example 2.

In this manner we shall have no more, nor less, than twelve modes, because these species cannot be matched with each other in any other way, except with great drawbacks, as is clear to anyone who has good judgment.

CHAPTER II   *Another Way of Demonstrating That the Number of the Modes Is Twelve*

{311}   WE can show that the modes number twelve also in another way, namely, through the harmonic and arithmetic divisions of the diapason. So as not to become confused, we shall keep the same order as the moderns, and thus we shall start with the fourth species of diapason and then proceed to the other species in order, dividing them first harmonically and then arithmetically.

If we take the fourth species of diapason, contained within D and d, and divide it harmonically into two parts by the note a, there is no doubt that we shall have the first species of diapente, D to a, below, and the first species of diatessaron, a to d, [above]. When these are joined together, as we saw and is shown in Example 3, they constitute the first mode. If we take the fifth species of diapason, located between E and e, and divide it harmonically by the note b-natural, we shall have the diapente E to b-natural, second species, and the second species of diatessaron, b-natural to e, which, joined together in the way that has been shown, yield the third mode. If we take the sixth species of diapason, F to f, and divide it harmonically by the note c, we shall have the fifth mode, which comes into being from the conjunction of the third species of diapente and the third species of diatessaron, which are F to c, and c to f, as stated above. [1] If we take the seventh species of diapason, contained within G and g, and divide it harmonically by the note d, we shall have the fourth species of diapente, G to d, joined to the first species of diatessaron, d to g, and thus the seventh mode. If we take the first species of diapason, contained within a and aa, and divide it harmonically by the note e, we shall have the first species of diapente, a to e, and the second species of diatessaron, e to aa, which, joined together, yield the ninth mode. We shall leave out the second species of diapason, placed between b-natural and bb-natural, because[2] it cannot be divided harmonically.[3] We shall take the third species

1. *Le Istit. harm.*, III, 13, 14; IV, 10.

2. Ed of 1573: . . . according to the Tenth Proposition of the Fifth [Discussion] of *Le Dimostrationi harmoniche.*

3. That is, without the use of accidental notes; in this case, f-sharp.

Example 3. [The authentic modes]

A table of the authentic, or odd-numbered, modes.

of diapason, c to cc, and divide it harmonically by the note g, from which division stem the fourth species of diapente, c to g, and the third species of diatessaron, g to cc, and thus the eleventh mode, as seen in Example 3.

All of these modes come into being through the harmonic division of the species of diapason; through arithmetic division we shall have six additional modes. For if we start with the first species of diapason, located between a and A, or between a and aa (for the difference is merely one of lower or higher pitch[4]), and divide it arithmetically by the note D (using here a to A), we shall have the first species of diatessaron, D to A, placed below, and the first species of diapente, a to D, placed above. When these are joined together in the manner shown in Example 4, they yield that mode which we call the second. If we take the second species of diapason, located between b-natural and B-natural, and divide it arithmetically by the note E, we shall have between E and B-natural the second species of diatessaron, and between b-natural and E the second species of diapente, which, joined together, yield the fourth mode. [312] The third species of diapason, c to C, divided [arithmetically] by the note F, will yield the sixth mode; for the third species of diatessaron, F to C, placed below, is joined to the third species of diapente, c to F, placed above. If we take the diapason d to D, the fourth species, and divide it arithmetically by the note G, we shall have the eighth mode; for G and D, the first species of diatessaron, is joined below to the fourth species of diapente [d to G]. If we take the fifth species of diapason, e to E, and divide it arithmetically by the note a, we shall have the second species of diatessaron, a to E, and the first species of diapente, e to a, which constitute the tenth mode. We shall leave out the diapason f to F, because[5] it cannot be divided arithmetically. We shall take the diapason g to G, the seventh species, and divide it [arithmetically] by the note c, and we shall have the twelfth mode; for from this division stems the third species of diatessaron, c and G, joined below to the fourth species of diapente, g and c, as may be seen in Example 4.

In this manner we arrive at twelve modes: six by harmonic division, and six by arithmetic division. To be sure, the second species of diapason, B-natural to b-natural, cannot be divided harmonically, [313] because if it were divided by the note

4. Ed. of 1573: . . . because according to the last Proposition of the Fifth [Discussion] of *Le Dimost. harm.*, every mode can be transposed up or down by a diapason.

5. Ed. of 1573: . . . according to the Twelfth Proposition of the Fifth [Discussion] of *Le Dimost. harm.*

Example 4. [The plagal modes]

A table of the plagal, or even-numbered, modes.

Example 5. [The twelve modes]

A general table of all the modes.

9th	2nd	4th	11th	6th	1st	8th	3rd	10th	5th	7th	12th
har.	ar.	ar.	har.	ar.	har.	ar.	har.	ar.	har.	har.	ar.

F we would have the semidiapente B-natural to F below and the tritone f to b-natural above. Nor can the sixth species of diapason, F to f, be divided arithmetically, because if it were divided by the note b-natural, a tritone would be heard below, between the notes b-natural and F, and the semidiapente f to b-natural would be heard above. Nevertheless, there have been some who have added other modes beyond the twelve shown, such as the thirteenth mode, according to harmonic division, and the fourteenth mode, according to arithmetic division. But really there cannot be more than twelve modes, as we have shown,[6] and these are arranged in Example 5.

6. Ed. of 1573: . . . and as we have demonstrated in the Fourteenth Proposition of the Fifth and last Discussion of *Le Dimost. harm.*

CHAPTER 12   *The Division of the Modes into Authentic and Plagal*

THE modes are divided into two groups: some are called principal and authentic, or odd numbered, and some are called lateral and plagal, or placal, or even numbered. To the first group belong the first, third, fifth, seventh, ninth, and eleventh modes; to the second group belong the second, fourth, sixth, eighth, tenth, and twelfth modes.

The modes of the first group were called principal, for honor and preeminence are always given to those things which are more noble. Hence the musician considers principally the consonances which are mediated harmonically, these being more nobly divided than those divided in another manner, and only then he considers those consonances which are divided in another way. The name "principal" has been attributed deservedly to the modes of the first group, because in these modes the harmonic mean is found between the two major parts of the diapason, namely, the diapente and the diatessaron, the former placed below and the latter above, whereas in the modes of the second group the harmonic mean is not found. But some prefer that the modes of the first group be called authentic, because these modes have more authority than those of the second group, or because they are augmentative, in that they can ascend higher above their final than can the modes of the second group. These modes are also said to be odd numbered, because when arranged with the second group in natural order in the manner 1, 2, 3, 4, 5, 6, 7, 8, 9, 10, 11, and 12, they occupy the place of the odd numbers.

The modes of the second group are called lateral, after the "sides" of the diapason, which are (as I have said elsewhere[1]) the diapente and the diatessaron; for when the parts generated by the division of the authentic or principal modes, namely, the diapente and the diatessaron, are placed in the contrary way (the diapente remaining common {to the two} and stationary), the lateral modes come into being. It can be seen in the first and second modes that when the diapente D to a remains stationary, the first mode, authentic, comes into being by the addition of the diatessaron a to d above, and the second mode, its collateral, comes into being by the placement of the diatessaron below, D to A. The same thing also happens in the other modes, as can be seen in Example 2.

Some have called the modes of the second group *plagii,* or *plagali,* which is appropriate, because these names derive from the Greek πλάγιον, which means "side," or from πλάγιος, which means "oblique" or "twisted," as if to say that these modes were oblique, twisted, or turned around, because they proceed from high to low, a manner contrary to the authentic modes, which proceed from low to high. Some have called them placal, as if they wanted to say placable, because the tune and harmony of these modes are gentler than those of their [respective] principal modes, or because the nature of these modes is contrary to that of their [respective] authentic modes. For if the harmony generated by the authentic mode disposes the soul to one passion, that of the plagal mode pulls it back in a different direction. These modes are said to be even numbered, because in the natural order of the numbers, shown above, they occupy the place of the even numbers.

But everything—be it natural or artificial—that has a beginning must also have an end, and so we bring the discussion of this matter to an end, as behooves a perfect thing. I now want to show in what manner each of the modes should end regularly, demonstrating at the same time the endings of the principal and collateral modes, and showing how much each mode may ascend and descend above and below its final. Thus we shall be able to write compositions with judgment and with good order, and, upon seeing a composition, we shall be able to determine in what mode and melodic system it is written.

1. *Le Istit. harm.,* IV, 2.

CHAPTER 13   *The Final Note of Each Mode; and How*
                         Far It Is Permissible to Ascend or Descend
                         above and below It

[314]   IT is easy to know the final note of each mode, considering
              its composition from the union of the diatessaron with the
              diapente, or considering its derivation from the division of
the diapason in the [harmonic and arithmetic] manners shown above.[1] Modern
musicians take as the final note of each mode the lowest note of each diapente,[2] and it
makes no difference whether the diatessaron is placed above or below it.

Since the lowest note of each diapente is common to two modes, as each
diapente itself is common to two modes, musicians usually match the modes two by
two. For example, the lowest note of the first species of diapente, being located on D
in both the first and second modes, and being common to these two modes, becomes
the final not only of the first but also of the second mode. By this bond and kinship
(so to speak) which is found between them, these modes are united in such a manner
that as much as one would like to separate them from each other, one would not be
able to do it, so strong is the union of these modes, as we shall see when discussing
what has to be done in accommodating the parts of [polyphonic] compositions.[3]

It is appropriate, then, that the first mode is matched with the second mode,
the third with the fourth, and so the others in order. For the common final note of the
first and second modes is D,[4] and the common final note of the third and fourth
modes is E, which is the lowest note of the second species of diapente. Musicians say
that F, the lowest note of the third species of diapente, is the common final of the
fifth and sixth modes, and they join these two modes because the third species of
diapente is common to both. They match the seventh mode with the eighth, for the
fourth species of diapente is common to both of them, and hence its lowest note, G,
becomes the final of these two modes. They make the note a the common final of the
ninth and tenth modes, for it is the lowest note of the first species of diapente, and
they join these two modes because this diapente is common to both of them. They
make c the common final note of the eleventh and twelfth modes because it is the
lowest note of the fourth species of diapente, and they match these two modes
together in view of this diapente common to both.

When these things are understood, no one concerned with this matter will fail
to match the authentic mode with its plagal, especially knowing that the final of the
first and second modes is D, the final of the third and fourth modes is E, the final of
the fifth and sixth modes is F, the final of the seventh and eighth modes is G, the

    1. *Le Istit. harm.,* IV, 9.
    2. Ed. of 1573: . . . as I have stated in the Seventeenth Definition of the Fifth Discussion of *Le
Dimost. harm.*
    3. *Le Istit. harm.,* IV, 31.
    4. Ed. of 1573: . . . which is the lowest note of the first species of diapente.

final of the ninth and tenth modes is a, and the final of the eleventh and twelfth modes is c, as seen in Example 6. And not only are the finals common [to each pair of modes], but also, as we shall see,[5] the places of the cadences.

It should be noted that a mode, when perfect, touches the eight notes of its diapason. The difference between the authentic and the plagal modes is that the latter ascend to the fifth note above their final, and descend to the fourth [note below their final], whereas the former touch the eighth note [above their final], and sometimes descend below their diapason by a whole tone or a semitone. In a similar way, the plagal modes may ascend above their diapente by a whole tone or a semitone, as is seen in many sacred compositions. Thus the authentic mode is found within eight notes divided harmonically, and the plagal mode within eight notes divided arithmetically, as may be seen in Examples 2, 3, 4, and 6.

The modes which extend above and below their finals in this way may be called perfect. Therefore we say that the Introit sung in the Mass of the fourth Sunday in Advent, *Rorate coeli desuper,*[6] is composed in the perfect first mode, and that the Introit sung in the Mass of the octave of Christmas, *Vultum tuum deprecabuntur,*[7] is composed in the perfect second mode.

But when plagal modes descend beyond [the fourth note below the final], or authentic modes ascend beyond [the eighth note above the final], such modes may be called superfluous, as Franchino Gaffurio calls them.[8] [Authentic modes] may be called imperfect or diminished when they do not reach the eighth note of their diapason, [315] or its first note. [Plagal modes may be called imperfect or diminished when they do not reach the fifth note above their final, or the fourth note below it.] We have an example of a superfluous mode in the Introit *Iustus es Domine,*[9] written in the first mode and sung in the Mass of the seventeenth Sunday after the Feast of Pentecost. There are almost innumerable examples of imperfect modes, among them the Introit *Puer natus est nobis,*[10] written in the seventh mode and sung in the third Mass on the most solemn day of the Nativity of Our Lord.

Here it should be noted once and for all that what I have said concerning the modes in plainsong should also be applied to the parts of the modes in mensural music, even though I have not given examples of the latter.

Since, as I have said above,[11] everything should be named according to its end, which is its most noble attribute, we should judge each mode by its final note. Thus we shall call perfect first mode that mode which ends on the note D and goes up to the note d. When the mode does not reach the note d we shall call it imperfect. In the same manner, we shall call perfect second mode that mode which ends on the note D, ascends to the note a, and decends to A; when it does not reach the note A, we shall

5. *Le Istit. harm.,* IV, 18.
6. *LU* 353.
7. *LU* 1229.
8. Gaffurio *Practica musice* I, 8.
9. *LU* 1047.
10. *LU* 408.
11. *Le Istit. harm.,* IV, 30.

Example 6. [The finals of the twelve modes]

call it imperfect. We shall use the terms "superfluous" or "abundant" when the first mode goes beyond the eighth note above its final, and when the second mode goes beyond the fourth note below its final.

What I have said pertains to those cases in which the modes end on their proper final notes and maintain their proper form. If the modes end on the notes called cofinals or on other notes, and the proper form is not found in them, we shall have to use other means to determine the mode of a composition, as I am going to show elsewhere.[12]

12. Ibid.

CHAPTER 14

Common Modes and Mixed Modes

THERE is also another distinction between modes. When both the odd- and even-numbered modes reach the fourth note beyond their diapason, the latter above and the former below, they should be called common,[1] for they are composed of the principal mode and its collateral. The entire composition written in such a mode would be contained within the eleven notes common to both the authentic and plagal modes, which have the same diapente and diatessaron in common. This can be seen in Example 6.

Many of the chants of the church have been written in these common modes, as, for example, the prose, or sequence (as they call it), *Victimae paschali laudes immolent Christiani*,[2] which is sung after the Epistle on the most holy day of the Resurrection of Jesus Christ, Son of God; the antiphon *Salve regina misericordiae*;[3] and the two responsories sung at Matins, *Duo Seraphin*[4] and *Sint lumbi vestri praecincti*.[5] All of these are

1. Glarean refers to them as "modes the systems of which can be connected," and deals with them in *Dodekachordon*, II, 29–35; III, 24. He once refers to "mixed modes" (*Dodekachordon*, I, 14), but they should not be confused with Zarlino's mixed modes.

2. *LU* 780, Glarean uses the same sequence as an example of a melody which includes the ambitus of both the authentic and plagal modes, and describes in detail the interval species used in it (*Dodekachordon*, I, 14).

3. *WA* 352.

4. That is, *Duo seraphim AR* 179.*

5. *PrM* 228.

named after the principal mode, namely, the first, because everything ought to be named after its most perfect, dignified, and noble attribute. These common modes may be called imperfect when they do not include the eleven notes mentioned above.

When in any of the modes set forth, whether authentic or plagal, perfect, imperfect, superfluous, or diminished, and also common, a diapente or diatessaron used in another mode is repeated many times, for example, if in the first, second or another mode were heard repeatedly the diapente or diatessaron of the third or fourth, the mode can be called mixed,[6] because the diapente or the diatessaron of one mode becomes mixed with the melodic line of another. This may be seen in the Introit *Spiritus Domini replevit orbem terrarum,*[7] which is sung in the Mass of the Feast of Pentecost. This Introit, composed in the eighth mode, has at its beginning the first species of diapente, which is used in the first mode. In the middle of this Introit, we see that the third species [of diapente], which is used only in the fifth and sixth modes, is repeated many times.

6. Gaffurio is more specific, explaining (*Practica musice,* I, 8) that the additional species has to belong to a mode different from the collateral and principal of the mode in which the composition is written. He says further that if the composition is written in a plagal mode, the added species must belong to an authentic mode other than its own.

7. *LU* 1279.

CHAPTER 15   *Another Way of Classifying the Modes; and What Should Be Observed in Each Mode in Composing Vocal Music*[1]

I T should be noted that the modes are twofold. There are those in which one sings the Psalms of David and the New Testament Canticles,[2] and those in which one sings antiphons, responsories, introits, graduals, and other similar things.

The latter may be called varied modes, because for each mode there is no single

1. Ed. of 1573: And in what manner the eight psalm tones are matched with the modes. [An equivalent to the addition in this chapter in the 1573 edition can be found in chapter 27 of the 1558 edition.]

2. Ed. of 1573: . . . and which are called psalmodies, as Dante Alighieri calls them at the beginning of Canto 33 of *Purgatory:*

Deus venerunt gentes, alternando
Hor tre hor quattro dolce Salmodia
Le Donne incominciaro lagrimando.

[Dante *Purgatory* 33. 1–3: "Now three, now four, alternating, the women weepingly began the sweet psalmody 'Deus venerunt gentes.'" Most editions have *Or* for Zarlino's *Hor,* and *e lacrimando* for his *lagrimando.*]

tune or fixed formula in which one must sing all the antiphons, responsories, and other similar things written in a mode, say the first, on a tenor or air in the manner [316] that the psalms or canticles are sung, and on another all those of the second mode, and so on for the rest, as may be seen in many examples. Rather there are many varied tunes, as can be seen in many chants. For example, the Introit *Gaudete in Domine*[3] is sung on one tenor or air on the third Sunday of the Advent of the Lord, while the Introit *Suscepimus Deus misericordiam tuam*[4] is sung on the eighth Sunday after the Feast of Pentecost on another tenor or air, although they are both composed in the first mode.

This does not happen in the psalms and canticles, the modes of which may be called stable, because everything in a particular mode is sung to the same tenor or air. For example, all the psalms of the first mode, with their verses, are sung to a single tenor, or fixed tune, without any change, and it is not permissible to vary such a tenor, because confusion would result. And although there are many different forms of these intonations or modes, such as the Patriarchan and the Monastic, nevertheless no more than eight are generally used in each church. These are called regular, and are determined by the antiphons contained in the first eight modes of the twelve shown. These intonations are sung in the offices. But when the psalm tones are sung in a mode outside the principal eight,[5] such a mode is called irregular. These intonations are different for each mode, although the tenor to which one sings one psalm of the first mode is not different from the tenor to which one sings another psalm of the same first mode.

Although one does not hear any difference in the singing of various psalms in the same mode, still there is another distinction, for churchmen have two sorts of psalm tones, namely, festive and ferial. This occurs because they sing the ferial psalms in a manner different and shorter than that in which they sing the festive ones, although there is but little difference between one and the other. Nor is there any difference between the tones, whether festive or ferial, to which the New Testament Canticles are sung, and those to which the psalms are sung, except that in the festive tones of the New Testament Canticle *Magnificat anima mea Dominum*[6] one may vary somewhat the beginnings of certain tones, such as those used in the second, seventh, and eighth modes, as may be seen in the first book of the *Practica* of Franchino Gaffurio, from chapter 8 to the end of the book, and in *Recanetto di Musica,* [Book I], in chapters 59 and 60.[7] One may also see in these books the manners in which churchmen usually end these psalm tones.

In the modes in which are sung the psalm verses in the Introit of the Mass, along with their *Gloria patri,* there are some formulas or tenors which are somewhat

3. *LU* 334.

4. *LU* 1361.

5. Ed. of 1573: . . . as is that psalm tone shown further below in chapter 26, which is used in the psalm *In exitu Israel de Aegypto.* [Tonus peregrinus.]

6. *LU* 213.

7. Stefano Vanneo, *Recanetum de musica* (Rome, 1533). Marco and Palisca, in Zarlino, *The Art of Counterpoint,* p. 266, note that a copy in the Newberry Library, Chicago, contains three pages at the end with writing in Zarlino's hand.

different from those used in the psalms of Vespers and the other Canonical Hours, as can be seen in [chapter 62 of] the *Recanetto* mentioned earlier. Nevertheless, [in each of these types of musical services, the psalms of a particular mode] are always sung to one tenor, without any change.[8]

I have wanted to say this so that a composer will know what to do when writing a vocal composition. For if he should want to write a composition based on the words of the New Testament Canticle *Magnificat anima mea Dominum,* which is sung at Vespers, it would be necessary for him to follow the mode and intonation of this canticle as it appears in plainsong.[9] The composer should do the same thing when writing a composition based on the words of any psalm sung at Vespers or at other [Canonical] Hours, whether the psalm is composed so that its verses may be sung with a second chorus in an alternating manner, as Jacquet [of Mantua][10] and many others have done, whether the verses [of the psalm] are sung entirely by one chorus, as in the psalms *In convertendo Dominus captivitatem Syon*[11] and *Beati omnes qui timent Dominum,*[12] composed by Lupus for four voices in the eighth mode, or whether the verses are composed for two choruses, as in the psalms by Adrian [Willaert], *Laudate pueri Dominum,*[13] *Laude Hierusalem Dominum,*[14] and many others, which are indicated "for divided choir" [*a choro spezzato*].

But when writing other compositions, such as motets or other similar things, the composer does not have to follow the chant, or tenor, of the psalm tones, for he is not obligated to do it. On the contrary, such a practice might be considered a shortcoming and be attributed to a lack of power of invention. Nor should he for any reason do what some composers do who, when composing, for example, in the eighth mode, do not know how to depart from the end of its psalm tone. This they also do in the other modes, so that it seems that they want us always to sing the Seuouae [saecula saeculorum. Amen] placed in antiphonaries at the end of each antiphon. When the composer wants to write compositions outside the psalm tones, he will be free and able to find an invention which will prove more suitable.

The composer in his modes should frequently sound the members of the diapason in which the mode is composed, namely, the diapente and diatessaron. I empha-

---

8. Ed. of 1573: The same thing can also be observed in the versets of the responsory which are sung at Matins, for they must be sung in a melodic line which is never changed, except in those places where the shortness or length of the words dictates such a change. But the *Gloria Patri* is always sung according to a prescribed tenor, taken from the versets mentioned above, as can be seen in chapter 64 of *Recanetto* [see n. 4].

9. *LU* 207. Ed. of 1573: This was gracefully observed by [Cristobal] Morales the Spaniard.

10. Nineteen such psalms either partly or entirely set by Jacquet are published in Willaert, *Opera omnia,* ed. Herman Zenck and Walter Gerstenberg (American Institute of Musicology, 1972), VIII, from *Di Adriano et di Iachet I Salmi appertinenti alli Vesperi per tutte le feste dell'anno* (Venice, 1550).

11. *Treize livres de Motets parus chez Pierre Attaingnant en 1534 et 1535,* book 9, ed. A. Tillman Merritt ([Paris, 1962]), p. 37.

12. No source known.

13. *Opera omnia,* VIII, 102, from *I Salmi appertinenti alli Vesperi* (Venice, 1550).

14. *Opera omnia,* VIII, 115, from *I Salmi appertinenti alli Vesperi* (Venice, 1550).

size that these should be the mode's own diapente and diatessaron and not those of another mode. For some composers proceed in one mode from the beginning up till the end of some of their compositions, touching frequently the diapente and diatessaron of this mode in every part, but enter irrelevantly into another mode when they arrive at the end of the composition, a practice which makes for a very sorry effect.

I see that some composers differentiate little between the procedure to be followed in a principal mode and that to be followed in its collateral. They use in the latter the same movements that they use in the former, so that one hears no variation of concentus, and there is little difference between them. [317] The composer who wants to do everything with reason will take care to lead the movements of the principal modes back down when they go up more than is allowed, especially the movements of the diapente and the diatessaron. He will also take care to lead the movements of the collateral modes back up when they go too far down, especially those movements which proceed through the diapente and the diatessaron. This is necessary because the diapente and the diatessaron are placed in an opposite manner in the principal and the collateral modes. In the principal mode the diapente is placed below and the diatessaron above, and in the collateral mode the diapente is placed above and the diatessaron below. This is really justifiable, for (as I have said[15]) the nature of the collateral is contrary to that of the principal. Being different in nature, they should also be different in movements, inasmuch as the difference comes from the [position of the] diapente and diatessaron, and also from the rapidity or slowness of the movements.

Hence if we attribute upward motion to the principal mode and downward motion to its collateral, everything will be done with reason, mainly because the principal mode is higher than its collateral by a diatessaron. Therefore slow movements, which make for gravity (as is mentioned elsewhere[16]), are suited to the collateral modes, and fast movements, from which high pitch is generated, are suited to the principal modes. Thus we shall accommodate everything to its proper place by using slow movements in the collateral modes and fast movements in the principal modes. I consider it completely inappropriate when composers use in the lower parts of their compositions movements that are too fast and too diminished, and in the higher parts movements that are too slow, with long durations of notes. However, I do not censure it if sometimes, when the subject matter calls for it, one uses slow movements in the high parts and fast movements in the low. But in everything one should use judgment, without which little good can be done.

Enough has been said concerning these subjects, but before I go on to other matters I would like us to see a mistake that is found among some who are not expert in music. After examining this mistake, we shall go on to a detailed discussion of each of the twelve modes named above.

15. *Le Istit. harm.*, IV, 12.
16. Ibid., II, 11.

CHAPTER 16
Whether by Removing the Tetrachord Diezeugmenon from Any Composition and Putting in Its Place the Synemmenon While the Other Tetrachords Remain Immovable, One Mode Can Be Changed into Another

THERE have been some who have felt that if one takes any species of the diapente or of the diatessaron which contains among its essential notes the tetrachord Diezeugmenon, and removes the said tetrachord, putting the Synemmenon in its place, such a change would not have the power to change the mode, for they say that the tetrachord Synemmenon is not natural but accidental and has no power to transform one mode into another in this manner.

I shall not argue as to whether this tetrachord is natural or accidental, but I shall say that if what they claim were true, it would follow that the semitone is superfluous in music and has no power to vary the species of the consonances. How untrue this is can be seen in Part III in many places,[1] where I have shown that it is because of the semitone that variety exists in the species of the consonances, a variety created by the transposition of the semitone from one place to another.

It is true that removing a tetrachord from a composition and putting another tetrachord in its place can be done in two manners. In the first manner, the note b-flat, that is, the Trite Synemmenon, found between Mese and Paramese, is placed once or twice in only one voice of the composition, as, for example, in a small part of the tenor, or of another voice. In this case we may say that by replacing the tetrachord Diezeugmenon, which begins on the note b-natural, that is, on Paramese, with the Synemmenon, which begins on the note a, thus placing the note b-flat in the composition, we do not transform one mode into another. We may also say that when the tetrachord Synemmenon is placed in the composition in this way, it is not natural, but, rather, accidental. In this case those who claim that the Synemmenon does not change the mode are right.

In the second manner the tetrachord Synemmenon is used in place of the Diezeugmenon throughout the whole composition, that is, in every voice, and instead of singing the composition according to the property of b-natural, it is sung according to that of b-flat. Thus when the second manner is used, those who claim that the Synemmenon does not change the mode are not right, because in this manner the tetrachord Synemmenon is not placed in the composition accidentally, but rather is natural, and the mode is said to be transposed, as we shall see below.[2] When used in this manner, the tetrachord Synemmenon has the power to transform one mode

1. *Le Istit. harm.,* III, 12, 13, 14, 16, 20, 21, 23.
2. Ibid., IV, 17.

into another. We can easily [318] see that this is true with the help of a suitable example.

The following tenor in the seventh mode [Example 7] is contained within its natural notes, that is, in its proper and natural place within the seventh species of the diapason. I would say that if in this tenor, or in a similar one, the note b-natural were changed into b-flat only once or twice, it would not cause this mode to be transformed, except in that small segment in which the note b-flat is placed. Thus this change would not have the power to change the mode, for although it is necessary to place the note b-flat in this way in order to regulate the melodic line, nevertheless this note, being accidental, does not change the form of the mode to the extent that it would not be recognized as the seventh. This can be seen in Example 8.

But if we place the sign b-flat at the beginning of this tenor, thus indicating that throughout the whole composition we should proceed through the notes of the tetrachord Synemmenon, I would then say that the note b-flat is natural and not accidental, and that it has the power to change the seventh mode into the first mode, for it changes the fourth species of diapente, between G and d, to the first species of diapente, between the same notes, as is shown in Example 9. It is true that in Example 9 the mode is not in its natural notes, for it is transposed up by a diatessaron. If it were returned to its proper place, it would be arranged in the manner seen in Example 10.

It is absolutely not true, then, that the replacement of the tetrachord Diezeugmenon by the tetrachord Synemmenon does not have the power to change one mode

Example 7.

In san-cti- ta- te ser-vi- a-mus Do-mi-no, et li-   be- ra-bit nos ab i- ni-   mi-cis no- stris.

Example 8.

Am- pli- us la- va me__ Do- mi- ne ab in- iu-   sti-   ti- a me- a.

Example 9.

In san-cti- ta- te ser-vi- a-mus Do-mi-no, et li-   be- ra-bit nos ab i- ni-   mi-cis no- stris.

Example 10.

In san-cti- ta- te ser-vi- a-mus Do-mi-no, et li-   be- ra-bit nos ab i- ni-   mi-cis no- stris.

into another. It is true, though, [that the Synemmenon does not change the mode] when placed according to the first manner. However, if a change of tetrachord is followed by a change [in the species] of diapason, and a change [in the species] of diapason brings about a change of mode, then proceeding from the former to the latter, we shall say that the tetrachord Synemmenon placed in the second manner has the power to change one mode into another. In this way Jean Mouton changed the mode in the Mass which he composed on the antiphon *Argentum, et aurum non est mihi*.[3] This antiphon is in the seventh mode, but by transposing the tetrachord, or changing it, Mouton transposed the composition to the eleventh mode.

We shall conclude, then, that whenever the note b-flat replaces b-natural throughout the composition, this note will always cause the mode to change. The same is true for the opposite change, that is, when the note b-natural replaces b-flat, and this is shown by experience.

3. *LU* 1515. *Opera omnia*, ed. Andrew C. Minor, V (American Institute of Musicology, 1974).

CHAPTER 17   *Transposition of Modes*

[319]   I T is possible, as has been shown,[1] to change one mode into another by putting the note b-flat in place of b-natural, that is, by changing the location of the semitone. If, therefore, the first mode can be changed to the seventh mode, and the seventh mode to the first, there is no doubt that any mode, be it the first, second, third, fourth, or any of the others, can be transposed up or down, as pleases us, with the help of any note that changes one [species of] diapason into another.

I shall leave it to anyone who has sense to judge how convenient this can be. These transpositions are useful and extremely necessary to every expert organist who accompanies choral music, and to players of other sorts of instruments as well, in order to accommodate the sounds of the instruments to the voices, which sometimes cannot ascend or descend as much as is dictated by the proper places of the modes on the said instrument. Such transpositions are now in use among modern musicians, as they also were among ancient musicians, such as Okeghem and his disciple Josquin, and innumerable others, as is seen in their compositions.

When out of necessity or under other circumstances the mode of a composition is transposed, musicians should be warned above all to arrange it in such a manner and place that, in both ascent and descent, all notes are present which are necessary for the constitution of the mode, that is, which yield the whole tones and semitones necessary for the mode's essential character.

Composers should observe this especially when they write for an instrument, for

1. *Le Istit. harm.*, IV, 16.

Example 11.

In san-cti-ta- te ser-vi- a-mus Do-mi-no, et li-   be-ra-bit nos ab i- ni-   mi-cis no- stris.

Example 12.

In san-cti-ta- te ser-vi- a-mus Do-mi-no, et li-   be-ra-bit nos ab i- ni-   mi-cis no- stris.

when they want to compose for voice only, it would not be a great mistake to mark with accidentals a few notes not found on some instruments (especially the clavichord), such as the enharmonic notes available on a few artificial instruments only.[2] I say this because the voice can reach high and low notes or can be used in any manner the singer wishes, whereas with instruments this cannot be done so freely.

In order to show the manner in which any composition can be conveniently transposed away from its natural notes, we shall take Examples 9 and 10 in the preceding chapter. These examples show best how every composition which proceeds through the note b-natural can be transposed up by a diatessaron with the help of the note b-flat, or, vice versa, how a melodic line proceeding through b-flat can be conveniently transposed down by the same interval with the help of b-natural.

Sometimes musicians, not simply out of necessity but rather as a joke and a caprice, or perhaps because they want, so to speak, to entangle the brains of singers, transpose the modes further up or down by a whole tone or another interval, using not only chromatic but also enharmonic notes in order to be able, when necessary, to transpose conveniently the whole tones and semitones to the places indicated by the proper form of the mode. I want to show how these transpositions are usually made.

Although musicians transpose modes in various ways, I shall discuss here only the two most common transpositions. These will be demonstrated in the first mode, from which everyone will be able to understand the manner to be adhered to in the other modes as well.

The first transposition [Example 11] is done with the help of notes marked by a flat, and the second [Example 12] with the help of notes marked by a sharp. The moderns [320] call these transpositions "modes transposed by false music," which they claim to be a transposition of a species from its proper place to another, meaning by this a transposition of the whole order found in each mode.

I leave it now to everyone expert in music to judge how useful this knowledge can be to an organist who is not very well instructed in music, inasmuch as the organist will be able from the examples given to know what to do if he has to transpose a composition while playing a church service in which various choral

2. Such as Vicentino's "archicembalo."

compositions are sung, not only at Mass and Vespers but also in the other [Canonical] Hours, both diurnal and nocturnal.

Let it be known above all that, although I have given examples of the first mode only, these transpositions can be made in compositions written in other modes, which I have not shown because I want to be brief.[3]

3. Ed. of 1573: I have clearly shown this in the Twenty-fifth [Proposition] of the Fifth [Discussion] of *Le Dimost. harm.*, hence I shall not speak further about this matter.

CHAPTER 18   *A Discussion of the First Mode in Particular: Its Nature, Its Initial Notes, and Its Cadences*

I SHALL now begin the discussion of each mode separately, starting with the first mode and proceeding in order. In discussing each mode, I shall first show that it is in use not only among churchmen but also among the whole community of musicians. Then I shall show the notes on which one can regularly begin a mode and those on which one can make cadences. Having done this, I shall discuss to some extent the nature of the mode.

The first mode, as I have shown,[1] is contained within the fourth species of diapason, found between the two extreme notes D and d, divided harmonically. Regarding this division, practitioners say that this mode is composed of the first species of diapente, D to a, and the first species of diatessaron, a to d, placed above the diapente.

There are innumerable sacred chants in this mode, such as introits, graduals, antiphons, responsories,[2] and other similar things. Among modern musicians there are also innumerable compositions written in this mode, including Masses, motets, hymns, madrigals, and other songs.[3] Among these compositions are the motets *Veni sancte spiritus*[4] and *Victimae paschali*,[5] composed for six voices, and the madrigal *Giunto m'hà Amor*,[6] composed for five voices, all by Adrian [Willaert]. I, too, wrote many compositions in this mode, among them[7] two motets for five voices, *O beatum*

1. *Le Istit. harm.*, IV, 10, 11.
2. Ed. of 1573: Halleluyas and prosae.
3. Ed. of 1573: . . . composed both in Latin and in the vernacular.
4. Adrian Willaert, *Opera omnia*, V, 88.
5. Ibid., V, 164.
6. Ibid., XII, 40.
7. Ed. of 1573: . . . the motets *Hodie Christus natus est* [Number 3 in *Josephi Zarlini Clodiensis musici . . . Modulationes sex vocum, per Philippum Iusbertum musicum Venetum collectae* (Venice, 1566)], *Victimae paschali* [Number 9 in *Modulationes* (1566)], and *Salve regina misericordiae* [Number 12 in *Modulationes* (1566)], for six voices.

pontificem[8] and *Nigra sum sed formosa.*[9] There are also many other compositions by many excellent musicians [in this mode] which, for the sake of brevity, I shall not name.

The true and natural initial tones of the first mode, as well as those of every other mode, are on the extreme notes of the diapente and diatessaron, and on the median note which divides the diapente into a ditone and a semiditone. Nevertheless, there are many compositions that begin on other notes, none of which I shall mention in order to be brief. Churchmen observed in their compositions some intermediate endings at the end of each clause, or sentence, and at the end of each complete thought. These they called "cadences," and they are very necessary for distinguishing the words which indicate that the sense of the sentence is complete. He who wishes to have a full knowledge of cadences can read chapter 53 of Part III, for there I have sufficiently discussed this matter.

It will suffice to say here, once and for all, that there are two sorts of cadences, namely, regular and irregular. The regular cadences are those which are always made on the extreme sounds or notes of the modes, and on the median note by which the diapason is mediated or divided harmonically or arithmetically. These are the extreme notes of the diapente and the diatessaron.[10] The regular cadences are also made on the median note by which the diapente is divided into a ditone and a semiditone. In other words, the regular cadences are made on the true and natural initial tones of each mode, and the cadences that are made on all the other notes are called irregular. The regular cadences of the first mode, then, are those which are made on the notes D, F, a, and d; the irregular cadences are those which are made on the other notes.

In order that what I have said may be understood more easily, I shall present an example for two voices [Example 13], by means of which the reader may know the proper places of the regular cadences and see the manner that should be adhered to in composing their melodic lines. I shall present similar examples for the other modes as well.[11] [321]

It must be noted, however, that the cadences of the psalms are always made on the note on which the end of the mediation of the intonation falls. Hence the cadences of the mediation, or midpoint of the psalm tone, of the first, fourth, and sixth modes will be made on a; those of the second, on f; those of the third, fifth, and eighth, on c; and those of the seventh, on e; for these mediations, or midpoints, end on these notes. This can be seen in the *Recanetto,*[12] in the *Thoscanello,*[13] and in many other books which contain similar psalm tones, or intonations, whichever name we want to use.

8. Number 2 in *Josephi Zarlini Musici quinque vocum moduli, motecta vulgo nuncupata . . . Liber primus* (Venice, 1549).

9. Number 6 in *Moduli* (1549). Printed in Luigi Torchi, *L'arte musicale in Italia* (Milan, 1897), I, 69.

10. Ed. of 1573: . . . into which the diapason is divided.

11. In Zarlino's examples of the modes the parts are labeled "soprano" and "tenore." These labels have been omitted.

12. See chapter 15, n. 7.

13. Pietro Aron, *Toscanello in musica* (Venice, 1523; and many later editions).

Example 13. [The first mode]

(Example 13 *continued*)

The finals are always placed on the note on which each verse of these psalm tones, or of each psalm, ends.

We should always take care to make the cadences principally in the tenor, inasmuch as this part is the principal leader of the mode in which the vocal composition is written, and it is from this part that the composer should derive the invention of the other parts. But these cadences are also made in the other parts of the composition when it is more convenient.

The first mode has a very close kinship with the ninth mode, because in the proper location of the first mode musicians write compositions of the ninth mode, outside its natural notes, transposing the ninth mode up by a diatessaron or down by a diapente, and replacing [322] the note b-natural by the note b-flat.[14] Morales the Spaniard did this in the motet *Sancta et immaculata virginitas,*[15] for four voices.[16]

The first mode has a certain effect midway between sad and cheerful because of the semiditone which is heard in the concentus above the extreme notes of the diapente and diatessaron, and because of the absence of the ditone in the lower part [of the diapente].[17] By nature this mode is religious and devout and somewhat sad; hence we can best use it with words that are full of gravity and that deal with lofty and edifying things. In this way the harmony is suited to the subject matter contained in the words.

14. Ed. of 1573: . . . which belongs to the tetrachord Synemmenon.

15. *Opera omnia,* ed. Higinio Angles, II (Rome, 1953), 17.

16. Ed. of 1573: And Jacquet [of Mantua] did this in the motet *Spem in alium,* also for four voices [*Celeberrimi maximeque delectabilis musici Jachet . . . motecta quatuor vocum* (Venice, 1539)].

17. Zarlino writes about the effect of the major and minor third in *Le Istit. harm.,* III, 10, 31.

CHAPTER 19   *Second Mode*

S OME have claimed that the second mode contains a certain severe and unflattering gravity, and that its nature is tearful and humble. Thus they have called it a lamentful, humble, and deprecatory mode. Hence churchmen, holding this to be true, used this mode for sad and lamentful occasions, such as Lent and other fast days. [323] They have said that it was a mode fit for words which represent weeping, sadness, loneliness, captivity, calamity, and every kind of misery. It is very much in use in their chants.

The principal and regular cadences of the second mode, as seen in Example 14, are placed on the notes a, F, D, and A (this mode being not very different from the first, as both are composed of the same species). The cadences placed on the other notes are irregular. Practitioners say that the second mode is composed of the first species of diapente, a to D, placed above, and the first species of diatessaron, D to A, placed below. They call it the collateral or plagal of the first mode.

Example 14. [The second mode]

(Example 14 *continued*)

There are many compositions in the second mode, composed by many ancient and modern musicians. These compositions include the motet *Praeter rerum seriem,* composed for six voices by Josquin,[1] and a motet of the same name composed for seven voices by Adrian [Willaert],[2] who also composed in this mode the madrigal *Che fai alma,*[3] for seven voices, as well as the motet *Avertatur obsecro Domine*[4] and the madrigal *Ove ch'i posi gli occhi,*[5] both for six voices, together with many other compositions. I myself composed in this mode the Sunday Prayer *Pater noster* with the Angelic Salutation *Ave Maria,*[6] for seven voices, as well as the motets *Ego rosa Saron*[7] and *Capite nobis vulpes parvulas,*[8] both for five voices. There are many other compositions in the second mode, written by various composers, but I do not mention them here because they are almost innumerable.

In mensural music the second mode is rarely found in its proper notes but most of the time is transposed up by a diatessaron, as can be seen in the motets mentioned above, for this mode can be transposed, as can the first mode, with the help of the Trite Synemmenon. And just as there is a close concurrence between the first and ninth modes, so there is an agreement between the second and the tenth.

1. Josquin des Pres, *Werken Van Josquin des Prez,* ed. A. Smijers, *Motetten* II, 21.
2. *Opera omnia,* V, 209.
3. Ibid., XIII, (1966) 114.
4. Ibid., V (1957), 100.
5. Ibid., XIII, 90.
6. Both under number 19 in *Moduli* (1549); also as number 13 in *Modulationes* (1566).
7. Number 16 in *Moduli* (1549).
8. Number 18 in *Moduli* (1549).

CHAPTER 20   *Third Mode*

THE third mode comes into being from the fifth species of diapason, divided harmonically by the note b-natural, or from the union of the second species of diapente, E to b-natural, placed below, with the second species of diatessaron, b-natural to e, placed above. This mode has the final note E in common with the fourth mode. Churchmen have innumerable compositions in this mode, as can be seen in their books.

The principal cadences of the third mode [324] are made on the notes of its regular initial tones, which are the notes E, G, b-natural, and e, as shown in Example 15. These notes are the extremes of the diapente and diatessaron, and the median of the diapente. The other cadences and initial tones, which are irregular, can be made on the other notes. Once those that are regular are known, the irregular can be recognized easily, and therefore we give an example of the former so that we can recognize the latter.

It should be noted that in this mode, as in the fourth, seventh, and eighth

Example 15. [The third mode]

modes, cadences are regularly made on the note b-natural, and since this note does not have a corresponding fifth above or fourth below, it sounds somewhat hard. Yet this hardness is tolerated in compositions written for more than two voices, because then the voices are kept in such an order that they produce a good effect, as may be seen among the cadences presented in chapter 61 of Part III.

There are many compositions written in the third mode, among them the motet *O Maria mater Christi,* for four voices, by Isaac,[1] the motets *Te Deum patrem,*[2] *Huc me sydereo*[3] and *Haec est domus domini,*[4] composed by Adrian {Willaert} for seven voices, and the madrigal *I mi rivolgo indietro,* composed by Adrian {Willaert} for five voices.[5] To these I would add *Ferculum fecit sibi rex Salomon,*[6] also for five voices, which I have composed in this mode, together with many other compositions.

If the third mode were not mixed with the ninth mode, and were heard by itself, its harmony would be somewhat hard, but because it is tempered by the

1. *Vier Marienmotetten,* ed. Martin Just, 17.
2. Adrian Willaert, *Opera omnia,* V, 270.
3. *Opera omnia,* V, 197, is for 6 voices.
4. *Opera omnia,* V, 188, is for 6 voices.
5. *Opera omnia,* XIII, 49.
6. Number 14 in *Moduli* (1549).

diapente of the ninth mode and by the cadence made on a, which is very much in use in it, some have been of the opinion that the third mode moves one to weeping. Hence they have accommodated to it words which are tearful and full of laments.

There is a great concurrence between the third mode and the ninth, for the second species of diatessaron is common to both of them. Modern musicians often transpose the third mode up by a diatessaron and away from its natural notes, with the help of the note b-flat. But most of the time it is placed in its proper and natural location.

CHAPTER 21   *Fourth Mode*

T HE third mode is followed by the fourth, which is contained within the second species of diapason, b-natural to B-natural, divided arithmetically by its final note E. This mode is composed of the second species of diapente, b-natural to E, placed above, and the second species of diatessaron, E to B-natural, placed below.

This mode is said by musical practitioners to be marvelously suited to lamentful words or subjects that contain sadness or supplicant lamentation, such as matters of love, and to words which express languor, quiet, tranquillity, adulation, deception, and slander. Because of this effect, some have called it a flattering mode. This mode is somewhat sadder than its principal, especially when it proceeds in a motion contrary [to that of its principal], namely, downward, and in slow tempo. I believe that the fourth mode would be somewhat more virile if it were used simply, without mixing in it the diapente [A to E] and·the cadence placed on a, which are used in the tenth mode. However, the fourth mode is frequently mixed in this way.

There are many compositions written in this mode, among them the motet *De profundis clamavi ad te Domine* for four voices by Josquin,[1] and the motet *Peccata mea Domine*[2] for six voices, the madrigal *Rompi dell'empio cor il duro scoglio*[3] for six voices, as well as the madrigal *Laura mia sacra*[4] for five voices, all composed by Adrian [Willaert].[5]

I, too, have written many compositions in this mode, among them the motet *Miserere mei Deus miserere mei*[6] for six voices,[7] and a Mass,[8] without using the condi-

1. *Werken, Motetten*, V, 177.
2. Adrian Willaert, *Opera omnia*, V, 119.
3. *La piu divina, et piu bella musica* (Venice, 1541) [1541^16].
4. Adrian Willaert, *Opera omnia*, XIII, 28.
5. Ed. of 1573: . . . and the madrigal *In qual parte del ciel* [*Opera omnia*, XIII, 79], for six voices, also by Adrian [Willaert].
6. Number 6 in *Modulationes* (1566).
7. Ed. of 1573: . . . and the motet *Misereris omnium Domine* [Das Chorwerk, ed. Friedrich Blume, 19], for six voices.
8. No source known.

Example 16. [The fourth mode]

(Example 16 *continued*)

tions [*osservanze*] shown in Part III,[9] and I have done this for no other reason than to show that those who would like to compose without departing from the given rules can compose easily without these conditions, when they want to do so, and they will compose much better than some do who do not know them.[10]

There are almost innumerable sacred chants in the fourth mode in which the note B-natural is touched very rarely, indeed, if I said never, I would not be wrong. Instead, the note c is reached upward, so that the semitone which ought to be heard below [between B-natural and C] is heard above [between b-natural and c], and the extremes of the mode come to be the notes c and C.

The irregular initial tones of the fourth mode, according to ecclesiastical authors, are to be found in many places, but its regular initial tones are to be found only on the notes B-natural, E, G, and b-natural, as are also its regular cadences, which are shown in Example 16. However, there are many irregular cadences as well. Most of the time practitioners transpose this mode up by a diatessaron, replacing the note b-natural by the note b-flat, as may be seen in innumerable compositions. This is done (as I have said) in the other modes as well. [325]

9. Zarlino refers to a set of rules presented in *Le Istit. harm.*, III, 63. These are exact instructions for writing imitative counterpoint at the unison, octave, and fifth, above and below, at a distance of a minim or a semiminim.

10. At the end of chapter 63 of Part III a similar statement is made to the effect that the composer should know the rules but need not stick to them rigidly.

CHAPTER 22   *Fifth Mode*

THE fifth mode is contained within the sixth species of diapason, F to f, mediated harmonically by the note c. Practitioners say that it is composed of the third species of diapente, F to c, and of the third species of diatessaron, c to f, placed above the diapente. The note F is the common final note of this mode and the sixth mode, its collateral. We derive only one mode, the fifth, from the sixth species of diapason, because this species cannot be divided otherwise than harmonically.

Some claim that, in singing, this mode brings to the spirit modesty, happiness, and relief from annoying cares. Yet the ancients used it with words or subjects that dealt with victory, and because of this some called it a joyous, modest, and pleasing mode.

The natural and regular initial tones of the fifth mode are placed on the notes F, a, c, and f, but among churchmen there are other initial tones, on various other notes, as can be seen in their books. The regular cadences of this mode are made on the four notes mentioned above, as seen in Example 17. The irregular cadences, when used, are made on the other notes.

Many compositions in the fifth mode are found in the sacred chant books,

Example 17. [The fifth mode]

(Example 17 *continued*)

although this mode is not much in use among modern composers, for they consider it harsher and more unpleasant than any other mode. Nevertheless there are quite a few [modern] compositions in this mode, such as the Hymn of Saint Francis, *Spoliatis aegyptiis,* by Adrian [Willaert],[1] two madrigals by Cipriano de Rore, *Di tempo in tempo mi si fà men dura*[2] and *Donna che ornata sete,*[3] and a madrigal by Francesco Viola, *Fra quanti amor,*[4] all composed for four voices. There are many more [326] which do not come to mind.

The fifth mode can be transposed down by a diapente with the help of the note b-flat, which replaces the note b-natural, as occurs when the other modes are transposed up. Here the final note is b-flat, as is evident.

1. *Opera omnia,* VII, 61.
2. *Opera omnia,* ed. Bernhard Meier, IV, 36.
3. Ibid., IV, 39.
4. No source known.

CHAPTER 23   *Sixth Mode*

T HE fifth mode is followed by the sixth, which is contained within the third species of diapason, c to C, divided arithmetically.[1] Practitioners say that this mode is formed and comes into being through the conjunction of the third species of diapente, c to F, placed above, with the third species of diatessaron, F to C, placed below. The note F is its final note.

The sixth mode, like its principal mode, was used very frequently by churchmen, and thus there are many compositions in their books which are written in this mode. They felt that the sixth mode was not very cheerful or elegant, and therefore they used it in serious and devout compositions containing commiseration, and accommodated it to matters containing tears. So they called it a devout and tearful mode to distinguish it from the second mode, which is more funereal and calamitous.

The regular initial tones of the sixth mode and its regular cadences [327] are made on the notes c, a, F, and C; the irregular initial tones and cadences are made on the other notes. When the former are known, it is easy to know the latter. Therefore it will not be inappropriate for us to give an example of the regular initial tones and cadences [Example 18] so that one may know the entire thing more readily.

I remember having seen many compositions written in this mode, but at present only the following come to mind: a motet by Mouton for four voices, *Ecce Maria genuit nobis Salvatorem,*[2] and a psalm by Adrian [Willaert] for two divided choirs in eight voices,[3] *In convertendo Dominus captivitatem Syon.*[4]

1. "Harmonically" in the 1558 edition; corrected in the 1573 edition.
2. *Motetti da corona,* book 1 (Venice, 1514).
3. Ed. of 1573: . . . composed on the sixth psalm tone.
4. *Opera omnia,* VIII, 160.

Example 18. [The sixth mode]

The sixth mode, like the other modes, can be transposed up by a diatessaron with the help of the note b-flat. Everyone will be able to see how easy this is from the two compositions mentioned above.

CHAPTER 24   *Seventh Mode*

THE seventh mode is contained within the seventh species of diapason, G to g, mediated harmonically. This mode, as the moderns say, comes into being from the conjunction of the first species of diatessaron, d to g, with the fourth species of diapente, G to d, the latter placed below and the former placed above.

The words which are appropriate to this mode are said to be those which are lascivious or which deal with lasciviousness, those which are cheerful and spoken with modesty, and those which express threat, perturbation, and anger.

The regular initial tones of the seventh mode and its principal and regular cadences are placed on the notes G, b-natural, d, and g, as is seen in Example 19. [328] The irregular initial tones and cadences of this mode are placed on the other notes.

There are many compositions written by musicians in the seventh mode, among

Example 19. [The seventh mode]

which are *Pater peccavi*[1] and *I piansi hor canto*[2] by Adrian [Willaert], both for six voices. This mode was much in use among churchmen, and in compositions of other musicians it is found most of the time within its natural notes. But many times, with the help of the note b-flat, it is transposed down by a diapente without any trouble.

1. Adrian Willaert, *Opera omnia*, V, 154.
2. Ibid., XII, 67.

CHAPTER 25   *Eighth Mode*

THE seventh mode is followed by the eighth, which is contained within the fourth species of diapason, d to D, divided arithmetically by the note G, and generated by the conjunction of the fourth species of diapente, d to G, placed above, with the first species of diatessaron, G to D, placed below. This mode has the final note G in common with the seventh mode.

Practicing musicians say that the eighth mode contains a certain natural softness and an abundant sweetness which fills the spirits of the listeners with joy combined with great gaiety and sweetness. They also claim that it is completely removed from lasciviousness and every vice. Hence they use it with words or subjects which are tame, civilized, and grave, and which contain profound, speculative, and divine thoughts, such as those suited for entreating the grace of the Lord.

In the chant books there are many compositions in this mode, which has its regular initial tones on the notes d, b-natural, G, and D. The irregular initial tones are placed on the other notes. The regular cadences are placed on the four notes named above, as may be seen in Example 20, [329] and the irregular cadences are placed on the other notes.

Example 20. [The eighth mode]

In the writings of other musicians there are many compositions [in the eighth mode], among them the motet *Benedicta es coelorum regina* for six voices by Josquin,[1] and the motets *Audite insulae*[2] for six voices and *Verbum supernum prodiens*[3] for seven voices, as well as the madrigal *Liete et pensose, accompagnate et sole donne*[4] for seven voices, all by Adrian [Willaert]. There are almost innumerable other compositions [in this mode].

This mode, like the others, can be transposed away from its natural notes by being moved up by a diatessaron with the help of the note b-flat, for otherwise transposition would be impossible.[5]

1. *Werken, Motetten*, III, 11.
2. Adrian Willaert, *Opera omnia*, V, 135.
3. Ibid., V, 253.
4. Ibid., XIII, 108.
5. Ed. of 1573: Here, however, I want to warn the reader about one thing, for this is the right place to discuss it. Churchmen usually applied the psalm tone of the psalm *In exitu Israel de Aegypto* (shown in the following chapter [*LU* 153]), to all the antiphons in this mode which begin on the notes C or D and end on the final G, such as *Nos qui vivimus* (*AM* 132, 133), *Martyres Domini* (*LU* 1154), and many other similar antiphons found in the old antiphonaries, as their Seuouae shows. I wanted to mention this in order not to leave out anything pertaining to the musician, and so that one will not be surprised if one happens to see such a thing. For it can be said that this psalm tone is more appropriate for these antiphons than the eighth psalm tone, which is applied to the other antiphons in this mode. This is so because the melodic line of this psalm tone concurs with the melodic lines of the aforementioned antiphons.

CHAPTER 26   *Ninth Mode*

T HE ninth mode, as practitioners say, comes into being through the conjunction of the first species of diapente, A to E, or a to e (whichever one chooses), with the second

Example 21. [The ending of Pater noster]

Sed li- be- ra nos a ma- lo.

species of diatessaron, E to a, or e to aa. I would prefer to say that the ninth mode is contained within the first species of diapason, A to a, or a to aa, mediated harmonically by the note E, or by e.

One could never truly say that this is a new mode. Rather, it is very ancient, even though until now it has been deprived of its name[1] and its proper place, for some have placed it among those modes which they call irregular, as if it were not subject to the same rules to which the other modes are subject, and as if its diapason were not divided harmonically, as is that of any other [authentic] mode, but in some other strange manner. It is true (as I have said elsewhere[2]) that the churchmen indicated only the first eight modes for the [330] intonations of the psalms,[3] as can be seen in their books. But one cannot say that the ninth mode is irregular simply because of this, inasmuch as the intonation of the psalms is one thing, and the melodic lines found in different modes, in plainsong as much as in mensural music, are another thing. I do not want to believe that, if an antiphon were found, composed in any of the last four modes, one could not apply to it one of the eight intonations[4] mentioned above; especially because each one of the intonations has diverse endings [i.e. *differentiae*], as is clear to all who are experienced in this matter.

Some have called the ninth mode open and terse, very suitable for lyric poetry. One can use this mode with words containing cheerful, sweet, soft, and sonorous subjects, because (as it is claimed) it possesses a pleasant severity, mixed with a certain cheerfulness and sweet softness. It is well known to all experts in music that this mode and the first mode conform with each other, for the first species of diapente is common to both of them, and one can pass easily from one to the other. This can also be said about the third and eleventh modes.

There are many chants in the ninth mode, and it would take much too long to refer to all of them. Among these compositions is the chant of the Sunday Prayer, *Pater noster,* which ends on the note A in some correct copies in the manner seen in Example 21.

The Nicene Creed, *Credo in unum Deum,* is also written in the ninth mode. The intonation of this chant begins on the note D, and, like the *Pater noster,* comes to an end on the note A, as may be seen in the correct copies [Example 22]. Contrary to what is seen [in modern usage], it does not end on the note b-natural or on the note E transposed up by a diatessaron with help of the note b-flat. This chant, when

1. This is surprisingly similar to Glarean's words about the same mode: "Old indeed, but deprived of a name for many years" (Dodekachordon, II, 17).

2. Le Istit. harm., IV, 15.

3. Ed. of 1573: . . . or psalm tones, whatever we want to call them.

4. Ed. of 1573: . . . or psalm tones.

Example 22. [The ending of Credo in unum Deum]

Et— vi-tam ven-tu- ri   se-   cu- li   A-   men.

Example 23. [Ave Maria gratia plena]

A- ve Ma- ri-   a gra- ti- a ple- na Do-mi-nus te-cum be- ne- di- cta tu

in— mu- li-   e-   ri- bus et be- ne- dic-tus frus- tus   ven- tris   tu- i.

Example 24. [In exitu Israel di Aegypto]

In— e- xi- tu Is- ra- el de Ae-gy- pto   do- mus Ia-cob de po-pu-lo bar-ba- ro.—

transposed, should end on the note D, but it has been spoiled and made incorrect by
the ignorance of the scribes, as happens also in other things of major importance. And
it is not only in the *Pater noster* and the *Credo in unum Deum* that the endings are found
away from their proper and natural notes, but it occurs as well in other chants that
have been spoiled and corrupted, but it would take too much space to give a
particular example of each. How easy it is to transform sacred chants from one mode
to another by varying only the final note or by transposing the chant up or down
without the help of the note b-flat is easy for those practiced in music to see, if they
examine closely the melodic lines and the procedures of these chants, and it would not
be very difficult to demonstrate this if one were willing to spend some time on it.

The antiphon *Ave Maria gratia plena* is composed in the ninth mode. In the
ancient books this antiphon is found within its natural notes, as is seen in Example
23, whereas in the modern books it is written lower by a diapente.[5] We may
understand that this is true from the fact that Pierre de la Rue composed a Mass[6] for
four voices on this antiphon in the true and essential notes of the ninth mode.

The introit *Gaudeamus omnes in Domino*[7] is also composed in this mode. No one

5. *LU* 1416.

6. Pierre de la Rue, Mass on the antiphon *Ave Maria gratia plena,* in *Les Maîtres musiciens de la
Renaissance française,* ed. Henry Expert, VIII, 77.

7. *LU* 1368.

Example 25. [The ninth mode]

should be surprised at this, even though the psalm tone of the psalm which follows it is in the first mode, for, as I have already stated [earlier in this chapter], it is not inappropriate to adapt each of the four last modes to the intonation of one of the eight psalm tones. And if the note b-flat, substituted for the note b-natural, has the power to change one mode into another, [331] there is no doubt that this Introit, being placed within the fourth species of diapason and sung with b-flat, is also in the ninth mode, as may be clearly seen by examining all I have said above in chapter 16. If one wanted to bring this Introit back to its true and natural notes, transposing it up by a diapente, it would be placed within the first species of diapason, a and aa. This was done by the learned Josquin, who, composing a Mass for four voices on this Introit,[8] took it back to its natural notes.

It now occurs to me that some were not mistaken when they judged that the intonation of the psalm *In exitu Israel de Aegypto* (shown in Example 24), was in the ninth mode, for they claimed that the antiphon *Nos qui vivimus benedicimus Dominum*[9] had been spoiled and transposed away from its [proper] place by a scribe who wanted to show himself more clever than the others, just as scribes have also done when copying other chants.

The ninth mode, like the others, has regular and irregular initial tones and cadences. The regular initial notes and cadences are placed on A, C, E, and a, as seen in Example 25. [332] The irregular initial tones and cadences are placed on the other notes.

There are various compositions in the ninth mode, among them the motets *Spem in alium nunquam habui* by Jacquet[10] [of Mantua] and *Sancta, et immaculata virginitas* by Morales the Spaniard,[11] both composed for four voices, as well as the two

8. Josquin des Pres, Mass on the Introit *Gaudeamus omnes in Domino*, in *Werken, Missen*, I, 57.
9. *AM* 132, 133. Written in the *tonus peregrinus*.
10. *Celeberrimi . . . Jachet . . . motecta quatuor vocum* (Venice, 1539).
11. *Opera omnia*, II, 17.

Masses I mentioned above.[12] I myself composed in this mode the motet *Si bona suscepimus de manu Domini*[13] and the madrigal *I vò piangendo il mio passato tempo*,[14] both for five voices, as well as other things which I do not name.[15]

The ninth mode, like the other modes, can be transposed down by a diapente with the help of the note b-flat.

12. See notes 6 and 8 above.

13. Number 12 in *Moduli* (1549).

14. Das Chorwerk 24.

15. Ed. of 1573: . . . and a Mass for six voices [no source known] on the motet *Benedicam Dominum* by Jean Mouton [Das Chorwerk 76].

CHAPTER 27   *Tenth Mode*

I T would take very long to show all the compositions in the chant books written in the ninth and tenth modes, and in the other two that follow. These chants are for the most part graduals, offertories, postcommunions, and others which are similar. They are not as easily recognized by people not very well instructed in music as are those chants which have intonations of psalm verses or *Gloria patri* after them, such as antiphons, responsories, and introits. From the endings of these latter chants and from the beginning of the notes placed over the Seuouae (these being the vowels of *saeculorum amen*) we can easily know in what mode each of these is written.

Thus, the following rules are used. When the chant ends on D and the beginning of the Seuouae starts on a, one knows that it is in the first mode. When the end of the chant is placed on D and the beginning of the Seuouae is placed on F, one knows that it is composed in the second mode. When the end of the chant is placed on E and the beginning of the Seuouae is on c, one knows that it is in the third mode. Similarly, one knows that a chant is in the fourth mode when it ends on E and the Seuouae begins on a; a chant is in the fifth mode when it ends on F and the Seuouae begins on c; a chant is in the sixth mode when it ends on F and the Seuouae begins on either F or a; a chant is in the seventh mode when it ends on G and the Seuouae begins on d; and a chant is in the eighth mode when it ends on G and the end of the psalm verse (which is no other than the Seuouae) begins on c.

By these rules one can easily recognize the modes and thus know how to intone the verse, or psalm, which follows the antiphon, for these chants are written in the first eight modes. But those chants which do not have such intonations are free, and may be composed in whatever mode one prefers. Their modes are not so easily recognizable as are those mentioned above. Therefore it is no wonder that some have not had perfect knowledge of the four last modes, for they cannot be recognized in such a manner.

But since we want to have perfect knowledge of the last four modes, we shall

Example 26. [The tenth mode]

return to the discussion of the tenth mode and shall note that this mode is contained within the notes of the fifth species of diapason, E to e, divided arithmetically by the note a, and that therefore some have said that this mode is composed of the first species of diapente, e to a, placed above, and the second species of diatessaron, a to E, placed below, joined at the note a, the final of this mode.

We may say that the nature of the tenth mode is not very different from that of the second and fourth modes, if such a judgment may be made from the harmony arising from it; for the tenth mode is composed of the diapente which is used in the second mode and the diatessaron which is used in the fourth mode.

The regular initial tones of the tenth mode are placed on the notes e, c, a, and E, and so are its regular cadences. Since from the knowledge of the regular cadences one can easily know the notes on which the irregular ones are made, I shall give an example of the former only in Example 26.

There are many compositions in this mode, such as *Gabriel archangelus locutus est Zachariae* by Verdelot[1] and *Flete oculi, rorate genas* by Adrian [Willaert],[2] both for four voices, as well as many others.

The tenth mode is transposed down by a diapente with the help of the note b-flat, without which very little would be good. [333]

1. *Treize livres de motets parus chez Pierre Attaingnant,* book 1, ed. A. Smijers (Paris, 1934), 99. The motet appears as *Gabriel archangelus apparuit Zachariae.*
2. *Opera omnia,* II, 62.

CHAPTER 28   *Eleventh Mode*

THE eleventh mode comes into being from the third species of diapason, C to c, mediated harmonically by the note G. Practitioners say that this mode is composed of the fourth

Example 27. [The eleventh mode]

species of diapente, C to G, placed below, and the third species of diatessaron, G to c, placed above.

The eleventh mode is by its nature very suitable for dances and *balli,* and therefore we find that most *balli* heard in Italy are played in this mode. Hence it has happened that some have called it a lascivious mode.

There are many chants in the eleventh mode in the sacred choirbooks, such as the Mass called *De Angelis*[1] and the antiphons *Alma redemptoris mater*[2] and *Regina coeli laetare Haleluiah.*[3] This mode is so much in use and so loved by the moderns that, induced by its sweetness and beauty, they have changed many compositions written in the fifth mode into the eleventh mode by putting the note b-flat in place of the note b-natural.

The regular initial tones of the eleventh mode are placed on C, E, G, and c, and so are its [regular] cadences [Example 27]. Its irregular initial tones and cadences are placed on the other notes.

Musicians have written many compositions in this mode, among them *Stabat mater dolorosa* by Josquin for five voices,[4] *O salutaris hostia,*[5] *Alma redemptoris mater,*[6]

1. *LU* 37.
2. *LU* 273.
3. *LU* 275.
4. *Werken, Motetten,* II, 51.
5. Adrian Willaert, *Opera omnia,* IV, 55.
6. Ibid., V, 109.

and *Pien d'un vago pensier*[7] by Adrian [Willaert], and *Descendi in {h}ortum meum* by Jacquet [of Mantua],[8] all composed for six voices, as well as the motet *Audi filia et vide* for five voices by Gombert,[9] and the motet *Ego veni in hortum meum,* also for five voices, which I myself composed many years ago.[10] There are innumerable other compositions in this mode, and it would take a long time to list them.

The eleventh mode is transposed away from its natural notes, up by a diatessaron or down by a diapente, with the help of the note b-flat, proceeding through the notes of the tetrachord Synemmenon.[11]

7. Ibid., XIII, 96.

8. *Treize livres de motets parus chez Pierre Attaingnant,* book 8, ed. A. T. Merritt (Paris, 1962), 155, where it is anonymous.

9. *Opera omnia,* ed. Joseph Schmidt-Görg, VII, 117.

10. Number 8 in *Moduli* (1549).

11. Ed. of 1573: . . . in which the note b-flat is found, as may be seen in all those compositions I have mentioned above.

CHAPTER 29   *Twelfth Mode*

[334]   THE twelfth mode, which is the last, is contained within the seventh species of diapason, g to G, divided arithmetically by the note c, its final. This mode (as practitioners say) comes into being from the conjunction of the fourth species of diapente, g to C, placed above, with the third species of diatessaron, C to G, placed below.

Among churchmen, in ancient times the twelfth mode was little used,[1] but more recently with the help of the tetrachord Synemmenon, that is, with the note b-flat, they have changed into the twelfth mode most of those chants which were written in the sixth mode. They have also written new chants in this mode, among them the antiphon *Ave regina coelorum,*[2] as well as many others.

The twelfth mode is suitable for expressing thoughts of love which contain lamentful things, for in plainsong it is a lamentful mode and according to the opinion of some it has something sad about it. Nevertheless, every composer who wishes to write a composition that is cheerful does not depart from this mode.

The regular initial tones of the twelfth mode and its regular cadences are placed on g, e, c, and G, as shown in Example 28. The irregular initial tones and cadences are placed on the other notes.

There are innumerable compositions in this mode written by many practicing musicians. These compositions include the motet *Inviolata integra et casta es Maria,* composed for five voices by Josquin,[3] a motet on the same text composed for seven

1. Ed. of 1573: . . . in its natural notes, as may be seen in their ancient books.

2. *LU* 278.

3. *Werken, Motetten,* II, 111.

Example 28. [The twelfth mode]

voices by Adrian [Willaert],[4] the motet *Mittit ad virginem*[5] for six voices, and the madrigals *Quando nascesti Amor*[6] for seven voices, *I vidi in terra angelici costumi*[7] for six voices, and *Quando fra l'altre donne*[8] for five voices, all composed by Adrian [Willaert]. To these we can add the motet by Jacquet [of Mantua] for five voices, *Decantabat populus,*[9] the motets [335] *Nemo venit ad me*[10] for five voices and *O quàm gloriosum est regnum*[11] for six voices, which I myself composed a long time ago,[12] and many others.

Although the natural notes of the twelfth mode are those shown above, musicians transpose it down by a diapente[13] with the help of the note b-flat.

4. *Opera omnia,* V, 223.

5. Adrian Willaert, *Opera omnia,* V, 173.

6. Ibid., XIII, 103.

7. Ibid., XIII, 85.

8. Ibid., XIII, 23.

9. *Nicolai Gomberti . . . Pentaphthongos harmonia, que quinque vocum Motetta vulgo nominatur, Liber primus* (Venice, 1541).

10. There is a *Nemo potest venire* a 5 in *Moduli* (1549), Number 3.

11. Number 7 in *Modulationes* (1566).

12. Ed. of 1573: . . . as well as the motet *Litigabant Iudaei* [Number 2 in *Modulationes* (1566)], which I composed to be sung in six voices.

13. Zarlino mistakenly has diatessaron.

But enough has been said about the nature and property of the modes, and about the use, the initial tones, and the cadences of each. It is necessary to discuss some other matters now. First we shall show what must be observed in composing and in judging the modes [of compositions], and second, the manner in which each part of a vocal composition should be accommodated to them, and how far the parts can ascend and descend, so that their extremes are defined, and all confusion is ended.[14]

14. Ed. of 1573: This having been done, we shall talk about the value of some of the written notes which are bound together. This done (God be willing), we shall end.

CHAPTER 30 · *What the Composer Should Observe When Composing, and How the Modes Should Be Judged*

[336]   FIRST, it should be noted that although there are almost innumerable compositions in each of the modes we have shown, many of them are composed not in simple modes but in mixed modes. We shall find the third mode mixed with the tenth, the eighth with the eleventh, and so forth with the others, as may be learned from examining vocal compositions, especially those of the third mode in which the second species of diatessaron, E to a, is found below, in place of the second species of diapente, E to b-natural, and the first species of diapente, a to e, is found above, in place of the second species of diatessaron, b-natural to e.

Even though these [two pairs of] species are contained within the same diapason, E to e, we find that in one mode this diapason is mediated harmonically and maintains the form of the third mode, whereas in the other it is divided arithmetically and maintains the form of the tenth mode. Since the species of the tenth mode [the diapente e to a and the diatessaron a to E], are heard so often and are repeated so many times, not only does the greater part of the composition no longer share anything with the third mode, but the entire composition turns out to be composed in the tenth mode. That this is true can be understood from the fact that if we join together the diatessaron E to a and the diapente a to e, placing the latter above and the former below, there is no doubt that we shall have the form of the tenth mode, contained within the fifth species of diapason divided arithmetically. In this way the composition that we judge to be in the third mode no longer has anything by which we can judge it to be in this mode, except for the final, for the composition ends on the note E.

Although we should judge a composition by its final note and not, as some would like, by what precedes it, for everything is rightly judged by its end, nevertheless we must not assume that by this note alone we can recognize the mode on which a composition is based. [1] Thus we must not believe that we may judge the mode by the last note alone, but rather we must wait for the composition to be led to its end, and then judge it rightly, inasmuch as the composition is then complete and has its true form, from which one is able to make the correct judgment.

It should be noted that the mode of a composition can be judged by two things: first, by the form of the entire composition, and second, by the ending of the composition, namely, by its final note. Since it is form which gives being to a thing, I would consider it reasonable to determine the mode of a composition not merely by the final note, as some have wanted, but by the whole form contained in the composition. Hence I say that if I had to judge a composition by its form, that is, by its manner of proceeding, as should be done, I would not consider it amiss for a principal mode to end on the median note of its diapason, divided harmonically, and, in a similar way, for a collateral mode to end on the extreme notes of its diapason, divided arithmetically, the final note having been laid aside [in both cases].

How elegantly this can be done may be learned from the motet *Si bona suscepimus de manu Domini*, composed for five voices by Verdelot, [2] and from the madrigal *O invidia nemica di virtute*, composed for five voices by Adrian [Willaert]. [3] Although these compositions have from beginning to end the procedure of the ninth and second modes respectively, nevertheless they do not end on their true finals but rather on their median notes. And what I say about the third and tenth modes can also be shown in the other modes, a task which I leave aside for the sake of brevity.

Thus one should not be surprised if one does not hear any difference between a composition which ends on the note E and another which ends on a, for they are composed in mixed modes in the manner described. If they were composed in simple modes, without any mixing, there is no doubt that one would hear a great difference in harmony between one and the other.

When we have to judge a composition, then we shall have to examine it carefully from beginning to end and see in what form it is composed, whether in the form of the first, second, or any other mode. This we can do by keeping an eye on the cadences, which throw a great light on this matter. In this way we shall be able to judge in what mode the composition is written, even if the composition does not end

---

1. According to Glarean, too (*Dodekachordon*, II, 1, 36), the mode of a composition should be determined not only by the final but also by the range of the octave and its division and by the characteristic melodic intervals (shown in *Dodekachordon*, I, 13). Pietro Aron also says (*Trattato della natura e cognitione di tutti gli toni di canto figurato*, 1) that the mode of a composition is determined by both the final and the interval species used in it. He says that man can be defined as an animal rational and mortal. The latter, symbolizing the *finalis*, is final and considered according to the end of man. The former, symbolizing the interval species, is formal and considered according to the specific and formal being of living man. The latter is not particular to man; the former makes the essence of man better known.

2. *Opera omnia*, ed. Anne-Marie Bragard, II, 1.

3. *Opera omnia*, XIII, 14.

on the proper final of the mode but rather on the median note,[4] or on some other note which has suited the composer's purpose.

If we should end [337] a composition on a note other than the final it would not be out of place, since churchmen also did this in their chants, as may be seen in the κύριε ἐλέησον appointed for Semidoubles or that known as *De Apostolis*,[5] the form of which (as is clear) is that of the first mode; nonetheless the last of these ends on the note a, which is called the cofinal and which is the median note of the diapason D to d that contains the form of the first mode. This manner of ending can also be seen in the Offertory sung in the Mass of the Wednesday (*quarta feria*) after the third Sunday in Lent, *Domine fac mecum secundum misericordiam tuam*,[6] which is contained within the extreme notes F and e. It can be seen in two other chants as well: the *Tollite hostias*,[7] sung after the Communion of the Mass of the eighteenth Sunday after Pentecost, and contained within the extreme notes mentioned above; and the *Per signum Crucis*,[8] sung on the solemn feasts of the Finding and Exaltation of the Holy Cross, and contained within the extreme notes F and g. These chants maintain the form of the seventh mode, for one finds in them the melodic line of the diapente G to d, and of the diatessaron d to g, and they end on the note b-natural, which is the median note of its diapente.

It is true that some moderns attribute these chants to the fourteenth mode, but this I shall leave to the judgment of anyone who has intelligence. In some of the modern books these chants are transposed down by the diapente, out of their natural notes, without the help of the note b-flat. This has been done through the ignorance or carelessness of the scribes or through the presumption of others who understood little. But in the good and correct copies (and to this day I have with me an old one, written by hand, which may still be seen and examined) these chants are contained within the notes mentioned above.

It should be noted that what I call the form of the mode is the diapason divided into its diapente and diatessaron, and the diapente and diatessaron which come into being from the harmonic or arithmetic division of the diapason and which are repeated many times in the proper modes.

Thus when we compose, we shall know from the above discussion how to shape the parts of a vocal composition and to put the cadences in places suitable for the articulation of the words. We shall also know how to judge a composition, in whatever manner it may be composed, whether in plainsong or in mensural music.

4. In authentic modes only, for in plagal modes the final and the mediating note of the diapason are the same note.

5. *LU* 25.

6. *GR* 133.

7. *LU* 1058.

8. *LU* 1058.

CHAPTER 31

The Parts of a Vocal Composition: How They Should Be Arranged, Their Range, and How Far the Highest Note of the Composition May Be from the Lowest Note

SOME [musicians] are at times so careless and use so little judgment in composing and arranging the parts of a vocal composition that they make the parts go up or down so excessively they can hardly be sung. With the object of removing all the rough places that might occur in this art and of making every vocal composition comfortable to sing, I shall show how to arrange the parts among themselves and how far they may ascend or descend as well as how distant from each other the extreme notes may be.

I would say, then, that whenever a musician proposes to compose a motet, madrigal, or any other kind of vocal music, he should first consider the subject matter, that is, the given words, and then choose the mode suitable to the nature of these words. Having done this, he should take care that the tenor proceeds regularly through the notes of the mode and makes cadences where the completion of the meaning and the end of the sentences of the text demand. Above all he should seek with all diligence to make the tenor (on which the composition is usually based) regulated and beautiful, graceful and full of sweetness, so that it becomes the sinew and bond for all the voices of the composition.

The voices should be joined in such a way that if the tenor occupies the notes of an [338] authentic mode, the bass ought to embrace the notes of the plagal, and vice versa. And even if the tenor goes up or down beyond the notes of the diapason which contains the mode by one or two steps, this would be of little import; for musicians do not worry whether the tenor and the other parts of their compositions are perfect, imperfect, or overabundant, provided that the parts are well suited to the melodic line and make good harmony. It would be good if each of the parts did not exceed eight notes and remained confined within the notes of its diapason. But parts do exceed eight notes, and it sometimes turns out to be of great convenience to the composer, and thus we shall ascribe this practice to a certain license and not to the perfection of the thing.

The mode in which a composition is written is established in the tenor, and the parts (as I have said) should be so arranged that if the tenor occupies the notes of an authentic mode, the bass will contain the notes of the collateral, or plagal, mode. And vice versa, if the tenor occupies the notes of a plagal mode, the bass ought to contain the authentic mode. When the tenor and bass are so arranged, the other parts will be accommodated in the best way, without any inconvenience to the composition.

Composers should be warned not to make the extreme notes of the bass more distant from the extreme notes of the tenor than by a diatessaron or a diapente, although it will not be an error to exceed the above by one more note, inasmuch as when placed in this way, the tenor and bass will be arranged in the manner mentioned above, namely, one will occupy the notes of the authentic mode and the other those of the plagal. When the tenor and the bass are linked in this manner, it will be easy to put the other parts in their places and arrange them in the composition. The extreme notes of the soprano will be distant by a diapason from the extreme notes of the tenor, and thus the soprano as well as the tenor will be sung in the notes of [the same mode, as, for example,] the authentic mode. Similarly, the notes of the alto will be placed in the same mode as those of the bass, distant from them by a diapason, and [in this example] both the alto and the bass will occupy the notes of the plagal mode.

All these parts being so arranged, the soprano will hold the highest place in the composition, and the bass, the lowest. The tenor and alto will be the middle parts, with the distinction that the notes of the alto will be higher than those of the tenor by a diatessaron, a little more or a little less. The extreme notes of the soprano will be as distant from those of the alto as the extreme notes of the tenor are from those of the bass. The parts (as I said earlier in this chapter) can at times be extended up or down by one step, and even, if necessary, by two or more steps beyond their diapason, but one should take care that the parts can be sung comfortably, and that they not exceed in their extremes the tenth or eleventh note, for then they would become forced, tiring, and difficult to sing, because of their ascent and descent.

In addition to this, one should note that the bass ought not to extend much below the notes of the diapason which contains its mode, nor ought the soprano to do the same above, for this would make the composition extreme, causing great inconvenience for the singers. Thus in computing the lowest note of the bass in a composition and the highest note of the soprano, a composer should take care not to exceed the nineteenth note, although it would not be very inconvenient if he reached the twentieth note, but not beyond that. When this is observed, the parts will remain within their limits and will be singable without any effort.

Sometimes one composes without the soprano, and this manner of composing is called by practitioners "composing for altered voices" [comporre à voci mutati], or, if it is only for tenor and bass, "composing for equal voices" [comporre à voci pari]. In the former compositions the contralto takes the place of the soprano, and the next highest voice becomes contained within the notes of the contralto, or within the notes of the tenor, so that such a composition will be written with two contraltos or three tenors. To be sure particular attention should be paid to the part taken for the soprano, because it is always somewhat higher than that taken for the alto, the latter proceeding in a somewhat more humble manner. But be that as it may, the parts of a composition should be arranged in such a way that the extremes do not exceed fifteen notes, including the lowest and the highest notes.[1]

Other parts besides the four mentioned above cannot be added except by

1. This refers only to compositions without a soprano part, for otherwise nineteen and even twenty notes are permitted between the highest and lowest notes of a composition.

doubling one of the four, and such a part would be called second tenor or second bass, and so with the others. That part which is consistently high rather than low and which reaches higher than the others can truly be called soprano. It should be noted that in all the modes the clefs for the sopranos and tenors are written as shown in the examples for each mode [Examples 13–20; 25–28]; for the bass clefs are written in such a way that their notes can be distant by a diatessaron or a diapente from the notes of the tenors; and I say the same thing concerning the distance between the sopranos [339] and the contraltos.

In the beginning of the second section of a vocal composition a part that enters alone resumes its melodic line on any regular initial tone of the mode on which the composition is based, or on any other note, provided that it is a natural note of that mode. For it is not commendable that at the end of a first section the contralto or tenor or soprano should conclude, for example, on the note b-natural, and begin in the second section on the note b-flat, or vice versa. A composer, then, is cautioned against such a thing, so that his compositions will be purged of every error and inconvenience, and he will gain a reputation as a good and perfect musician.

CHAPTER 32   *How Harmonies Are Accommodated to Given Words*

I T remains now to see (for the time and place require it) how harmonies are accommodated to a given text. There is a reason why I speak about accommodating harmonies to words [and not words to harmonies]. In [chapter 12 of] Part II I declared, in accordance with Plato's opinion,[1] that *melos* is a compound of words, harmony, and rhythm. Although it seems that in such a combination none of these things takes priority over another, the fact is that Plato places the words before the other components as the principal thing, and considers the other two components to be subservient to it. For after he has shown the whole by means of the parts, he says that harmony and rhythm should follow the words and not the words follow the rhythm or harmony. And so it should be. For if a text, whether by way of narrative or imitation, deals with subjects that are cheerful or sad, grave or without gravity, and modest or lascivious, a choice of harmony and rhythm must be made in accordance with the nature of the subject matter contained in the text, in order that these things, combined with proportion, may result in music that is suited to the purpose.

We should note what Horace says in the Epistle of the *Art of Poetry:*

Versibus exponi Tragicis res Comica non vult.[2]

1. Plato *Republic* 398D.

2. Horace *Ars poetica* 89: "A comic theme refuses to be set forth in tragic verse." The edition by H. Rushton Fairclough, Loeb Class. Lib., p. 458, has *volt* for Zarlino's *vult.*

If poets are not permitted to write a comedy in tragic verse, it is not permissible for a musician to combine harmony and words in an unsuitable manner. Thus, it will not be appropriate for him to use sad harmony and grave rhythms for cheerful subjects, and he is not permitted to use cheerful harmony and light or fast rhythms, call it what we may, where funereal matters are treated. On the contrary, he should use cheerful harmonies and fast rhythms for cheerful subjects and sad harmonies and grave rhythms for sad subjects, so that everything may be done with proportion.

I think that everyone will know how to accommodate the harmonies to the words in the best way possible when he has studied what I have written in Part III[3] and has considered the nature of the mode in which he wishes to write a composition. He should take care to accompany each word in such a manner that, when the word denotes harshness, hardness, cruelty, bitterness, and other things of this sort, the harmony will be similar to these qualities, namely, somewhat hard and harsh, but not to the degree that it would offend. Similarly, when any of the words express complaint, sorrow, grief, sighs, tears, and other things of this sort, the harmony should be full of sadness.

When a composer wishes to express harshness, bitterness, and similar things, he will do best to arrange the parts of the composition so that they proceed with movements that are without the semitone, such as those of the whole tone and ditone. He should allow the major sixth and major thirteenth, which by nature are somewhat harsh, to be heard above the lowest note of the concentus, and should use the suspension [*sincopa*] of the fourth or the eleventh above the lowest part, along with somewhat slow movements, among which the suspension of the seventh may also be used. But when a composer wishes to express effects of grief and sorrow, he should (observing the rules given) use movements which proceed through the semitone, the semiditone, and similar intervals, often using minor sixths or minor thirteenths above the lowest note of the composition, these being by nature sweet and soft, especially when combined in the right way and with discretion and judgment.

It should be noted, however, that the cause of the various effects is attributed not only to the consonances named, used in the ways described above, but also to the movements which the parts make in singing. These are of two sorts, namely, natural and accidental. Natural movements are those made between the natural notes of a composition, where no sign or accidental note intervenes. Accidental movements are those made by means of the [340] accidental notes, which are indicated by the signs ♯ and ♭. The natural movements have more virility than the accidental movements, which are somewhat languid. From the accidental movements there arises a kind of interval called accidental, whereas from the natural movements originate those intervals which are called natural. We should note that the natural movements make the composition somewhat more sonorous and virile, and the accidental movements make it sweeter and somewhat more languid. For this reason the former movements can serve to express effects of harshness and bitterness, and the latter movements can serve for effects of grief and sorrow. Combining with some judgment the intervals of the

3. *Le Istit. harm.*, III, 31.

major and minor consonances with the natural and accidental movements made by the parts, we shall succeed in imitating the words with a well-understood harmony.

As to the observance of rhythms, the primary consideration should be the subject matter contained in the text. If it is cheerful, one should proceed with powerful and fast movements, namely, with note values that convey swiftness of movement, such as the minim and the semiminim. But when the subject matter is tearful, one should proceed with slow and lingering movements. Adrian [Willaert] has shown both manners in many compositions, among them [the madrigals] *I vidi in terra angeli costumi*,[4] *Aspro core e selvaggio*,[5] and *Ove ch'i posi gli occhi*,[6] all composed for six voices, *Quando fra l'altre donne*[7] and *Giunto m'ha Amor*,[8] for five voices, and innumerable others, together with innumerable motets which I do not name in order to be brief.

This is not the only consideration concerning rhythm (something which the ancients understood in a way different from the moderns, as is clearly seen in many places in Plato[9]), for we should also take care to accommodate the words of the text to the written notes in such a manner and with such rhythm that no barbarism is heard, such as when in a vocal piece a syllable that should be short is made long, or vice versa, a syllable that should be long is made short, something heard every day in innumerable compositions and really a shameful thing. This vice is found not only in mensural music but in plainsong as well, as is obvious to all who have judgment. Indeed there are few chants not full of similar barbarisms and in which repeatedly a length of time is given to the penultimate syllable of the words *Dominus, Angelus, Filius, Miraculum, Gloria,* and to many other syllables that pass quickly. It would be very commendable to correct this, and it would be very easy, for by a very small change the composition would be adjusted. Nor would its original form change by this, for the difficulty lies only in a ligature of many notes, placed over short syllables, which makes them inappropriately long, when a single note would have sufficed.

In order that the sense of the words be complete, care should also be taken not to separate any parts of the text by rests while a clause, or any of its parts, remains unfinished, as is done by some of little intelligence. Furthermore, one should not make a cadence, especially a principal one, nor put in rests larger than a minim, unless the sentence or the full sense of the words is completed. Nor should a minim's rest fall in mid-sentence, for this is really a pernicious thing; and although it is practiced by some undiscerning musicians, everyone willing to put his mind to this thing will be able to see and recognize it easily.

4. *Opera omnia*, XIII, 85.
5. Ibid., XIII, 54, from *Musica nova di Adriano Willaert* (Venice, 1559).
6. Ibid., XIII, 90.
7. Ibid., XIII, 23.
8. Ibid., XII, 40.
9. Plato *Republic* 397B–401E; *Laws* 653E–654A, 664E–665A, 798D–E, 802D–E; *Timaeus* 47E.

As this matter is of great importance, a composer should open his eyes and not keep them closed, so that he does not gain the reputation of being ignorant of something so essential. He should take care to put a rest of a minim or semiminim (whichever suits him) at the head of intermediate points of a text, because there the rest will serve as a comma. But at the head of sentences he should put whatever length of rest is convenient, for it seems to me that when rests are placed in such manner the parts of a sentence can best be distinguished from one another, and the perfect sense of the words heard without any discomfort.

CHAPTER 33   *How to Assign Note Values to Words*

WHO would ever be able to describe the lack of order and grace that many musical practitioners maintain and have maintained and the confusion they have caused in assigning note values [*figure cantabili*] to words of a proposed text? It can be described, surely, but only with great difficulty. When I reflect that a science which has given laws and good order to the other sciences is at times so confused in some things as to be barely tolerable, I cannot pretend it does not sadden me.

It is really astonishing to hear in vocal compositions not only confused sentences, incomplete clauses, misplaced cadences, singing without order, innumerable errors in applying harmonies to words, [341] little attention to the modes, passages without grace, rhythm without proportion, and movements without purpose,[1] but to find also durations so assigned to words that a singer cannot discover or decide on a suitable way of performing the composition. In one place a singer sees many notes over two syllables, in another many syllables under two notes. Sometimes a singer hears in another part vowels contracted or elided, as the words require, and, wishing to do the same in his own part, will come short of a beautiful and elegant style of singing by giving a long value to a short syllable, and vice versa. Or he will hear in other parts a syllable made long which in his own part must of necessity be short, so that, hearing so much diversity, he does not know what to do and remains completely bewildered and confused.

The whole task consists of assigning note values to given words, and it is essential in a composition that by this means the notes be described and notated in such a way that the sounds and tones can be performed in every melodic line. It is by means of such written note values that we can perform the rhythm, namely, the length and brevity of the syllables contained in a text, and over these syllables are often found not only one, two, or three, but even more written notes. Therefore, lest confusion arise in assigning notes to syllables of given words, and so that all disorder

1. Ed. of 1573: . . . as well as notes that are badly arranged in time and prolation, and innumerable other disorders.

may be removed (if possible), I shall now—in addition to the many rules given in various places, in accordance with the requirements of my materials—propose the following rules, which will serve not only the composer but also the singer and will suit my purpose.

1. Over a long or a short syllable put a corresponding note value, so that no barbarism will be heard. For in mensural music, each separated musical note, not in ligature (except for the semiminim and all notes smaller than the semiminim), carries its own syllable. This rule is observed in plainsong as well, for a syllable is assigned to each square note, except sometimes for the middle notes of a ligature, which are performed like minims and also like semiminims, as seen in many chants, especially in the *Credo in unum Deum* called the Cardinal Credo.[2]

2. No more than one syllable should be assigned to the beginning of a ligature of several notes, whether in mensural music or in plainsong.

3. No syllable should be assigned to the dot placed next to notes of mensural music, even though the dot is singable.

4. Generally, one only rarely places a syllable under a semiminim or under notes that are smaller than the semiminim, or under a note which immediately follows it.

5. It is not customary to assign any syllable to notes which immediately follow a dot of a semibreve or minim when the following notes are of less value than these dots, as the semiminim after the dot of a semibreve, or the chroma after the dot of a minim, and the same is true for notes which immediately follow these.

6. When[3] a syllable is placed under a semiminim, another may be placed under the following note.

7. Any note, whatever it may be, placed at the beginning of a melody, or in the middle after a rest, will by necessity carry the pronunciation of a syllable.

8. In plainsong, no word or syllable should ever be repeated, although some musicians do this, something truly reprehensible. But in mensural music such repetitions are tolerable; I do not mean repetition of a syllable or word, but repetition of some part of a text of which the sense is complete. This may be done when there are notes in such quantity that text may be repeated conveniently, although (according to my judgment) repeating something many times is not very good unless it is done in order to emphasize words that bear a serious message worthy of consideration.

9. When all syllables that are in one sentence or in one part of a text have been assigned to note values, and only the penultimate and last syllables remain, the penultimate syllable may have above it several small notes—two, three, or some other quantity—provided, however, that this penultimate syllable is long and not short; for if it were short, a barbarism would be committed. The reason for this is that this manner of singing gives rise to what many call a neume, which occurs when many notes are sung to one syllable. So placed, however, these notes violate the first rule given here.

2. Credo IV of the modern *Graduale Romanum. LU* 71.
3. Ed. of 1573: . . . out of necessity.

10. The last syllable of a text must end, in observance with the rules given, on the last note of the melody.

Innumerable examples of these rules may be found by examining the learned compositions of Adrian [Willaert] and of those who truly have been and are his disciples. Therefore, without giving another example, I shall proceed to discuss ligatures, which are made from several notes, and which serve our purpose.

CHAPTER 34   *Ligatures*

[342]   LIGATURES are really necessary in mensural music for many reasons, not only because they are useful to composers for assigning values or notes to syllables of a proposed text, but also because composers sometimes take as a subject an antiphon of plainsong in which there are many tied notes. If they want to base their composition on the antiphon and to imitate it, they must necessarily use the ligatures as well. They would not use all of them, however, because it sometimes proves to be inconvenient, but only some of them, and not even with the same note values, but with different ones, according to what seems right to the composer. Therefore, in order to have full knowledge of this subject and to know in what manner ligatures should be written and which notes should be tied and what their value should be, we shall now deal with these matters. But first we must see what a ligature is.

Practitioners say that a ligature is a certain tying together, or conjunction, of simple notes, made with suitable strokes or lines, in which each note that can be tied has a square or oblique shape. Ligatures are made with three note values, namely, maxim, long, and breve.[1] The two extremes of these notes, the maxim and the breve, change their value according to the different ways in which they are tied.[2] The maxim is a passive note, subject to a diminution of its value, but can never be augmented. The breve is also passive and can be augmented and diminished according to how it is written and the place it holds within the ligature. The long, however, is not subject to augmentation or diminution, for it is always written in a ligature without any variation of its form, no matter in what part of the ligature it is placed.

Every ligature is considered in two ways: first, when the second note in the ligature is placed higher than the preceding note; and second, when the first note in the ligature is placed higher than the subsequent note. When the notes are placed in the first way, the ligature is called ascending; when they are placed in the second way, the ligature is called descending. It is true, as we shall see, that one may make a ligature with notes that are tied in both ascending and descending manners.

One should note that the maxim is written in a ligature in two manners: first,

---

1. Meaning the shape of the note rather than its value (which can be that of a semibreve).
2. Ed. of 1573: . . . and according to the various contingencies which they receive.

in accordance with its true form, namely, with a long straight body; second, with a long oblique, or slanted, body, whatever we want to call it. When not oblique, the maxim is written in two ways: either with a tail, or leg, whatever we want to call it, on the right side, or without a tail. And whether or not it is tied to other notes, and whether it is at the beginning, the middle, or the end of the ligature, it always keeps its value, that is, it is worth four breves.[3] When the maxim is oblique, it is also written in two ways: either ascending from below, that is, from its first part, which is placed on the left side, to its second part, which is placed on the right side; or descending from above, from left to right.

There are two kinds of oblique ligatures: those with a tail on the left, and those without a tail. If the ligature has a tail, the tail goes either upward or downward. When the tail goes downward and the ligature is oblique and descending, the first and second parts of the ligature are each worth one breve; and the same is true when the ligature is oblique and ascending, although this is no longer in use. When the tail is turned upward and the ligature is oblique, whether descending or ascending (although the latter is not used), the first and second parts of the ligature are always worth one semibreve each. When an oblique ligature does not have a tail, and its second part goes downward, the first part is worth one long, and the second part one breve; but when the second part goes upward (a form which musicians do not use any longer), both the first and the second parts are worth one breve each.[4] And this applies when these two parts are not accompanied by, or tied to, other notes, for when they are accompanied by, or tied to, other notes, there are other considerations.

As for the breve, it is placed in the previously mentioned ligatures[5] in two ways, namely, without a tail and with a tail. When it has a tail, we find it written in two manners: either with tail on the left turned downward, or with the tail turned upward.

There is another consideration [concerning the value of the notes in a ligature], for each tied note can be placed in the ligature in three ways: at the beginning, the middle, and the end; and so by the beginning, middle, and end, one knows the value of the parts of each ligature. In order to impart perfect knowledge of the value of these parts, several rules will be given.

1. Every note placed without a tail at the beginning of a ligature, be it square or oblique, with the second note descending, will always have the value of one long[6] [343] (except for the maxim with or without a tail, and not oblique).

3. Ed. of 1573: . . . or two longs.

4. Zarlino follows here the interpretation of Gaffurio (as expressed in *Practica musice*, II, 5), which is that the ligature ▢ represents the values breve-breve. The same ligature is interpreted as LB by Tinctoris, *Tractatus de notis et pausis*, 1, 10 (ed. Albert Seay, Corpus scriptorum de musica, 2, 1975, p. 114) and by Adam von Fulda (Gerbert, *Scriptores ecclesiastici de musica*, 3, p. 365).

There is an inconsistency in Zarlino's interpretation: Gaffurio, who interprets the ligature ▢ as breve-breve, interprets the ligature ◻ as long-breve, but Zarlino uses the interpretation of Gaffurio concerning the ligature without a tail, and that of Tinctoris and Adam von Fulda concerning that with a tail. Thus Zarlino interprets both ▢ and ◻ as breve-breve.

5. Meaning *ligatura binaria*.

6. Exemplified in the first three ligatures in Ex. 29.

2. Every first note, or first part of a [two-note] figure, be it square or oblique; which has the tail on the left turned downward, will always have the value of one breve.[7]

3. When any note without a tail is placed at the beginning [of a ligature], and the second note, which follows it, ascends, the first note will always have the value of one breve.[8]

4. When a note is placed at the beginning of any ligature, be it square or oblique, with the tail turned upward on the left side and with the second note ascending or descending, both the first note and the following one will each always have the value of one semibreve,[9] as may be seen in Example 29.

Example 29.

Longs   Breves   Semibreves

The above examples concern the first notes of the ligatures, but there is another consideration concerning the middle notes, because all middle notes, whether square or oblique, except for the semibreves mentioned, will always have the value of one breve [Example 30].

Example 30.

Middle breves

Final notes, when square and descending,[10] will all have the value of one long.[11] If they are placed after the second part of an ascending or descending oblique figure, and if they themselves ascend, they will always have the value of one breve;[12] if they descend, they will have the value of one long,[13] [as may be seen in Example 31].

Example 31.

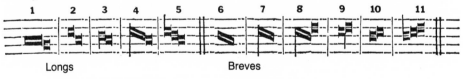

Longs   Breves

7. Exemplified in the fifth and sixth ligatures in Ex. 29.
8. Exemplified in the fourth and seventh ligatures in Ex. 29.
9. Exemplified in the eighth, ninth, and tenth ligatures in Ex. 29.
10. Zarlino neglects to mention square ascending final notes.
11. Exemplified in the first five ligatures in Ex. 31. Zarlino neglects to mention the exception, namely, the last note in a *ligatura binaria* the first note of which has a tail turned upward, giving the last note the value of a semibreve.
12. Exemplified in the eighth ligature in Ex. 31.
13. Exemplified in the fourth ligature in Ex. 31.

But two things must be noted: first, the discussion of these notes concerned the form of their body, and not other things; and second, any note placed in the ligatures is subject to the same contingencies to which simple, untied notes are subject, although some people have maintained the opposite. [14]

The ligatures (as I believe) have been arranged in these manners by their first inventor, and have been given certain quantitative values according to the various ways in which the notes in them are written, and according to the different placements of the notes, as seemed right to the inventor. Thus everyone should content himself with what I have said concerning ligatures and not seek to find out why the inventor wanted to give more value to one note than to another and to order these ligatures in one way rather than in another, for this would be a vain thing. [15]

14. Ed. of 1573: There is an additional consideration, which is that each ligature contains its *tempora,* whether subject to perfect or to imperfect *tempus,* provided that their nature is not altered by some contingency. Thus in perfect *tempus,* if the note placed first in the ligature is worth a semibreve, the next note will be worth an imperfect breve, for this note will always be interpreted as altered. But the middle notes will always be worth a perfect breve, and the last note will always be perfect, provided that the notes are not made imperfect by some other contingency.

15. Ed. of 1573: Moreover, it matters little whether we know it or not. But no more of this.

CHAPTER 35   *What Anyone Must Know Who Desires to Arrive at Some Perfection in Music*

Now that I realize that I have arrived, with Divine help, at the desired end of my efforts, I would like to do two things before concluding this discussion. One of them is to show what is required of anyone who desires to arrive at the ultimate level of this science. The other is to show that we should not surrender judgment of musical matters to the senses alone, for they are fallible, but rather we should accompany the senses with reason. Whenever these two parts are joined together in concordance, there is no doubt that no error can be committed, and perfect judgment will be made.

Beginning then with the first matter, I would say that he who desires to arrive at that perfection which can be achieved in musical matters and to see all that is permitted in this science, must possess knowledge of many things, so that without help from someone else he can easily arrive at an understanding of these matters, which are hidden from many in this discipline. For when one of these things is missing, one cannot hope to arrive at the designated goal.

It should be known that music is a science subordinate to arithmetic, as I have stated in chapter 20 of Part I, because the forms of the consonances [344] are contained within determinate proportions comprised of numbers. In order to know the reasons for all the contingencies that may befall the proportions, it is necessary to be well instructed in arithmetic and in the handling of numbers and proportions. If someone desires to learn from my efforts only those things essential for this task, it is necessary that he know at least the handling of shopkeeper numbers, so that when he arrives at the use of proportions, he can easily do what he desires.

Since the ratios of sounds cannot be known except by means of sonorous bodies, which are quantities that can be divided and are really what provides the material of the consonances, it is necessary to be instructed in matters of geometry, or at least know how to operate the compass or ruler to divide a line, and know that which concerns a point, a line (be it crooked or straight), a plane, a solid, and other similar things that pertain to continuous quantity. Thus, in such speculations the help of this science can be turned to good account in dividing any sonorous quantity.

The aspiring musician should also know how to play the monochord or the harpsichord, if not perfectly, then at least moderately well; the harpsichord, because it is more stable and perfect in its tuning than any other instrument; the monochord, so that he may gain from it the knowledge of the sonorous and dissonant intervals and be able to put into practice and to prove those things which he finds out anew every day. Through these instruments he will know how to investigate the effects of the sonorous numbers with proof in hand. But this presupposes that he knows how to tune such an instrument perfectly and that he has perfected his hearing; so that when he desires (as happens at times) to investigate the differences between intervals, he will be able to make a perfect judgment without committing an error; and when he desires to tune any other instrument, he will know what should be done.

It is also necessary to be instructed in the art of singing in particular, and in the art of counterpoint or composing as well, and to have a good knowledge of these arts, in order to know how to carry out everything that occurs in music and to judge whether or not it could be successful. For bringing things of music to life is really nothing other than leading them to their ultimate end, or perfection, as also happens in other arts and sciences (such as medicine) which contain both speculative and practical aspects.

I shall not discuss now, for the sake of brevity, how useful knowledge of other sciences can be. Grammar is important, for through it we gain perfect knowledge of languages, by means of which we can understand distinctly the authors who deal with music, and can satisfy a desire to write something about it; and sometimes reading history, in which there are many things of great help, gives much light when an exact knowledge of the things of this science is sought. Dialectics is also of great advantage, for it enables us to debate and discuss this with firm grounds.[1] Rhetoric, too, can be very useful to scholars of our science by permitting them to express their ideas in an orderly way.

I shall leave it to everyone who has a bit of judgment to assess how useful instruction in matters of natural science can be, for, as I have stated elsewhere,[2] music is subordinate not only to mathematical science but also to natural philosophy.

1. Ed. of 1573: . . . and to arrive at demonstrations, without which little or no good is done; for music is a mathematical science, which uses demonstrations, as may be seen in all five Discussions of *Le Dimostrationi harmoniche*.

2. *Le Istit. harm.,* I, 20.

Other sciences as well are useful to the musician, because, really, they cannot but help. And although the aim of music consists in the operation, that is, in the putting [of theory] into practice, and although hearing, when refined, cannot be easily deceived by sound, nevertheless at times some things can happen in such a way that when a man is deprived of the sciences mentioned above (which are very useful for knowing the reasons for these things), he is left greatly betrayed.

If someone desires, then, to acquire a perfect knowledge of music, it is necessary that he be equipped with all these things; for the greater his ignorance in matters mentioned above (which are of major importance and are very necessary), so much the less will he be able to arrive at the desired level, and with so much more difficulty will he be able to accomplish this.[3]

3. Ed. of 1573: But since I have dealt with this extensively in the book entitled *The Perfect Musician,* therefore at present it will suffice to touch on, and merely hint at, these few things. For he who desires to see more minutely the necessity of these things will be able to satisfy himself fully by reading this book.

Two years before he died Zarlino promised again to bring out a book entitled *Melopeo, o Musico Perfetto* at the end of his *Sopplimenti musicali* (Venice, 1588), VIII, 14, p. 330, along with a work in twenty-five books, *De re musica.* There is evidence that the latter work did exist at least in a draft, for Artusi in *Seconda parte dell'Artusi* (Venice, 1603) at the end of the prefatory letter "A gl'amici lettori" promises to put in order Zarlino's book, *De re musica;* elsewhere in the same book (p. 55) Artusi cites chapters from Books 18 and 19 of Zarlino's *De utraque musica,* which may be the same work.

CHAPTER 36   *The Senses Are Fallible, and Judgments Should Not Be Made Solely by Their Means, but Should Be Accompanied by Reason*[1]

THE proposition that a sense never errs concering its proper sensible, or its proper object, is very famous among philosophers. But if this proposition were understood simply and literally, it would sometimes be false. For one may take the proper object for two different things. First, for that which is not perceived by another sense, and which by itself affects the sense and contains all those things which by themselves are [345] apprehended only by that sense. Color, for example, or any visible thing, is the proper object of sight, and sound, the proper object of hearing, and so with the others, as I stated in chapter 71 of Part III. Second, one may take the proper object for that which affects a sense alone and which cannot be felt or understood by another sense. The species contained in the proper object as taken in the first way is called

1. This chapter heading is surprisingly similar to one from Boethius' *De inst. mus.* 1. 8: *Non omne iudicium dandum esse sensibus, sed amplius rationi esses credentum; in quo de sensum fallacia.*

proper sensible, as are, for example, whiteness or blackness, for they affect the sense of sight, imprinting on it their species, and they are not understood except by the sense of sight; and this applies similarly to the species of sounds and other things. Hence, although a sense does not err concerning the proper object as taken in the first way, it can very well err when the object is taken in the second way, especially when the necessary conditions do not exist, these being that the sense [organ] be suitably close to the object, that the organ be suitably disposed, and that the medium be pure and unspoiled.

Although (as the Philosopher [Aristotle] understands) a sense would not err concerning its proper object[2] as taken in the second way if the conditions already stated exist, it can nonetheless err concerning the subject of the proper sensible object, that is, concerning the object's location and position; for this belongs not to external, but to internal sense, like virtue and cognitive power, which are the most noble things among sensitive powers because they are closer to the intellect than any other thing.

I have wanted to say this because many believe that since the sciences originated in the senses, we should trust the senses more than anything else, for they cannot be deceived concerning their proper objects. But those who believe that the senses cannot err are really very far from the truth, for although it is true that every science has had its beginning in the senses, nevertheless it is not through them that science has acquired its name, and it is not through them that is gained the certainty sought in science, but rather it is through reasoning and through demonstrations made by way of the internal senses, that is, through the work of the intellect, which is reasoning. And if the intellect can sometimes err in reasoning, as it actually does, how much more can the senses err? Hence I say that neither the senses without reason, nor reason without the senses, can give good judgment of any scientific object, but rather it is necessary for these two parts to be joined together.

We can easily know that this is true from the fact (to give an example) that if we wish to divide anything into two equal parts solely by means of the senses, we shall never be able to divide it perfectly. Even if it happened that, the division having been made, the parts turned out to be equal, this would have been owed to chance, and we could never be certain of such a thing unless other proof were obtained. And every division into equal parts done solely by means of the senses will grow more difficult with the number of parts into which a thing is divided. Although such divisions will be done as needed, the intellect will never be able to accept these divisions until reason shows that they have been done well. This happens because the senses cannot recognize the smallest differences that exist between things, for they become confused by too much and too little, and also become corrupted. In the realm of sounds, we learn this from the sense of hearing, which is offended by a large quantity, namely, by some great uproar, and does not grasp too little sound or a minimal quantity. Therefore, deliberate reasoning is needed for determining such differences. For exam-

2. Aristotle *De anima* 2. 7. 418a.

ple, if twenty-five or fifty grains were taken away from a large heap of grain, the sense of sight would not be capable of distinguishing [the loss of] this quantity, which is imperceptible in respect to the heap, just as one could not make any judgment if the aforesaid number of grains were added to this heap. Thus, if someone desires to know such a thing, he needs to proceed other than by means of the senses. Indeed the same thing happens concerning sounds, that is, although the sense of hearing cannot err in the first way in distinguishing consonant intervals from dissonant ones, nevertheless its function is not to judge how much one interval is distant from another, or by what quantity one interval surpasses another or is surpassed by it. For if the senses could not err concerning such things, the use of the discovered measures and weights and similar other things would have been in vain. But really they were not discovered in vain, because the ancient philosophers knew very well that the senses may be mistaken in measurements.

Let us say then that although the science of music had its origin in the sense of hearing (as stated in the first chapter of Part I), and although the ultimate perfection and end of this science consists in carrying out and exercising [the theory], and although sound is the proper sensible or object of hearing, nevertheless the function of judging matters concerning sounds and voices should not be given solely to the sense of hearing, but should always be accompanied by reason. Nor should one give this judgment entirely to reason, leaving aside the sense of hearing, because the one without the other can always be cause for error.

In order to have perfect knowledge concerning music, it does not suffice to appeal to the sense of hearing, even if it is most keen, [346] but rather one should seek to investigate and know the whole, so that reason is not discordant with sense, nor sense with reason; and then everything will be well.

But just as it is necessary that sense and reason concur in order to make judgment in things of music, so it is necessary that he who wants to judge anything pertaining to art have two capabilities: first, that he be expert in things of science, that is, of speculation; and second, that he be expert in things of art, which consists of practice. He must know how to compose, because no one can rightly judge that which he does not know, for it is really inevitable that, not knowing something, he will judge it badly.

Hence, just as one who is learned only in that part of medicine called theoretical and who has not had a hand in practice will never be able to make perfect judgment of an illness, and can always err by relying solely on science, so the practical musician without [the capacity for] speculation and the speculative musician without [experience in] practice can always err and make bad judgments in musical matters. Accordingly, just as it would be insane to rely on a physician who does not have the knowledge of both practice and theory, so it would be really foolish and imprudent to rely on the judgment of [a musician] who was solely practical or had done work only in theory.

I have wanted to say this because there are some people who have so little judgment and who are so reckless and presumptuous that although they do not have either of these two faculties, they want to judge that which they do not know. And there are some others who, because of their mean nature, and in order to show that they are not ignorant, condemn as much the good as the bad efforts of everybody. There are some others who, having neither judgment nor knowledge, follow that which pleases the ignorant common people and sometimes want to make judgment of someone's adequacy by virtue of his name, country, native land, those he serves, and his appearance. So if being excellent and outstanding in a profession consisted in one's name, country, native land, service, appearance, and other similar things, I am sure that not many years would pass before no ignorant man would be found. For every father would open his eyes to this thing and would do everything possible in order to have sons who are distinguished in a profession, whatever it be, because (as I believe) there is no father who does not have the natural desire that his sons be superior to everyone in any science or profession. But in truth the opposite is the case: those who are great and famous in a profession are rare in number, and for each one of them, thousands and thousands of obscure, ignorant, clumsy, and crazy men are born, as one can see from any discussion.

I have said this because sometimes public acclamation and adoration (and not only among men of judgment) are so strong that no one dares to say anything against the common opinion, even though at times it is understood to be manifestly false; on the contrary, people are silenced, and remain indecisive and mute. For example, I remember that while reading once in the second book of *Il Cortegiano* of Count Baldassare Castiglione,[3] I discovered that when some verses presented at the court of the Duchess of Urbino went under the name of Sannazaro, everyone judged them to be most excellent, and praised them highly. Then it became known for certain that they had been composed by someone else, and suddenly they lost their reputation and were judged to be less' than mediocre. Similarly, I discovered that a motet which was sung in the presence of the aforementioned lady did not please, nor was it ranked among the good compositions, until it became known that the composition was written by Josquin.[4]

In order to show what the malignity and ignorance of men can sometimes do, I shall now relate what I have heard said many times about the most excellent Adrian Willaert, namely, that a motet for six voices, *Verbum bonum et suave,*[5] sung under the name of Josquin in the Papal Chapel in Rome almost every feast of Our Lady, was considered one of the most beautiful compositions sung in those days. When Willaert came from Flanders to Rome at the time of Leo X and found himself at the place where this motet was being sung, he saw that it was ascribed to Josquin. When he said that it was his own, as it really was, so great was the malignity or (to put it more mildly) the ignorance of the singers, that they never wanted to sing it again. In the book mentioned above, Count Baldassare adds another example of those who are

3. Castiglione *Il Cortegiano* II, 35.

4. Ed. of 1573: . . . for then it was immediately ranked in accordance with the lofty reputation which Josquin had at that time.

5. *Opera omnia*, V, 16.

without any judgment, and tells of a man who, drinking of one and the same wine, at one time said that it was most perfect, and at another, that it was most insipid, for he was convinced that he had been drinking two sorts of wine.[6]

Everyone can now see that judgment is not given to all, and from this one should learn not to be rash in praising or condemning anything, in music as much as in any other science or art, because for diverse reasons, judging is a very [347] difficult and dangerous thing, for there are many obstacles that may occur and many things of which the reasons cannot be known. Furthermore, there are different appetites, so that what pleases one does not please another, and while one man is delighted by sweet and smooth harmony, another would like it somewhat harder and harsher. Musicians should not despair when hearing such judgments, even if they hear people condemn their compositions and say everything bad about them. Rather they should take heart and be comforted, for the number of those who have no judgment is almost infinite, and few are those who do not judge themselves worthy of being numbered among prudent and wise people.

Many things can be said beyond this, but I am aware of
having already said more about this subject than was perhaps
appropriate, and therefore, rendering thanks to God,
the greatest Giver of all Blessings, to
this discussion I shall put an

END.

6. Castiglione *Il Cortegiano* II, 35.

Bibliography

GREEK AND ROMAN SOURCES

(Here are listed English translations when available, otherwise the critical edition.)

Ammonius Hermeiou. *In Aristotelis Categorias commentarius*. Edited by Adolph Busse. Berlin, 1895.

Apuleius, Lucius. *The Florida*. In *The Apologia and Florida of Apuleius of Madaura*, translated by H. E. Butler. 1909; reprinted. Westport, Conn.: Greenwood Press, 1970.

———. *The Golden Ass: Being the Metamorphoses of Lucius Apuleius*. Translated by W. Adlington (1566), revised by S. Gaselee. Loeb Classical Library. Cambridge: Harvard University Press; London: W. Heinemann, 1965.

Aristides Quintilianus. *De musica libri tres*. Edited by R. P. Winnington-Ingram. Leipzig: B. G. Teubner, 1963.

Aristotle. *Metaphysics*. In *Aristotle*, vols. 17–18. Translated by Hugh Tredennick. Loeb Classical Library. London: W. Heinemann, 1968.

———. *Politics*. Translated by H. Rackham. Loeb Classical Library. London: W. Heinemann, 1967.

Aristoxenus. *Harmonics*. Translated by Henry Stewart Macran. Oxford: Clarendon Press, 1902; reprinted. Hildesheim: G. Olms, 1974.

Athenaeus. *The Deipnosophists*. Translated by Charles Burton Gulick. Loeb Classical Library. London: W. Heinemann, 1970.

Basilius, Saint. *Opera omnia*. Edited by J.-P. Migne. In *Patrologia cursus completus. . . . Series graeca*, vols. 29–32. Paris: Migne, 1857.

Capella, Martianus. *De nuptiis philologiae et mercurii*. In *Martianus Capella and the Seven Liberal Arts*, vol. 1. Translated by William H. Stahl and Richard Johnson. New York: Columbia University Press, 1971.

Censorinus. *De die natali liber*. Edited by Otto Jahn. Berlin: G. Reimer, 1845; reprinted. Hildesheim: G. Olms, 1965.

Cicero, Marcus Tullius. *De oratore*. Translated by E. W. Sutton, completed with an introduction by H. Rackham (books 1–2); and by H. Rackham (book 3). 2 vols. Loeb Classical Library. Cambridge: Harvard University Press; London: W. Heinemann, 1942.

———. "The Speech in Defense of Lucius Flaccus." In *The Speeches: In Catilinam I–IV, Pro Murensa, Pro Sulla, Pro Flacco*. Translated by Louis E. Lord. Loeb Classical Library. Cambridge: Harvard University Press; London: W. Heinemann, 1959.

———. *Tusculan Disputations*. Translated by J. E. King. Loeb Classical Library. Cambridge: Harvard University Press; London: W. Heinemann, 1966.

Clemens Alexandrinus. *Miscellanies or Stromata: The Writings of Clement of Alexandria*. Translated by William Wilson. Ante-Nicene Christian Library: Translations of the Writings of the Fathers, vols. 4, 12. Edinburgh: T. & T. Clark, 1867, 1869.

Cleonides. *Harmonic Introduction*. In *Source Readings in Music History*, pp. 34–46. Edited and translated by Oliver Strunk. New York: W. W. Norton, 1950.

Dio Chrysostomus. *Discourses on Kingship*. In *Dio Chrysostom*, vol. 1, pp. 1–233. Translated by J. W. Cohoon. Loeb Classical Library. London: W. Heinemann, 1971.

Diodorus Siculus. *Bibliotheca historica*. Translated by C. H. Oldfather. Loeb Classical Library. London: W. Heinemann, 1933.

Ennius, Quintus. *Annals*. Edited by Ethel Mary Steuart. Cambridge: Cambridge University Press, 1925.

Gaudentius. *Harmonica introductio*. Edited by Karl von Jan. In *Musici scriptores graeci*, pp. 327–55. Leipzig: B. G. Teubner, 1895.

Horatius Flaccus. *Odes and Epodes*. Translated by C. E. Bennett. Loeb Classical Library. Cambridge: Harvard University Press; London: W. Heinemann, 1968.

————. *Satires, Epistles, Ars poetica*. Translated by H. Rushton Fairclough. Loeb Classical Library. Cambridge: Harvard University Press; London: W. Heinemann, 1970.

Josephus Flavius. *Jewish Antiquities*. In *Josephus*, vols. 1–8. Translated by H. St. J. Thackeray. Loeb Classical Library. London: W. Heinemann, 1930.

Lucianus. *Dialogues of the Dead*. In *Lucian*, vol. 7, pp. 1–175. Translated by M. D. Macleod. Loeb Classical Library. London: W. Heinemann, 1961.

————. *Harmonides*. In *Lucian*, vol. 6, pp. 215–225. Translated by K. Kilburn. Loeb Classical Library. London: W. Heinemann, 1959.

Manasses, Constantinus. *Compendium chronicum*. Edited by J.-P. Migne. In *Patrologiae cursus completus. . . . Series graeca*, vol. 127. Paris: Migne, 1864.

Ovidius Naso, P. *The Art of Love, and Other Poems*. Translated by J. H. Mozley. Loeb Classical Library. Cambridge: Harvard University Press; London: W. Heinemann, 1962.

————. *Fasti*. Translated by James George Frazer. Loeb Classical Library. London: W. Heinemann, 1967.

————. *Heroides and Amores*. Translated by Grant Showerman. Loeb Classical Library. Cambridge: Harvard University Press; London: W. Heinemann, 1963.

————. *Tristia. Ex Ponto*. Translated by Arthur Leslie Wheeler. Loeb Classical Library. Cambridge: Harvard University Press; London: W. Heinemann, 1931.

Pindarus. *Odes*. Translated by John Sandys. Loeb Classical Library. London: W. Heinemann, 1968.

Plato. *Laches*. In *Plato*, vol. 4, pp. 1–83. Translated by W. R. M. Lamb. Loeb Classical Library. London: W. Heinemann, 1962.

————. *Republic*. Translated by Paul Shorey. Loeb Classical Library. London: W. Heinemann, 1969.

Plinius Secundus, Caius. *Natural History*. 10 vols. Translated by H. Rackham (1–5), W. H. S. Jones (6–9), and D. E. Eichholz (10). Loeb Classical Library. Cambridge: Harvard University Press; London: W. Heinemann, 1938–62.

Plutarchus. *On Music*, in *Moralia*, vol. 24, pp. 352–455. Translated by Benedict Einarson and Phillip H. De Lacy. Loeb Classical Library. Cambridge: Harvard University Press; London: W. Heinemann, 1967.

Pollux, Julius. *Onomasticon*. Edited by Heinrich Bethe. 3 vols. Leipzig: B. G. Teubner, 1900–1937.

Ptolemy, Claudius. *Harmonics*. Edited by Ingemar Düring. In *Die Harmonielehre des Klaudios Ptolemaios*. *Göteborgs Högskolas Årsskrift*, 36 (1930). Göteborg: Elanders Boktryckeri Aktiebolag, 1930.

Quintilianus, Marcus Fabius. *Institutio oratoria*. Translated by H. E. Butler. Loeb Classical Library. London: W. Heinemann, 1969.

Seneca, Lucius Annaeus. *Agamemnon*. In *Seneca's Tragedies*, vol. 2, pp. 1–87. Translated by Frank Justus Miller. Loeb Classical Library. Cambridge: Harvard University Press; London: W. Heinemann, 1961.

Statius Publius Papinius. *Silvae*. In *Statius*, vol. 1, pp. 1–337. Translated by J. H. Mozley. Loeb Classical Library. London: W. Heinemann, 1955.

––––––. *Thebaid*. In *Statius*, vol. 1, pp. 339–571; vol. 2, pp. 1–505. Loeb Classical Library. London: W. Heinemann, 1955.

Strabo. *Geography*. Translated by Horace Leonard Jones. Loeb Classical Library. London: W. Heinemann, 1960.

Valerius Maximus. *Factorum et dictorum memorabilium*. Revised by C. Kempf. Stuttgart: B. G. Teubner, 1966.

Virgilius Maro, P. *Eclogues, Georgics, Aeneid*. In *Virgil*, vol. 1, pp. 1–77; 80–237; 240–571; vol. 2, pp. 1–365. Translated by H. Rushton Fairclough. Loeb Classical Library. London: W. Heinemann, 1978.

MEDIEVAL SOURCES

Boethius, Anicius Manlius Severinus. *The Consolation of Philosophy*. Translated by S. J. Tester. Loeb Classical Library. London: W. Heinemann, 1973.

––––––. *De institutione musica libri quinque*. Edited by Gottfried Friedlein. Leizpig: B. G. Teubner, 1867.

Cassiodorus Senator, Flavius Magnus Aurelius. *Institutiones*. Edited by R. A. B. Mynors. Oxford: Clarendon Press, 1937.

––––––. *The Letters of Cassiodorus, Being A Condensed Translation of "Variae epistolae."* Translated by Thomas Hodgkin. London: H. Frowde, 1886.

Gerson, Joannes. *Tractatus de Canticis*. In *Oeuvres complètes*, vol. 9, pp. 524–602. Edited by Msgr. Glorieux. Tournai: Desclée & Cie., 1973.

Index of Classical Passages Cited

General Index

CAMPAIGN • 223

OPERATION *NORDWIND* 1945

Hitler's last offensive in the West

STEVEN J ZALOGA   ILLUSTRATED BY JIM LAURIER

Series editor Marcus Cowper

First published in Great Britain in 2010 by Osprey Publishing,
Midland House, West Way, Botley, Oxford OX2 0PH, UK
443 Park Avenue South, New York, NY 10016, USA
E-mail: info@ospreypublishing.com

A CIP catalog record for this book is available from the British Library.

ISBN: 978 1 84603 683 5
PDF e-book ISBN: 978 1 84603 898 3

Editorial by Ilios Publishing Ltd, Oxford, UK (www.iliospublishing.com)
Page layout by Mark Holt
Index by Sandra Shotter
Typeset in Sabon and Myriad Pro
Maps by Bounford.com
3D bird's-eye views by The Black Spot
Battlescene illustrations by Jim Laurier
Originated by PDQ Digital Media Solutions Ltd
Printed in China through Worldprint

10 11 12 13 14   10 9 8 7 6 5 4 3 2 1

AUTHOR'S NOTE

The author would like to thank the staff of the US Army's Military History
Institute (MHI) at the Army War College at Carlisle Barracks, PA and the staff
of the US National Archive, College Park for their kind assistance in the
preparation of this book. Thanks also go to Art Loder for his help on
Luftwaffe issues.

For brevity, the traditional conventions have been used when referring to
units. In the case of US units, 1/179th Infantry refers to the 1st Battalion,
179th Infantry Regiment. The US Army traditionally uses arabic numerals
for divisions and smaller independent formations (70th Division, 781st Tank
Battalion), roman numerals for corps (VI Corps), spelled-out numbers for
field armies (Seventh Army) and arabic numerals for army groups (12th
Army Group).

In the case of German units, 2./Panzer-Regiment 7 refers to the 2nd
Company, Panzer-Regiment 7; II./Panzer-Regiment 7 indicates 2nd
Battalion, Panzer-Regiment 7. German corps have two accepted forms,
the formal version using roman numerals (LXXXIV Armee Korps) or the
shortened 84. AK which is the preferred form used here for clarity. Likewise,
the German field armies are contracted in the usual fashion (e.g. AOK 19
for Nineteenth Army).

THE WOODLAND TRUST

Osprey Publishing are supporting the Woodland Trust, the UK's leading
woodland conservation charity, by funding the dedication of trees.

Key to military symbols

Key to unit identification

CONTENTS

6th Army Group advance to the Rhine, November 14 to December 16, 1944

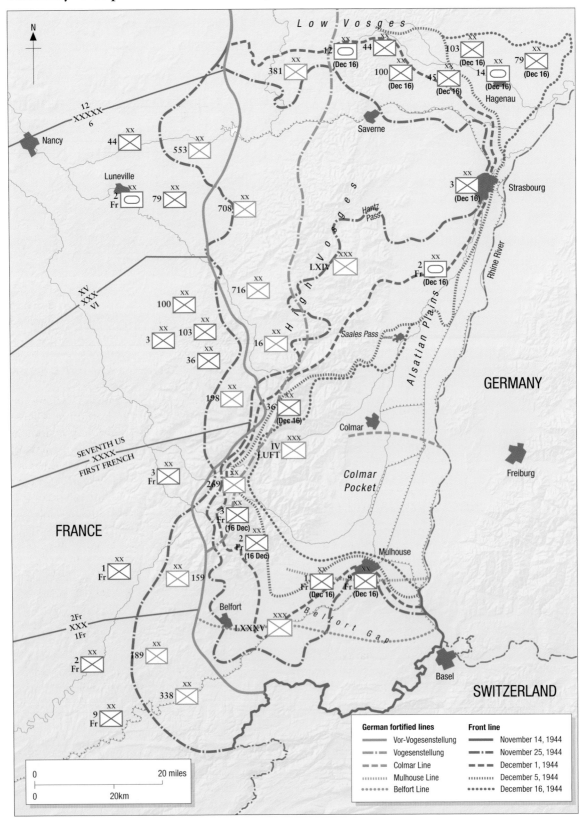

N

Low Vosges

12
44
103 (Dec 16)
79 (Dec 16)
381
100 (Dec 16)
45 (Dec 16)
14 (Dec 16)
Hagenau

Saverne

12 XXXXX 6

Nancy

44
553
79
2 Fr
Luneville

High Vosges

Hantz Pass

3 (Dec 16)
Strasbourg

708
716

LXIV

2 Fr (Dec 16)

Rhine River

100
3
103
36
16

Saales Pass

Alsatian Plains

XV XXX VI

198
36 (Dec 16)

GERMANY

Colmar

IV LUFT

Colmar Pocket

Freiburg

SEVENTH US XXXX FIRST FRENCH

3 Fr
269
3 Fr (16 Dec)
2 Fr (16 Dec)

Mulhouse

FRANCE

1 Fr
159

1 Fr (Dec 16)
9 Fr (Dec 16)

2Fr XXX 1Fr

Belfort
LXXXV

Belfort Gap

2 Fr
189
Basel

338

SWITZERLAND

9 Fr

German fortified lines	Front line
Vor-Vogesenstellung	November 14, 1944
Vogesenstellung	November 25, 1944
Colmar Line	December 1, 1944
Mulhouse Line	December 5, 1944
Belfort Line	December 16, 1944

0   20 miles
0   20km

ORIGINS OF THE BATTLE

In the waning hours of New Year's Eve 1944, the Wehrmacht launched Operation *Nordwind*, the last German offensive of World War II in the west. It was an attempt to exploit the disruptions caused by the Ardennes offensive further north in Belgium. When Patton's Third Army shifted two of its corps to relieve Bastogne, the neighboring Seventh US Army was forced to extend its front lines. This presented the Wehrmacht with a rare opportunity to mass its forces against weakened Allied defenses. At stake was Alsace, a border region that had been a bone of contention between France and Germany for the past century. Taken from France by Germany in the wake of the 1870 Franco-Prussian war, it returned to France after World War I in 1918, only to be retaken by Germany after France's 1940 defeat.

The fate of Alsace was of no particular concern to Eisenhower and the Anglo-American forces in north-west Europe, and the initial plans were simply to withdraw the Seventh US Army to more defensible positions in the Vosges mountains until the more crucial Ardennes contest was settled. However, the forfeit of the Alsatian capital of Strasbourg was completely unacceptable to de Gaulle and the Free French forces, resulting in a political firestorm that forced a reconsideration of Allied plans for dealing with the German attacks. Hitler saw Alsace as the last tangible reminder of Germany's great victory in 1940 and Strasbourg was the symbol of German control on the west bank of the Rhine; he insisted the city be retaken. The failure of the Ardennes offensive convinced Hitler that some new tactic had to be employed when dealing with the Allies. Instead of a single large offensive, Hitler decided to launch a series of smaller, sequential offensives. As a result, some German commanders called the Alsace campaign the "Sylwester offensives" after the central-European name for the New Year's Eve celebrations.

The initial *Nordwind* offensive emanated out of the fortified border city of Bitche, but made little progress in the face of stiff American resistance. The American battle cry became "No Bulge at Bitche!" US units were pulled off the Rhine near the Strasbourg area to reinforce the Bitche sector, providing the local German commanders with another temporary opportunity. A hasty river-crossing operation was staged at Gambsheim and the bridgehead gradually expanded in the face of weak American opposition. In view of the failure of the initial *Nordwind* offensive around Bitche, Hitler shifted the focus of the Alsace operation farther east towards Hagenau, attempting to link up the two attack forces and push the US Army away from the Rhine. This led to a series of extremely violent tank battles in the middle of January around the towns of Hatten-Rittershoffen and Herrlisheim, which exhausted both sides. An experienced German Panzer commander later called these winter battles the fiercest ever fought on the Western Front.

When the Red Army launched its long-delayed offensive into central Germany on January 14, the possibilities for further Wehrmacht offensives in Alsace drew to an end. Panzer units were transferred to the Eastern Front, and German infantry units began to establish defensive positions. With the Wehrmacht exhausted and weakened, it was the Allied turn for action. A large pocket of German troops was trapped on the west bank of the Rhine around Colmar, and Eisenhower insisted that the Colmar Pocket be eradicated. The 1ère Armée did not have the strength to do it quickly, so in late January, additional American divisions were moved into Alsace from the Ardennes front. In two weeks of fierce winter fighting, the German Nineteenth Army was decisively defeated and its survivors retreated over the Rhine.

The January 1945 Alsace campaign fatally damaged one German field army and severely weakened a second. This became startlingly clear in March 1945 when the US Army's lightning campaign crushed Heeresgruppe G (Army Group G) in the Saar-Palatinate, later dubbed the "Rhine Rat Race." The obliteration of the Wehrmacht's exhausted southern field armies was the root cause of Patton's dramatic advance through southern Germany in April and May 1945.

Alsatian civilians return to the ruins of the village of Mittelwihr on the eastern slopes of the High Vosges following the elimination of the Colmar Pocket in February 1945. The wrecked PzKpfw IV/70(A) was probably from Panzer-Brigade 106, which fought in these final battles. (NARA)

CHRONOLOGY

1944

August 15, US Seventh Army lands in southern France in Operation *Dragoon*, starting the campaign to push Heeresgruppe G out of southern and central France.

November 13 6th Army Group begins offensive with Seventh US Army overcoming the High Vosges defenses and the French 1ère Armée the Belfort Gap.

November 19 1ère Armée reaches the Rhine after pushing across the Belfort Gap.

November 23 Strasbourg is liberated by French 2e Division Blindée.

November 28 1ère Armée captures Mulhouse and Belfort, opening access to the Alsatian plains.

December 10 Himmler takes over the new Heeresgruppe Oberrhein command, which controls the isolated Colmar Pocket.

December 16 Wehrmacht begins Ardennes offensive.

December 19 6th Army Group is instructed to take over part of Patton's Third Army sector and go over to a defensive posture.

December 23 General Balck sacked as head of Heeresgruppe G; Blaskowitz returns to command.

December 27 Eisenhower warns Devers to be prepared to pull back off the Alsatian plains to the Vosges Mountains if the Germans attack.

Night December 29/30 Heeresgruppe G units begin moving into their attack positions.

Midnight December 31 Operation *Nordwind* is launched shortly before the start of the new year.

1945

January 4 Hitler admits the Ardennes offensive has failed; Heeresgruppe Oberrhein is ordered to begin attacks over the Rhine.

January 5 Heeresgruppe Oberrhein creates bridgehead over the Rhine north of Strasbourg near Gambsheim.

January 6 Focus of Operation *Nordwind* shifts from Bitche sector to Hagenau; Kampfgruppe Feuchtinger begins movement towards Hagenau forest.

January 8 Combat Command B, 12th Armored Division begins initial attack against Gambsheim bridgehead but is pushed back in a day of fighting.

January 9 Kampfgruppe Feuchtinger begins attacks against Hatten, starting a week-long battle with 14th Armored

Division over control of Hatten-Rittershoffen and the gateway through the Hagenau forest.

January 14	Red Army launches Oder offensive into central Germany, quickly forcing the transfer of prime divisions to the Eastern Front.
January 16	The 12th Armored Division resumes attacks on Gambsheim bridgehead near Herrlisheim but is beaten back.
January 17	The 10. SS-Panzer Division intervenes in Herrlisheim fighting; two US battalions are wiped out.
January 19	Attempts to push out of the Gambsheim bridgehead are frustrated and 10. SS-Panzer Division is shifted to Hagenau front.
January 20	1ère Armée launches opening phase of Operation *Cheerful* – the reduction of the Colmar Pocket.
January 20	Major-General Patch authorizes VI Corps' withdrawal from positions north of Hagenau forest to the Moder river line after dark on the night of January 20/21.

January 20/21	The 3rd Division, US XXI Corps begins attacking towards Colmar.
January 22	Heeresgruppen G and Oberrhein meet on Alsatian plain but are unable to overcome the Moder river line; French II corps begins attack on the Erstein bulge on northern shoulder of the Colmar Pocket.
January 25	Hitler calls off offensive operations around Hagenau.
February 2	Allied forces reach outskirts of Colmar; 5e Division Blindée captures center of the city the next day.
February 5	US and French troops link up at Rouffach, cutting off the western portion of Colmar Pocket.
1445hrs February 8	Hitler authorizes withdrawal from the Colmar Pocket, which is now less than two miles deep.
0800hrs February 9	German pioneers blow up Rhine bridge at Chalampe, marking the end of the Colmar Pocket.

THE STRATEGIC SETTING

By the late autumn of 1944, Allied forces in the European Theater of Operations (ETO) consisted of three army groups: Montgomery's British and Canadian 21st Army Group in the Netherlands, Bradley's US 12th Army Group from Belgium to Lorraine, and Devers' Franco-American 6th Army Group in Alsace. Of the three army groups, Eisenhower afforded priority to the two northernmost, Montgomery's and Bradley's. The inclusion of Devers' 6th Army Group to the force structure had come later than the other two, and was a source of considerable friction between Washington and London. General George C. Marshall, the US chief of staff, had insisted that the Mediterranean theater be de-emphasized after the capture of Rome in June 1944, and that the resources be freed for use in France. Churchill continued to push for further Allied operations in the Mediterranean, but Washington had the final word. As a result, the Seventh US Army and the French 1ère Armée staged an invasion of southern France on August 15, 1944 to clear the Wehrmacht out of southern, western, and central France. Operation *Dragoon* succeeded beyond

Men from the 398th Infantry, 100th Division move through the woods near Raon l'Etape during the fighting for the High Vosges mountains on November 17, 1944. This newly arrived unit has the later-style battledress based on the M1943 field jacket. (NARA)

the wildest expectations of its planners, liberating two-thirds of France in a lightning one-month campaign that destroyed half of the Wehrmacht's Heeresgruppe G in the process. By mid-September, the Seventh US Army had met up with Patton's Third Army near Dijon, creating a solid Allied front from the North Sea to the Mediterranean.

The Allied supply crisis in late September 1944 halted Devers' 6th Army Group and gave Heeresgruppe G a short lull to rebuild its defenses in Alsace. By mid-October 1944, Heeresgruppe G included three field armies, with 17 divisions, 500,000 troops, and 40,000 horses. The conduct of the fighting in Alsace was shaped by its geography, especially its mountainous terrain. The Vosges Mountains ran north–south alongside the Rhine River, creating a formidable natural barrier that had never been successfully overcome by an army in modern times. The High Vosges stretched from the Swiss frontier near Belfort northwards along the Rhine to elevations of over 5,000ft (1,524m) before gradually moderating near Strasbourg and the Saverne Gap. At this point they transitioned to the Low Vosges. The French and American components of Devers' 6th Army Group each had their own assignments. De Lattre's 1ère Armée was assigned the task of penetrating the Alsatian plains via the lowlands of the Belfort Gap, an approach so obvious that the Wehrmacht stoutly defended it. Major-General Patch's Seventh US Army was given the forbidding task of overcoming the High Vosges from the west, either over the mountains or through several key passes. In order to block the Allied advance, the Wehrmacht began an extensive fortification program in September 1944 beginning with the Vor-Vogesenstellung in the foothills of the Vosges, and the main Vogesenstellung in the Vosges mountains themselves.

Once 6th Army Group was reinforced with the remainder of its forces from the southern French ports, the offensive resumed in early October. The French 2e Corps d'Armée attempted to skirt the main German defenses in the Belfort Gap with a penetration of the mountain passes on its northern shoulder, but the attack was not entirely successful due to a vigorous German counterattack and difficulties with both the terrain and the rainy autumn

Wehrmacht engineer formations began creating the Vor-Vogesenstellung defensive belt in September 1944 to block the main Vosges mountain passes. In the haste to create these defenses, 88mm guns intended for the Jagdpanther tank destroyer were fitted to improvised field mounts and emplaced as static defenses to cover key areas such as this gun positioned near Phalsbourg in the Saverne Gap. (NARA)

weather. The US VI Corps initiated Operation *Dogface*, an attempt to push through the German defenses in the foothills of the Vosges approaching Bruyères before they could solidify. A punishing battle of attrition ensued in the forested mountains. Even if the October battles did not result in a breakthrough, the Sixth Army Group had positioned itself for a renewed offensive. In neighboring Lorraine, Patton's Third Army resumed its attacks towards Metz on November 8, which was the trigger for the 6th Army Group offensive which started on November 13. The poor weather provided little opportunity for Allied air support, and the 6th Army Group did not enjoy a significant force advantage in infantry over the Wehrmacht.

In the south, the French 1ère Corps d'Armée attacked over the lowlands of the Belfort Gap towards Mulhouse, and into the face of some of the stiffest German defenses of 85. AK (LXXXV Armee Korps). The French 2e Corps d'Armée went over the Vosges against 4. LK (IV Luftwaffe Korps) towards Colmar. Heeresgruppe G was uncertain about French plans, with AOK 19 (Armeeoberkommando 19) commander General der Infanterie Wiese arguing that the French would make the main drive directly into the fortified Belfort Gap while the army group commander, General Balck, argued that the French would attack over the Vosges towards Colmar. French deception efforts suggested the Vosges approach and when the attack came a day after a snowstorm on November 14 the German defenses in the Belfort Gap were surprised by the ferocity of the French attack. After securing a modest penetration, the tanks of the 1ère Division Blindée (1st Armored Division) began racing for the Rhine near the Swiss border with the French colonial infantry widening the breach. Lead tank patrols reached the river on

The 1ère Armée was the first Allied army with a firm foothold on the Rhine. Here, a .50-cal. heavy machine-gun team is seen in action in Huningue along the Rhine at the junction of the French, German, and Swiss borders north of Basel on November 30, 1944. (NARA)

November 19, the first Allied troops to do so. German counterattacks on November 22/23 failed to halt the French advance. The French attack continued until November 28, somewhat short of their goals but with the Belfort Gap in their hands and the cities of Mulhouse and Belfort liberated.

In the center, the US VI Corps penetrated the High Vosges via the Salles Pass opposite Selestat and achieved a second penetration towards Strasbourg through the Hantz Pass. In less than two weeks of fighting, the infantry succeeded in overwhelming the German mountain defenses, debouching on the eastern side of the mountain range. In the north, Haislip's XV Corps penetrated into the Saverne Gap and ground through substantial German defenses. On reaching Saverne on November 22, Haislip unleashed his exploitation force, the French 2e Division Blindée, which aggressively raced for Strasbourg. The boldness of the French tank attack found the Strasbourg defenses unprepared and the Alsatian capital fell on November 23. The Wehrmacht attempted to counterattack by striking XV Corps in the flank using the Panzer-Lehr-Division, but this effort was stymied by a prompt intervention by Patton's neighboring Third Army, sending a combat command of the 4th Armored Division into the fray which stopped the Panzer attack.

Following the loss of Strasbourg on November 23, the focal point of German actions in late November and early December was the defense of the Colmar Pocket, which was the last major German foothold on the west bank of the Rhine in Alsace. The November campaign separated AOK 1 from AOK 19, which had become confined in the Colmar Pocket. On November 24, General Rundstedt and General Balck recommended that AOK 19 be withdrawn over the Rhine to a new defense line in the Black Forest; Hitler was infuriated by the idea that a major portion of Alsace would be handed back to the French without a fight and grimly instructed that the forces trapped around Colmar would fight or die on the Alsatian plains.

The advance of Leclerc's 2e Division Blindée was so sudden and unexpected that when the French tanks burst into Strasbourg on November 23, its citizens were going about their business with no expectation of the drama that was unfolding. This photo was taken a few days after the liberation with the damaged Notre Dame cathedral in the background. (NARA)

An M4A2 tank of the French 5e Division Blindée with infantry support moves into the outskirts of Belfort on November 20, 1944 during the efforts to penetrate the Belfort Gap onto the Alsatian plains along the Rhine. (NARA)

Hitler placed the defense of this sector under SS-Reichsführer Heinrich Himmler, and under a new Oberrhein (Upper Rhine) command as a rebuke to the defeatism of the army.

With the High Vosges barrier penetrated, Devers began preparations to cross the Rhine, even though he had not yet received formal permission from Eisenhower to do so. The spectacular progress of the 6th Army Group in November 1944 raised the issue of the role it would play in the forthcoming

Panzer support for AOK 19 in the Belfort Gap was scant. The badly depleted Panzer-Brigade 106 Feldherrnhalle served as its fire brigade, rushing from spot to spot in hope of averting catastrophe. One of their PzKpfw IV tanks is seen on fire after being hit by bazooka fire during a skirmish with the French 4e Division Marocaine de Montagne in the Hardt woods near Pont-du-Bouc, north of Mulhouse, during the fighting for the Belfort Gap in the first days of December 1944. (NARA)

The 1ère Armée attempted to break into the Belfort Gap in November and December both on the Alsatian plains as well as through the High Vosges as seen here. This is a patrol of the 3e Division d'Infanterie Algérienne, an Algerian division that had previously seen combat in Italy. (NARA)

operations in Germany. Eisenhower had generally accepted the British view that the emphasis should be on the northern wing, and especially Montgomery's 21st Army Group mission to seize Germany's vital Ruhr industrial region, with Bradley's 12th Army Group providing a supporting role against the Saar industrial basin. Under such a scheme, Devers' 6th Army Group did not have a significant role besides a vague part in Eisenhower's "Broad Front" strategy. Part of the issue was the geographic details of Alsace and the corresponding terrain on the German side of the Rhine. Beyond the Rhine plain, Alsace faced Germany's Black Forest, a mountainous and wooded expanse that did not appear to be especially suited to mobile offensive operations. The 6th Army Group, with its long experience in mountain operations, was not intimidated by such prospects, having just overcome the most substantial mountain obstacle in the ETO in a stunning two-week campaign. However, Eisenhower was still enmeshed in the disastrous Hürtgen forest campaign in the First US Army sector, a bloody attritional battle with few signs of progress. As a result, the thought of a potential repeat of this campaign in the Black Forest gave Eisenhower considerable pause.

Besides the issue of the suitability of the Black Forest as an operating theater in the early winter of 1944, Eisenhower was also tentatively committed to supporting a projected operation by Patton's Third Army into the Saar, aimed towards Frankfurt. Operation *Tink*, scheduled to begin on December 19, would not be possible unless German defenses in the

On November 23, 1944, Panzer-Lehr-Division staged a counterattack from Saar-Union against the Seventh Army, hitting two regiments of the 44th Division. This Panther Ausf. G was knocked out during the fighting with the 114th Infantry near Schalbach on November 25; a bazooka hit is evident on the hull side immediately below the turret. The Panzer-Lehr Division was forced to abandon the attack when Combat Command B, 4th Armored Division launched a flank attack from Fénétrange. (NARA)

Palatinate on the west bank of the Rhine were loosened. As a result of these considerations, Eisenhower vetoed Devers' plan to strike across the Rhine in late November or early December. Instead, the 6th Army Group was given a supporting role. The northern wing of Patch's Seventh US Army was assigned to push north into the Low Vosges to help Patton's Third Army in its assault to the Rhine. In the south, the French 1ère Armée was directed to eliminate the Colmar Pocket.

Eisenhower's new directives led to a series of brutal mountain offensives in early December. The US XV Corps' attack north towards the Saar faced a

During December, the Seventh Army's main task was penetrating the Low Vosges and gaining access to the Alsatian plain. This is the entrance to the Saverne Gap looking west, one of the main access routes out of the mountains towards the Rhine. (NARA)

TOP

By mid-December, the Seventh Army was bumping into the trace of the Maginot Line around Bitche. Here, GIs of the 71st Infantry, 44th Division inspect the Ouvrage du Simsershof on the outskirts of Bitche after the garrison there from the 25. Panzergrenadier-Division had finally withdrawn on the night of December 18/19 after days of intense artillery bombardment. (NARA)

BOTTOM

Devers and Patch planned to jump the Rhine near Rastatt in early December to roll up behind the Westwall. Although Seventh Army units began training for river crossings in late November, Eisenhower vetoed the plan. The Seventh Army got their next chance three months later and this photograph shows a training exercise by the 157th Infantry of the 45th Division moving a 57mm anti-tank gun in a DUKW amphibious truck on March 11, 1945. (NARA)

heavy concentration of Maginot Line defenses around the old fortress city of Bitche while VI Corps to the east faced the Hagenau forest followed by the Westwall (Siegfried Line). The penetration of the Hagenau forest was successful enough that VI Corps committed its mechanized exploitation force, the 14th Armored Division. In contrast, XV Corps had a hard time on the approaches to Bitche and had not captured the city by the third week of

December when operations were halted by the Ardennes offensive. Farther south, the Colmar Pocket was assaulted on three sides but the Wehrmacht retained firm control through the end of December.

The most influential event in the Alsace fighting transpired farther north in the Belgian Ardennes where Heeresgruppe B launched its surprise offensive on December 16. The ferocity of this attack stunned Eisenhower and Bradley and led to a scramble to mount a counterattack. Patton's Third Army, already on the verge of launching Operation *Tink* towards Frankfurt, instead sent two of its corps northwards to help relieve Bastogne. This had immediate implications for the neighboring US Seventh Army, which was now expected to cover the 27-mile (43km) gap created by Patton's shift without any additional reinforcements. As a result, the Seventh US Army had to cover 126 miles (203km) of front with six infantry divisions, much too thin a defensive line by usual US Army standards. By way of comparison, the VIII Corps sector in the Ardennes which the Germans had found so attractive for their offensive had four infantry divisions on a front 60 miles (96km) long, a concentration about a third denser than the Seventh Army's front in Alsace. By December 19, all Allied offensive operations in Alsace were brought to a halt and a defensive reorientation began.

Having been ruthlessly engaged by the 6th Army Group for five months of continual fighting, Heeresgruppe G was looking for revenge. The senior German commanders in Alsace had been kept in the dark about the Ardennes offensive. When news of the initial German successes arrived, there was some optimism that the tide might be turned in Alsace with a bold attack. These plans eventually crystallized into Operation *Nordwind* at the end of December 1944.

A scene repeated in many Alsatian towns in the autumn and early winter of 1944/45. A series of road obstructions have been erected to block major thoroughfares, consisting of two vertical log walls with the center filled with earth and rocks. These obstructions were usually built by impressing local civilians. Here, an M10 3in. GMC of the 645th Tank Destroyer Battalion is supporting 45th Division actions near Lembach on December 14 during the attempts to penetrate the Low Vosges. (NARA)

THE OPPOSING COMMANDERS

GERMAN COMMANDERS

Generaloberst Johannes Blaskowitz, commander of Heeresgruppe G during Operation *Nordwind*. (NARA)

General der Infanterie Hans von Obstfelder, commander of AOK 1 during Operation *Nordwind*. (MHI)

In December 1944, German forces in the western theater were under the command of Oberbefehlshaber West (OB West) headed by **Generalfeldmarshall Gerd von Rundstedt. Generalfeldmarshall Walter Model's** Heeresgruppe B controlled three field armies from the North Sea to the area around Nancy in Lorraine, and Heeresgruppe G directed the three field armies from Lorraine southwards through Alsace to the Swiss frontier. One of its three field armies, Manteuffel's 5. Panzerarmee, was transferred out of Heeresgruppe G in November 1944 for the Ardennes offensive.

During the summer of 1944, Heeresgruppe G had been commanded by **Generaloberst Johannes Blaskowitz** who was relieved on September 21 due to Hitler's displeasure over the high cost of the retreat from southern and central France. He was replaced by **General der Panzertruppe Hermann Balck,** who had been commanding 4. Panzerarmee on the Eastern Front. Balck was one of the best known Panzer commanders of the Eastern Front and he had been elevated from corps to army command only at the beginning of August. His rise was unusually rapid and was part of Hitler's effort to reinvigorate key command positions in the west with an infusion of young blood from the east. Balck did not show any particular aptitude for infantry warfare in the Vosges Mountains and he was on the wrong side of the argument with AOK 19 commander Wiese over French operations in November. The French penetration of the Belfort Gap and the capture of Strasbourg undermined Hitler's confidence in him. The disappointing performance of Heeresgruppe G in November and December 1944 led to substantial command changes from army group to corps level.

The first to go was the AOK 1 commander, Otto von Knobelsdorf. He was unhappy with the lack of Panzer support provided for his army during the fighting for the Saverne Gap in November, and at the end of the month he had complained vigorously about the extent of transfers from his command to support the forthcoming Ardennes offensive. When he reported that he was ill on December 2, Rundstedt used this as an excuse to relieve him, and **General der Infanterie Hans von Obstfelder** was his replacement. Obstfelder had served during World War I in France and was a *Hauptmann* (captain) by the war's end. Obstfelder was in command of 28. Infanterie-Division during the 1939 Polish campaign; he was promoted to *General der Infanterie* on June 1, 1940 leading 29. AK (XXIX Armee Korps) in France in 1940 and in southern Russia, including the fighting in the Caucasus and the Mius river campaign in 1941/42.

He was transferred to lead 86. AK on August 25, 1943, which was originally part of AOK 1 in southern France, but which was transferred to Normandy during the summer of 1944 where it was encircled in the Falaise Pocket.

The fall of Strasbourg on November 23 infuriated Hitler, and the capture of a bridge over the Saar River by the US 395th Infantry led to another outburst. This river crossing was significant because it compromised the Westwall defensive belt, and Hitler demanded an immediate inquiry. The first to fall victim to Hitler's tirade was Balck's chief of staff, Generalmajor F. W. von Mellenthin on December 5, but a "witch-hunt" ensued which eventually claimed more senior commanders in a few weeks' time. The next affair to roil Heersgruppe G was triggered by intrigue in Berlin. Since the July 1944 bomb plot against Hitler, **Reichsführer-SS Heinrich Himmler** had been involved in a series of power grabs to assert more control over the army. Since most of the coup plotters had been in the Ersatzheer (Replacement Army), Himmler engineered a takeover of this command. The growing importance of his Waffen-SS and control over the Ersatzheer whetted his appetite for greater power over the rest of the armed forces. The fall of Strasbourg provided the pretext, and a scheme was floated in November to establish an Upper Rhine High Command (Oberkommando Oberrhein) to direct the defense of the Colmar Pocket and to retake Strasbourg. The proposed command was extremely unusual in that it reported directly to Berlin and would not be subordinate to Rundstedt's Western Front command. In the event, the new command was established as Heeresgruppe Oberrhein and it took over control of AOK 19 from Heeresgruppe G as well as units of the Ersatzheer in the neighboring Wehrkreis V (Military District V). Himmler was formally given control of the new command on December 10. He had absolutely no military command experience, and his tenure as Heeresgruppe Oberrhein commander would prove to be a source of endless aggravation for the army commanders in the sector. One German commander described Himmler's military understanding as "childish."

Within days of his appointment, Himmler traveled to Alsace to monitor the progress of defensive operations against the French attacks on the Colmar Pocket. A Tunisian detachment had captured the Hohneck, the highest peak in the High Vosges on the night of December 3/4. Himmler became fixated on this minor skirmish and concocted a scheme to recapture the mountain peak, melodramatically codenamed Operation *Habicht* (hawk). On December 12, Himmler visited the headquarters of the 189. Infanterie-Division in Wintzenheim where he encountered the AOK 19 commander, **General der Infanterie Friedrich Wiese**, who was supervising the operation. The attack on Hohneck failed, and Himmler decided that Wiese was insufficiently ardent in his task. He was relieved a week later and replaced by General der Infanterie Siegfried Rasp, an officer with few conspicuous qualifications for the task. Rasp had served primarily as a divisional or army staff officer through August 1943 when he was assigned to command the 3. Gebirgsdivision; this lasted two weeks and he was transferred to the 335. Infanterie-Division which saw heavy fighting in southern Russia until it was destroyed near Kishniev in August 1944 shortly after Rasp had been transferred. He led the reconstruction of the 78. Sturm-Division, which had been annihilated by the Red Army's summer 1944 offensive, but he was transferred to another staff post before the unit was again committed to the front. He had only been elevated from the rank of Generalleutnant earlier in December. His sudden rise to field army command suggests that Himmler wanted a less experienced and more pliant commander

Oberstgruppenführer Paul Hausser, one of the few experienced senior Waffen-SS commanders on the Western Front, was brought in on January 23 to clean up the mess created by Himmler with his disruptive Heeresgruppe Oberrhein headquarters in the midst of the collapse of the Colmar Pocket. (NARA)

General der Infanterie Friedrich Wiese, commander of AOK 19 until late December 1944 when he was sacked by Himmler. (MHI)

who would not question his orders as Wiese did during the Hohneck affair. The actual military leadership of Heeresgruppe Oberrhein remains obscure; French accounts suggest that Himmler appointed the World War I hero and SS stalwart, 64-year-old Obergruppenführer Heinrich von Maur as his main military adviser.

The final command change in Heeresgruppe G was the top position, and Balck was relieved on December 23. The change was not particularly surprising given Hitler's aggravation over the loss of Strasbourg and Balck's failure to prevent a penetration of the formidable High Vosges barrier. In his place returned Johannes Blaskowitz, who had been replaced by Balck only two months before. He was no favorite of Hitler's. His return was engineered by his old comrade, Gerd von Rundstedt, who wanted a reliable hand in command of Heeresgruppe G, especially now that Wehrmacht control was being poached by "former chicken farmer" Himmler with his disruptive Oberrhein command.

Blaskowitz was born in East Prussia in 1883, not from a traditional military family but as the son of a Lutheran minister. He served in the infantry in World War I and remained in the Reichswehr after the war, advancing in rank and becoming a *Generalmajor* in October 1932. He was apolitical but strongly nationalistic, so his career continued to advance after the rise of the Nazis. General Günther Blumentritt later recalled that he was "rigorously just and high-minded ... with a strong spiritual and religious turn of mind." This would not serve him well with the Nazis. Blaskowitz led the Eighth Army during the invasion of Poland, fighting the most intense battle of the campaign during the Polish counterattack on the Bzura River and the subsequent siege of Warsaw. In the wake of the campaign, he complained about the atrocities against Poles and Jews by the SS. Hitler dismissed his complaints about SS brutality as "childish ideas" and Blaskowitz was sidetracked to occupation duty in France instead of being assigned to a major command slot in the Russian campaign. He commanded AOK 1 on the Bay of Biscay for most of the war, a sleepy backwater by Wehrmacht standards. Although not favored in Berlin, he retained Rundstedt's confidence and in May 1944 Blaskowitz was placed in command of Heeresgruppe G.

The command situation at corps level was more stable than at higher levels, with only one of the five corps commanders in Heeresgruppe G removed in December. The 89. AK commander, **General Werner von und zu Gilsa**, was relieved on November 23 when his headquarters was overrun in Saverne by the tanks of the French 2e Division Blindée. Although he escaped, Balck replaced him with **General Gustav Höhne**, an experienced Eastern Front commander. The remainder were all veteran Eastern Front commanders, most of whom had been assigned during the autumn of 1944.

AMERICAN AND FRENCH COMMANDERS

The 6th Army Group and Seventh US Army were the "red-haired stepchildren" of the US Army in Europe. Eisenhower and his SHAEF (Supreme HQ Allied Expeditionary Force) headquarters generally treated the 6th Army Group operations as an afterthought, and relations between the senior commands were strained.

Lieutenant-General Jacob "Jake" Devers was the 6th Army Group commander. A classmate of George Patton's at West Point, he spent most of his early career in the field artillery. He was stationed in Hawaii in 1917/18,

A portrait photograph of Gen. Jacob Devers after the war; Devers received his fourth star at the end of March 1945. (NARA)

and as a result saw no combat duty during World War I. His assignments in the interwar years included teaching posts at West Point and a stint with the Army G-3 (Operations) Office of Artillery in Washington, where he had his first contacts with the future Army chief of staff, George C. Marshall. At the outbreak of World War II in 1939 he was chief of staff of the Canal Zone (Panama). He had developed a reputation as an excellent organizer and in October 1940 he was assigned to create one of the army's main new training bases at Fort Bragg by General Marshall, becoming the Army's youngest major-general. When the pioneer of the US tank force, Major-General Adna Chaffee, became ill in 1941, Devers was transferred to lead the Armored Force on August 1, 1941. His superior performance in this demanding assignment reinforced Marshall's confidence in him and in May 1943 he was assigned to lead ETOUSA (European Theater of Operations, United States Army). This command in Britain was responsible for building up the US Army in preparation for the eventual landings in France in 1944. While his rank and experience made Devers a contender for senior US field commands in the 1944 campaigns, his prospects were hobbled by several factors. Unlike

Maj. Gen. Wade Haislip, XV Corps commander, had originally served under Patton's command in Normandy and in the race to the Seine before his corps was shifted to the Seventh Army in the autumn of 1944. (NARA)

other candidates such as Dwight Eisenhower, Omar Bradley, George Patton, and Mark Clark, he had no combat experience. He also proved to be less adept at the political aspects of senior command, and, unlike Eisenhower, he was not especially liked by Churchill or other key British officials. He also managed to alienate Eisenhower on several occasions in 1943, refusing various requests for troop dispositions from the ETO to the Mediterranean theater while Eisenhower was in charge of the Italian campaign.

There was really no contest for the position of Supreme Headquarters Allied Expeditionary Force, which went to Eisenhower due to his far more extensive experience and his broad support not only among American commanders, but amongst senior British leaders, especially Churchill. Devers was never considered for a place in Eisenhower's coterie of senior commanders, who came mostly from Ike's Mediterranean theater veterans. Nevertheless, Devers' sterling performance in administrative commands left Marshall indebted to him and confident of his leadership abilities. When Marshall was finally able to push through the Operation *Dragoon* plan for the amphibious landings in southern France, Devers was the obvious pick. The French had mooted the idea of a French commander for the 6th Army Group, a notion that was rejected out of hand by both the US and British chiefs of staff. The 6th Army Group was activated in September 1944 following the successful conclusion of the Operation *Dragoon* landings in southern France.

Relations between Devers and Eisenhower were strained, due in no small measure to Eisenhower's personal dislike of Devers. Ike and his inner circle such as Bradley often disparaged Devers as ".22 caliber," an allusion to the small-caliber rifles given to teenage American boys for target practice. The animosity was misplaced given the 6th Army Group's exemplary track record since the August Operation *Dragoon* landings, and the challenges Devers faced in coordinating the activities of his joint US–French command. The sterling performance of Major-General Patch's Seventh Army in overcoming the Vosges in November stands in marked contrast to the performance of Bradley and Hodges in the Hürtgen forest, and the 6th Army Group had a far better measure of their Wehrmacht opponent, as was evident in comparing the intelligence failure in the Ardennes with the intelligence success in *Nordwind*.

VI Corps commander, Maj. Gen. Edward Brooks is seen briefing SHAEF commander Dwight Eisenhower at 6th Army Group headquarters during the Alsace fighting; Patch is behind him. Brooks had previously commanded the 2nd Armored Division in Normandy until sent to Alsace in October 1944 to fill in for Lucian Truscott. (MHI)

The two components of Devers' 6th Army Group were the Seventh US Army and the 1ère Armée. The Seventh US Army was led by **Lieutenant-General Alexander "Sandy" Patch**. He was born at Fort Huachuca in the Arizona territory, the son of a 4th Cavalry Regiment officer, and graduated from West Point in 1913. He served in Pershing's Mexican Expedition in 1916 and commanded an infantry battalion in France in 1918. In 1942/43, Patch led the American Division and later XIV Corps during the Army's first major offensive campaign on Guadalcanal. Patch returned to the United States to train the new IV Corps, which was sent to the Mediterranean in early 1944. Seventh Army had been commanded by **General George S. Patton** during Operation *Husky* on Sicily in the summer of 1943, but Patton was transferred to England in January 1944 to command Third Army under Eisenhower. Patch was not especially favored by either Marshall or Eisenhower, but he was championed by Eisenhower's chief of staff, **General Walter Bedell Smith**, and highly regarded by Devers as well. The combination of Devers and Patch proved to be an excellent match.

Lt. Gen. Alexander "Sandy" Patch was commander of the Seventh US Army. (NARA)

The senior 1ère Armée commander was the talented and flamboyant **Général Jean de Lattre de Tassigny**. He graduated from Saint Cyr in 1911 and saw extensive combat in World War I, being wounded four times including a nearly fatal lance wound to the chest during a cavalry skirmish. Like many ambitious French officers of the postwar army, he transferred to North Africa and took part in the pacification campaigns there. In 1931, he was posted to the general staff under General Weygand; his rival for the post was Charles de Gaulle. He led the 14e Division d'Infanterie in the battle of France in 1940, which put up a spirited defense near Rethel. De Lattre was not captured by the Germans but due to his loyalty to Weygand, he decided to remain in France rather than join de Gaulle's Free French movement abroad. He served in the Vichy French Armistice Army in metropolitan France and Tunisia, siding with anti-German factions. De Lattre was arrested by the Vichy government in November 1942 after the Wehrmacht occupied Vichy France but in September 1943 he broke out of prison and escaped to Britain. De Gaulle recognized his talent and dispatched him to Algeria to help raise the expanding French army there, commanding Army B, the core of the later 1ère Armée. As a preliminary

Allied commanders celebrate the reduction of the Colmar Pocket in February 1945. Here, Gén. Jean de Lattre de Tassigny congratulates Maj. Gen. Frank Milburn who led XXI Corps, the principal US formation in the operation. To the left is Major-General Norman Cota, commander of the badly battered 28th Division which had fought in the Hürtgen forest and the approaches to Bastogne before being transferred to the Seventh Army for the Comar operation. (NARA)

operation, de Lattre led the capture of Elba on June 17, 1944 by a combined force of the Royal Navy and French troops. De Lattre had displayed remarkable bravery on the battlefield and was a perceptive and talented commander. He had a theatrical and demanding personality that rivaled that of other prima donnas of World War II like Patton and MacArthur. He was extremely energetic and mercilessly micromanaged his corps and divisional commanders. In his diary, Devers recalled that de Lattre would fly off on a tirade about twice a week. Devers employed former senator Henry Cabot Lodge Jr. as his liaison with de Lattre on account of his fluent French and his tactful diplomatic skills. Although the 6th Army Group staff found de Lattre difficult to work with, they concluded that it was probably even worse for his French staff who called him "le roi Jean," or King John.

Relations between the senior American and French commanders within the 6th Army Group were about as good as could be expected. The ambiguous relationship of the French Army with senior Allied commands was the source of inevitable friction, and the French dependence on American material support was a source of endless frustration and misunderstanding on both sides. The French were not fully represented in senior Allied command organizations such as the Combined Chiefs of Staff, and de Lattre's loyalty was inevitably torn between the military necessity to obey commands from Devers along with the political necessity to recognize the demands of de Gaulle's provisional government in France. As will be detailed later, this issue came to a head over the fate of Strasbourg in January 1945.

The French command had its share of internal antagonisms, most notably the breach between Gaullist stalwarts like Général Jacques Leclerc of the 2e Division Blindée and the 1ère Armée commanders. Leclerc had been with de Gaulle from the outset and regarded the senior 1ère Armée commanders as a bunch of opportunists who switched sides out of convenience rather than conviction. Many of the senior 1ère Armée commanders regarded Leclerc as an upstart captain who had seen a rapid rise in rank solely on account of his political connections. The animosity between both factions was bitter enough that the US Army found it prudent to keep Leclerc's 2e Division Blindée away from the 1ère Armée, and so it served under an American corps command through most of the campaign.

OPPOSING PLANS

GERMAN PLANS

The OB West staff proposed that Heeresgruppe G be assigned a supporting role in the Ardennes offensive, consisting of a strike towards Metz, but both Hitler and Rundstedt quickly dismissed this idea as preposterous given the army group's meager resources. In November 1944, Heeresgruppe G was informed that a major offensive in the west would take place sometime in the immediate future, but was not informed of the date, location, or other details. On December 15, the Heeresgruppe G headquarters opened sealed orders that explained that the offensive would take place in the Ardennes the following day, but few details were provided. Berlin expected that the Ardennes offensive would create a lull in Alsace and so under such circumstances, Heeresgruppe G should plan and conduct a local offensive to further relieve pressure from the Ardennes offensive. The date and objective of the offensive were left up to the local command, but the plan had to be approved by Hitler.

When the Seventh US Army front went dormant on December 19/20, this gave Heeresgruppe G the cue to begin an offensive. The first step was to pull back the 21. Panzer-Division and 25. Panzergrenadier-Division for refitting, since they would be needed as the army group's mobile reserve. Two potential operations were considered. The first option was an attack out of the "Orscholz switch" area southwest of Trier against the overextended remainder of Patton's Third Army, XX Corps. This operation was on the northern fringe of the army group's forces and would require extensive regrouping of forces, which would be vulnerable to US air power, so this plan was rejected. The second option was a strike through the Low Vosges to recapture the Saverne Gap with the objective of re-establishing contact with AOK 19 in the Colmar Pocket. On December 23, Berlin approved the Saverne option. The only major reinforcement offered for the attack was 6. SS-Gebirgsdivision "Nord," which was being transferred from Finland and which was expected to arrive between Christmas and New Year; the bulk of the forces for the offensive would have to come from those already available since all theater reserves were committed to the Ardennes fighting. There was also a promise that Himmler's Heeresgruppe Oberrhein would stage its own attack against the Alsace bridgehead, although the Heeresgruppe G staff was not convinced that AOK 19 had the forces necessary to conduct any sort of offensive action in view of the desperate situation in the Colmar Pocket.

The Festung Kommandant Oberrhein constructed several defensive lines in Alsace starting in September 1944 with two lines in the Vosges Mountains and several shorter lines on the Rhine Plain. The Germans absorbed some of the older French defenses into their own defense lines around Colmar, such as this machine-gun pillbox. (NARA)

The plan was refined during the final week of December before receiving Hitler's final approval. The three potential avenues of attack were to the west of the Low Vosges along the Saar River, through the Low Vosges south of Bitche, or to the east of the Vosges on the Alsatian plains via Wissembourg. The western avenue was the best for rapid movement since the road network would support mechanized forces and the Saar River could serve as a defensive shield. On the other hand, this was the center of gravity for the US XV Corps and the open terrain would make the attack vulnerable to US air attack if the weather was favorable. The center approach offered good assembly areas for German infantry, and Heeresgruppe G still held the concentration of Maginot Line forts around Bitche. In addition, the forested and mountainous terrain would mask the German attack and make US air attack difficult. On the other hand, the mountainous terrain of the Low Vosges had poor roads and could not easily support Panzer forces in bad winter weather. The eastern avenue had a good road network and relatively weak American forces. On the other hand, on this front the terrain was well suited to defense, the US Army controlled several Maginot forts in the area and had extensively mined the sector, and the layout of the rivers and the presence of the Hagenau forest presented significant terrain obstructions. As a result of these considerations, Heeresgruppe G selected the center route through the Low Vosges from Bitche and this was approved by Blaskowitz and Rundstedt on December 24; it received the codename *Nordwind* (north wind) at this time.

Hitler's attitudes towards the plan were more critical, based on the lessons of the recent Ardennes offensive. The initial infantry penetrations had gone badly and the premature commitment of Panzers (especially in the 6. Panzerarmee sector) had led to heavy tank losses and a stalled attack. As a result, Hitler doubted that the Heeresgruppe G plan would succeed and in particular he was skeptical that the infantry would do well in the forested mountains in winter conditions, so he favored the western avenue in more open terrain. In the end, a compromise was reached with Rundstedt and Blaskowitz. The western approach, labeled "Sturmgruppe 1," became an area of advance together with the center approach, now dubbed "Sturmgruppe 2." Hitler was also insistent that neither Panzer division be committed, not even parts of the divisions, until a breakthrough had been made. In view of the terrain, he directed that the remaining armor support, consisting of about 90 assault guns and tank destroyers, be provided to the 17. SS-Panzergrenadier-Division which would form the core of the western thrust. Hitler selected the night of December 31 to January 1 for the attack on the presumption that New Year's Eve would be celebrated behind American lines. A planned diversionary attack from the Orscholz switch against Patton's XX Corps was limited to a divisional feint because of a lack of forces.

After the Ardennes failure, Hitler had become convinced that massive offensives at army group level were no longer feasible in the west, and that a better option would be to stage smaller, sequential offensives at field army or corps level, and to exploit any of these when they showed promise. As a result, he made it clear to Rundstedt and Blaskowitz that *Nordwind* was only the first stage of a sequence of Alsace attacks. There would be further attacks by Himmler's Oberrhein command, and a follow-up offensive codenamed *Zahnarzt* (dentist) would take place when *Nordwind* was complete.

The Heeresgruppe G staff was not pleased with the changes, though they were prudent enough not to complain directly to Hitler or to the recently arrived Blaskowitz, who had been present when the final decisions were made. Their main concern was that Hitler's version of the plan had two centers of gravity, which would disperse the force of the effort and was against doctrine. The forces available were hardly capable of a single main thrust, and removing armored support from the center thrust would further weaken its chances.

The plan presumed that surprise would be absolutely essential to the success of the operation, so strict security measures were established. Access to details of the plan was restricted to corps and divisional commanders as well as their staffs and some selected officers; no information was to be passed by radio or telephone, only through written communications. No major troop movements were permitted until the night of December 29/30 for fear of disclosing the plans, providing only a day to mass the forces. Reconnaissance missions were prohibited except for normal patrol activities. No preliminary artillery bombardment was allowed, as experience of the Ardennes fighting showed that the artillery preparation had simply alerted forward US units without causing significant casualties.

Heeresgruppe G hoped to activate a supporting operation by Himmler's neighboring Oberrhein command, but since AOK 19 had been taken from their control in early December, they had no power to coordinate such plans. Hitler's version of the *Nordwind* plan also included a supporting Heeresgruppe Oberrhein operation. The objective of this attack was to establish bridgeheads on either side of Strasbourg as a preliminary step to recapturing the city. There have been hints that Himmler deliberately interfered with attempts to coordinate the attacks as part of an effort to disentangle the two efforts so that his command could take the credit when Strasbourg was recaptured. In the event, the plan to start the Heeresgruppe Oberrhein attack 48 hours after *Nordwind* was changed on December 27 when a specific date was dropped in favor of initiating the attack after Heeresgruppe G committed its Panzer exploitation force.

AMERICAN PLANS

Patch's Seventh US Army was frequently called upon to support Patton's Third Army to the north. When Third Army was sent to relieve Bastogne in late December 1944, Patch was instructed to take over Patton's sector. This is Patton and Patch at Seventh Army headquarters in Sarrebourg on December 4, 1944. (NARA)

On December 19, Eisenhower held a meeting at Verdun with all senior US commanders to plan a response to the Ardennes offensive. Patton offered to shift one corps immediately to relieve Bastogne, followed by a second within a few days' time. After Eisenhower concurred, Devers was instructed that the 6th Army Group would have to halt all offensive operations and that Patch's Seventh Army would have to cover part of Patton's former front line. During follow-up discussions on December 26, Eisenhower told Devers that he wanted him to pull VI Corps back from the Rhine and to straighten out his

extended line by withdrawing to the Vosges Mountains. Devers pointed out that both his staff and Patch's headquarters did not expect the main German attack to come against VI Corps due to the nature of the terrain and the Maginot forts, but instead against XV Corps along the Saar River. Devers left with the impression that there was no urgency to the withdrawal and he instructed Patch to plan three phased withdrawals of VI Corps in the event of a heavy attack, but only if an attack developed. Whilst SHAEF continued to press for a withdrawal, Devers and Patch were not willing to give up defensible positions simply because of SHAEF's skittish assessment of the threat after the Ardennes intelligence fiasco. This argument would eventually come to a head, but only after the Wehrmacht launched *Nordwind*.

Although there have long been stories that the Allies learned of Operation *Nordwind* by Ultra signals intelligence, official histories of the intelligence effort have categorically denied that any such messages were intercepted. As mentioned above, the Wehrmacht had strict instructions that no messages related to *Nordwind* were to be passed by radio, so any intelligence gathered by signals intercepts would have simply been inferences made from traffic patterns. Around Christmas, the Seventh Army G-2 officer, Colonel William Quinn, concluded from suspicious German activity that an attack was likely. For example, aerial photo reconnaissance in the Bitche area around Christmas had shown that the Germans had prepared forward artillery positions that were not yet occupied, and patrols sent to collect prisoners for interrogation were running into unusually strong German forces. Although Ultra did not provide any specific evidence of the attack, the shifting order of battle also suggested an attack was imminent. Quinn briefed Patch about his suspicions, and when Quinn suggested the attack would come on New Year's Eve, Patch asked why. Quinn replied: "German stupidity: they know we are New Year's Eve addicts and will all be drunk and this will be the finest time for a penetration." Patch agreed with the assessment and convinced Devers of the threat.

Patch and the Seventh Army staff was convinced that the most dangerous avenue of a German attack, and the most likely, was the western approach down the Saar River. The Germans had already attempted to use this avenue in mid-December when they had launched a spoiling attack with Panzer-Lehr-Division. Although they recognized that a more direct thrust through the Low Vosges was a possibility, the Seventh Army viewed the terrain as far less trafficable, especially since the onset of hard winter weather in late December. They were not at all convinced that a major attack would be launched along the Alsatian plains around Lauterbourg, as US troops held chunks of the Maginot Line and had established significant defenses in the sector already.

Their superiors at SHAEF were insistent that Seventh Army divert adequate reserves to handle the anticipated assault. Devers gave this task to the 12th Armored Division and the 36th Division. In addition, the French 2e Division Blindée (which had garrisoned Strasbourg) was brought nearer to the Low Vosges as a potential counterattack force. On New Year's Eve, Patch met his two corps commanders and warned them to expect an attack within 24 hours; all holiday festivities would be postponed. On the afternoon of December 31, aerial reconnaissance reported that German troop movements had started all along the front. But as snow clouds gathered, further reconnaissance was curtailed and there was no precise information on the focus of the German actions.

THE OPPOSING ARMIES

WEHRMACHT

The Wehrmacht in Alsace was starved of forces due to the shift of resources to the Ardennes in November and December 1944. As a result, Heeresgruppen G and Oberrhein both had to make do with badly depleted infantry divisions and a minimum of Panzer formations. These units were reinforced by a motley selection of improvised units including various march battalions, police, and *Volksturm* units.

Germany's precarious manpower situation in 1944 led to the creation of Volksgrenadier divisions as an alternative to conventional infantry divisions. The new organization was intended to offer maximum firepower with minimum personnel and equipment. They were intended primarily for defensive missions on elongated fronts, and were not optimized for offensive missions due to inadequate mobile resources and a stripped-down organizational structure. Of the 173 infantry divisions nominally in the Wehrmacht order of battle in January 1945, 51 were *Volksgrenadier* divisions. In the case of Alsace, AOK 1 was composed primarily of *Volksgrenadier* divisions with six of the seven infantry divisions in this configuration. The opposite was the case with AOK 19, with only one of its eight infantry divisions in this form.

The Festung Kommandant Oberrhein was responsible for constructing the Vogesenstellung fortification line in the High Vosges, starting in September 1944. This surplus Panther tank turret was being emplaced in the defense line in the Saales Pass but was overrun by the Seventh Army in late November before it was completed. (NARA)

Casualties in 1944 had far outstripped the ability of the Wehrmacht to make up for losses with trained personnel. The Wehrmacht typically allowed infantry divisions to be burned out in combat, and when they had lost the majority of their infantrymen, the division would be hastily rebuilt with raw recruits and then sent back into the line without proper tactical training. The principal manpower resource in late 1944 was the large number of surplus Luftwaffe ground crews and Kriegsmarine personnel since so many aircraft and warships were derelict due to a lack of fuel. Although the morale and capabilities of these young troops were often quite good, they were usually sent into battle with only the most rudimentary sort of infantry training. An additional source of cannon fodder came from men who were combed out of industry after having been given exemptions earlier in the war; they were usually older and less fit than the Luftwaffe and Kriegsmarine transfers.

A typical example in Alsace was the 256. Volksgrenadier-Division in the Bitche sector. The original 256. Infanterie-Division was annihilated in the July 1944 Red Army offensive. As was often the case, a small cadre of headquarters, support troops, and artillerymen survived the division's destruction, leaving a "shadow division" which could serve as a kernel from which to grow a new division. It was reformed in Saxony in September 1944 by combining the Eastern Front survivors with elements of the newly created but incomplete 568. Volksgrenadier-Division. The majority of the new recruits in the division came from industrial, economic, and administrative posts in Germany who had previously been exempted from service, and the divisional commander complained that they were too old and lacked the endurance needed for infantry combat. The rest came mainly from Kriegsmarine personnel who were "young, healthy and strong men of high morale … who later constituted the backbone of the infantry regiments particularly because of their untapped physical and emotional resources." With virtually no individual training or unit tactical training, the division was rushed to the Netherlands at the end of September and committed to the fighting along the Scheldt estuary against

British and Canadian troops at the beginning of October. The divisional commander noted that only one of the three regimental commanders had command experience; the battalion commanders were eager for action but young and inexperienced. After a month of fighting, the division was pulled out and sent to the Hagenau sector in Alsace against US forces, where it was again bled white. By the time of Operation *Nordwind* at the beginning of 1945, the rifle companies were down to only 40 percent of their strength, and in the opinion of their divisional commander, only fit for defense. As was typically the case, the other elements of the division were in somewhat better strength with the engineers at about 70 percent strength and the artillery at about 90 percent strength. Its *Panzerjäger* (tank destroyer) battalion had only three assault guns instead of the authorized 14 and only eight towed 75mm anti-tank guns. The signals units were weakened by the need to divert divisional troops to the rifle units to make up for combat casualties, and the radio units were only marginally capable of conducting their tasks in combat due to a lack of training. The divisional commander concluded that the unit was "decisively impaired" and needed at least two weeks out of the line for rebuilding; instead, it was assigned an offensive mission in harsh winter conditions. The only reinforcements received were a "march battalion" of about 250 poorly trained replacements. There was a general shortage of winter clothing and waterproof boots, and heavy infantry weapons were in short supply, especially mortars and heavy machine guns.

Panzer support in Alsace was weak, since so many units had been shipped to the Ardennes sector. The only mechanized unit earmarked for the initial *Nordwind* attack was 17. SS-Panzergrenadier-Division "Götz von Berlichingen," a formation that had been in continual combat with the US Army since Normandy, and which had been burnt out and rebuilt on several occasions. The neighboring army commanders felt that its main problem was poor leadership, and it had lost several divisional commanders and numerous junior commanders during the autumn. The field army staff labeled the current commander as incompetent. Its main armored element, SS-Panzer-Abteilung 17 Bataillon was equipped mostly with assault guns instead of tanks, with 45 StuG III assault guns, three PzKpfw III command tanks, six Flakpanzer 38(t) vehicles, and four Flakpanzer IV Wirbelwinds on hand, of which 84 percent were operational. The SS-Panzerjäger-Abteilung 17 Bataillon was similarly equipped with 31 StuG III assault guns, two Jagdpanzer IVs, one Marder III and eight towed 75mm PaK 40 anti-tank guns; only 67 percent of the vehicles were operational with many of the old StuG III assault guns being worn out or damaged in combat. Their strength was later increased by 57 assault guns that arrived after Christmas, but the reinforcements had been sitting out in the open for months and only a few could be rendered serviceable before the attack. The division's two *Panzergrenadier* regiments were burned out and at less than half strength in the middle of December, but some additional troops were received in the last week before the offensive, mainly of "an inferior type" of German (ethnic Germans from eastern Europe). Senior officers at AOK 1 were so unimpressed by the poor performance of the 17. SS-Panzergrenadier-Division in the autumn fighting that they wanted to strip it of its assault guns to re-equip the 21. Panzer-Division, but Berlin refused.

The two other mechanized formations earmarked for *Nordwind* were the 21. Panzer-Division and the 25. Panzergrenadier-Division, both of which were placed in army reserve and not committed during the initial fighting. The 21. Panzer-Division had been badly beaten up in the autumn fighting, but was

Artillerie-Stab 485 was the artillery arm of Wehrkreis V, responsible for Alsace. It raised a number of fortress artillery battalions for Festung Kommandant Oberrhein using captured heavy artillery like this 203mm Haubitze 503/5(r), the Soviet B-4 203mm Howitzer M.1931. This particular howitzer was deployed near Sarrebourg for the defense of the Low Vosges under an elaborate camouflage cover which has mostly been stripped away in this view after the battery was overrun by the Seventh Army in late November 1944. (NARA)

rebuilt in late December. Panzer-Regiment 22 was re-equipped and had a full tank strength of 38 Panthers and 34 PzKpfw IV tanks, but only four of its authorized 21 Jagdpanzer IV tank destroyers. It was particularly weak in armored infantry half-tracks having no light SdKfz 250s and only 29 of the 57 authorized SdKfz 251 troop-carrying half-tracks. It had to make do with civilian trucks. Manpower strength in the *Panzergrenadier* regiments was fair: Panzergrenadier-Regiment 125 was at 70 percent strength and Panzergrenadier-Regiment 192 was at 56 percent strength. The 25. Panzergrenadier-Division was not fully pulled out of the line until Christmas Eve and its rebuilding was less extensive. Panzer-Abteilung 5 had only six Panthers, five Jagdpanzer IV tank destroyers, and 3 Möbelwagen Flakpanzers; which was only 23 percent of its authorized strength. Its Panzerjäger-Abteilung 25 was in only marginally better shape with 14 StuG III assault guns, at 33 percent of authorized strength. Its two *Panzergrenadier* regiments were in better shape so far as infantry half-tracks were concerned with 131 SdKfz 251s on hand, or 82 percent of authorized strength; manpower in the two regiments had been reduced to barely a quarter of their full strength early in the month and both regiments were hastily filled to partial strength by early January.

Since so much of the Panzer strength was being held in reserve, the attacking infantry had to depend on supporting assault guns, with about 80 in AOK 1. The schwere-Panzerjäger-Abteilung 653 (Heavy Tank Destroyer Battalion 653) was equipped with the monstrous Jagdtiger, which proved virtually useless because of its poor mechanical reliability. At the beginning of *Nordwind*, only two vehicles were at the front due to numerous breakdowns during transit. A few more arrived during the fighting and were attached to the 17. SS-Panzergrenadier-Division. Two flame-thrower tank companies, Panzer-Flamm-Kompanien 352 and 353, were attached to Heeresgruppe G due to the presence of so many Maginot Line bunkers in this sector. There was also a single Jagdpanzer 38(t) tank destroyer battalion under Heeresgruppe G, Panzerjäger-Abteilung 741, committed during Operation *Nordwind*. Besides these separate Panzer units, a very modest number of assault guns were organic to the infantry divisions.

Due to the significant number of Maginot Line fortifications in the battle-zone, AOK 1 was allotted two companies of flame-thrower tanks, equipped with the new Flammpanzer 38(t), a version of the better-known Jagdpanzer 38(t) Hetzer assault gun. This one from Flammpanzer Kompanie.353 was captured while supporting the attacks of the 17. SS-Panzergrenadier-Division near Gros-Réderching against the American 44th Division. (NARA)

The AOK 1 had an attached Volks Artillery Gruppe with a pair of Volks Artillerie Korps and two artillery rocket brigades. While the presence of two artillery corps may seem impressive, in reality these so-called "corps" were in fact reinforced regiments consisting of five medium and heavy artillery batteries and a single heavy anti-tank battery with 88mm guns. The *Volks-Werfer* brigades had been created in mid-December 1944 and each consisted of two regiments with a total of 18 batteries and 108 210mm multi-barrel *Nebelwerfer* rocket launchers. The army-level artillery support was divided between the two main attacks. The Luftwaffe's 9. Flak-Division was in the area and was ordered by Berlin to cooperate, but it was barely able to provide anti-aircraft cover for the massing of forces and it had only a limited capability to provide some additional artillery support during the offensive itself.

The new Panzergrenadier divisions were supposed to be allotted a company of 14 assault guns for organic armored support. One of the more common types in Alsace was the Jagdpanzer 38(t), popularly called the Hetzer, which was a low-cost expedient in place of the older and more durable StuG III. This particular example in Oberhoffen on February 13, 1945 is being examined by a GI from F/142nd Infantry, 36th Division and was probably from Kampfgruppe Luttichau, which fought in the Gambsheim bridgehead. (NARA)

Beyond the principal tactical units, the Wehrmacht in Alsace also had to make do with a remarkably motley assortment of rear-area units that were often rushed into defensive positions to plug gaps. Due to the proximity to the Westwall there were a variety of fortress infantry and fortress artillery units that could be cannibalized for platoons and companies. Besides combat units under tactical command, the Wehrmacht also had rear-area organizations within Germany to manage the recruitment and training of new units such as the Ersatzheer. Wehrkreis V, headquartered in Stuttgart, managed the creation of replacement units with the administrative Division 405 in Alsace. Besides these training units, there were rear area field commands to manage local security including military police, and the *Landes Schützen* units which were regional defense units made up of 45–60-year-old men. Feldkommandant 987 was responsible for the district behind AOK 1, and besides security it was also responsible for organizing rear-area non-combatant troops into "alarm units" which, in theory, could be called up in the event of emergency. In addition to the field commands, major cities had their own *Wehrmacht Kommandant* with defensive responsibilities in time of emergency. In practice, these rear area commands had little defensive value as their modest security forces and military police were pilfered by the tactical commands before the arrival of Allied units, leaving them with only a minimum of military police, unarmed administrative personnel, local construction troops, and fixed flak batteries.

The local defense forces were supposed to be supplemented by *Volksturm* units. The *Volksturm* was a pet project of propaganda minister Goebbels to create a Nazi-party militia with enough political fervor to overcome the lack of training and weapons. While the *Volksturm* showed some promise in

These prisoners captured by the 143rd Infantry, 36th Division in Rohrwiller on February 4, 1945 were fairly typical of German infantry in Alsace, all former members of the Luftwaffe who had been transferred to the army in the autumn of 1944 after so many Luftwaffe squadrons were grounded by a lack of fuel. (NARA)

eastern Germany, its performance in western Germany was pathetic. The *Volkssturm* concept was generally opposed by the regular army as a waste of weapons. Since the local population had already been thoroughly combed for troops, the *Volkssturm* was recruited either from boys too young for conscription, or old men who the army felt had little use in uniform even in the marginally useful *Landes Schützen* battalions. The *Volkssturm* also tended to undermine local civil defense efforts, which had come to depend on this same source of manpower to deal with local emergencies. As an example, a *Volkssturm* battalion raised in Freiburg and dispatched to the front in Alsace had to be recalled to Freiburg in the aftermath of an RAF raid on the city. To further sour the army on the whole idea, the *Volkssturm* were under the command of local political authorities, the local *Kreisleiter*, which made them even less useful in defense.

OPERATION *NORDWIND* (JANUARY 1, 1945)

UNIT	COMMANDER	HEERESGRUPPE G ASSESSMENT
Heeresgruppe G	**Generaloberst Johannes Blaskowitz**	
1. Armee	Generalleutnant Hans von Obstfelder	
25. Panzergrenadier-Division	Oberst Arnold Burmeister	Weakened by recent combat, and equivalent to reinforced regiment in infantry strength
21. Panzer-Division	Generalleutnant Edgar Feuchtinger	Battle-weary but could still field a regimental *Kampfgruppe* in mobile role
6. SS-Gebirgs-Division "Nord"	SS-Gruppenführer Karl Brenner	Excellent but not yet fully in theater
Sturmgruppe I		
XIII SS-Infanterie Korps	**Obergruppenführer-SS Max Simon**	
19. Volksgrenadier-Division	Generalleutnant Walter Wißmath	Battle-weary
36. Volksgrenadier-Division	Generalmajor Helmut Kleikamp	Combat strength equivalent to an infantry regiment, morale good
17. SS-Panzergrenadier-Division	SS-Standartenführer Hans Lingner	Strongest division in army group but its achievements failed to match its strength
Sturmgruppe II		
XC Infanterie Korps	**General der Flieger Erich Petersen**	
559. Volksgrenadier-Division	Generalleutnant Kurt Freiherr von Mühlen	Battle-weary
257. Volksgrenadier-Division	Generalmajor Erich Seidel	Full strength but incomplete training
LXXXIX Armee Korps	**General der Infanterie Gustav Höhne**	
361. Volksgrenadier-Division	Generalmajor Alfred Philippi	Combat strength equal to about two regiments, good morale
245. Infanterie-Division	Generalleutnant Erwin Sander	Completely worn out and used as tactical reserve
256. Volksgrenadier-Division	Generalmajor Gerhard Franz	Good, experienced division equal to three weakened regiments

OPERATION *SONNENWENDE*

Heeresgruppe Oberrhein	**Reichsführer-SS Heinrich Himmler**	
19. Armee	General der Infanterie Siegfried Rasp	
LXIV Armee Korps	**General der Infanterie Hellmut Thumm**	
189. Infanterie-Division	Generalmajor Eduard Zorn	
198. Infanterie-Division	Generalmajor Otto Schiel	
708. Volksgrenadier-Division	Generalmajor Wilhelm Bleckwenn	
16. Infanterie-Division	Generalmajor Alexander Moekel	
LXIII Armee Korps	**General der Infanterie Erich Abraham**	
338. Infanterie-Division	Generalmajor Konrad Barde	
159. Infanterie-Division	Generalmajor Heinrich Bürcky	
716. Infanterie-Division	Generalmajor Wolf Ewert	
269. Infanterie-Division	Generalleutnant Hans Wagner	

US ARMY

The US Army in Alsace was stretched very thinly but was in substantially better shape than the Wehrmacht. Although US infantry divisions were fewer in number than their Wehrmacht counterparts, they were kept closer to authorized strength. For example, in the initial operations in the Vosges in early October, Seventh Army deployed three infantry divisions and a separate regiment with a total of 17,695 infantry, while the opposing AOK 19 had 10–12 divisions but only 13,100 infantry. During the fighting in the Low Vosges in mid-December 1944, the four US infantry divisions involved had 77 percent of their authorized strength in their rifle companies, ranging from a high of 88 percent (103rd Division) to a low of 66 percent (45th Division).

The Seventh Army Divisions fell into roughly three categories: experienced but battle-weary, new but partly battle-experienced, and new and unprepared. Three infantry divisions had served with the Seventh Army since the Operation *Dragoon* landings and had previously served in the Mediterranean theater seeing their combat debut in North Africa (3rd Division), Sicily (45th Division), and Salerno (36th Division). These three were amongst the most battle-tested in the US Army in Europe, and were accustomed to the rigors of mountain combat. Three other divisions had seen their combat debut in Normandy with Haislip's XV Corps (44th and 79th Divisions, and 2e Division Blindée). Two divisions had entered combat recently, the 100th Division which entered combat in the Vosges in early November 1944 and the 103rd Division which entered combat in the Vosges in mid-November. While not having the experience of the veteran divisions, these new divisions had seen enough combat in the autumn fighting that they were prepared for the upcoming German offensive.

SEVENTH US ARMY, 1 JANUARY 1945

XV Corps	**Maj. Gen. Wade Haislip**	
103rd Division	Maj. Gen. Charles Haffner	409th, 410th, 411th Infantry
44th Division	Brig. William Dean	71st, 114th, 324th Infantry
100th Division	Maj. Gen. Withers Burress	397th, 398th, 399th Infantry
Task Force Harris (63rd Div.)	Brig. Gen. Frederick Harris	253rd, 254th, 255th Infantry
VI Corps	**Maj. Gen. Edward Brooks**	
Task Force Hudelson	Col. Daniel Hudelson	94th CRSM, 62nd AIB, 117th CRSM
45th Division	Maj. Gen. Robert Frederick	157th, 179th, 180th Infantry
Task Force Herren (70th Division)	Brig. Gen. Thomas Herren	274th, 275th, 276th Infantry
Task Force Linden (42nd Division)	Brig. Gen. Henry Linden	222nd, 232nd, 242nd Infantry
79th Division	Maj. Gen. Ira Wyche	313th, 314th, 315th Infantry
XXI Corps/SHAEF Reserve	**Maj. Gen. Frank W. Milburn**	
12th Armored Division	Maj. Gen. Roderick Allen	23rd, 43rd, 714th TB; 17th, 56th, 66th AIB
14th Armored Division	Maj. Gen. Albert Smith	25th, 47th, 48th TB; 19th, 62nd, 68th AIB
36th Division	Maj. Gen. John Dahlquist	141st, 142nd, 143rd Infantry
2e Division Blindée	Gen. Div. Jacques Leclerc	12e RC, 12e RCA, 501er RCC, RMT

AIB = Armored Infantry Battalion: CRSM = Cavalry Reconnaissance Squadron (Mechanized)
Infantry = Infantry Regiment: TB = Tank Battalion: (*See below for French abbreviations*)

The sudden extension of the Seventh Army to cover parts of the Third Army sector in late December forced Devers to commit elements of three divisions that had recently arrived in Marseilles: the 42nd, 63rd, and 70th Divisions. While still in the United States, these divisions had been heavily cannibalized for precious riflemen in the spring and summer of 1944 due to shortages in the ETO. These divisions were in such rocky shape that they were not supposed to be deployed until training was complete in July 1945; instead they were hastily shipped to France in December 1944. The 63rd Division had received 1,374 new replacements since the autumn while the 70th had received a whopping 3,871 new troops; neither division had completed the standard 12-week large-scale maneuver phase of training. To make matters worse, none arrived intact with all its component elements. Due to the desperate need for infantry, Devers ordered the infantry regiments of these two divisions forward. Since they were not ready to participate in the fighting as divisions, they were temporarily deployed as task forces, and subordinated to more experienced divisions. Typically, their component regiments were thrown into combat separately. These formations were by far the weakest and least prepared of the US infantry units to take part in Operation *Nordwind*, and were derisively referred to as "American *Volksturm* Grenadiers" by some of the more experienced US infantry units. While the three late-arriving American infantry divisions were of poor quality compared with the rest of Seventh Army, they were certainly no worse than the vast majority of the Wehrmacht infantry taking part in Operation *Nordwind*.

The US infantry formations had numerous advantages over their German opponents in terms of armored and artillery support. In contrast to the German infantry divisions, which were lucky to have a company of 14 assault guns, all US infantry divisions had a tank battalion and a tank destroyer battalion attached. The tank battalions were organized in a standardized fashion with three companies of M4 (Sherman) medium tanks and a company of M5A1 (Stuart) light tanks. The tank destroyer battalions were mainly equipped with the M10 3in. GMC (gun motor carriage) and one battalion had the new M36 90mm GMC, the most powerful tank destroyer in service at the time. Only a single battalion was equipped with the inferior towed 3in. guns. The newly arrived 827th Tank Destroyer Battalion (Colored) had the new M18 76mm GMC; this was one of a small number of segregated

Unlike the VI Corps divisions, which came into France from the Mediterranean theater, the 44th Division was one of three XV Corps units that landed in Normandy and joined the Seventh Army in Lorraine in the autumn after taking part in Patton's race to the Seine. During Operation *Nordwind*, the division was on the Seventh Army's left flank and helped defeat the assault by the 17. SS-Panzergrenadier Division. Here, the divisional commander, Brig. Gen. William Dean, inspects a 57mm anti-tank gun position at the front lines near Herbitzheim on January 24, 1945. Dean is better known as the commander of the 24th Infantry Division in Korea in 1950, when he won the Medal of Honor for conspicuous bravery in trying to stem a North Korean attack. (NARA)

African-American units in the Seventh Army. The US infantry divisions enjoyed significantly better artillery support than the Wehrmacht both in terms of better divisional artillery, more corps artillery, a far more ample supply of ammunition, and better radio-coordinated fire direction.

SEVENTH ARMY, DIVISIONAL ARMOR ATTACHMENTS – JANUARY 1, 1945

Infantry Division	Tank Bn.	Tank Destroyer Bn.
3rd	756th	601st (M10 3in. GMC)
36th	753rd	636th (M10 3in. GMC)
44th	749th	776th (M36 90mm GMC)
45th	191st	645th (M10 3in. GMC)
79th	781st	813th (M10 3in. GMC)
100th		824th (towed 3in.)

In terms of armor, the Seventh Army could count on three armored divisions compared with the Wehrmacht's one Panzer and two *Panzergrenadier* divisions. The American and French units were substantially better equipped and near full strength. Of the three Allied divisions, the French 2e Division Blindée was by far the most experienced. The 14th Armored Division had been committed to small-scale action in November 1944 but was not yet fully seasoned. Devers was not happy with its progress, but at least it had some combat exposure. The 12th Armored Division had only recently arrived in theater and was completely inexperienced, as would become painfully apparent in the January fighting. As of the second week of January 1945, the Seventh Army had 704 medium tanks of which 167 were M4A3 (76mm), 50 were M4 (105mm), and the rest were the standard 75mm versions. There were also 376 light tanks, mostly the M5 and M5A1 in US units and the M3A3 with the French 2e Division Blindée. The 6th Army Group as a whole had substantial armored forces when the French 1ère Armée and separate tank battalions are considered. As of mid-December 1944, the 6th Army Group had 1,131 Sherman medium tanks, 697 light tanks, and 504 self-propelled tank destroyers.

The other extemporized unit deployed by Seventh Army in late December was Task Force Hudelson, which was created to cover the gap between XV and VI Corps immediately south of Bitche. This consisted of three units from the 14th Armored Division: the 94th Cavalry Squadron, 62nd Armored Infantry Battalion, and 400th Armored Field Artillery Battalion, plus the Seventh Army's reconnaissance unit, the 117th Cavalry Squadron, and a variety of supporting engineer and other units. This hastily created unit was assigned to screen a wide 15-mile (24km) stretch of the Low Vosges from Bitche to Drachenbronn, a heavily forested and mountainous sector which Patch considered the easiest to defend. While this later proved to be true, this sector also happened to be the focus of one of the two major German thrusts and Task Force Hudelson would initially be outnumbered by a ratio of more than ten to one.

6th Army Group's air support was not especially generous by US standards although certainly more extensive than the non-existent Luftwaffe support of Heeresgruppe G. The 1st Tactical Air Force (Provisional) was created in October 1944 to coordinate the American XII Tactical Air Command with the French 1er Corps Aérien Français. The XII TAC included four P-47 fighter-bomber groups, each numbering about 36 aircraft, and two B-26 medium bomber groups. The French units were in the process of being re-equipped from a hodgepodge of British and American cast-offs and eventually included three P-47 and two B-26 *escadres* (groups).

FRENCH ARMY

The Free French Army was in the midst of transition in the autumn of 1944 and faced some unique problems. The first two divisions of de Gaulle's Free French movement were the 1ère Division Motorisée d'Infanterie (1re DMI) raised with British help, and the 2e Division Blindée (an armored division) raised with US support. Both divisions relied heavily on volunteers, especially from the French colonies in North Africa. The remainder of the divisions were created out of the former Vichy Army of Africa, which switched sides after the November 1942 Allied invasion of French North Africa. The matter of recreating the French army was taken over by the United States due to the bitter relations between Britain and France after the 1940 debacle and the subsequent British sinking of the French fleet. Under the Anfa Plan approved by President Franklin Roosevelt during the Casablanca conference in January 1943, the US pledged to raise and equip nine infantry and three armored divisions.

Four French infantry divisions were committed to Italy under Général Alphonse Juin with the Corps Expéditionnaire Français (CEF) and fought with considerable distinction in the tough mountain fighting to the east of Monte Cassino in early 1944. In the meantime, Gén. Jean de Lattre de Tassigny raised three more divisions, the 1ère and 5e Divisions Blindées and the 9e Division d'Infanterie Coloniale (DIC). De Gaulle wanted all French units committed to the liberation of France, so the CEF was extracted from Italy and amalgamated with de Lattre's forces, which became the 1ère Armée (First Army) alongside Patch's US Seventh Army. With the exception of the 1ère DMI, which was equipped by the British, the Free French units raised in North Africa in 1943/44 were armed and equipped by the US Army and followed US organizational patterns while at the same time retaining distinctly French regimental lineage. This can lead to some confusion as the infantry divisions bore the traditional French designations of mountain division, colonial division and so on while in fact they all had the same organization; tank units retained their regimental designations though in fact they followed US tank battalion organization.

The new divisions were formed from a mixture of sources, in some cases absorbing units from the Army of Africa, and in other cases being formed

The colonial units of the French army still relied heavily on horses and mules for transport, which were archaic but very effective in the Vosges, as can be seen here with a supply column of the veteran 3e Division d'Infanterie Algérienne in the hills near Rupt on October 4, 1944. (NARA)

through conscription in the North African colonies. French conscription policy recognized two categories, "*européens*" and "*indigènes*", referring to French settlers in North Africa and the indigenous Algerian, Tunisian, and Moroccan population. Sub-Saharan colonial troops were usually designated as "*sénégalais*" though in fact they came from a variety of French colonies including Madagascar, the Ivory Coast, and Senegal. The mobilization brought in more "*indigènes*" than French, amounting to 105,700 by the end of 1944 compared with 48,400 French settlers.

The colonial troops had fought with distinction in both Italy and in the summer and early autumn fighting in France, but there was growing political pressure to reorganize the French army with more troops from metropolitan France. The colonial units had borne an unfair and heavy burden from 1942 to 1944, suffering considerable losses amongst their rifle companies. There was resistance in the colonies to dispatching large additional levies after the liberation of most of metropolitan France in the summer of 1944. Casualties amongst experienced French colonial officers had also been high, and the hardened colonial troops were often surly and uncooperative under the direction of green French officers who knew little of their language or customs. Furthermore, there were some concerns that the African troops, and especially the Senegalese units, would have a hard time coping with the winter conditions in Alsace.

The obvious sources for fresh troops were the numerous FFI (Forces Françaises de l'intérieur) resistance units, which had grown wildly in number in 1944. De Gaulle's government was insistent on amalgamating these units into the regular army, as there was some concern that they would be used as political militias to impose their own parties in power in various localities; the groups were not well disciplined and had been a source of civil disorder after the liberation. This process began in the summer of 1944 and many of the newly formed units were deployed in the sieges at the Atlantic ports still in German hands such as Lorient, St Nazaire, and Royan. Only one of the FFI divisions, the 10e Division d'Infanterie under Général Bilotte, was committed to the fighting in Alsace.

"Les indigènes," France's North African colonial troops, bore the brunt of the infantry fighting in Alsace in the autumn and winter of 1944/45. These are Algerian troops of the experienced but weary 3e Division d'Infanterie Algérienne, which had fought in Italy in 1943/44, then again in southern France and Alsace in 1944/45. (NARA)

To relieve the excessive dependence on France's North African colonies for the supply of troops, the 1ère Armée began a process of "whitening" in the autumn of 1944, first reinforcing the colonial regiments with supplementary units formed from FFI resistance units, then substituting FFI troops for colonial troops in the regular regiments. (NARA)

By the end of October 1944, the 1ère Armée had already absorbed about 60,000 FFI troops into its ranks, in many cases by attaching FFI battalions as a supplementary fourth battalion to existing infantry regiments. In addition, a process had begun to integrate individual FFI members and volunteers into the Army. The process of "*blanchisement*" (whitening) of the 1ère Armée continued through most of the autumn. The 1ère Division de Marche d'Infanterie (DMI) received about 6,000 FFI troops, while the 9e DIC was reorganized first through the adoption of FFI sub-units, then by direct replacement of its 9,200 Senegalese troops. The three North African mountain divisions (2e, 3e, and 4e DIA) were kept at strength by replacing one regiment in each division with FFI troops. The process was a prolonged and complicated affair as the French commanders did not want to substitute

The US supply of arms to the rejuvenated French Army was not limitless, so de Gaulle's government made efforts to develop its own sources, especially the use of refurbished arms from the 1940 arsenals left behind by the Wehrmacht during its retreat from France in 1944. A total of 72 of the 155mm Grande Puissance Filloux (GPF) guns were in service with the 1ère Armée by 1945, and this battery is seen in action during the reduction of the Colmar Pocket in February 1945. (NARA)

poorly trained and ill-disciplined FFI troops for tough and well-disciplined North African troops in the midst of combat operations. Since the US was reluctant to supply numerous ad hoc 1ère Armée units with weapons, supplies, and equipments, the French army attempted to generate equipment through French channels such as the use of 1940 French equipment left behind by the Germans. By 1945, some 137,000 FFI troops were absorbed into the 1ère Armée. Many of the colonial troops replaced in the infantry divisions were reassigned to other areas, such as the new units assigned to the French–Italian border.

De Lattre continually complained to Devers about the imbalance in supplies between the lavishly equipped Seventh Army and the ragtag 1ère Armée. While the US did give priority to the Seventh Army in some areas, the problem was partly the result of French decisions to focus on the combat elements of the 1ère Armée at the expense of logistical support. Its logistics agency, Base 901, numbered 29,000 troops when a comparable US organization would have numbered 112,000 to support the army's eight divisions.

To complicate matters further, de Gaulle had been pressing Eisenhower to divert some of de Lattre's forces to help clear the Gironde estuary on the approaches to the port of Bordeaux. The Allies had priority for ports on the Atlantic, and de Gaulle wanted the port freed from the German garrisons to provide a port for French civil use. This effort was codenamed Operation *Liberty*, and Devers was instructed to free the 1ère DMI and 1ère Division Blindée for this operation in late 1944. Not only did he object to this diversion, but de Lattre and his corps commanders continued to drag their feet since it would disrupt their combat operations in the Belfort Gap.

1ère ARMÉE, LATE JANUARY 1945*

1ère Armée Française	Gén. Jean de Lattre de Tassigny	
1er Corps d'Armée	**Gén. Antoine Béthouart**	
1ère DMI (Division de Marche d'Infanterie)	Gén. Diego Brosset,	1er BI, 2e BI, 4e BI, 1er RA
2e DB (Division Blindée)	Gén. Jacques Leclerc	12e RC, 12e RCA, 501 er RCC, RMT
3e DIA (Division d'Infanterie Algériénne)	Gén. Augustin Guillaume	3e RTA, 7e RTA, 4e RTT, 67e RAA
2e Corps d'Armée	**Gén. Joseph de Goislard de Monsabert**	
1ère DB (Division Blindée)	Gén. Aimé Sudré	2e RC, 2e RCA, 5e RCA, 1er DBZ, 68e RAA
9e DIC (Division d'Infanterie Coloniale)	Gén. Joseph Magnan	4e RTS, 6e RTS, 13 RTS, RACM
2e DIM (Division d'Infanterie Marocaine)	Gén. Marcel Carpentier	4e RTM, 5e RTM, 8e RTM, 63e RAA
4e DMM (Division Marocaine de Montagne)	Gén. René de Hesdin	1er RTM, 2e RTM, 6e RTM, 69e RAM
5e Division Blindée	Gén. Henri de Vernejoul	1er RC, 1er RCA, 6e RCA, RMLE, 62e RAA
10e Division d'Infanterie	Gén. Pierre Bilotte	5e RI, 24e RI, 46e RI, 32e RA

*Does not include attached US Army XXI Corps

BI = Brigade d'Infanterie; DBZ = Demi-Brigade de zouaves; RA = Régiment d'artillerie; RAA = Régiment d'artillerie d'Afrique; RACM = Régiment d'artillerie colonial du Maroc; RAM = Régiment d'artillerie marocaine; RC = Régiment Cuirassiers; RCA = Régiment de Chasseurs d'Afrique; RCC = Régiment de chars de combat; RFM = Régiment de Fusiliers-Marins; RI = Régiment d'infanterie; RMLE = Régiment de marche de la Légion Etrangère; RMT = Régiment de marche du Tchad; RTA = Régiment de tirailleurs algériens; RTM = Régiment de tirailleurs marocains; RTS = Régiment de tirailleurs sénégalais; RTT = Régiment de tirailleurs tunisiens

THE CAMPAIGN

OPERATION *NORDWIND*

The main *Nordwind* attack by the 17. SS-Panzergrenadier-Division in the Saar Valley went badly from the start. On January 5, 1945, a few of the monstrous Jagdtigers from schwere-Panzerjäger-Abteilung 654, accompanied by a captured M4 medium tank, supported the attack near Rimling. An M36 90mm GMC from the 776th Tank Destroyer Battalion carefully moved into a flanking position and at a range of 900m, put a single armor-piercing round into the side of Jagdtiger number 134, causing an internal ammunition fire which destroyed the vehicle in a catastrophic explosion, blowing off the superstructure sides. (NARA)

"German offensive began on Seventh Army front about 0030am. Krauts were howling drunk. Murdered them." So wrote the Seventh Army chief of staff, Brigadier-General Arthur White in his diary.

The *Nordwind* offensive began on New Year's Eve, a half-hour before midnight. With the ground covered in most areas with a foot of snow, it took the German units some time to move up to the front lines, and so most attacks did not begin until midnight. More often than not, American accounts recall that the German soldiers attacked drunk, screaming and shouting as they advanced into their fire.

The main assault by Sturmgruppe 1, Simon's 13. SS-AK with the 17. SS-Panzergrenadier-Division and the 36. Volksgrenadier-Division, ran into the deep defenses of the 44th and 100th Infantry Divisions in the Saar Valley. A narrow penetration was made towards Rimling and Achen, but in general, the attack in this sector was stopped dead in its tracks with heavy casualties. Sturmgruppe 1 had very little success in bringing up its armored support due to the poor road conditions and the weather. On the night of January 3 the offensive in this sector was halted.

Operation *Nordwind*, December 31, 1944 to January 20, 1945

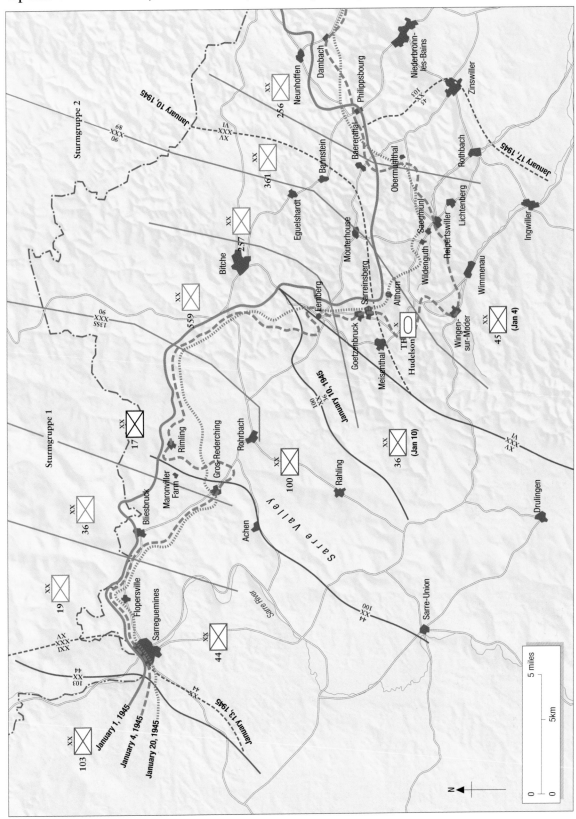

The target for the main German thrust was Task Force Hudelson south of Bitche, a weak cavalry screen with little hope of even delaying the onrush of a German infantry corps. These are survivors from the 117th Cavalry Squadron, the Seventh Army's reconnaissance element, seen a month later near the Gambsheim bridgehead. (NARA)

More succccess was gained by Sturmgruppe 2, the four divisions of Petersen's 90. AK and Höhne's 89. AK out of the Bitche fortified area. This section of the Low Vosges was mountainous and forested, and so poorly suited for attack that Patch had left it screened by the entirely inadequate Task Force Hudelson. As a result, the German advance confronted little or no opposition. Having been forbidden to conduct reconnaissance before the attack, as a result several of the newly arrived divisions stumbled around in the difficult terrain. The 361. Volksgrenadier-Division showed the most progress, as it had retreated through the area weeks before and so at least had some sense of the terrain. These corps ploddingly advanced about ten miles (16km) during the course of the next four days.

As it became clear that the Germans were making a major attempt to push through the Low Vosges, Brooks and the VI Corps began to shuffle forces to cover the yawning gap left by Task Force Hudelson. Brooks tried to plug up various exits out of the mountains along the Moder River by filling the narrow mountain passes with infantry regiments stripped from other sectors of the front. This created a confusing checkerboard of units from different commands; the 45th Division pushed two of its regiments into the gap, reinforced with a regiment from Task Force Herren (70th Division) and a regiment from the 79th Division. Within a few days, Major-General Frederick of the 45th Division was commanding eight regiments instead of his usual three, half of which had never seen combat.

Realizing that the Saar assault by Sturmgruppe 1 had failed, Blaskowitz and Obstfelder decided to reinforce success and try to continue the momentum in the Bitche sector instead. While Patch and Brooks were hastily reinforcing the Vosges mountain defenses, Blaskowitz was trying to push new units south from Bitche into the mountains. The most important source of German reinforcements was the 6. SS-Gebirgsdivision "Nord," which began arriving in bits and pieces in the days after New Year. This division was undoubtedly the best in the theater and was well accustomed to winter mountain warfare. The first of its regiments to arrive was SS-Gebirgsregiment 12, which proceeded south through the 257. Volksgrenadier-Division and 361. Volksgrenadier-Division towards the hamlets of Wingen-sur-Moder and Wimmenau around midnight of January 2/3. Two of its battalions managed to infiltrate through scattered elements of the 179th Infantry and stormed into Wingen-sur-Moder on the morning of January 4, capturing the battalion headquarters of 1/179th Infantry. Infantry companies under the 45th Division began counterattacks against Wingen that afternoon, but the attacks were far too small to rout the 725 sturdy troops in the town; the US commanders were under the impression that the town had been occupied by only 50 Germans. Although Wingen was the deepest penetration made during Operation *Nordwind*, the German troops were out of touch with headquarters after losing their radio truck. The 45th Division was conducting counterattacks all around Wingen, which made reinforcement or relief

The deepest German penetration during the initial phase of Operation *Nordwind* was at the town of Wingen-sur-Moder, captured by elements of SS-Gebirgs-Regiment 12. This view of the town was taken on January 6, the final day of the fighting, when elements of Task Force Herren were attacking the town again. (NARA)

TOP

A US Army machine-gun team armed with a water-cooled .30-cal. machine gun is seen at a window opening during the fighting in Wingen-sur-Moder on January 6, 1945. (NARA)

BOTTOM

A GI escorts prisoners from SS-Gebirgs-Regiment 12 as the defenses began to collapse on January 6, 1945 in Wingen-sur-Moder. (NARA)

impossible even had Blaskowitz and Obstfelder had a better appreciation of the situation. An attack on Wingen by the inexperienced 276th Infantry on January 5 failed to recapture the town but the German troops were now surrounded with little hope of relief. In view of the hopeless situation, the surviving German forces were authorized to withdraw and did so after dark on the night of January 6/7, with only 205 out of the original 800-man force

TOP
An M4A3 (76mm) medium tank of Company B, 781st Tank Battalion advances past a column of destroyed US vehicles on January 7 while supporting the 274th Infantry during its clean-up operations inside Wingen-sur-Moder, which had been abandoned by SS-Gebirgs-Regiment 12 the night before. (NARA)

BOTTOM
The SS-Gebirgs-Regiment 12 also captured the village of Wimmenau near Wingen, later retaken by the 180th Infantry. These are two young prisoners captured in the town. (NARA)

escaping. The recapture of Wingen marked the end of the first phase of Operation *Nordwind*. The 89. AK estimated it had suffered about 2,500 casualties in the fighting and casualties in the neighboring corps were probably worse.

American assessments of the *Nordwind* attack focused on its poor execution. A senior staff officer from Berlin visited Blaskowitz's headquarters on January 6/7 and concluded that: "The evident waning fighting strength of our own troops is explicable not only by the brevity and insufficiency of training time together in the Reserve Army, but also the absence of old reliable NCOs and competent battalion and company officers. A prerequisite for any new assault would be personnel replacements. Also the artillery has proven to be insufficient, likewise its forward observers and their radio equipment."

US UNITS
45th Division

179th Infantry Regiment
1 HQ, 1/179th Infantry
2 3/179th Infantry

274th Infantry Regiment
3 E/274th Infantry
4 F/274th Infantry
5 G/274th Infantry

276th Infantry Regiment
6 1/276th Infantry
7 A/276th Infantry
8 B/276th Infantry
9 C/276th Infantry
10 3/276th Infantry
11 I/276th Infantry

781st Tank Battalion
12 B/781st Tank Battalion

45 FEDERICK

2 HOCHBERG

▼ EVENTS

1 During the pre-dawn hours of January 4, the SS-Gebirgsregiment.12 *Kampfgruppe* approaches Wingen-sur-Moder over the hills to the north via the Fischback creek. Two companies from I.Battalion head west towards Heideneck while the remainder of the force heads into the town itself.

2 The German forces overwhelm the headquarters of the 1/179th Infantry located in Hotel Wenk.

3 In the afternoon and evening of January 4, elements of the 2/276th Infantry approach Wingen down the main road but are stopped short of D'Hutt. Two companies of II/274th Infantry make another approach south of the railroad but are also stopped.

4 On January 5, 3/276th Infantry fights its way as far as the railroad overpass on the west side of the town, but is forced to withdraw due to losses.

5 The 2/274th Infantry reorients its attacks from the southwest of town and stages company-sized attacks around noon and mid-afternoon of January 5. In the evening, Kampfgruppe Wingen finally makes contact with higher headquarters and is authorized to withdraw.

6 Co. B, 781st Tank Battalion provides fire support for the attacks from the Kirchberg Heights south of the town.

7 The 3/276th Infantry continues its attempts to push into the town via the main road on January 6, but is halted again short of D'Hutt.

8 The 2/274th Infantry again presses its attacks into the town from the southwest and G/274th Infantry fights its way close to the St Felix Catholic Church near the town center.

9 The penetration by the US infantry into the town center leads to a night counterattack by Kampfgruppe Wingen's sole reserve, the pioneer platoon of the 3rd Battalion.

10 The 2/274th Infantry again renews its attacks into the town on January 7. German casualties are now nearing a critical point, and the regiment has been authorized to withdraw.

11 In the pre-dawn hours, starting at around 0200hrs on January 8, the survivors of Kampfgruppe Wingen (about 205 of the original 800 troops) manage to withdraw up a mountain road towards Kohlhutte.

WINGEN-SUR-MODER: JANUARY 4–8, 1945

The 6. SS-Gebirgsjäger-Division storms Wingen-sur-Moder, but is driven back by the US 45th Division.

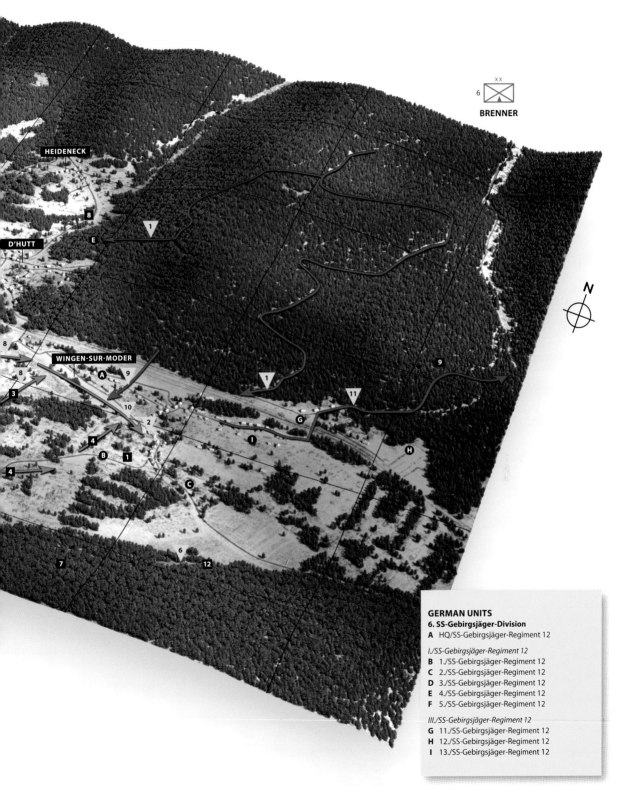

BRENNER

HEIDENECK

D'HUTT

WINGEN-SUR-MODER

N

GERMAN UNITS
6. SS-Gebirgsjäger-Division
A   HQ/SS-Gebirgsjäger-Regiment 12

I./SS-Gebirgsjäger-Regiment 12
B   1./SS-Gebirgsjäger-Regiment 12
C   2./SS-Gebirgsjäger-Regiment 12
D   3./SS-Gebirgsjäger-Regiment 12
E   4./SS-Gebirgsjäger-Regiment 12
F   5./SS-Gebirgsjäger-Regiment 12

III./SS-Gebirgsjäger-Regiment 12
G   11./SS-Gebirgsjäger-Regiment 12
H   12./SS-Gebirgsjäger-Regiment 12
I   13./SS-Gebirgsjäger-Regiment 12

51

THE STRASBOURG CONTROVERSY

After his December 27 meeting in Paris with Eisenhower, Devers wrote in his diary: "I was impressed with the idea that Strasbourg and Mulhouse should be held if at all possible." Eisenhower's staff recalled otherwise and Ike thought he had made clear that Strasbourg would be abandoned. Devers and the Seventh Army were not keen on withdrawing from the Alsatian plain as they felt that the existing defensive positions were better than the ones offered by withdrawing. Devers was especially reluctant to retreat from Hagenau since the defenses were firmly planted in Maginot Line fortifications with extensive barbed wire and minefields; SHAEF on the other hand thought the disposition of the divisions was of "some concern" as they "were liable to be severely handled or cut off in the event of a successful enemy penetration south towards Sarrebourg or north from the Colmar Pocket." Although the Hagenau front might have looked precarious on a map, Devers and Patch were well aware of the actual conditions on the ground and were skeptical of a threat in this sector; the Germans concurred with their viewpoint and initially had rejected an attack in this sector precisely because of its defensive advantages.

In the event, the main Seventh Army effort in late December was in extending its lines to cover the gap left by the withdrawal of Patton's corps as well as preparing for the expected German offensive in the Saar Valley. On the afternoon of January 1 following the opening of the German attack, Devers received a blistering phone call from Eisenhower's chief of staff, General Walter Bedell Smith, who complained that Seventh Army was disobeying orders and not falling back to the Vosges. Devers responded that he was doing so, but that it would take time in view of the circumstances on the ground. In a meeting with Patch later in the afternoon, Devers conceded that Strasbourg would have to be abandoned and that the objective would be to withdraw to the Vosges by January 5. Word of the Strasbourg withdrawal had been conveyed to French liaison officers, and that evening Général Touzet du Vigier visited Devers with a letter from de Gaulle. The French government demanded that Strasbourg remained in Allied hands and the French army planned to turn the city into another Stalingrad before letting the Germans have it; du Vigier had been appointed to head the Strasbourg defense. Devers appreciated the French position, and instructed his chief of staff, Major-General Barr, to fly to Paris on January 2 with du Vigier to clarify instructions from Eisenhower; de Gaulle had already told Gén. Juin to visit Bedell Smith and reiterate their firm position.

The French government was absolutely adamant about the retention of Strasbourg. Alsace had long been a bone of contention between Germany and France and had already changed hands four times in the past century; Strasbourg was its capital and the symbol of Alsace for both countries. Aside from being a matter of prestige, the French had begun rounding up Germans in the city after its liberation on November 23, and there was some concern that if the city fell back into German hands, there would be bloody reprisals against French civilians. The Germans had adopted a scorched earth policy in parts of Alsace in November, and the only reasons that this had not already occurred in Strasbourg was that the city had fallen so quickly; the German commander of Strasbourg had been sentenced to death *in absentia* for his failure to demolish the city. De Gaulle personally intervened with both Roosevelt and Churchill to reverse Eisenhower's rash decision.

Generalmajor Franz Vaterodt, the Wehrmacht Kommandant of Strasbourg, had been ordered to demolish Strasbourg before its capture but had neither the means nor the inclination to do so. Hitler's destructive plans were a major source of anxiety to the French government over the city's fate in January 1945. Vaterodt is seen here to the left with Major R. McIntire from Seventh US Army HQ and Vaterodt's chief of staff, Oberst Willi Kaiser. (NARA)

The political firestorm brewing over Strasbourg came to a head on January 3 during a special meeting in Paris of Eisenhower, de Gaulle, and Juin, along with their staffs; Winston Churchill personally attended as a mediator. De Gaulle described the decision as a potential "national disaster." Eisenhower insisted his orders would stand, and unfairly blamed the situation on the failure of the 1ère Armée to clear out the Colmar Pocket. Infuriated by Eisenhower's charges, de Gaulle threatened to withdraw French forces from SHAEF command and Juin hinted that France might deny the Allies the use of the French railroad network. Eisenhower finally appreciated the depth of the French concern over Strasbourg and backed down, earning Churchill's praise for defusing the escalating acrimony. Major-General Barr, who had attended the meeting, informed Devers of the change of policy almost immediately, which was formally confirmed in a top secret communiqué on January 7 which stated that "Having regard to the political and moral significance of the Strasbourg area, you will defend it as strongly as possible consistent with the overriding necessity for maintaining the integrity of your forces which will not be jeopardized." The Strasbourg controversy had become a major political headache for Eisenhower due to his ill-conceived decision to abandon the city. In the event, it benefited Devers in his relations with the 1ère Armée. His advocacy of retaining Strasbourg, done for sound military reasons as well as his appreciation of the French predicament, was deeply appreciated by de Lattre as well as the senior French commanders.

SHIFTING THE *SCHWERPUNKT*

The poor results from the initial phase of Operation *Nordwind* left Blaskowitz in a quandary about what to do next. The plan had been to exploit the anticipated breakthrough in the Saar Valley with Operation *Zahnarzt*, a thrust by the Panzer reserve into the relatively open country west of the Low Vosges. In view of the failure of Simon's 13. SS-Korps to even dent the heavy US defenses, *Zahnarzt* was abandoned. Since the terrain south

AIR STRIKE ON STRASBOURG, JANUARY 13, 1945 (pp. 54–55)

The Luftwaffe was almost invisible in the skies over Alsace in January 1945, except for mysterious hit-and-run raids by jet fighters. These left some impression on American troops who recalled their unusual sound and speed, but their poor bombing accuracy created little concern. The culprits were the Me-262A-2a fighter-bombers **(1)** of I./KG51 "Edelweiss," the first Luftwaffe Gruppe converted to use the new jet bombers in the summer of 1944. The new jet was on the bleeding edge of technology and the pilots paid the price with no fewer than six aircraft being lost shortly after takeoff due to pernicious engine shortcomings that would plague its career.

This bomber unit had been ordered by Hitler not to fly below 4,000m (13,000ft) for fear that one of the secret aircraft would be lost over Allied lines, and as a result, they tended to use cluster bombs in their initial operations which were neither accurate nor especially effective. The order was finally cancelled in December 1944 in time for operations over the Ardennes where the group took an active if not notably successful role. On January 10–14, the jets were ordered into action in the Strasbourg region. The usual tactic was to put the aircraft into a shallow dive from an altitude of 4,000m and release the

bombs no lower than 1,000m; when used with Revi sights the tactic was supposed to offer 35–40m accuracy but this was under ideal conditions and not the harsh winter conditions of Alsace. On the return flight to base, the aircraft would often attack any visible Allied bombers. During the Strasbourg missions, three of the aircraft were lost, two to fighters patrolling near their base and one to anti-aircraft fire. There was another spurt of attack missions over Alsace in early February 1945 during the reduction of the Colmar Pocket, ending with nearly two dozen sorties on February 8.

The fighter-bomber version of the Me-262 was its most controversial type, largely forced on the Luftwaffe by Hitler. It was a thoroughbred being wasted as a plow-horse, with exceptional speed but mediocre payload or accuracy. The aircraft had originally been designed as a fighter and lacked a dedicated bomb-aiming system. While the regular fighter version of the aircraft was armed with four 30mm cannon, on the Me-262A-2a it was reduced to two cannon **(2)**. Pylons were fitted under the nose, and the aircraft would typically carry a pair of 250kg bombs **(3)**.

of Bitche was so unfavorable for Panzers, by January 9 Blaskowitz urged a shift of the *Schwerpunkt* (main effort) to the east with 21. Panzer-Division and 25. Panzergrenadier-Division debouching out of the Vosges near Rothbach and into the open country east of Hagenau. Other developments along the Rhine complicated this plan.

With AOK 19 now independent of Heeresgruppe G and under Himmler's control, planning for operations around Strasbourg took place entirely independently of Heeresegruppe G. Heeresgruppe Oberrhein had been reporting to Berlin that US forces were pulling out of the area north of Strasbourg; the area was considered a quiet section of the front and had been entrusted to a thin screen of the green troops of Task Force Linden under the direction of the 79th Division, with the French 3e Division d'Infanterie Algérienne moving to take control of the northern suburbs of Strasbourg on January 5. Himmler saw this as a chance to carry out the promised supporting mission for Operation *Nordwind*, and ordered AOK 19 in the Colmar Pocket to strike towards the south of Strasbourg in an operation codenamed *Sonnenwende* (Winter Solstice). Forces on the east bank of the Rhine under Bach's 14. SS-Korps were assigned a similar mission north of Strasbourg. The aim of both attacks was to recapture Strasbourg, which Himmler intended to be a present for Hitler on the 12th anniversary of his accession to power on January 30. In the event, the attacks around Strasbourg were weak and badly coordinated and led in unexpected directions.

Rather than wait for the anticipated *Sonnenwende* attack out of the Colmar Pocket, on January 4 Berlin ordered an immediate river crossing operation by 14. SS-Korps. The forces used for the operation were an incredibly ragtag assortment, even by 1945 Wehrmacht standards. The force was under the direction of Generalmajor Gerhard Hüther's 553. Volksgrenadier-Division, which had been crushed in the Saverne Gap in November. The division was supposed to be withdrawn to Stuttgart to rebuild, but instead was sent back to the Rhine front in December to hold the east bank of the river while rebuilding. The division had only one of its three infantry regiments (Grenadier-Regiment 1119) anywhere near to full strength and it was hastily reinforced using personnel and troops from the NCO training school at Esslingen. The neighboring 405. Division training division transferred one of its improvised regiments, Regiment Marbach, and SS-Polizei-Regiment 2 was also attached. The division had only a single surviving artillery battery so reinforcements were scoured from eight batteries of fortress artillery using an assortment of captured foreign field guns. The corps commander, Erich von dem Bach-Zelewski, was well aware that such a formation had no offensive power at all, and using Himmler's influence he scraped together an improvised Panzer formation, Jagdpanzer-Abteilung von Lüttichau. This unit had originally been slapped together in late November 1944, and consisted of Hauptman Hannibal von Lüttichau's Pz.Kpfw IV company from II./Panzer-Regiment 2, two companies of Nashorn tank destroyers, and three companies of Jagdpanzer 38(t) Hetzer assault guns.

The Gambsheim bridgehead was established in the early morning hours of January 5 against little opposition. The initial landings were conducted by infantry using rubber assault boats, and once the bridgehead was secured, they were followed by 8-tonne ferries and eventually a 70-tonne Rhine ferry for the armored vehicles. After establishing a perimeter around Gambsheim, Lüttichau's *Kampfgruppe* began sending Panzers out to the neighboring towns of Herrlisheim and Offendorf. The towns were then secured with

Operation *Sonnenwende*, January 5–12, 1945

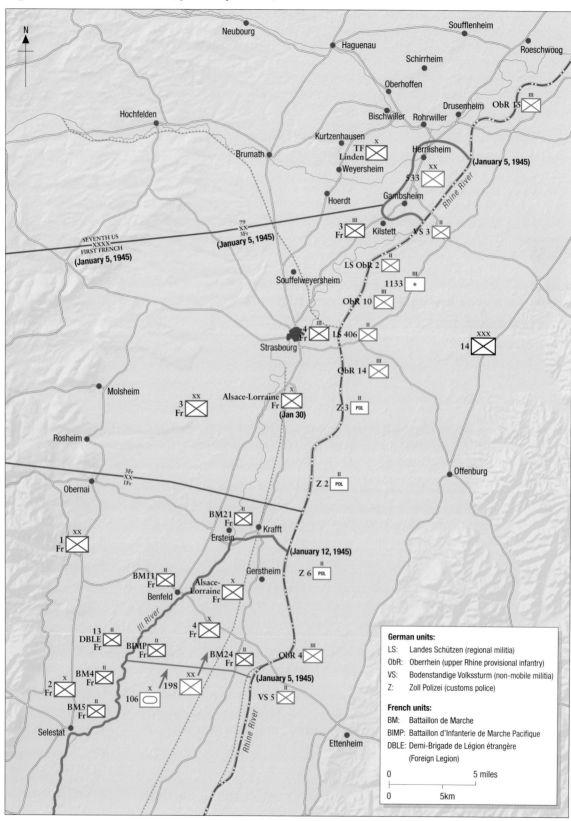

N

Soufflenheim

Neubourg

Roeschwoog

Haguenau

Schirrheim

Oberhoffen

ObR 15 | III

Drusenheim

Hochfelden

Bischwiller · Rohrwiller

(January 5, 1945)

Kurtzenhausen

Brumath

Herrlisheim

TF | X
Linden

533 | XX

Weyersheim

Gambsheim

Hoerdt

Rhine River

79 | XX | 3Fr
(January 5, 1945)

3 | III
Fr | Kilstett

VS 3 | II

SEVENTH US
XXXX
FIRST FRENCH
(January 5, 1945)

LS ObR 2 | II

Souffelweyersheim

1133 | III

ObR 10 | III

4 | III
Fr | LS 406 | II

14 | XXX

Strasbourg

ObR 14 | III

Molsheim

3 | XX
Fr

Alsace-Lorraine | X
Fr
(Jan 30)

Z 3 | POL | II

Offenburg

Rosheim

3Fr
XX
1Fr

Obernai

Z 2 | POL | II

BM21 | II
Fr

1 | XX
Fr

Krafft

Erstein

(January 12, 1945)

Z 6 | POL | II

BM11 | II
Fr

Gerstheim

Benfeld

Alsace-
Lorraine | X
Fr

Ill River

13 | II
DBLE
Fr

4 | X
Fr

BIMP | II
Fr

BM24 | II
Fr

ObR 4 | III

2 | X
Fr

BM4 | II
Fr

198 | XX

(January 5, 1945)

106 | X

VS 5 | III

BM5 | II
Fr

Selestat

Ettenheim

Rhine River

German units:
LS: Landes Schützen (regional militia)
ObR: Oberrhein (upper Rhine provisional infantry)
VS: Bodenstandige Volkssturm (non-mobile militia)
Z: Zoll Polizei (customs police)

French units:
BM: Battaillon de Marche
BIMP: Battaillon d'Infanterie de Marche Pacifique
DBLE: Demi-Brigade de Légion étrangère
(Foreign Legion)

0 _____ 5 miles
0 _____ 5km

infantry troops and an assortment of police and *Volksturm* units while the Panzer force moved south towards Kilstett. A flak regiment was positioned on the east bank of the river with 88mm guns and 20mm automatic cannon for air defense, but the 88mm guns also provided anti-tank protection. River crossing was undertaken only under the cover of darkness or fog. In the event, US air operations in the area were very limited and the crossing operations were held up due to US air attacks only once. Although the US Seventh Army became aware of the bridgehead almost from its inception, it was judged too minor a threat in view of problems elsewhere in the VI Corps sector. No serious efforts to contain the bridgehead were made for several days.

Operation *Sonnenwende* was kicked off three days later on January 8 primarily by the 198. Infanterie-Division, which managed to push back weak French forces southeast of Erstein until the French re-established firm defenses on the Ill River and its subsidiary canals by January 12. Among the defending units was Brigade Indépendente Alsace-Lorraine, a volunteer formation created by author and adventurer André Malraux. Operation *Sonnenwende* proved to be the least successful of all the Sylwester offensives, pushing the Colmar Pocket a few miles closer to Strasbourg, but only exacerbating the overextension of AOK 19.

The success in expanding the Gambsheim bridgehead north of Strasbourg led Himmler to interfere with Blaskowitz's planning. With *Sonnenwende* a failure, Himmler promoted an opportunistic shift in tactics, refocusing the bridgehead's mission from the capture of Strasbourg to a plan to cut off the US VI Corps in the Hagenau area. Instead of deploying the Heergesgruppe G armor out of Rothbach east of Hagenau as Blaskowitz was proposing, he proposed that it be directed farther northeast around Wissembourg with an objective of pushing through the open country between the Bienwald and the Hagenau woods, down along the Rhine where it could join up with his Gambsheim bridgehead. Heeresgruppe G was not happy with this scheme, expecting that the area would be heavily mined and fortified and that the area east of Hagenau did not provide enough maneuver room. Furthermore, the US defenses, although thin, were anchored in a number of Maginot Line fortifications. Regardless of these objections, Berlin ordered the stalled attack by 89. AK from the Bitche area to be suspended in favor of shifting the focus of *Nordwind* farther east to the Hagenau sector.

HATTEN-RITTERSHOFFEN

The understrength 21. Panzer-Division and 25. Panzergrenadier-Division were combined as Kampfgruppe Feuchtinger and began moving out of the Bienwald at 0200hrs on January 6, with an aim to seize several Maginot forts by surprise. In the pre-dawn darkness, the attack proceeded quickly against very light opposition from Task Force Linden, but the advance columns eventually ran into minefields, slowing their progress. The push resumed on January 7 in the midst of a snowstorm, and eventually came to a halt in the Maginot Line defenses near Oberroedern, held by the 3/313th Infantry (79th Division). The US forces in this sector were in the process of withdrawing by phase lines back to the Vosges, and by now were generally located along the trace of the Maginot Line. General der Panzertruppe Karl Decker's recently arrived 39. Panzer-Korps headquarters was now put in charge of the attack towards Hagenau.

The 21. Panzer-Division continued its attacks on the scattered Maginot fortifications with engineer and tank support, finally penetrating the defenses north of Oberroedern on January 8. In spite of this, Blaskowitz threatened Feuchtinger and two regimental commanders with courts martial for their continued defiance of his explicit tactical instructions, later leading to Feuchtinger's relief. That evening, the 25. Panzergrenadier-Division was moved into position farther south with the aim of penetrating the Maginot Line defenses towards Hatten and Rittershoffen, two neighboring towns that would earn a very grim reputation over the next week amongst both German and American troops. The initial attack began around midnight, attempting to overcome the substantial barbed-wire and minefield defenses using pioneers reinforced with Panzergrenadiers and supported by StuG III assault guns.

In spite of heavy losses caused by American artillery, the pioneers overcame several bunkers using flame-throwers and flame-thrower tanks. By sunrise, Panzergrenadier-Regiment 119 reached the eastern outskirts of Hatten, encountering 1/242nd Infantry from Task Force Linden. Around noon, Kampfgruppe Huss, a Panzergrenadier force on half-tracks with Panzer support, tried to envelop the town on either side. By this time, Combat Command A, 14th Armored Division had been moving from its blocking position near Rothbach to the Hatten-Rittershoffen sector. Its lead element, a platoon of four tanks of Company A, 48th Tank Battalion, had taken up defensive positions to the south-east of Rittershoffen. Blinded by the snow and overcast, the German columns didn't spot the American tanks until it was too late and the first six German tanks were knocked out in rapid succession; the Kampfgruppe Huss attack completely collapsed when brought under artillery fire. The 48th Tank Battalion supported a counterattack by the 2/242nd Infantry to relieve the decimated 1/242nd Infantry in Hatten, who had already sustained about 300 casualties in the day's fighting in the bunkers and in the town. These were the opening moves in a week-long series of seesaw battles. Both sides repeatedly attacked and counterattacked each other in the rubble of the two towns, gaining a momentary advantage only to be pushed back by another round of attacks. On January 10, the 2/315th Infantry arrived and attempted to reinforce the American attacks in Hatten. The American attacks on January 10 were beaten off by Panzergrenadier-Regiment 119 and 2/242nd Infantry took such heavy casualties that it was withdrawn to Rittershoffen to recuperate. This led to the isolation of 2/315th Infantry, but 3/315th Infantry was moved forward to reinforce the American positions in Hatten. While this was going on, the two German divisions were still trying to widen the breach by overcoming US defenses in Maginot Line bunkers on the approaches to Hatten.

Two GIs from the 14th Armored Division inspect the wreckage in Hatten after the town was recaptured in March 1945. In the background is an M4A3 medium tank of the 14th Armored Division while in the foreground is an M18 76mm GMC of the 827th Tank Destroyer Battalion (Colored). (NARA)

EVENTS

1 In the pre-dawn hours of January 9, Kampfgruppe Pröll attacks Maginot forts east of Hatten with Panzergrenadier-Regiment 35 on the right and II./Panzergrenadier-Regiment 119 on the left. With engineer support and flame-throwers, they manage to overcome several of the bunkers held by 1/242nd Infantry.

2 Kampfgruppe Huss is ordered to reinforce the attack and proceeds to send 16 PzKpfw IV tanks from Panzer-Regiment 5 along with Panzergrenadiers in SdKfz 251 half-tracks to envelop the town on either side. This advance is stopped by the arrival of a platoon of four tanks of Co. A, 48th Tank Battalion to south-east of Rittershofen, which quickly knock out the first six German tanks in rapid succession.

3 The 48th Tank Battalion supports a counterattack by the 2/242nd Infantry trying to re-establish control of Hatten.

4 On January 10, the 2/315th Infantry arrive and attempt to reinforce the American attacks in Hatten. The American attacks on January 10 are beaten off by Panzergrenadier-Regiment 119, and 2/242nd Infantry take such heavy casualties that it is withdrawn to Rittershofen to recuperate. This nearly leads to the isolation of 2/315th Infantry, but 3/315th Infantry is moved forwards to reinforce the American positions in Hatten.

5 Before dawn on January 11, two *Kampfgruppen* swing wide of the town and try to take Rittershofen further west. They consist of Kampfgruppe von Luck and Kampfgruppe Huss. The observation bunker outside Rittershofen is taken first, then some of the buildings on the north-east side of town. By the evening of January 11, the remnants of 2/315th Infantry are clinging to the rubble of Hatten along with their sister battalion, the 3/315th Infantry, in Rittershofen.

6 Combat Command A of 14th Armored Division moves forward from Niederbetschdorf and fights its way into the northwest section of town in late afternoon of January 11.

7 On January 12, Combat Command A makes another attempt to push the Germans out of Rittershofen, with little success.

8 Combat Command B arrives in the sector and attempts to push into Hatten from the north but is stopped by elements of the 21. Panzer-Division.

9 On the night of January 12/13, I./Fallschirmjäger 20 begins arriving in Hatten to take over the positions held by the 21. Panzergrenadier-Division. At dawn, Combat

Command R's 14th Armored Division, including A/47th Tank Battalion and A & B/19th Armored Infantry Battalion, moves along the railroad track and attacks Hatten from the south. Combat Command A attacks Rittershofen from the north. A second attack by Combat Command R in the late afternoon of January 13 finally re-establishes contact with 2/315th Infantry. Attacks by Combat Command A continue into the western side of Rittershofen, but Combat Command B attacks to the north continue to be frustrated.

10 The III./FJR 20 arrives in the outskirts of Rittershofen prior to midnight and launches an attack with the support of Flammpanzer 38(t) flame-thrower tanks but the attacking forces takes heavy losses in the night skirmish.

11 The stalemate in Hatten-Rittershofen continues with indecisive fighting on January 14. On January 15, Panzer-Regiment 22 tries to re-establish links between the two towns using tank patrols; the 47. Volksgrenadier-Division is put into motion to replace the units in the towns.

12 14th Armored Division launches an attack on January 17 in Rittershofen that initially overwhelms one of the German headquarters. Elements of Panzer-Aufklärungs-Abteilung 21 and II./Fallschirmjäger 20 counterattack and reclaim the position.

13 As the weather clears on January 18, both sides stage air attacks. American P-47 Thunderbolts bomb and strafe Hatten, while Me-262 jet fighter-bombers of Kampfgruppe 51 drop bombs on Niederbetschdorf.

14 During the evening of January 19, the first elements of the 47. Volksgrenadier-Division begin arriving in both villages to begin the switch of forces.

15 The 21. Panzergrenadier-Division and 21. Panzer-Division withdraw from both villages; the handover to the 47. Volksgrenadier-Division is completed that day. Brooks orders the 14th Armored Division and other units in the villages to withdraw to the Moder river line on the night of January 20/21, with rearguards to remain in place until 0500hrs on January 21.

HATTEN-RITTERSHOFFEN: JANUARY 9–20, 1945

Battles rage over control of Hatten-Rittershoffen and the gateway through the Hagenau forest.

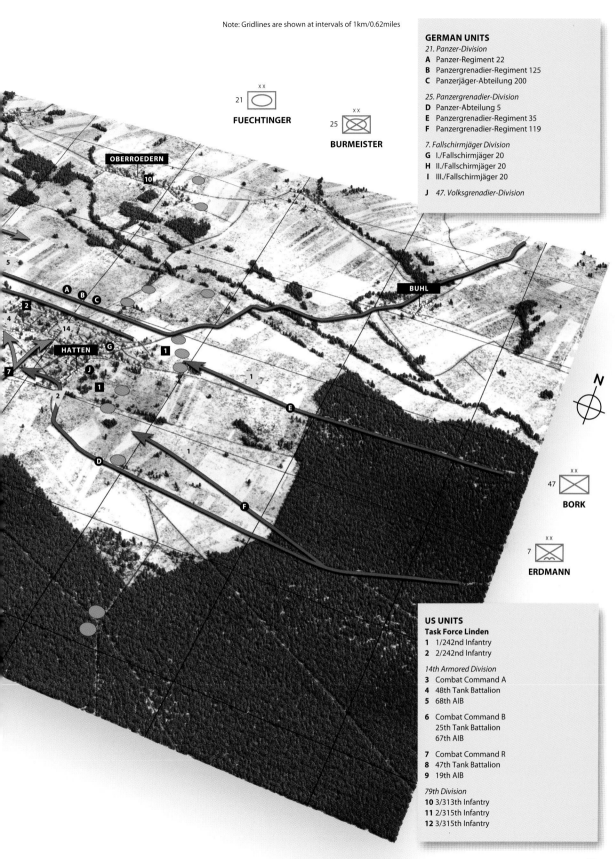

Note: Gridlines are shown at intervals of 1km/0.62miles

FUECHTINGER

BURMEISTER

OBERROEDERN

BUHL

HATTEN

BORK

ERDMANN

Decker attempted to circumvent the vicious stalemate inside Hatten by directing two *Kampfgruppen* from the 21. Panzer-Division to swing wide of the town and take Rittershoffen farther west. This attack took place on January 11 amidst a considerable amount of confusion on both sides. The flat area between the two towns, called the "pool table" by the US troops, became a killing ground for both sides whenever the weather was clear enough to pick out targets in the open fields. By the evening of January 11, the remnants of 2/315th Infantry were clinging to the rubble of Hatten, with their sister battalion the 3/315th Infantry hunkered down in Rittershoffen. Both sides decided to commit more forces to the fray, with Decker's 39. Panzer-Korps receiving elements of the 7. Fallschirmjäger-Division and Brooks committing the remainder of the 14th Armored Division, its Combat Command B and Combat Command R, which began arriving on January 13. The injection of Combat Command R into the fight on the morning of January 14 was quickly beaten back; a renewed counterattack later in the day left much of the town in American hands, but a night attack by *Panzergrenadiers* restored the stalemate. The fighting intensified on January 15 as more troops of the 7. Fallschirmjäger-Division entered the battle and Flammpanzer 38, were used in an effort to burn out the stubborn US infantry positions in the stone cellars of the town.

Like a pair of punch-drunk boxers, neither side was willing to give up. On January 14, the Red Army launched its long-anticipated Oder offensive towards Berlin, and Hitler ordered all available mechanized forces shifted from the west to the east; Decker began substituting the 47. Volksgrenadier-Division for the *Panzergrenadier* units on January 16. Brooks committed the

A knocked-out PzKpfw IV in the ruins of Hatten following the fighting. (Patton Museum)

A destroyed M4A3 medium tank of the 14th Armored Division in the ruins of Rittershoffen after the fighting. The level of violence within the town is evident from the sheer number of hits on this tank, with at least five hits visible from the rear alone. (NARA)

last battalion from the 315th Infantry, 1/315th, on January 17, which restored the violent stalemate. The commander of one of the *Panzergrenadier Kampfgruppen*, Hans von Luck, recalled that the fighting in these two obscure towns "was one of the hardest and most costly battles that had ever raged on the Western Front." While the human toll has never been precisely calculated, a US survey of the battlefield in March 1945 found the burned-out wrecks of 31 M4 medium tanks, 9 M5A1 light tanks and 8 half-tracks along with 51 Panzers and assault guns and 12 half-tracks; the Germans had recovered at least six Panzers before withdrawing. The final outcome of this inconclusive skirmish was determined elsewhere.

THE GAMBSHEIM CANCER

While Brooks' VI Corps was fighting the battle for Hatten-Rittershoffen north of Hagenau, an equally violent confrontation had erupted to the south. Late on January 6, Patch had ordered the "Gambsheim cancer" eradicated, allotting Combat Command B of the 12th Armored Division from the SHAEF reserve for this task to reinforce the badly overstretched 79th Division and Task Force Linden along the Rhine. The 12th Armored Division was not combat experienced, and, in particular, it had not worked out the usual

ATTACK ON THE MAGINOT LINE, JANUARY 9, 1945 (pp. 56–57)

The advance by Kampfgruppe Feuchtinger towards the Hagenau forest was blocked by a string of Maginot Line fortifications built by the French Army in the 1930s. Hatten had several casemates **(1)** on its eastern side, as well as observation bunkers and personnel shelters behind the town in the direction of Rittershoffen. When 25. Panzergrenadier-Division was given the assignment of breaking through this line on January 9, they began their preparations by calling forward their divisional *Pionier* units (engineers), who were equipped with man-portable flame-throwers and explosive charges. In addition, Panzer-Flamm-Kompanie 352, equipped with ten Flammpanzer 38(t) tanks **(2)**, had been attached to the *Kampfgruppe* specifically for these contingencies. The usual tactics for dealing with these pillboxes was to attempt to cut through any barbed-wire obstructions in the pre-dawn hours, as well as to make a preliminary sweep for mines. Minefields posed an unusual threat in the January fighting as the autumn rain has thoroughly soaked the ground, and the sudden frost that arrived in the third week of December 1944 solidly froze the ground and the mines along with it.

The US infantry defenses on the outskirts of Hatten did not rely on the casemates alone, but on infantry trenches and emplaced 57mm anti-tank guns. These were suppressed in advance by German artillery, and there were often assault guns or tanks present to deal with any surviving defenses outside of the bunkers. Once it appeared that the exterior defenses had been suppressed, the bunkers would be attacked either by a *Pionier* team, or in some cases, by a Flammpanzer 38(t) as seen here. The Flammpanzer 38(t) in the background has a *Pionier* team **(3)** accompanying it as it was often necessary to use explosive charges to pry the American defenders out of the bunkers, even after being hit repeatedly by flame-throwers.

The Flammpanzer 38(t) had been ordered by Hitler specifically for *Nordwind* on November 27, 1944. It consisted of the usual Jagdpanzer 38(t) but with a Köbe Flammenwerfer fitted in place of the usual 75mm gun. It was fed from a 185-gallon tank inside the vehicle which was enough for about 60–70 flame bursts **(4)** and it had an effective range of about 50m. The Hatten attack was the first use of these vehicles by this company, which took heavy losses during the Hatten-Rittershoffen fighting and several were later used in street fighting in Rittershoffen where two of them were lost to American fire.

problems of conducting combined-arms missions in urban areas, particularly in regard to coordination between tank and infantry units. The US armored divisions were especially weak in infantry, containing barely a third of the riflemen found in an infantry division, and these ferocious town battles chewed up infantry companies at an appalling rate.

At the time, the German bridgehead around Gambsheim had about 3,330 troops from the 553. Volksgrenadier-Division; the defenses of Herrlisheim were centered in the town and the fields on either side were covered by several emplaced anti-tank guns along a railroad embankment. VI Corps seriously underestimated the size of the force in Herrlisheim as comprising only 500–800 "disorganized" infantry, and so struck at the town in a weak and piecemeal manner.

Combat Command B/14th Armored Division was deployed in textbook combined-arms fashion, consisting of Task Force Power based on the 714th Tank Battalion with an attached armored infantry company, and Task Force Rammer based on 56th Armored Infantry Battalion with an attached tank company, both supported by the 494th Armored Field Artillery Battalion with M7 105mm howitzer motor carriages (HMCs). The force was not well suited to such a mission, being outnumbered by German infantry about two-to-one in terrain where its superiority in tank strength gave it little advantage. Combat Command B launched its attack on Herrlesheim around 1000hrs on January 8 from the north around Rohrwiller. There had been no time for reconnaissance and the tanks became stalled along the Zorn River, which bisected the battlefield. Two armored infantry companies moved across a footbridge and secured positions in the outskirts of the town by evening. After repelling a German counterattack on the night of January 8/9, the attack resumed the following day with the tank companies taking up position as close to the western side of the town as possible to provide fire support. Four tanks were lost during the day's fighting to 85mm flak guns positioned along the railroad embankment, as well as some supporting assault guns. Contact with the infantry within the town was lost due to radio problems, and casualties began to mount. The situation became so confused that in the early morning hours of 9/10 January, Combat Command B decided to withdraw its infantry from Herrlisheim.

This was the site of the Gambsheim bridgehead over the Rhine in January 1945; the picture was taken shortly after the war. AOK 19 relied on the use of Rhine ferries during the long winter nights to resupply its forces on the western bank, realizing full well that tactical bridges would be vulnerable to Allied air strikes. (MHI)

January 16, 1945

1 Task Force 2, based on the 66th AIB, attempts to penetrate and seize the Steinwald and then proceed into Offendorf. The pre-dawn attack comes under intense small-arms and mortar fire and suffers significant losses. The force withdraws to the cover of the Landgraben canal.

2 Task Force 1, based on the 43rd Tank Battalion, sets off towards Offendorf around 1030hrs in spite of the repulse of Task Force 2 earlier in the morning. The tank battalion's three medium-tank companies fan out in the open fields on the approaches to the railway embankment, but are hit by 75mm and 88mm fire from eight emplaced anti-tank guns and several assault guns along the embankment and in the Stainwald.

3 Task Force 3, based on the 17th AIB, dismounts from its half-tracks and follows the tanks of Task Force 1

KURTZENHAUSEN

XX
12

ALLEN

US DEFENSIVE LINE, NIGHT OF JANUARY 17/18

WEYERSHEIM

6

12

4

5

12

4

1

11

15

14

10

13

towards the Herrlisheim–Gambsheim railway embankment, where they are hit by small-arms and mortar fire. They also fall back later in the day due to the repulse of the 43rd tank Battalion attack.

4 The 66th AIB makes another attempt to punch into the Stainwald, using B/66th AIB supported by engineers of the A/119th Armored Engineer Battalion and medium tanks of B/23rd Tank Battalion. The attack kicks off in the pre-dawn hours but immediately comes under intense German fire. The lead wave of medium tanks encounters a minefield blocking the D94 road and the northwest approach into the woods, which halts the advance. By 0700hrs the attack has failed.

January 17

5 The 17th Armored Infantry Battalion begins to advance into Herrlisheim, starting at around 0500hrs on January 17, and makes good progress. They are soon bogged down in the town, confronted by an estimated 500 German infantry. By the end of the day, that number grows to about 1,500 as 553. Volksgrenadier-Division is reinforced from the neighboring sectors as well as by the arrival of troops of the 11. SS-Panzer-Division.

6 The remaining 29 medium tanks of the 43rd Tank Battalion, with attached engineers of C/119th Armored Engineer Battalion serving as improvised infantry, proceed to the south of Herrlisheim in the pre-dawn hours. The tanks begin to move into the town around 0850hrs in an attempt to support the advance of the 17th AIB, but both groups fail to make contact. The last radio message from the unit around 1100hrs describes the town as a "circus" and far worse than the day before with an estimated 2,000 infantry in the town. The tanks are gradually destroyed piecemeal, primarily by Panzerfausts.

7 The recently arrived SS-Panzer-Abteilung 10 sends out a tank company from Offendorf towards Herrlisheim in the morning to counterattack the American forces, but it is beaten back by artillery and tank fire.

8 In the afternoon, SS-Panzer-Abteilung 10 sends a Panther tank company back into Herrlisheim, approaching the town from the quieter northern sector. They knock out or capture the remaining Sherman tanks still in Herrlisheim, and are credited with destroying seven Shermans and capturing 12 more.

9 23rd Tank Battalion attempts to intervene in the fighting in Herrlisheim in order to support the 17th AIB, and spends the night in defensive positions on the south-west side of the town.

10 By 1700hrs, Major Logan's headquarters in Herrlisheim is completely surrounded and the 19th AIB task force is down to about 200 men, mostly hiding out in the cellars. The headquarters is finally overwhelmed at around 0400hrs on January 18 and Logan is amongst the wounded prisoners.

11 In the early morning hours of January 18, unable to make any contact with the 17th AIB, the survivors of the 23rd Tank Battalion pull back further away from Herrlisheim and set up a defensive perimeter.

12 In the early morning hours of January 19, Co. C, 23rd Tank Battalion moves south from the Bruchwald to set up a defensive perimeter on the Zorn river, shielding Weyersheim.

13 The 3rd platoon, C/23rd Tank Battalion is sent to reinforce US positions in the Langenau woods later on January 19.

14 A push by SS-Panzergrenadier-Regiment 21 on January 19 is beaten back by emplaced tanks of 23rd Tank Battalion.

15 An afternoon attempt to push out of Gambsheim by SS-Panzergrenadier-Regiment 21 supported by tanks is stopped by US artillery and tank fire.

16 SS-Panzer-Regiment 10 attempts to push out of Herrlisheim to the west with Panzergrenadier support but is beaten back by tank fire from Lt. Sadler's platoon from C/23rd Tank Battalion in the Langenau woods and by artillery fire.

HERRLISHEIM: JANUARY 16–19, 1945

US armored forces attempt to reduce the German bridgehead around Herrlisheim.

Note: Gridlines are shown at intervals of 1km/0.62miles

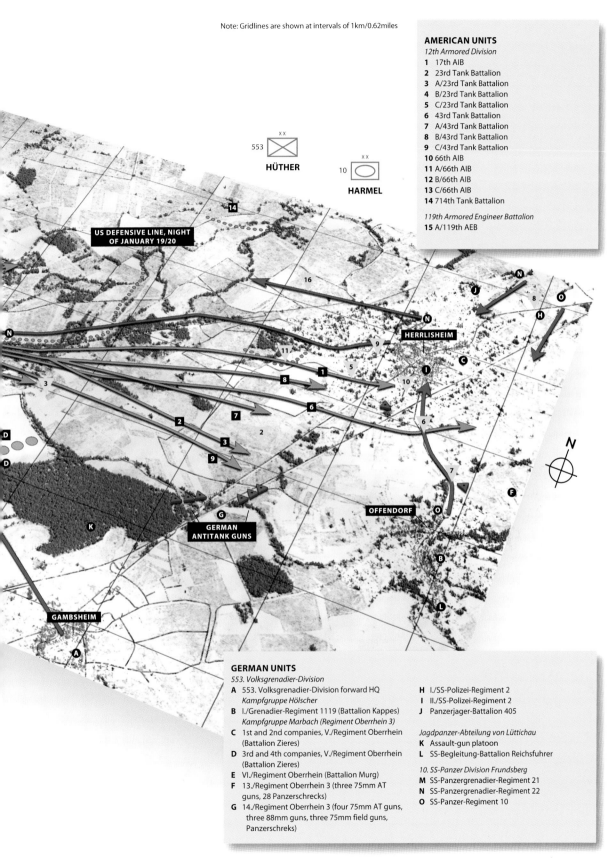

553 [unit symbol]
HÜTHER

10 [unit symbol]
HARMEL

US DEFENSIVE LINE, NIGHT
OF JANUARY 19/20

HERRLISHEIM

OFFENDORF

GERMAN
ANTITANK GUNS

GAMBSHEIM

AMERICAN UNITS
12th Armored Division
1   17th AIB
2   23rd Tank Battalion
3   A/23rd Tank Battalion
4   B/23rd Tank Battalion
5   C/23rd Tank Battalion
6   43rd Tank Battalion
7   A/43rd Tank Battalion
8   B/43rd Tank Battalion
9   C/43rd Tank Battalion
10 66th AIB
11 A/66th AIB
12 B/66th AIB
13 C/66th AIB
14 714th Tank Battalion

119th Armored Engineer Battalion
15 A/119th AEB

GERMAN UNITS
553. Volksgrenadier-Division
A   553. Volksgrenadier-Division forward HQ
        Kampfgruppe Hölscher
B   I./Grenadier-Regiment 1119 (Battalion Kappes)
        Kampfgruppe Marbach (Regiment Oberrhein 3)
C   1st and 2nd companies, V./Regiment Oberrhein
        (Battalion Zieres)
D   3rd and 4th companies, V./Regiment Oberrhein
        (Battalion Zieres)
E   VI./Regiment Oberrhein (Battalion Murg)
F   13./Regiment Oberrhein 3 (three 75mm AT
        guns, 28 Panzerschrecks)
G   14./Regiment Oberrhein 3 (four 75mm AT guns,
        three 88mm guns, three 75mm field guns,
        Panzerschreks)

H   I./SS-Polizei-Regiment 2
I   II./SS-Polizei-Regiment 2
J   Panzerjager-Battalion 405

Jagdpanzer-Abteilung von Lüttichau
K   Assault-gun platoon
L   SS-Begleitung-Battalion Reichsfuhrer

10. SS-Panzer Division Frundsberg
M   SS-Panzergrenadier-Regiment 21
N   SS-Panzergrenadier-Regiment 22
O   SS-Panzer-Regiment 10

A column of tanks from the 12th Armored Division moves towards the Gambsheim bridgehead in January 1945. The battle for Herrlisheim was the first significant combat for this inexperienced division. (NARA)

Brooks realized that a single combat command was inadequate to deal with the Gambsheim bridgehead, and so, on January 13, the entire 12th Armored Division was assigned to the mission. The second phase of the attack began early on the morning of January 16, with the newly arrived Combat Command A attacking south of Herrlisheim towards Offendorf and the Steinwald, while Combat Command B tried to attack Herrlisheim again across the Zorn River. The 43rd Tank Battalion of Combat Command A lost 12 tanks during the attack on Offendorf mainly due to emplaced anti-tank guns, but the 17th Armored Infantry Battalion managed to fight its way into Herrlisheim, occupying about a third of the town by nightfall. The German infantry in the town counterattacked, pushing the US force out.

Unknown to the 12th Armored Division, Decker's 39. Panzer-Korps had been allocated the 10. SS-Panzer-Division to spearhead a breakout from the Gambsheim bridgehead, and the Panzers had begun their transfer over the river by ferry from the Freistatt area on January 15/16 after dark. The division set up headquarters in Offendorf and planned to begin their assault with a tank attack by I./SS-Panzer Abteilung 10, equipped with about 50 PzKpfw IVs and over 40 Panther tanks. The German tank attack collided with a two-pronged American attack. Combat Command B attempted to push into Herrlisheim again from the north, while at the same time, Combat Command A launched two attacks from the south. The attacks began in the pre-dawn hours of January 17 and did not go well for either side. In the early morning fog, the German tank column took heavy losses to US tank guns on the approach to Herrlisheim and withdrew to Offendorf. The American attacks against the northern corner of Herrlisheim and against the Steinwald failed with heavy losses. The 43rd Tank Battalion moved between Steinwald and Herrlisheim, taking anti-tank fire from both locations, but managed to fight its way into Herrlisheim from the south. The tanks and their supporting infantry and engineers came under unrelenting attack by German infantry armed with Panzerfaust rockets. The battalion commander, Lieutenant-Colonel Nicholas Novosel, radioed back that "Things are hot" but radio contact then went dead. The 23rd Tank Battalion was instructed to reorient its attack towards Drusenheim farther to the north, passing through Herrlisheim in the process, but was stopped cold on the outskirts of the town by heavy fire without linking up with the infantry.

Back at Offendorf, the 3./SS-Panzer-Abteilung 10 under the regimental adjutant Obersturmbannführer Erwin Bachmann, set off again for Herrlisheim with a Panther tank company. They knocked out or captured most of the remaining Sherman tanks still in Herrlisheim; Bachmann was later awarded the Knight's Cross for his actions that day. By the end of the day the 12th Armored Division headquarters had no idea of the fate of the 43rd Tank Battalion; the 17th Armored Infantry Battalion positions in Herrlisheim were overrun in the pre-dawn hours of January 18 and the battalion commander captured. The following day, the 12th Armored Division sent a rescue party to find any survivors from the missing 43rd Tank Battalion or 17th Armored Infantry Battalion, but they were brusquely pushed back by heavy German fire. An artillery spotter plane discovered a field full of charred Shermans south of Herrlisheim so further attacks were called off. In February, when the area was retaken by the US Army, 28 destroyed Shermans of the 43rd Tank Battalion were found in and around the town. The 10. Panzer-Division had captured more than ten Shermans and these would later serve with the division when it was sent east to fight the Red Army in February.

The southern end of Herrlisheim was a ruin of burned-out 12th Armored Division tanks and wrecked buildings, as is evident from this scene taken after the fighting. (MHI)

The 10. SS-Panzer-Division had no more luck over the next few days, beaten bloody during attempts to push out towards Kilstett on January 18. Its Panzer regiment lost 8 PzKpfw IVs and 21 Panthers during the fighting between January 17–21. The fighting on January 19 was especially costly, accounting for 22 of the 29 Panzer losses, so that evening the attacks were halted.

The impasse around Hagenau finally broke on January 20. Devers and Patch had been pushing SHAEF to release more troops to the Seventh Army, mainly to deal with the Colmar Pocket to the south. Now that the Ardennes bulge had been erased, reinforcements were arriving, which included the 101st Airborne Division and 28th Division. The stalemates at Hatten-Rittershoffen and Herrlisheim convinced the senior American commanders that it was time to fall back to a more defensible position rather than waste more troops in the village stalemates north of the Hagenau forest. As a result, Brooks' VI Corps ordered a withdrawal to the Moder river line south of the Hagenau forest starting after dark on January 20/21.

Devers' assessment of the fighting was summed up in his January 17 diary entry: "Ted Brooks has fought one of the great defensive battles of all time with very little… There have been instances when, because of the long front weakly held, commanders have not risen to the tremendous responsibilities placed upon them. This has permitted the Germans to gain a bridgehead on the Rhine. Our efforts to take this bridgehead out have gone slowly and been disappointing."

In view of the poor weather and the lack of aerial reconnaissance, Decker's 39. Panzer-Korps was largely unaware of the withdrawal until after it happened, and so failed to pursue. Once the withdrawal to the Moder was

A column of tanks of the 23rd Tank Battalion, 12th Armored Division returns to Herrlisheim on February 4 as part of the effort to stamp out the remnants of the Gambsheim bridgehead. The German car in the foreground was a booby-trapped roadblock that detonated when struck by one of the passing tanks. (NARA)

Battles around Hagenau, January 6–21, 1945

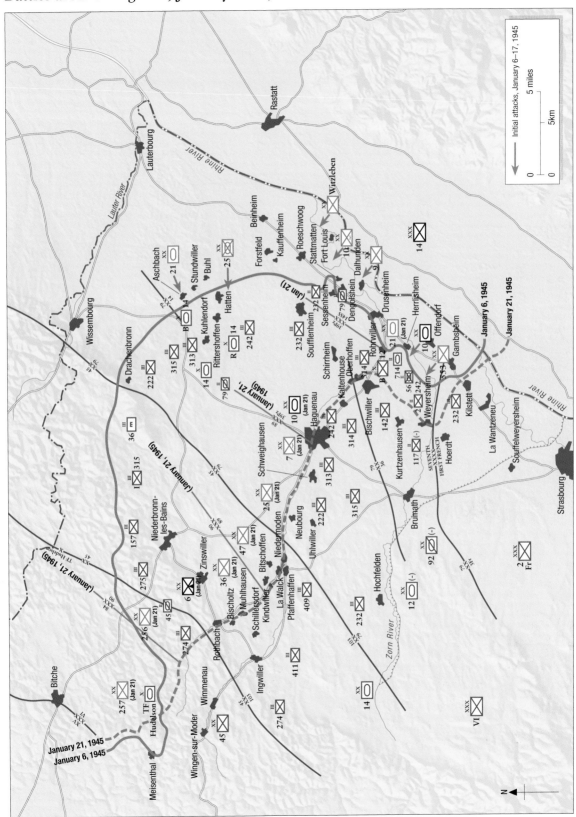

Initial attacks, January 6–17, 1945

5 miles

5km

Rhine River

Lauter River

Lauterbourg

Rastatt

Witzleben

Beinheim

Roeschwoog

Kauffenheim

Forstfeld

Stattmatten

Fort Louis

Dalhunden

Drusenheim

Herrlisheim

Offendorf

Gambsheim

Aschbach

Stundwiller

Buhl

Kuhlendorf

Hatten

Rittershoffen

Sessenheim

Soufflenheim

Schirrheim

Rohrwiller

Weyersheim

Kilstett

La Wantzeneu

Souffelweyersheim

Drachenbronn

Wissembourg

Kaltenhouse

Oberhoffen

Bischwiller

Hagenau

Kurtzenhausen

Hoerdt

Strasbourg

Schweighausen

Bischoltz

Niederbronn-les-Bains

Zinswiller

Bischoffen

Niedermoden

Neubourg

Uhlwiller

Hochfelden

Brumath

Muhlhausen

Kindwiller

La Walck

Pfaffenhoffen

Rothbach

Wimmenau

Ingwiller

Bitche

Wingen-sur-Moder

Meisenthal

January 6, 1945

January 21, 1945

Rhine River

Zorn River

SEVENTH
FIRST FRENCH

January 6, 1945

January 21, 1945

N

A GI from the 12th Armored Division runs past a burned-out M4A3E2 assault tank of the 43rd Tank Battalion during the recapture of Herrlisheim in February 1945. (NARA)

recognized, German units from around Rittershoffen pushed southwards to link up with the Gambsheim bridgehead, which occurred on January 22. Overconfident from the sudden gains, the Germans attempted to push into Bischwiller and Hagenau, but suffered heavy casualties in the process. By this stage of the battle, Allied Ultra intelligence access to German communications had improved due to Hitler's order on January 11 that attacking corps in this sector report directly to Berlin as quickly as possible, meaning more use of encrypted radio. It was becoming clear that the Soviet offensive in the east was removing any possibility of significant reinforcements arriving in Alsace. The Germans secured a few bridgeheads over the Moder river line, but they were quickly extinguished. On January 26, the attacks were halted and on January 27, the 21. Panzer-Division and 25. Panzergrenadier-Division were ordered out of the line in preparation for their movement east. The Sylwester offensives had finally come to an end.

The exhaustion of the Sylwester offensives led to numerous shake-ups in the German command. Rundstedt expected that the Allies would bring their offensives over the Rhine in February and he was not confident that Generaloberst Kurt Student, commander of Heeresgruppe H in the Netherlands, was adequate to the task. With Alsace cooling down, he engineered the transfer of Blaskowitz to the Heersgruppe H slot, and he was replaced on January 27 with Oberstgruppenführer Paul Hausser, who had taken over Heeresgruppe Obberrhein several days before; Heeresgruppe Oberrhein now disappeared. Himmler's interest had shifted east and his minions moved to Silesia to command Heeresgruppe Weichsel.

In the end, the Sylwester offensives had gained the Wehrmacht a little ground on the Alsatian plains around Hagenau, but at enormous cost. They had completely failed to achieve their operational objectives. As a battle of attrition, the balance sheet was largely in favor of the US Army with total combat casualties being around 14,000 in the Seventh Army compared to about 23,000 German casualties in Heeresgruppe G. These losses, combined with the drain of forces out of Alsace to the east in late January and early February, left Heeresgruppe G very vulnerable to future Allied operations in this sector, as would become clear at Colmar.

This unremarkable farmland on the Alsatian plains was the scene of some of the most intense tank fighting of Operation *Nordwind*. The terrain on the outskirts of Herrlisheim is littered with the burned wreckage of tanks from the 12th Armored Division and 10. SS-Panzer-Division, seen on February 8, two weeks after the battles after some of the snow had disappeared. (NARA)

OPERATION *CHEERFUL*: STRANGLING THE COLMAR POCKET

Eisenhower had been urging Devers to eliminate the Colmar Pocket since December when de Lattre's 1ère Armée had run out of steam. Plans to restart the attacks were delayed due to Operation *Nordwind* and the related shift of French resources to defend Strasbourg, especially the experienced 3e Division d'Infanterie Algérienne. Planning between Devers and de Lattre resumed on January 11 with Devers promising significant Seventh Army support as soon as forces could be freed from rebuffing the German attacks in northern

Crews from 12th Armored Division recover a damaged M4A3 medium tank from the 43rd Tank Battalion, which had been knocked out two weeks earlier in the ferocious fighting around Herrlisheim that had destroyed the battalion in two days of fighting. (NARA)

TANK GRAVEYARD IN HERRLISHEIM, JANUARY 17, 1945 (pp. 78–79)

Mechanized operations in urban terrain, currently known as MOUT, is one of the most difficult of all tank tactics. It proved to be the undoing of the 43rd Tank Battalion, which was poorly trained and inexperienced in such fighting techniques. Urbanized environments are particularly difficult for tank operations since the tanks are nearly blind and they can be attacked from nearly any direction by enemy infantry. The tactical solution to this problem is careful tank–infantry cooperation, with the infantry providing the eyes for the tanks and helping to protect them from close-in enemy infantry attack, and the tanks providing the infantry with the firepower needed to pry out enemy defenders in the semi-fortified expanses of stone buildings and cellars. The problems confronted by the 43rd Tank Battalion were twofold. On the one hand, the unit had received little or no MOUT training; experience might have solved this problem as it did for most US armored divisions. In addition, its supporting force that day came primarily from divisional engineers impressed into service as improvised infantrymen due to the heavy losses of infantry in the previous days' fighting. Besides the tactical and training shortcomings of the units, the 12th Armored Division suffered from a lack of suitable technical means for tank–infantry cooperation since infantry and tank radios were incompatible. The technical solution elsewhere in the ETO had been to install field telephones on the back of the tanks so that accompanying infantry could talk to the tank crew. This had not yet been done in the inexperienced 12th Armored Division.

From the German side, the arrival of rocket anti-tank weapons had dramatically improved the ability of infantry to defend itself against tanks, especially in confined urban or forested terrain. The more powerful and accurate of these weapons was the 88mm Raketenpanzerbüchse, more popularly called the Panzerschreck (tank terror) or Ofenrohr (stovepipe) (1). It was an enlarged copy of the American 2.36in. bazooka and could easily penetrate the armor of a US Sherman tank (2). It was a cumbersome two-man weapon with a loader carrying additional rockets (3). On paper, each infantry regiment was allotted 36 of these, and each Volksgrenadier regiment as many as 72. Another attempt to increase infantry firepower was the Sturmgewehr 44, the first modern assault rifle in widespread use (4).

The difficulties of operating in towns were not confined to the 12th Armored Division. The 12. SS-Panzer-Division had become entrapped in a similar killing ground in the Belgian villages of Krinkelt-Rocherath a month earlier on December 18, 1944, and their heavy losses there were one of the causes of the German failure in the Ardennes offensive.

Alsace. With the Ardennes campaign winding down, Eisenhower promised the transfer of the 10th Armored Division and the 28th Division. The latter was a mixed blessing as it had been badly beaten up in the Hürtgen forest, only to be steamrolled on the approaches to Bastogne at the beginning of the Ardennes offensive. It was now rebuilding and Eisenhower admitted it would be good only for defensive actions. In the end the 10th Armored Division was committed elsewhere. Devers had created XXI Corps under Major-General Frank Milburn to manage the SHAEF reserve early in the month, and it was assigned to command the various US divisions committed to the campaign. It was subordinated to de Lattre's 1ère Armée for the Colmar operation, codenamed Operation *Cheerful*. Besides the weak 28th Division, the corps was allotted "Iron Mike" O'Daniel's refreshed 3rd Division, arguably the best Allied division in the theater, and later the 75th Division. The 12th Armored Division was still licking its wounds but would be added to the mix later as an exploitation force. The corps was supported by the combat commands of the French 5e Division Blindée when needed.

Ideally, Devers and de Lattre would have taken the obvious approach and struck the shoulders of the pocket to trap as many German troops as possible. This was complicated by the Erstein bulge along the Ill River, which had been taken by 198. Infanterie-Division in its short-lived Operation *Sonnenwende* offensive earlier in the month. The 2e Division Blindée was assigned to deal with this problem. Instead of the obvious approach, the plan called for the French to begin the assault in the southern Mulhouse sector to draw away German reserves. Once this was under way, the main offensive punch provided by Milburn's corps would be directed directly against Colmar, aimed at rapidly penetrating the pocket and seizing the main river crossing at Neuf-Brisach. Tactical planning aside, the real issue was the substantial logistical difficulties of conducting the operation in the dead of winter. For example, French fuel supplies were at dangerously low levels after the Doubs River froze, blocking the usual fuel barge traffic; the US fuel pumping lines likewise were blocked by the frigid winter weather. The French attempted to complicate German

A light machine-gun team from 142nd Infantry, 36th Division in a defensive position near Bischwiller on January 24 after the VI Corps had pulled back behind the Hagenau forest to the Moder river line. (NARA)

supply problems by floating mines down the Rhine from Kembs to damage the two main bridges at Brisach and Neuenberg, but this scheme faltered due to the ice; air attacks against the Brisach bridge had failed so often that the bridge had been awarded an honorary "Iron Cross" by the local German garrison. An extensive series of ferry sites on the Rhine were relied upon to supplement the bridges.

The German garrison in the Colmar Pocket was under the command of Himmler's Heeresgruppe Oberrhein and consisted of Gen. Rasp's AOK 19 with two corps: 63. Armee-Korps, which controlled the *Südfront* and Gebirgsfront in the Vosges mountains facing the French 1er Corps d'Armée, and 64. Armee-Korps on the *Nordfront* facing Milburn's XXI Corps and the French 2e Corps d'Armée. Armeeoberkommando 19 was supposed to be reinforced with two divisions in December 1944 and January 1945 – the 269. Infanterie-Division and the 2. Gebirgsjäger-Division from Finland – but only the latter arrived; it was stationed around the vital Neuf-Brisach bridgehead. The two corps controlled about 8 divisions, but most units were understrength, with relatively weak infantry companies, few anti-tank guns, and the usual shortages of artillery ammunition. Their total strength was around 22,500 men, although there may have been as many as 70,000 personnel in the pocket early in January. Armored support was very limited and totaled 189 tanks and assault guns. Panzer-Brigade 106 was the main fire brigade for 64. Armee-Korps, and the only other major armored formations were the Sturmgeschütz-Abteilung 280 and schwere-Panzerjäger-Abteilung 654. The latter unit was by far the strongest in terms of equipment with about 30 Jagdpanthers operational, and it was assigned to corps reserve and its companies doled out to hot spots as needed. Hitler declared Colmar a *Festung* (fortress city), to be defended to the death; its garrison comprised two fortress engineer battalions, two construction battalions, and two field penal battalions – hardly the substance of a crack defense.

A snow camouflaged M4A3 (76mm) tank of the 709th Tank Battalion is seen moving up to the front with troops of the 75th Division near Riedwihr on January 31, 1945 during the operations in the Colmar Pocket. (NARA)

Operation *Cheerful* started on schedule on January 20 in the midst of a heavy snowstorm. The weather helped mask the attack by the French 1er Corps d'Armée out of the Mulhouse area, but also slowed the attackers. Rasp shifted his modest reserves south, including elements of the fresh 2. Gebirgsjäger-Division and his paltry Panzer reserve. In view of the weather, neither Himmler nor Rasp thought this was the start of a major offensive, but rather a diversionary attack to take pressure off the Strasbourg sector. The French 1er Corps d'Armée attack stalled, but had accomplished its mission of distracting the Germans.

The next phase of Operation *Cheerful* was an attack on January 22 by Monsabert's 2e Corps d'Armée, aimed at eliminating the Erstein bulge created by the aborted Operation *Sonnenwende* a few weeks before. With a force density of hardly 50 infantrymen per kilometer of front, General der Infanterie Thumm, the 64. Armee-Korps commander, recommended pulling back to a more reasonable defensive line. This was refused and the Erstein bulge was ground away.

At 2100hrs on January 21, O'Daniels launched Operation *Grandslam*, the American element of Operation *Cheerful*. The 3rd Division had been heavily reinforced for the attack, including the attachment of a fourth infantry regiment. The main tactical challenges of the offensive were the numerous north–south river and canal barriers. After having pushed through a thin German screen on January 21–23, the 30th Infantry of the 3rd Division reached the Ill River near Maison Rouge and found an old wooden bridge intact. Instead of waiting for the engineers to erect a treadway bridge sufficient for armor as planned, the infantry regiment proceeded over the river on the wooden bridge while the engineers frantically tried to reinforce it. The first attempt to move a Sherman tank across the bridge led to a partial collapse. On the afternoon and evening of January 23, elements of the 708. Volksgrenadier-Division attacked the 30th Infantry, with armored support from Sturmgeschütz-Abteilung 280. Lacking any anti-tank weapons and unable to dig into the frozen ground, the 30th Infantry took heavy casualties and some of its companies were routed. Another German attack the next day nearly overran the small bridgehead, but eventually the 15th Infantry managed to secure a river crossing farther north and arrive at Maison Rouge with tank support, which broke up the German attacks. During the fighting in the Riedwihr woods on January 26, the commander of Company B,

Aside from the badly depleted Panzer-Brigade 106, the only major Panzer formation in AOK 19 during the Colmar fighting was schwere-Panzerjäger-Abteilung 654, which had 44 Jagdpanthers and 22 Nashorn 88mm tank destroyers at the beginning of the fighting. The regiment was involved in heavy fighting through the last weeks of January and by early February had no tank destroyers operational. This is one of the regiment's Jagdpanthers lost during the Colmar fighting. (Author's collection)

Reduction of the Colmar Pocket, January 19 to February 9, 1945

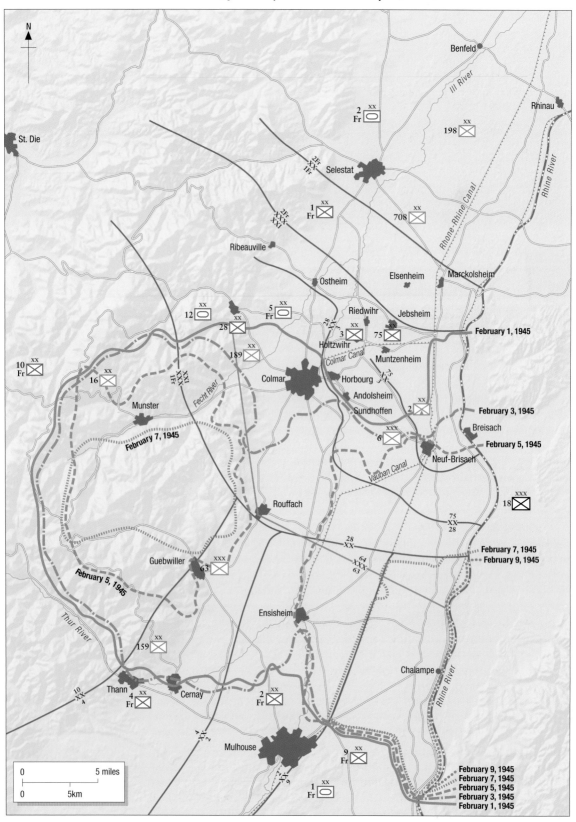

N

Benfeld

Ill River

Rhinau

2
Fr   XX

198   XX

St. Die

2Fr
XX
1Fr

Selestat

Rhone-Rhine Canal

Rhine River

2Fr
XXX
2Fr

1
Fr   XX

708   XX

Ribeauville

Ostheim

Elsenheim

Marckolsheim

12   XX

5
Fr   XX

Riedwihr

Jebsheim

February 1, 1945

10
Fr   XX

28   XX

189   XX

28
XX

Holtzwihr

3   XX

75   XX

16   XX

Fecht River

XXVI
XXX
1Fr

Colmar

Colmar Canal

Muntzenheim

Munster

Horbourg

75
XX

Andolsheim

February 3, 1945

February 7, 1945

Sundhoffen

2   XX

Breisach

6   XX

February 5, 1945

Neuf-Brisach

Vauban Canal

18   XXX

Rouffach

75
XX
28

28
XX

February 7, 1945

February 9, 1945

Guebwiller

63   XX

64
XXX
63

February 5, 1945

Thur River

Ensisheim

159   XX

Chalampe

Rhine River

10
XX
4

Thann

4
Fr   XX

Cernay

2
Fr   XX

XX
4
2

Mulhouse

9
Fr   XX

February 9, 1945
February 7, 1945
February 5, 1945
February 3, 1945
February 1, 1945

XX
9

1
Fr   XX

| 0 | 5 miles |
| 0 | 5km |

84

This Nashorn 88mm tank destroyer of schwere-Panzerjäger-Abteilung 654 was knocked out in a duel with a French M10 3in. GMC tank destroyer of the 2e Division Blindée during the fighting near Riedwihr on January 26 in the Elsenheim woods during the final skirmishes in the Colmar Pocket, one of six that were knocked out that day after blocking the sector with their long-ranged guns. (NARA)

15th Infantry, Second Lieutenant Audie Murphy, won the Medal of Honor after beating back German infantry attacks using the machine gun on the turret of a burning M10 tank destroyer; the incident was later immortalized in a popular book and movie (*To Hell and Back*) with Murphy playing himself in the film. The initial objective, the Colmar canal, was reached on the night of January 29/30.

The arrival of Hausser in command of Heeresgruppe G and the reunification of command of both AOK 1 and AOK 19 under this army group led to a reassessment of German operations in Alsace. The staff of Heeresgruppe G had already concluded that the Colmar Pocket was doomed and that it would be prudent to withdraw forces over the Rhine to bolster the defense of the Black Forest across the river in Germany. Hitler partially agreed to a pull-out in the north but wanted the main portion of the pocket held as long as possible; Rundstedt also wanted the pocket held as a means to divert Allied forces from an anticipated offensive against the Saar.

The weakness of the units within the pocket prevented Rasp from creating a plausible defense against the Franco-American offensive, which was steadily gaining strength from the addition of units from the Ardennes and American units freed of commitments in the Hagenau sector after the halt of the Sylwester offensives there late in January. The 3rd Division advance was reinforced by the newly arrived 28th, 75th and 12th Armored Divisions. On February 1, Rasp began pulling German units out of the Vosges front in spite of orders from Berlin, in the hope that AOK 19 would be authorized to withdraw over the Rhine while there was still time. Instead, at 1719hrs that night, he received instructions from Hitler to hold fast. On February 2, the 28th Division began clearing the suburbs of Colmar and on February 3, tanks of the French 5e Division Blindée began moving into the heart of the city against weak opposition. By February 5, the fortress city of Neuf-Brisach on the Rhine had been reached by the 3rd Division, cutting off the main ferry

A pair of French M10 3in. GMCs of the 11e Regiment de Chasseurs d'Afrique, 5e Division Blindée pass through the ruined village of Bettenhoffen on their way to Gambsheim on February 1, 1945 during the final clean-up battles along the Rhine. (NARA)

and bridge site. That day, French and US forces linked up in Rouffach, encircling the western half of the pocket, and trapping the remnants of four German divisions. Without permission from Berlin, Rasp continued moving forces over the Rhine by ferry or over the Neuenberg bridge, and instructed units to try to fall back to the bridge at Chalampe, which was still in German hands. The 1ère Armée spent the next several days clearing the pocket of numerous German holdouts, but by the first week of February, AOK 19 no longer had any coherent defenses left in the pocket except for isolated *Kampfgruppen*. On February 8 at 1445hrs, Hitler finally gave permission to withdraw the remnants of AOK 19 over the river, but by that stage the final pocket was only seven miles (11km) wide and two miles (3.2km) deep and was on the verge of annihilation. On February 9, Gén. Leclerc's 2e Division Blindée from the north met elements of the 9e Division d'Infanterie Algérienne from the south at the final Rhine bridge at Chalampe, and the German demolition of this bridge at 0800hrs marked the symbolic end of the Colmar Pocket.

Total Allied casualties in the fighting for the pocket were 13,390, of which 2,317 were killed in action and the remainder wounded, taken prisoner or missing. The French suffered the majority of the casualties, with 1,595 killed and 8,583 wounded or missing (76 percent), and there were a further 7,115 Allied non-combat casualties, mostly to trench foot and frostbite. The French infantry companies in the battle suffered 35–40 percent casualties. During the fighting from November 14 to February 20, AOK 19 had lost over 24,000 men taken prisoner and an unknown number of men killed and wounded; during the reduction of the Colmar Pocket from January 20 to February 8, the army lost over 25,000 troops of whom 16,438 were captured during the fighting; fewer than 10,000 troops escaped the pocket and most of its surviving divisions were down to 400–500 riflemen. AOK 19 had ceased to exist as a fighting force and its fighting power had been obliterated.

As the Colmar fighting came to a conclusion in southern Alsace, the US Seventh Army conducted clean-up operations in the low Vosges in northern Alsace. By January 31, the Gambsheim bridgehead area was retaken,

A French M4A2 medium tank with accompanying infantry of the 5e Division Blindée moves towards the center of Colmar on February 2, 1945 during the fighting that led to the city's capture the following day. (NARA)

including Herrlisheim and Offendorf. Some areas in the Hagenau sector, including the martyred villages of Hatten-Rittershoffen, were not retaken until the March offensive into the Saar.

German prisoners are escorted back by troops of the 75th Division during the fighting near Bischwiller to the northeast of Colmar on February 1, 1945. The M4A1 medium tanks are from the 709th Tank Battalion, which was supporting the 75th Division during the Colmar fighting. (NARA)

AFTERMATH

The German Sylwester offensives were the death rattle of the Wehrmacht in the west. After these misguided attacks, the Wehrmacht would never again be able to conduct anything but local counterattacks in the west because all of its operational reserves had been spent or shipped off to the east. The attacks were originally conceived as an adjunct to the Ardennes offensive with an aim towards tying down US forces. This mission became moot when Patton's Third Army shifted its forces against Bastogne starting on December 19, long before Heeresgruppe G could initiate any actions in Alsace. By this stage of the war, the US Army had far quicker operational response times than the Wehrmacht, which was hamstrung both by a lack of fuel and predatory Allied air attacks against its transportation network. By the time that *Nordwind* started in Alsace on New Year's Day, Devers' 6th Army Group was already in a defensive posture and the fate of the Ardennes offensive had already decisively shifted against Germany. The original rationale for the Sylwester offensives had evaporated. The Wehrmacht reflexively continued its Alsace counteroffensive heedless of whether it had any plausible operational goal.

After a two-week lull while the Colmar Pocket was being cleared, VI Corps stepped up its efforts to clean up unfinished business in early February by clearing the northern end of the Gambsheim bridgehead while the French 3e Division d'Infanterie Algérienne cleared the south. Oberhoffen, held by 10. SS-Panzer-Division during the process of being relieved by a *Volksgrenadier* division, was the center of much of the fighting that involved the 14th Armored Division and 36th Division on the American side. Here, an M4A3 (76mm) burns in the foreground as medics evacuate casualties under the cover of an M10 3in. GMC on February 3, 1945 during an action by the 142nd Infantry, 36th Division. (NARA)

Hitler had grown increasingly nihilistic after the failure of the Ardennes attack, and accepted a bloody battle of attrition as reason enough to continue the Alsace fighting. This made little sense in the conditions facing the Wehrmacht in Alsace in January 1945 where the Allies had artillery superiority as well as good defensive positions, and the Wehrmacht was attacking with weak, second-rate infantry in adverse terrain and weather conditions with little Panzer support and pathetically thin stocks of artillery ammunition. Such fighting inevitably caused significant casualties on both sides, but the outcome was seldom in doubt. As an attritional struggle, the Sylwester offensives cost the Wehrmacht far more than it cost the Allies.

The fighting in Alsace in January also deprived the Wehrmacht of the time and the resources to prepare for the inevitable battle for Germany. This was most clear in the case of AOK 1 in the Saar on the north of Patch's Seventh Army. AOK 1 had been bled white in the *Nordwind* fighting, and in February and March began to face the simultaneous encroachment of both Patton's Third Army from the west and Patch's Seventh Army from the south. Furthermore, because of the geography, Patch's penetration of the Westwall meant that the Seventh Army could roll up the Rhine Valley behind the sector being attacked by Patton's Third Army, completely undermining the last major defensive barrier in front of Patton's troops. The result was the disastrous "Rhine Rat Race" in mid-March when AOK 1 simply disintegrated in front of Patton, vacating the entire Saar-Palatinate in hardly a week of desultory fighting. The destruction of AOK 19 in January 1945 and AOK 1 in March 1945 left southern Germany completely exposed to the advance of Patton's Third Army and Patch's Seventh Army and it is little surprise that the deepest and fastest Allied advances in April–May 1945 were in southern Germany.

LEFT
Following the reduction of the Colmar Pocket, the Seventh Army stepped up its efforts to erase the German advances in the initial stages of Operation *Nordwind*. The fortress city of Bitche was finally taken and this heavily camouflaged Jagdpanzer 38(t) Hetzer assault gun was knocked out during the fighting there in early March 1945 by XV Corps. (NARA)

RIGHT
In March, Seventh Army continued its thrust northwards through the Low Vosges into the Saar. Here, troops of Combat Command A, 14th Armored Division pause in Oberlauterach on March 18, 1945. The heavy losses of tanks to German Panzerfaust anti-tank rockets during street fighting in Alsatian towns like Hatten, Rittershoffen, and Hillersheim prompted the Seventh Army to start a crash program to fit sandbag armor to its tanks as seen here. (NARA)

THE BATTLEFIELD TODAY

The bitter fighting in the winter of 1944/45 is not as widely memorialized in Alsace as the Ardennes campaign in Belgium. The outcome of the war was far more ambiguous than in Belgium or the rest of France due to the confused matter of national identity in this border region. The best-known World War II museums in the province are preserved sections of the extensive 1940 Maginot fortifications. Some of these museums coincide with bunkers that were involved in the *Nordwind* campaign, such as the Esch casemate and the Hatten bunker, both located in the eastern outskirts of Hatten. These museums include displays devoted to the 1945 fighting, though the main focus is the fortifications themselves and their role in the Maginot system. There is a military museum dedicated to the Colmar Pocket fighting in Turckheim to the west of the city. Many of the regional history museums in the area contain exhibits on the war years as well. The towns that were the center of some of the fiercest battles have been rebuilt since the war. Wingen-sur-Moder is best known as the home of the Lalique glass works on the eastern side of the town. Hatten has the two bunker museums as mentioned above. There are numerous small memorials scattered through the region. The most prominent of these are a dozen or more tanks which have often been set up to commemorate particular events. For example, a postwar French Army M4A1E8 (76mm) is located in the center of Rosenau village to commemorate the French Army's arrival at the Rhine; there is another Sherman tank at Place Lacarre in Colmar as a war memorial.

FURTHER READING

There is an extensive literature on Operation *Nordwind* and the Sylwester offensives. Aside from the numerous US and French official histories and unit accounts, the US Army's Foreign Military Studies program after the war managed to collect accounts by a significant number of senior German commanders about the Alsace campaign in 1944/45. I have used the collections at the US Army Military History Institute at Carlisle Barracks, Pennsylvania, and the US National Archives and Records Administration (NARA II) at College Park, Maryland. In addition, there are some very good published histories of the campaign. Keith Bonn's account was part of a broader trend in revisionist histories that appeared in the 1980s and 1990s in reaction to the excessively pro-German slant of American military history writing in the previous decade; Aberjona Press has also published several other significant histories of the Alsace campaign. In spite of the volume of material available about the Alsace campaign, there are some notable gaps in the historical record. Himmler's Heeresgruppe Oberrhein left few records and even the US Army's Foreign Military Studies program had less success in collecting accounts from these units compared with Heeresgruppe G, as is evident in the Foreign Military Studies list below. The National Archives and Records Administration has a modest collection of documents from Heeresgruppe Oberrhein, which were useful in preparing the maps here. The Heersgruppe G records at NARA are more extensive, but peter out after December 1944. Another noticeable gap is the lack of a major biography of Jacob Devers. Although on a par with Montgomery and Bradley, who have been the subject of scores of biographies, there is still no full-length biography of this important American commander.

There are a number of excellent small unit accounts, of which the Zoepf memoir is one of the more remarkable since not only was the author a participant in the battle, but Aberjona Press went to considerable lengths to provide him with documentation from both the American and German side to permit the writing of a well-balanced account of the brutal battle for Wingen-sur-Moder; his account is further amplified by Cheves' memoir, which examines the same battle from the perspective of a US battalion commander.

Besides the published accounts and government studies, I used some of the after-action reports and other unit records of 6th Army Group, Seventh Army, and divisions at NARA II. The US Army Military History Institute has some notable resources such as Gen. Jacob Devers' diary, and a collection of documents collected by Devers regarding the Strasbourg controversy.

US Army Foreign Military Studies

Albert, Ekkehard, *XIII SS Corps: 13 Jan–25 Mar 1945* (B-711)
Bach-Zelewski, Erich von dem, *XIV SS Corps: Nov 1944–Jan 1945* (B-252)
Beisswänger, Walter, *Artillery Headquarters Strasbourg-Sarrebourg:
      8 September–23 October 1944* (B-474)
Brandstäder, Kurt, *Nineteenth Army* (B-463)
——, *Defensive Battle* (B-789)
Brenner, Karl, *6. SS-Gebirgs-Division: 26 Jan–28 Feb 1945* (B-586)
Britzelmayr, Karl, *19th Volksgrenadier-Division* (B-527)
Botsch, Walter, *Nineteenth Army: 14 September–7 November 1944* (B-766)
——, *Nineteenth Army: 8 November 1944–10 January 1945* (B-263)
Eckstein, Walter, *Upper Rhine Fortifications: 19 Oct 1944–8 Apr 1945* (B-835)

Eimler, Robert, *Fortress Engineer Commander XXI: September 1944–April 1945* (B-064, B-291)

Emmerich, Albert, *First Army: 20 Dec 1944–10 Feb 1945* (B-786)

Franz, Gerhard, *256th Volksgrenadier Division: November 1944–8 April 1945* (B-089)

Feuchtinger, Edgar, *21st Panzer Division in Combat Against American Troops in France and Germany* (A-871)

Grimmeis, Max, *LXIV Corps: 28 January–7 February 1945* (B-430)

Hackel, Ernst, *16th Infantry Division* (B-452)

Hartmann, Hermann, *Mulhouse Wehrmacht Commander: July 1944–January 1945* (B-083, B-497, B-498)

Hausser, Paul, *Army Group G: 25 Jan–21 Mar 1945* (B-600)

——, *Effects of the Ardennes Offensive on Army Group G* (B-026)

Höhne, Gustav, *Reconnaissance of the Vosges Positions: 8 Aug–15 Oct 1944* (B-043)

——, *LXXXIX Army Corps: The Attack in the Vosges: 1 January–13 January 1945* (B-077)

Hold, Kurt, *First Army: 20 Dec 1944–15 Jan 1945* (B-767)

Hüther, Gerhard, *553rd Volksgrenadier Division: Dec 1944–Mar 1945* (B-177)

Ingelheim, Ludwig Graf von, *LXXXII Corps: 2 Dec 1944–27 Mar 1945* (B-066)

Kögel, Bernhard, *256th Volksgrenadier Division: 10 Oct 1944–2 Feb 1945* (B-537)

Krieger, Josef, *708th Volksgrenadier Division* (B-451)

Mellenthin, Frederich von, et al., *Army Group G: 20 Sep–8 Nov 1944* (A-999)

Mönch, Hans, *Feldkommandant 987: 19 October 1944–25 March 1945* (B-059)

Mühlen, Kurt von, *559th Volks Grenadier Division: 17 December 1944–15 January 1945* (B-429)

Peterson, Erich, *IV Luftwaffe Corps-XC Corps: 18 Sep 1944–23 Mar 1945* (B-071/B-117)

Philippi, Alfred, *361st Volksgrenadier Division: 31 August–16 December 1944* (B-626)

——, *361st Volksgrenadier Division: 24 December 1944–12 January 1945* (B-428)

Reinhardt, Hellmuth, *Volksgrenadier Division and Volkssturm* (P-065B)

Reschke, Kurt, *LXXXIX Corps: 14–23 Jan 1945* (B-826)

——, *LXXXIX Corps: 20 Dec 1944–13 Jan 1945* (B-765)

Schramm, Percy, *The German Wehrmacht in the Last Days of the War: 1 January–7 May 1945* (C-020)

Simon, Max, *13. SS-Corps: Comment on Operation Nordwind* (C-039)

Taglichsbeck, Hans, *LXIV Corps Defensive Construction: 16 Sep 1944–25 Feb 1945* (B-504)

Thumm, Helmut, *LXIV Corps: 28 August 1944–28 January 1945* (B-050)

——, *LXIV Corps: 1 November–31 December 1944* (B-468)

——, *LXIV Corps: 6 Dec 1944–28 Jan 1945* (B-550)

Vaterodt, Franz, *Defense of Strasbourg 1944: 23–25 November 1944* (B-545)

Veiel, Rudolf, *Wehrkreis V: 1 Sep 1943–15 Apr 1945* (B-193)

Wiese, Friedrich, *The Nineteenth Army in the Belfort Gap and Alsace September–December 1944* (B-781)

Witek, Otto, *Army Group G Supply: 26 Oct 1944–6 May 1945* (B-366)

Wilutsky, Horst, *Army Group G: Nov 1944–Jan 1945* (B-095)

Official Army Reports and Unit Histories

Le 2e CA dans la Battaille pour la Libération de la France (1945)
The Fighting 36th: A Pictorial History of the Texas Division in Combat (1945)
History of the 14th Armored Division (1946)
History of the Third Infantry Division in World War II (1947)
*The Initial Assault on Herrlisheim by Combat Command B, 12th Armored
        Division* (US Armor School: 1949)
*Initial Assault on Herrlisheim by the 56th Armored Infantry Battalion and the
        714th Tank Battalion of the 12th Armored Division during the Period
        8–11 January 1945* (1945)
*The Seventh United States Army: Report of Operations, France and Germany
        1944–45*, Vols. 2 and 3 (1946)
The Story of the Century (1946)
Clarke, Jeffrey and Smith, Robert, *US Army in World War II: Riviera to the Rhine*
        (US Army Center of Military History: 1993)
Vigneras, Marcel, *US Army in World War II: Rearming the French* (US Army
        Center of Military History: 1993)

Books

Bernage, Georges and Lannoy, F., *Leclerc Libère Strasbourg: Novembre 1944*
        (Heimdal: 1991)
Bernage, Georges et al., *Battaille d'Alsace 1944–45* (Heimdal: 1992)
Bernier, Jean-Pierre, *La Libération de Strasbourg et de l'Alsace* (Lavauzelle: 1984)
Bonn, Keith, *When the Odds Were Even: The Vosges Mountains Campaign
        October 1944–January 1945* (Presidio: 1994)
Cheves, Wallace, *Battle of Wingen-sur-Moder: Operation Nordwind* (Merriam
        Press: 2008)
Colley, David, *Decision at Strasbourg: Ike's Strategic Mistake to Halt the Sixth
        Army Group at the Rhine in 1944* (Naval Institute Press: 2008)
Engler, Richard, *The Final Crisis: Combat in Northern Alsace, January 1945*
        (Aberjona: 1999)
English, John, *Patton's Peers: The Forgotten Allied Field Army Commanders of the
        Western Front 1944–45* (Stackpole: 2009)
Gaujac, Paul, *L'Armée de la Victoire: du Rhin au Danube 1944–45*
        (Lavauzelle: 1986)
Giziowski, Richard, *The Enigma of General Blaskowitz* (Hippocrene: 1997)
Hinsley, F. H. et al., *British Intelligence in the Second World War, Vol. 3, Part 2*
        (HMSO: 1988)
L'Huillier, Fernand, *Libération de l'Alsace* (Hachette: 1975)
Lattre, Jean de, *The History of the French First Army* (George Allen & Unwin:
        1952)
Le Clair, Yves and Kolb, Brigitte, *L'armée de l'air dans la bataille de la poche de
        Colmar* (Musée Mémorial de Colmar: 2004)
Luck, Hans von, *Panzer Commander* (Praeger: 1989)
Markey, Michael, *Jake: The General from West York Avenue* (Historical Society of
        York County: 1998)
Pierre, Perny et al., *Operation Nordwind: Janvier 1945 Alsace du Nord*
        (Heimdal: 1985)
Perrigault, Jean-Claude, *21. Panzer-Division* (Heimdal: 2002)
Pommois, Lise, *Winter Storm: War in Northern Alsace November 1944–March
        1945* (Turner: 1991)

Rigoulot, Pierre, *L'Alsace-Lorraine pendant la guerre 1939–1945* (Presses Universitaires de France: 1997)

Rittgen, Francis, *Opération Nordwind: Dernière offensive allemande sur la France* (Pierron: 2006)

Tieke, Wilhelm, *In the Firestorm of the Last Year of the War: II.SS-Panzerkorps with the 9. and 10. SS-Divisions* (Federowicz: 1999)

Vonau, Jean-Laurent, *La Bataille de Hatten-Rittershoffen, Janvier 1945* (Revue d'Histoire de l'Alsace du Nord: 1985)

Wahl, Jean, *La Ligne Maginot en Alsace* (Editions du Rhin: 1987)

White, Nathan, *From Fedala to Berchtesgaden: A History of the Seventh US Infantry in World War II* (Keystone: 1947)

Wyant, William, *Sandy Patch: A Biography of Lt. Gen. Alexander Patch* (Praeger: 1991)

Yeide, Harry and Stout, Mark, *First to the Rhine: The 6th Army Group in World War II* (Zenith: 2007)

Zoepf, Wolf, *Seven Days in January: With the 6th SS-Mountain Division in Operation Nordwind* (Aberjona: 2001)

INDEX

Figures in bold refer to illustrations, figures in brackets refer to plate captions.